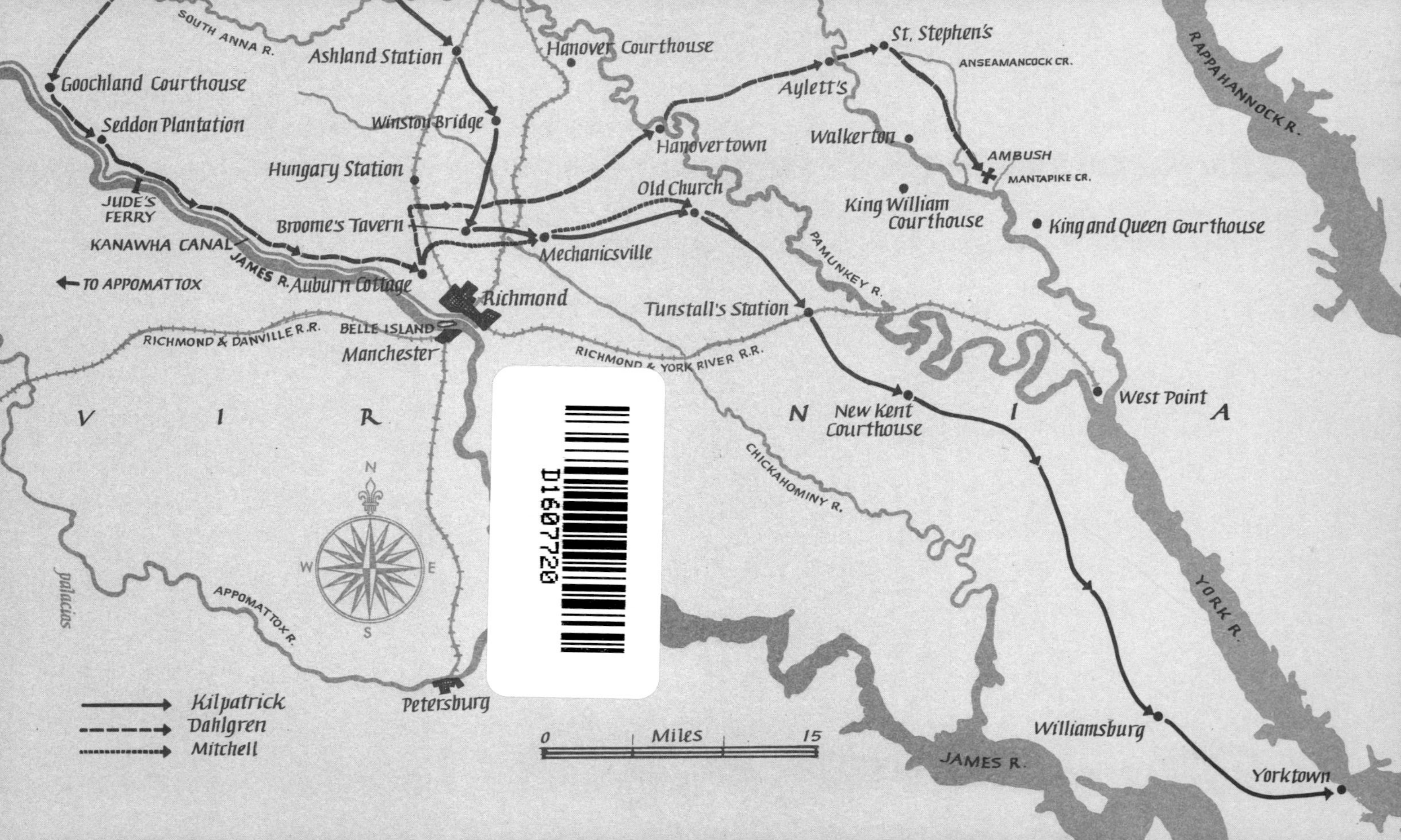

SOUTH ANNA R.
Ashland Station
Hanover Courthouse
St. Stephen's
ANSEAMANCOCK CR.
RAPPAHANNOCK R.
Goochland Courthouse
Aylett's
Seddon Plantation
Winston Bridge
Walkerton
Hanovertown
AMBUSH
MANTAPIKE CR.
Hungary Station
Old Church
JUDE'S FERRY
King William Courthouse
King and Queen Courthouse
Broome's Tavern
KANAWHA CANAL
Mechanicsville
PAMUNKEY R.
JAMES R.
Auburn Cottage
← TO APPOMATTOX
Richmond
Tunstall's Station
BELLE ISLAND
RICHMOND & DANVILLE R.R.
Manchester
RICHMOND & YORK RIVER R.R.
West Point
V I R G I N I A
New Kent Courthouse
N
W
E
S
CHICKAHOMINY R.
YORK R.
APPOMATTOX R.
palacios
Petersburg
Kilpatrick
Dahlgren
Mitchell
0 Miles 15
Williamsburg
JAMES R.
Yorktown

The Richmond Raid

The Richmond Raid

A Novel by

JOHN BRICK

Doubleday & Company, Inc.
Garden City, New York

Printed in the United States of America

For LOWELL KERR and BILL CARLSON

Part One

1

The long bar in Willard's Hotel at Fourteenth Street in Washington wasn't as crowded as it would be later in the afternoon. Hank Stephens had a long section of the dark mahogany to himself, with plenty of elbowroom. It had been a long time since he'd had a chance to have a drink in a well-appointed and well-managed saloon. He lounged easily against the bar.

While he waited for one of the barkeepers to swab a path down to him, Stephens carefully took a long cigar from his shirt pocket and inspected it to see that it wasn't broken.

The barkeeper struck a match on the undersurface of the bar and held the flame to the tip of the cigar.

"What's your pleasure, Major?" he asked.

"Whiskey," Stephens said, "and a glass of water."

"Right you are, Major."

Stephens pulled strongly on the dark cigar, taking the smoke into his lungs. It was a good cigar, rich in flavor. It had cost him twenty cents at the stand in the hotel lobby.

The man brought the whiskey, setting it on the bar with a flourish. Stephens downed it in two swallows, then nodded that the glass be filled again. This time the barkeeper left the bottle on the bar.

The man seemed inclined to talk. His gaze took in Stephens' worn and faded uniform that still carried traces of Virginia's red dust and mud in spite of the brushing that had been given it by one of the Willard's porters.

"Just come up from down below, Major?" the barkeeper asked.

Stephens nodded. He sipped at the second glass of whiskey. The first one had satisfied his craving for a drink; this one would fill his desire to savor good whiskey in a fine saloon. He would enjoy this one. All he'd had lately had been the raw applejack run off by the troopers at any one of a half-dozen stills in the woods around Stevensburg. Fifty cents a quart, and it would pop your skull and leave splinters in your tongue.

He looked around, seeking to avoid for the time being the barkeeper's obvious desire to talk. The man was hovering, waiting to catch Stephens' eye again.

At the far end of the bar a half-dozen civilians stood talking loudly about railroad equipment. They all beamed with prosperity. Nearer to Stephens, two surly-looking fellows discussed the shipment of remounts from the West. They gruffly cursed the new Chief of the Cavalry Bureau, General James H. Wilson. They seemed unconcerned with the close presence of a major of cavalry. Stephens wondered if it would make any difference to them if they knew that he had once roomed with Wilson at the Academy. He figured it wouldn't.

Alone at the bar beyond the horse contractors, a lean-faced lieutenant of artillery glowered into his drink, looking as if his battery had just been captured by the rebs. Several young Army officers talked over drinks at a table against the far wall. Three naval officers sat at another table, and alone in a corner, a bearded man in seedy clothing scribbled busily on yellow foolscap, occasionally stopping to lift a glass to his lips. During one of these pauses he nodded pleasantly toward Stephens, who nodded in return. Stephens recognized him as a correspondent for the New York *Herald*.

The barkeeper stroked the mahogany with his folded towel. "It's been pretty quiet down there, ain't it, Major?"

"That's right. Usually is in winter."

"Reason I'm interested is I got a boy down there," the man said. "Cavalry, like you, Major. Happen you might know his regiment. He's in the 2nd New York."

"That's my regiment," Stephens said, looking up in surprise. "What's his name?"

"Johnny Watkins," the man said eagerly. "I'm John Watkins, Senior. He's a big boy, got yellow hair like his mother. Big and husky. You know him?"

Stephens nodded. "I think so. I'm not sure. Company B?"

"That's it. It's a small world, ain't it, Major? You walk in here and you know my son in the Army. He's a good boy, Major. Writes to his ma–she's up home in Tarrytown–once a week, regular. Writes to me, too. He sends a nice letter. Full of real interesting items you don't read in the paper. He thinks the world and all of your general. Makes a joke on his name–changes Kilpatrick to Kill Cavalry. Not to be a smart aleck, you understand. You can tell Johnny thinks the general is something, all right."

Stephens grinned briefly. "He is something, all right. Yes, indeed, he is."

"Like Johnny says," the man agreed. "I sure would like to get a look at him. Most of 'em comes in here when they're up in Washington, and they all know me. But I never seen General Kilpatrick in here."

Stephens looked at the massive clock at the end of the bar. "You'll see him in here inside a half hour. He'll come down to drag me away from this bottle. He's upstairs now."

The barkeeper beamed. "I'll be proud to serve him a drink, Major."

"No, you won't," Stephens said. "Not to Jud Kilpatrick. He's teetotal. Don't even suggest it. You'll get a temperance lecture."

"He'll take a cigar, won't he?"

Stephens grinned. "The general's vices are not the usual ones, Mr. Watkins."

They were interrupted by the newspaperman, who stepped to Stephens' side. "Afternoon, Major," he said affably. "Haven't seen you in some time."

Hank greeted the man and offered him a drink.

"Thank you. I never check a generous impulse. You came in with Kilpatrick, didn't you, Major?"

Stephens nodded shortly.

"What's he up here for? Saw him this morning ducking into the War Department. Anything doing that I can use?"

"You'll have to ask him, sir. He doesn't tell me what he has in mind."

The reporter grinned. "I will," he said. "Never asked him a question yet that I didn't get an answer to fill a whole column. He'd like the whole country to share Kilpatrick's admiration for Kilpatrick."

"Perhaps it should," Stephens said. "Perhaps it will."

The man eyed him sharply. "Why do you say that? He up to something?"

Stephens shrugged, covering casually the remark the reporter had snapped up. "You'd have to ask the general. He doesn't tell me his plans."

"I will. Thanks for the drink. You know his room number?"

Stephens shook his head. "The desk will probably tell you."

Let Jud answer the questions, Hank told himself as he watched the man walk out of the saloon. Just so he doesn't tell him something that will be printed in the *Herald* on Monday and be read with interest in Richmond on Thursday. That *Herald* man would love to find out what we're doing here.

Stephens turned at the approach of a slim young man in the uniform of a colonel of cavalry. He walked stiffly, using a pair of canes to support his weight. He had been sitting with the Army officers at the table in the rear. Hank hadn't noticed him. The colonel was a most handsome boy, no more than twenty-one, with light thin hair and sparse goatee and mustache.

"Major Stephens, isn't it?" he said with a smile that added to his bright good looks. He tucked one of the canes under his left arm so that he could shake hands. "You remember me, Major?"

"Dahlgren," Stephens said, extending his hand. "Those eagles have perched on your shoulders since the last time I saw you."

"After Gettysburg," Dahlgren said. He spoke in a quick clear youthful voice. He tapped his right leg with one of his canes; it sounded hollowly of wood. "Traded this for them." His voice changed suddenly; it was touched with challenge: "I manage fine, Major. I can ride a horse as well as any man with two legs."

"Sure," Stephens said. "Why not?"

Dahlgren smiled boyishly. "Exactly. Why not? And I'm coming back to field duty. Soon. Very soon." He grinned at Stephens as if they were partners in a conspiracy. "You know what I mean, don't you, Stephens?"

Hank stared levelly into the bright eyes. He didn't trouble to word an evasive answer. He didn't give any answer at all, but said: "Join me in a drink, Colonel?"

Dahlgren shook his head. "I've been with friends at the table yonder. Saw that newspaper fellow talking to you, so I waited until he left. I wanted to talk to you since I saw you come in. Where's Kilpatrick?"

"Upstairs."

Dahlgren nodded. "Is he going back right away? You think he's free for dinner?"

"You'll have to ask him."

"I certainly will. I'm going to get in on this thing, Stephens."

Stephens looked down at the glass cradled between his hands.

"When will it be? Do you know, Major?"

Hank looked at the barkeeper, who was listening with interest. The man flushed and moved away.

Hank spoke evenly: "I don't know just what it is that you're talking about, Colonel."

Dahlgren laughed. "Hell, man, I know why he's here. It's hard to keep a secret in this town."

"I don't know any secrets," Stephens said, twirling his whiskey glass. Goddammit, why didn't this boy stop talking?

"I can ride," Dahlgren said softly. "When he takes you out, I'll be along. I'll go make that date for dinner right now. Care to join us, Major?"

"Thank you, but no. I have an engagement."

Dahlgren moved away, thumping clumsily toward the door leading into the hotel lobby.

Hank thought sourly that here was another fire-eater who had to have field duty even with only one leg. There were enough of them already, goddammit, and Hank considered that most of the fire-eaters managed only to get good men killed to no purpose. What were they: heroes or fools? Or both? Hank thought that only God knew, and He had never seen fit to inform Hank Stephens, who had given up a long time ago trying to find out the difference between a hero and a fool. Maybe there wasn't any.

He wondered how many others in Washington knew about Kilpatrick's scheme. Maybe it didn't matter how many. One would be enough if he talked in the right places. And somebody probably would.

It will be splendid, he told himself, to have them know we are coming. To have them sitting behind the guns, waiting. It will be fine. Who talked to Dahlgren? Which one of the dozen or two dozen or three dozen people that Jud has already told? I'm the only one I'm sure of. I didn't even tell my horse, and he's got a right to know. He's going, too.

Maybe this afternoon will be the end of it. Maybe the man up the street will say no. Maybe he'll turn the whole thing down. Not likely. Not with Kilpatrick talking to him. Jud's a good talker. Always was.

Stephens drained his glass and picked up the bottle the barkeeper had left in front of him. He poured another drink, knowing that he shouldn't, but not really giving a damn. He raised his glass in slight salute to the sign, neatly lettered, that was hanging above the mirror back of the bar: NO LIQUORS SERVED TO SOLDIERS. Only to officers, he thought, by order of the Secretary of War and the management of Willard's.

Slowly he finished his cigar, puffing it gently. From time to time, he sipped at the whiskey. He could feel its glow soaking him, relaxing him, numbing the raw ends of the nerves that had been abraded so long. This is just right, he thought. I don't need another, and I'd better not have one.

He wondered if he ought to try talking to the barkeeper again, to see if his speech had started to slur. How can you tell, he thought. You sound normal to yourself. Just don't have another one. Not until later. Not until after Jud and I have gone to get the Word. He corrected himself: until Jud gets the Word. I don't need any. I just follow orders.

There was a mirror along the length of the back of the bar. He looked at himself, wondering if he seemed to others to be as old as he felt. Twenty-nine last month. A year older than Jud, and they call him the Boy General. He and Custer and Merritt and Wilson. All at the Point together, all in the cavalry, all brigadier generals. And another cadet–Hank Stephens, permanent civilian and temporary major of cavalry.

He watched himself in the mirror, seeing a smile curl on his lips. Maybe you won't get the chance to grow any older, Stephens. Not on this wild one that Jud is planning.

He saw in the glass a pair of broad but not heavy shoulders topped by a lean face with bones just a bit too heavy, too prominent in brow and jaw. His hair was dark and thick. His eyes were dark blue and hollowed in his face. He looked worn and thin. He looked as if he needed a long rest.

I do, he thought. Until the day the war ends.

He looked at the bottle again, wondering if he should pour just one more. He wanted it, but he decided not to take it. Even in a hard-drinking army, a man ought to use a little judgment when he was about to see the Commander in Chief. He sipped carefully at the finger or so of whiskey in the tumbler, trying to make it last.

After a time, he heard a quick thumping of boots on the saloon floor. A swift sharp voice spoke at his shoulder: "All right, Stephens."

He put down the glass and turned slowly, picking up his hat and his heavy buckskin gauntlets from the bar. "Ready, General," he said easily. He was sure that all the syllables came out properly.

The young man who faced him with a frown of disapproval was undersized, his eyes at the level of Stephens' chin. He was lean and wiry, with thin Burnside whiskers the color of fresh bank-run gravel. His face was out of proportion with the rest of him–he had a long heavy jaw and a thin straight mouth. He was odd-looking, even ugly, but men caught by his hard eyes would never smile at his out-sized jaw and his bantam size. He seemed to spark with energy.

His voice cracked out his displeasure: "How many glasses of that stuff have you had, Major?"

Stephens' face tightened. He answered softly. "As many as I wanted, General."

The general seemed to rise an inch above himself, then suddenly shrugged one star-crested shoulder. He laughed shortly without humor. "Don't get hard with me, Hank. I've known you too long."

"That's right, General," Stephens said evenly. "Just as long as I've known you. So it won't pay you to get hard either."

Anger stirred for an instant, then the general laughed again quickly. "It's just that I can't see how you can pour that stuff into yourself, Hank. What's more, he'll smell it on your breath."

"He'll know what it is," Stephens said. "Each man has his own notions of pleasure, General. One of mine is whiskey. One of yours is a battle line. You can't stomach mine and I can't stomach yours."

The general looked steadily into Stephens' eyes, then said flatly: "And that, Hank, is exactly why you're not commanding a brigade."

"That's why I don't want to command a brigade. We've had about enough of this, Jud. Let's stop it before we get ugly."

"All right, Hank," the general said quietly. "You saw young Dahlgren? The admiral's son?"

Stephens nodded. "He was down here. Wanted to see you. Seemed to know all about it."

The general shrugged. "So I gathered. He wants to have dinner with me tonight, to talk about it. Wonder how he heard?"

"Somebody told him," Stephens said dryly.

"It's hard to maintain absolute secrecy about a thing like this," Kilpatrick said. "He wants to go along, I suppose. He's got a lot of fire, and he's smart, too."

"Bayard reborn," Stephens said softly.

"What?"

"Once more unto the breach, dear friends," Hank said, wondering if that last glass should not have been left in the bottle. "Why don't we get Custer in on it, too?"

"Custer? What the devil are you talking about, Hank? Good Lord, Custer! I wouldn't want Custer with me in a sham battle."

"All right," Hank said. "Don't mind me. Dahlgren seems a little young for those eagles, that's all. This thing isn't going to be a child's game, you know."

"I'm young. So are you. What difference does age make?" The general glanced at the clock on the back wall. "Let's go. He's waiting to see us."

"One thing, first," Hank said. He motioned to the attentive barkeeper.

"Not another, Hank?" the general said harshly. "Don't make a fool of yourself, now."

"Man wants to meet you, Jud. His boy is in the 2nd New York."

"Am I supposed to know him?" Kilpatrick asked softly.

"Just a trooper named Watkins. Big boy with blond hair. Johnny Watkins."

Stephens presented the barkeeper to the general, who vigorously pumped the man's hand. "Your boy is a good trooper, Mr. Watkins. Fine lad."

"You know my Johnny, General? You've noticed him among so many?"

"I make it a point, sir, to try to know all my men. A commander's duty, sir."

"This is a real pleasure, General. I can't wait to tell the missus in my next letter to her that I met Johnny's general. She lives up at Tarrytown. That's where we're from."

Kilpatrick nodded and smiled genially. Hank grinned, thinking that Jud was disappointed the fellow wasn't from New Jersey. The general never missed a chance to chat at length with citizens of New Jersey. After the war, they would remember the Boy General. Since Watkins was from New York, however, Kilpatrick wheeled for the door without saying anything further. Hank took some greenbacks from his blouse pocket. The barkeeper waved them away. "My treat, Major. Come in again."

"I hope I can do that, Mr. Watkins."

When they were through the door, Hank said quietly: "You don't know that boy, Jud."

"I didn't exactly say I did," the general said shortly. "Just said he was a good trooper. Can you, offhand, pick out any bad ones in the 2nd New York? Of course you can't. Let's go. Johnston is holding the horses for us on Fourteenth Street."

"Horses? We're not walking? It's practically across the street."

The general shook his head vigorously. "The commander of a cavalry division doesn't walk to the Executive Mansion."

"Oh, that's it," Stephens said, turning away to hide a grin. There were a few things that Jud learned at the Academy that I never picked up, he told himself. Maybe it was that last year, the one I missed. He learned how to be a general, while I learned the joys of marriage.

A couple of minutes later they rounded the corner of the President's Park along the muddy width of Pennsylvania Avenue. Traffic was heavy, with riders and carriages and wagons all slinging mud in every direction. The general rode slightly ahead of Stephens and Sergeant Johnston. Kilpatrick was a good rider, as most Pointers were apt to be, and he had no trouble with the big bay horse, controlling the animal with one gauntleted hand while, with the other, he returned the salutes of passing officers and the waves of civilians. His light-red whiskers fluttered thinly in the breeze. His black campaign hat, with its single star, was worn in the distinctive style that marked the officers of his command, the brim tilted high on the left and low on the right. Stephens' hat, worn in place of the forage cap he usually favored, was cocked in the same fashion, though not so rakishly. "Tilt your hat, Hank," Kilpatrick had said on the cars coming north from Brandy Station. "Let 'em know you're a Kilpatrick man."

Sergeant Johnston, a burly redhead, grinned at the major on his left as Kilpatrick steadied his horse when the animal shied at a scurrying dog. "Ain't he comical, Major?" Johnston said softly. "Just as slick as goose grease, ain't he?"

Stephens smiled absently, thinking of the hold that Kilpatrick had over the troopers. They didn't especially like him, most of them, but they swaggered when they said they were "Kilpatrick men." They would grouse and grumble as much as–indeed, more than–any other soldiers in the Army, for the little general was not known for his tight rein on the troopers, but when Jud gave the word, they'd saddle up and ride after him to hell if that was where he wanted to go. There were other generals in the Army of the Potomac who had more to offer to the mind's eye of the trooper looking for the ideal cavalry commander. There were Buford and Gregg and Merritt, for example, and even Custer, if one sought flamboyance and theatrics. Jud Kilpatrick generally looked as if he ought to be tending store or milling wheat back home in New Jersey instead of commanding a cavalry division. But he strutted and pranced and capered, and he fought like a tiger most of the time when he was committed to a battle line. The men called him "Kill Cavalry" with some justification. They made jokes about him, and they grinned behind his back, but they were proud to be identified with him.

"Not so comical, Sergeant," Hank said quietly. "Don't let him hear you say that."

Johnston sobered immediately, shaking his head in quick denial. "Don't you think I ever would, Major. Nossir. I'd as lief charge a reb battery all alone as tell the general there was things about him that make me laugh." Johnston paused. His grin returned. "You see them boots he's got on, Major?"

Stephens looked at the expensive leather that reached the general's knees.

"He sent me to have 'em fixed this morning, when we got here to town. Said he wanted new heels on 'em. The others was all right, I told him. Not worn down or nothing. He gives me that look that would freeze a lightning bolt. Says he wants an extra half inch on 'em. You know why?"

Stephens said he didn't.

"I figgered it out while I was waiting for the shoemaker to fix 'em.

You're going to see the President, ain't you, Major? You reckon the general wants the President to stoop way over and talk to him? Hell, no. The general will go up a little hisself, so at least they're talking eye to collar, you might say."

Johnston chuckled happily to himself.

"By the way, Major," he said after a moment, "how come you and him is going to see the President? He seen Mr. Stanton this morning, and he come out looking like a sutler on payday. Now the President. What's going on, Major? I asked him, the general, but he just says button your lip, Johnston. So I buttoned it. But the boys will be asking me when we get back to Stevensburg. What's he up to, Major?"

Stephens looked at the easy-going face of the sergeant, a fellow neither bright nor dull, a capable soldier without too much imagination. What the hell, Stephens thought, he won't believe whatever I tell him unless it happens to coincide with whatever the camp rumor was when we left yesterday. And if I tell him the truth, that will be one tale he will not tell to the men when we get back to the division, because he simply will not believe me.

"What he's going to do, Sergeant," he said softly, "is go in to ask the President if he can take the division down to capture Jeff Davis and put an end to the war."

"Ah, hell, Major," Johnston said aggrievedly, "you known me too long to pile horseshit on me. I just asked you a simple question. Maybe you can't tell me the truth, but you oughtn't to be a wiseacre, neither. You and me has come too far in this lousy cavalry for that." Johnston lapsed into grumpy silence as their horses followed the general's bay into the President's Park.

Stephens smiled. *While you live, tell truth and shame the devil!*

He remembered the cold night less than a week ago, when Kilpatrick had summoned him to headquarters. The general cleared the place of all officers and soldiers, then waved a War Department letter at Hank. He jumped up and down, doing a variation of an Irish jig. "I've been waiting for this, Hank. Right over Meade and Pleasonton, straight from Washington."

"What is it, Jud?"

"They want me to come up and talk to them. They're interested in my plan to capture Richmond with the Third Division."

Hank remembered his reactions as the plan unfolded. His stomach muscles had twitched and fluttered, as if the Minié balls were already screaming by. Then he grew angered at the wildness of it, a crazy scheme that would get good men killed. Finally, however, he began to relax while Kilpatrick rattled away with the plans–remounts, artillery, supplies, routes. Hank was sure that Mr. Stanton and the President would reject this nonsense. They hadn't carried this war forward so grimly into February of 1864 to throw away a cavalry division on a wild dream like Kilpatrick's.

Now, a few days later, they were approaching the Executive Mansion, carrying with them Mr. Stanton's approval. Kilpatrick needed only the word of the troubled man who awaited them.

Kilpatrick beamed his confidence.

Good Lord, Hank thought, he may just talk the President into it.

2

"This is Major Henry Stephens, Mr. President. He will command the troops who swing into the city from the other side, sir."

Hank stepped forward and shook the large firm hand that was held out to him. "Major Stephens," the President's voice acknowledged quietly. "Won't you both sit down, please?"

Kilpatrick wasted no time when he got the word to start. He rattled it off briskly: four to five thousand men, a few guns but no wagon train. . . . Stephens and a picked force to swing to the south and come in through Richmond's back door while the main force hammered the clerks and bookkeepers aside and poured into the city . . . yes, clerks and bookkeepers and young boys would man the city's poor defenses . . . the prisoners from Belle Isle to be brought to the mainland and hustled toward the coast to Butler's army on the Peninsula . . . the President's amnesty proclamation to be put into the hands of every citizen of Richmond . . . who could say? Some important rebs caught up in the sweep, maybe Old Sourpuss Davis himself . . . ships blazing in the river . . . warehouses flaming . . . just imagine, Mr. President, the Tredegar Iron Works burned to the ground!

The President spread his hands gently to stem the torrent. "Haul back on the reins, General. Slow down and get your breath. Now this sounds like a fine rabbit stew you're preparing to cook for us, but first, let's make sure of the rabbit. While you and the major here are doing all this, what is our old friend General Lee going to be doing? Won't he have a welcoming party for you, perhaps headed by Jeb Stuart or Wade Hampton?"

"The rebs will have their hands full until it's too late, sir. As you know, I have suggested a large force of infantry and a body of cavalry, starting a day ahead of us, to swing over toward Charlottesville–that general direction over the Rapidan. Lee will watch them. He may even move troops to oppose. Stuart's cavalry will head that way. They'll never suspect a deep raid in the winter. We'll be pounding into Richmond before they know we've started."

The President got up from his chair. "Let's go to the map, General. Show me the route in detail, how you will go down and how you will come back."

Stephens watched from the background as the tall figure of the President leaned down to the map, while Kilpatrick's wiry body jabbed upward at it. The words flowed again in a stream of confidence: Ely's Ford over the Rapidan . . . Spotsylvania . . . Hanover Junction . . . thrust into Richmond itself . . . main force here and Stephens there. . . .

Finally the quiet voice interrupted again: "You seem to do it most admirably on the map, General. Now tell me what General Meade and General Pleasonton have to say about all this."

Stephens was wryly amused to see the flicker of concern on Jud's face, and to hear the haste in which the reply was given: "They'll approve it, sir, as soon as they get word from you."

"I daresay they will," the President said dryly. "But what do they say about it now?"

Go ahead, Jud, Stephens thought. Answer that one.

Hank knew very well that Jud had committed a cardinal sin in the eyes of West Point and Army tradition—he had played leapfrog over his superiors with this plan. Hank suspected, seeing a momentary mobility of the President's lips as if a smile was being controlled, that Mr. Lincoln knew it very well, too.

"Frankly, Mr. President," Kilpatrick said boldly, "they haven't said much because they don't know much about it. Oh, they know I have a plan to raid Richmond. Who hasn't? You just give the word, sir, and it will have their best attention."

"It must have, if you are to succeed, General."

"Then you approve, sir?" Kilpatrick said eagerly.

"We'll talk some more, General, if you don't mind. Now, Major Stephens, let's have your views on your part of the expedition."

Hank hesitated as several seconds went by. He fixed his eyes on the broad wall map of the Virginia battlegrounds, as if he might be finding his answer there.

What's the use, he asked himself. If I say it's a damn-fool scheme that may get us all killed or captured, then Jud will replace me. If he gets permission, I can do it, if it can be done. I can do it as well as any field officer he can find.

"If everything goes well, sir," he said slowly, "we can go down and come back without excessive losses."

The President regarded Hank steadily, motioning with his hand to quiet Kilpatrick, who started to interrupt in his high-pitched, intense voice.

"Just a moment, General. I'd like to ask the major another question. What would you regard as excessive losses, sir?"

There it is, Hank thought. Tell him now and be quit of the whole business. Tell him what you really think, and Kilpatrick will fire you, old friend or not. You'll finish the war in the remount stables at Stevensburg, sweeping up after the horses. The words formed in his mind, even though he wasn't saying them, but seemed instead to be merely phrasing his answer:

> For a successful raid, sir, I would regard losses above two hundred men and five hundred horses as excessive. I say that because I don't think this war will come to an end until we smash their army to pieces. We could raid Richmond a dozen times without effect on the secesh army. The second part of my answer, sir, concerns an unsuccessful raid. I would, in that event, regard the loss of one man as excessive, Mr. President.

He didn't say anything, however.

He didn't look at Kilpatrick, who must have known what he was thinking. Hank had damned the idea bitterly when Jud had told him that he would command the secondary force. It's not a game any more, Jud. It's not West Point with the sham battles on the Plain, nor even Bull Run with its picnic air. It's not even Gettysburg, although that was only seven months ago, when the cavalry guidons streamed on the third day as we charged and countercharged and fought for glory. We're coming to the hard and bitter end of it, and there's no place any more for glory.

"Well, Major?" the President said softly.

Stephens made his decision then, swiftly and bitterly. A field officer couldn't pick and choose his operations. If the troopers of the 2nd New York went to Richmond, he'd have to go too. "Perhaps I shouldn't have used the phrase, sir," he said slowly. "On raids of this type, we would always normally expect some losses. They would be offset by the advantages gained. You know what those will be, sir."

"Yes," the President said musingly. "It's possible, if you achieve the proper speed and surprise, that you might draw Mr. Davis and some of his Cabinet into your net. We would be delighted to have them as guests here in Washington. But primarily, General, your three main objectives should be those we discussed: the destruction of war installations and supplies, the distribution of the amnesty proclamation widely among the civilian populace, and finally, the task that must lie closest to all our hearts–the release of the prisoners on that dreadful island in the James. All right, gentlemen. Anything else that we must discuss? They keep me on a busy schedule, you know."

"I'll have to see Mr. Stanton again," Kilpatrick said. "I take it, Mr. President, that you will give him the necessary orders?"

"I will. What date have you set?"

"Weather permitting, the last day or so in February, sir. That gives us time to get the division ready, and to launch the proper diversions."

"All right, then. Good luck to you, General, and to you, Major. We will anxiously await the word of your success."

"Thank you, Mr. President," Kilpatrick said, briskly shaking hands.

Stephens stepped forward in his turn to shake the hand that was offered him.

"I wish you a happy birthday, sir," he said.

"Why, thank you, Major. It's good of you to remember."

"Yes," said Kilpatrick hastily, "a happy birthday to you, Mr. President."

"Thank you. Good-bye, gentlemen."

3

The general had to guard his words on the steps of the Executive Mansion, for many people were passing in and out. Just below, Johnston held the horses. Even though he kept his voice low, Kilpatrick left no doubt of his anger.

"I should have left you in Virginia, Hank! I thought for a minute there that you were about to let go with that balderdash you fed me last week."

"I almost did, General."

"It was plain to see on your face. You might have finished the whole plan right there. Casualties! Of course we'll have 'em. You didn't expect to go all the way to Richmond without 'em, did you?"

"That's not the point in question, Jud."

"What is the point, then? You were about to put the kibosh on the whole business if you could. And you know what that would have meant, as far as you're concerned."

Stephens nodded. "You'd have given me the ax. I thought of that, too."

"All right! All right! No harm done, because you didn't say it." Kilpatrick grinned savagely. "We got the word, Hank. And now we'll go. We'll fill up the front pages of every newspaper in the country. That's what counts for us, Hank. That and the effect on the rebs, of course. Meade has to go along whether he likes it or not, and Pleasonton may growl and yowl, but he's got to support me. We're on our way, Hank! This will be the greatest single operation of the whole war. Our names will be household words. School children a hundred years from now will read in their history books how Kilpatrick took Richmond and knocked the Confederacy into a cocked hat."

Kilpatrick was standing on the last step, keeping his voice low, but perhaps not low enough. Stephens glanced at Sergeant Johnston, who had his head cocked, as if trying to catch the general's words. "You'd better watch what you say, Jud. Too many people know about this already."

Kilpatrick sobered. He nodded vigorously. "Right, Hank. Now I'm off to see Stanton again, and then Jim Wilson in the Cavalry Bureau. Why don't you go to see Wilson first? You know as well as I do what we'll need in the way of remounts and equipment, and you were a good friend of his at the Academy. You can soften him up. We'll need a lot of new horses."

"Shall I tell him what we need 'em for?"

Kilpatrick shrugged. "He knows. The Secretary of War told him this morning." Kilpatrick laughed. "Hank, you can't keep this thing a secret between you and me. By the way, would you like to join Dahlgren and me for dinner? You can size him up for the job. I like him," the general said with a grin. "Maybe because we're birds of a feather. You're the sobersides, the cautious one. If you think he's unsteady in any way, I'll drop him. I don't have to take him along just because his father's an admiral."

No, Stephens thought, but that's one of the reasons he's going.

Hank shook his head. "No, sir. He's a good officer, from all I've heard. The only objection I would have would be his youth, and that means little so long as he's experienced. If it's all the same with you, Jud, I'll beg off for the rest of the day, after I talk with Wilson. I shouldn't have any trouble with him, now that you have the President's blessing."

Kilpatrick looked critically at Stephens. "I forgot about that. Kate Farnham lives in Washington now."

"That's right, Jud. And I'd like to spend another day here, if you don't need me back at camp right away."

Kilpatrick shrugged, as if to indicate that Stephens' personal affairs were no concern of his. "All right. This is Friday. Come in on the Sunday-night train or that early one Monday morning."

"Thanks, Jud."

"Give Kate my best regards. And, Hank—one thing more."

"Yes, General," Hank said quietly, knowing what was coming.

"I don't like to say it, but until this is over, let up on the whiskey, will you? Any man is apt to talk—"

Stephens flushed and interrupted. "I haven't talked about this one, General, but you know damned well it's being tossed around like a beanbag."

"All right, Hank," Kilpatrick said shortly. He started down the steps again, then twisted his long face around in a scowl. "Damn it, Hank! Why didn't you remind me before we went in there that it was his birthday?"

The general didn't wait for an answer, but strutted in his bantam fashion to the big bay. Stephens came more slowly, mounting his own horse while the general was already riding down the drive. Johnston looked inquiringly at the major.

"Go ahead after him, Sergeant. He's going across the street to the War Department. So am I, but as usual, he's in a hurry."

"I can catch him. What's the news, Major? The boys will want to know."

"You can tell the boys to go to hell, Sergeant," Stephens said shortly. "Now that's an order. I don't want wild rumors back in Stevensburg. When you get back there, you just tell 'em that this trip was for remounts and equipment."

"Remounts? That means action. In the wintertime, action means a raid of some kind, Major. The boys will know that."

"Just you be sure that they don't know any more, if you want to keep those stripes. You'd better get after him, Sergeant. If you're not there to grab that horse when he wants to get off, you'll be Private Johnston so fast it'll make your head swim."

Johnston laughed. "I known him too long. His bark is worse'n his bite." The sergeant saluted and pressed his horse down the drive after Kilpatrick's receding figure.

Hank spent about twenty minutes with his old friend of Academy days, the quick and capable Brigadier General James H. Wilson, who was brand new in the job of Chief of the Cavalry Bureau, but who handled the matter of the coming raid in one crisp remark: "Kil will have what he wants when he wants it, Hank, and I sure to God hope this scheme of his works."

"He has no doubts whatever."

"He wouldn't." Wilson grinned engagingly. "He never counted odds. Remember the time he offered to fight every cadet from South Carolina and Georgia, one at a time or all together, no holds barred?"

Hank shook his head. "I was gone then, Jim."

"That's right. I'd forgotten." Wilson spoke diffidently, but with the privilege of friendship: "How is your wife, Hank?"

"I expect she's all right. I don't know. We don't write much to each other."

There was a somewhat awkward pause of a few seconds, then Wilson said in an attempt at casualness: "Kate Farnham lives in Washington, Hank. I met her at a dinner party the other night. And Royce is with the rebs in Virginia."

"I know," Stephens said. He changed the subject abruptly: "Congratulations on the stars, Jim."

"Thank you, Hank. You would have had a pair yourself if you'd stayed to graduate. Good God, George Custer is a general. I'll tell you this—if you and Kil bring Jeff Davis back here for tea, you'll have a pair of stars and Kil will double his."

"I'll be satisfied to get back in one piece, Jim. It's been good to see you again. Send us four-legged horses, will you?"

"Sure enough, Hank. Good-bye, and the best of luck on your little trip."

Major Stephens did not have far to go, but now that the time had come which gave his trips to Washington their treasured rich hours, he felt an odd resistance to hurrying. He had only to leave the War Department, cross Pennsylvania Avenue and ride through Lafayette Square. A few short blocks away, on Seventeenth Street, he would be there. Instead, he rode around the corner, past the State and Treasury Departments, back to Willard's Hotel. As many times as he had seen Kate Farnham here in Washington, he was never sure that wisdom and prudence would not triumph over passion. Someday the door might not open to him.

At the hotel, he dismounted and turned his horse over to one of the crew of young Negro boys that Willard's kept handy to the hitching rack. Kil had hired the horses at a livery stable near the B. & O. Station at New Jersey Avenue and C Street, so the animal wasn't of prime concern to Stephens. However, he knew well that an unattended horse at any hotel hitching rack was an easy mark for the capital's horde of thieves. A good remount was bringing one hundred and fifty-nine dollars from the Cavalry Bureau.

He went into the saloon, now beginning to crowd as the afternoon grew longer. He managed quickly to get a drink from the friendly Watkins, as well as a sheet of hotel stationery and pen and ink. He wrote swiftly in a full plain hand:

My dear Kate:

I came up with Kil on division business. I will be here for the weekend. Send answer by the boy, if you are free to see me.

Hank

He went outside to the street after he had sealed and addressed the envelope to Mrs. Kathleen Palmer Farnham at the Seventeenth Street address. He called one of the Negro boys and directed him to deliver the note and bring an answer back to the saloon. He went back to his drink at the bar.

He wondered why he was always afraid—afraid that this would be the time when she would say: "No, Hank. No more. Never again. There's no hope in it." That was why he wrote the note asking to see her, so that she would have the chance to refuse him by pen and ink rather than to his face.

It had been two years now. How much longer would it be? Until the end of the war, maybe? Or today, maybe. She would have to be the one to decide it. He would not. He would keep coming as long as she would have him.

He gripped the bar rail tightly with his free hand, thinking that he had been a goddam fool. He could have had her. He could have graduated from West Point and married her in the chapel. Instead, she had married Royce Farnham.

At least he had something, however—a few hours now and a few hours then. While the war lasted, he would have his few hours every so often. Then it would end.

He knew what would happen when the war was over. Farnham would put down his sword with the rest of the rebels. Farnham would do whatever all the Confederates would have to do in order to live in defeat, and then Kate would go back to him. They would grow rice or indigo or whatever the hell it was on the plantation in South Carolina that Royce had talked about all the time at West Point. They would grow little rebels who would hear the stories about how Father rode with Wade Hampton and with Jeb Stuart in the Great War.

Hank told himself to stop crying about it. Farnham was just a handsome rebel who had been a friend at the Academy and now was a Confederate colonel. He had married Hank Stephens' girl, and now he had lost her also because she was a Yankee. At least until the war was over.

Royce Farnham was somewhere in Virginia, with either Stuart or Hampton, while Hank Stephens was in Washington with Jud Kilpatrick, planning to spend as many hours as he could with Mrs. Royce Farnham, who didn't love her husband any more because he was a rebel. Except that perhaps she would send word this time that she didn't love Hank Stephens, either.

"Mr. Watkins," he said quietly, "bring me another whiskey when you get the chance, please."

"Sure thing, Major."

The boy would be back before he finished this one. He had been told to hurry. Hank vowed not to take an extra drink until the answer came.

He kept looking toward the door, to see if the boy was back. Maybe the youngster had stopped to watch a parade.

He would have her until the war ended. He thought of his own inconsistency. One side of him said that war was a rotten dirty business. The other side of him was willing to let it go on forever—to let Farnham stay in Virginia, to let Mrs. Henry Stephens stay in Peekskill, New York.

He was thankful for a whole weekend. He was thankful to Kilpatrick, who gave it to him.

He wished that Kil didn't know all about Kate. Kil knew Farnham, and he knew her father, Colonel Palmer. Jud was a talker; he'd never stopped talking since the first day that Hank had seen him strutting on the Plain at the Point.

Stephens turned to look at the door. Christ, what was keeping that boy?

As if in answer to the plea, the slight figure of the boy slipped through the doorway. He paused to look for the major. In his hand was a small blue envelope. Stephens took three quick steps. He dropped a handful of change into the eager paw, taking the envelope with his other hand. He ripped it open.

The blue paper carried only four words: *Of course. Come quickly.*

He took his hat and gloves from the bar, stepped into the lobby of the hotel and told the clerk that his horse should be returned to the livery stable and that his room should be held for him through Saturday night.

"Right you are, Major," the clerk said. "Suppose General Kilpatrick asks for you?"

"He'll know where to find me."

He walked happily, briskly, across the near end of Lafayette Square, where children of Senators and generals and Cabinet members played under the iron eye of the statue of Andrew Jackson, mounted, eternally doffing his hat to those who passed through the square.

The farther he went from Pennsylvania Avenue, the less elegant the houses became. "Like West Point," Kate had said, "where the distance of the house from the Plain identifies the rank of the occupant. This is colonels' country here. A block further along, you'll see nothing but captains."

The house was a three-story brick building set a few yards back from the street behind a high trimmed hedge. Similar houses lined the block, but most of them fronted on the sidewalk. A neat plate on the heavy door was lettered: COLONEL ALFRED D. PALMER. Below it was a small white calling card inserted in a metal bracket. This was printed in neat script: MRS. KATHLEEN PALMER FARNHAM.

Hank rapped the brass knocker once. It was opened almost immediately by an elderly Negro, who bowed Stephens inside.

"Good evening, sir," he said. "A nice evening."

Stephens nodded. "How are you, Howard?"

"Pretty fair, sir, for an old man. Miss Kate will be right down. She told me to show you into the library and to serve you a drink. What will you have, Major?"

"Nothing, Howard. Not now."

The servant led the way into the dark library. He lit the gas jet with a show of caution, as if he expected it to explode in his face.

"What have you heard from the Colonel, sir?" Howard, who had worked for Colonel Palmer for a quarter century, believed that every cadet who had ever studied military topography under Palmer at the Point was in constant communication with the colonel, who was presently serving as one of Grant's engineers in the Department of the Mississippi.

"Nothing lately, Howard. Things have been quiet down there, just as they have in Virginia."

Howard wrinkled his nose, as if to indicate that the war in Virginia was of little moment, without Colonel Palmer. "Have you visited the Academy lately, Major?" The old man also expected every West Pointer to return to the shrine as often as possible.

Hank smiled. "You always ask me that, Howard, and you always get the same answer. I don't go back. I didn't quite make it."

"I remember quite well, sir," the old man said. "But you ought to visit once in a while, Major. We all have friends at the Academy, sir."

Hank nodded absently, thinking that he ought to go look at the records sometime. He knew what they said. "Stephens, H. W., Class of May 1861, resigned." He could still hear Colonel Delafield's dry voice putting an end to his career: "If the young woman is in that condition, Mr. Stephens, then you have no choice. That's all, Mr. Stephens."

That's all. It didn't matter that he didn't love her and she didn't love him. It didn't even matter that she'd never been pregnant in the first place. He married her in Peekskill in the fall of 1860, while a Presidential campaign was raging, while little Kil was strutting around the Academy a few miles away across the river, poking Southrons in their aristocratic noses, while Kate Palmer was already planning her wedding to 2nd Lieut. Royce L. Farnham, U.S.M.A., Class of 1860.

I've never thought to ask Jud, Hank thought. I wonder if he ever had a chance to poke Farnham in the nose?

Howard spoke again. "The cavalry, Major, has proved to be a fine branch of service for your friends and classmates. Mister Kilpatrick is a general, and Mister Merritt, and Mister Wilson. Even Mister Custer, the young gentleman from Michigan who liked to play jokes."

"He still does," Hank said dryly. "You ought to see his uniforms."

"We sometimes see newspapers from the other side," Howard said. "The young gentlemen of your time at the Academy are doing well there, also. Mister Rossiter and Mister Pelham. Mister Farnham is a colonel now, sir."

"I know that," Hank said.

"Won't you let me get you something to drink while you wait, Major?"

"No need for waiting," said a low-timbred voice from the doorway. "I'm here. How are you, Major?"

Stephens turned quickly, feeling his blood racing as it always did when he heard her voice. He saw her smiling at him with eyes crinkled, face bright with pleasure, dark hair tumbling forward on the right side of her brow. She was dressed in dark-red silk, without hoops or other cumbersome paraphernalia beneath it, so that her body was slim and straight yet so female that he caught his breath in quick anticipation. He knew how sleekly that cloth would slide, with the pressure of his hand, on the warm firm flesh beneath. God, how long had it been since he'd held her—more than a month since he'd managed a day and a night away from the division, and in truth that had amounted to only a few hours because of the traveling time.

"Kate," he said softly, "how well you look." His voice shook with love and desire. Surely, he thought, old Howard knows what is between us. If I turn now I'll find him frowning.

"I can't say the same for you, Major," she said gently, still not coming toward him. "You look worn and tired, as if you and Kil are trying to finish the war all by yourselves. And how is Kilpatrick, H. J.?" she asked, smiling as she used her favorite form of address for the bantam cadet who had once bowed stiffly to her in the living room of her father's quarters and had introduced himself as "Kilpatrick, H. J."

She came all the way into the room, gracefully and quickly as she always moved, bringing some fragrance with her that Stephens could not identify. "Let Howard get you a drink before he leaves," she said.

Hank shook his head, watching her, his eyes moving from face to body. "I stopped at Willard's," he said. "I don't need a drink."

She was wearing a new perfume, he was sure. She always tried to have an innovation for his visits—a new way to wear her hair, some new style of dress or jewelry. Suddenly and vividly he remembered the night last fall when her surprise for him had been saved until she called him to her room and displayed herself in a diaphanous nightdress the like of which he supposed might be found only in the brothels of Paris. There was scarcely anything to it beyond a few yards of filmy lace and a couple of satin bows. When, later, he'd asked her how she'd summoned the nerve to buy it, she'd laughed and said that her French dressmaker had imported a dozen of them, for the mistresses of generals and politicians.

"All right, Howard," she said quietly. "You and Mabel can leave us as soon as you're ready. I won't need you until Monday. Have a good visit with your grandchildren. Be sure to take them some cake and pie and cookies from the kitchen."

"Yes, Miss Kate," Howard said evenly. "We will see you on Monday morning."

He knows, Hank thought. He knows very well, and he is shocked to the center of his proper soul. I wonder if he has ever contemplated telling Colonel Palmer about us.

Howard left them, going through the hall to the kitchen, where his wife was finishing the preparations for dinner. Hank took Kate into his arms swiftly, kissing her with harsh passion stored in a month's absence, with all the fire that had been subdued for weeks by the mud and freezing rain and biting winter winds of northern Virginia. They stood for a minute or two, holding each other and whispering words of love.

"Let me go, dearest," she said finally. "I'll have to go see to dinner. Unless you want to take me out to Gautier's for dinner?"

"To hell with that!" he said harshly, reaching for her slim body again. She dodged quickly and laughed at him.

"Fix yourself a drink," she said. "Howard and Mabel are still here. I'll go see if I can't hurry them along."

"You tell me to drink and Jud tells me not to," he said abruptly. "It's getting so I can't even look at a bottle of whiskey without hearing voices in my ear."

She stopped smiling and looked soberly at him. "What's wrong, Hank? What's bothering you? The war again? You're quiet down there. What is it?"

He shook his head, not answering.

"Hank, I've never said anything to you about how much you drink, have I? It's your problem, if it is a problem. And we both know it will be solved the day Lee surrenders and men stop killing each other."

He shook his head again in sudden weariness. "No, Kate. I didn't mean to sound sharp. It's this thing that Jud has got us into. It's too much on my mind."

"What is it, Hank?"

"An idea that Jud has worked out to put his name in headlines throughout the country. I'll tell you later. Jud's been telling everybody, so I might as well tell you. But it will keep." He smiled suddenly, shaking off the momentary depression. "Go hurry them along."

"And put dinner on the table?"

"My God, no. That will keep too, Kate."

She left the room. In spite of himself, he looked at the sideboard that held glasses and decanters of whiskey and wine. ". . . it will be solved the day Lee surrenders . . ." That's what she had said about his drinking problem. Would it? That would be the day when he believed she would take the first tentative step toward rejoining her husband, when he would have to think about returning to his bleak life in Peekskill, New York. He walked to the sideboard and fixed himself a drink.

As soon as the elderly Negro couple had left in the swift-falling winter twilight to walk the few blocks to the house of their son and his family, Hank and Kate needed only a long fierce embrace and a whispered agreement to abandon the dinner that was keeping warm on the back of the kitchen stove. They raced up the stairs through the shadows beyond the reach of the gaslight. In the early darkness they loved each other wildly, as if it were the first time and as if, perhaps, it were the last.

Later came the quiet talking about small matters that had happened since he'd been in Washington. Then he told her about Kil's grand design to end the war in a spectacle of glory. She sorrowed with him for the men who might die for no purpose, but she agreed that he had to follow where Kilpatrick led, that he had been right in not telling the President his doubts.

They spoke soft words of love that effortlessly removed the great unseen barriers between them, the words seeming to prove that because there was so much pleasure and splendor in being together as lovers now, therefore they would be together always. They loved each other again, gently and happily, with never a thought during the long evening for the colonel of South Carolina cavalry somewhere in the lean gray ranks of the Army of Northern Virginia, nor for the pretty and petulant wife in the big house above the Hudson who sometimes complained in her infrequent letters that she thought that "Kil ought to let you come home at least once in a while."

4

The fire jumped and flickered in the big fireplace opposite the bed. Hank had brought the dinner up from the kitchen, and served it at a bedside table, where now the inch or so of wine that remained in the bottle of burgundy caught the fire's reflection in a glow of color.

She was sleeping, her face relaxed and her hair tumbled prettily. Her arm lay across his chest. He didn't move, for fear of rousing her. All his tension, all his anxiety, all his weariness of mind had slipped away in the euphoria of the quiet hours. He smiled softly, vowing that he would, during this weekend, look neither to the past nor to the future, but would let love and peace and pleasure have their ways. And having made the promise to himself, he proceeded immediately to break it.

He turned his head to watch her sleeping. How different they were now than they had been in the wild fervor of the hours gone by. How peaceful it was, here alone with her and far from the savage world that had so torn his soul and his mind that he despaired of having them heal. He thought of lonely nights gone by, in winter quarters or in the field, when the vicious, blind, mindless brutality of the war seized and racked him. Those were the times when the whiskey bottle came in handy.

When had it all started? When had he first started to slide into the depths of horror and dread and hatred for the slaughter? Maybe when he looked upon the windows of torn flesh at Fredericksburg; maybe at Chancellorsville, in the bloody fields and shattered wood lots. Perhaps after Gettysburg, when his mind finally grasped the enormity of meaning in those three terrible days–that the Army of Northern Virginia was beaten but not crushed, and that it would fight again and again, until in the end it was reduced to a mass of blood and bone and rags.

He was fairly certain that he had seen it then, had known that the war was about to take a new turn, that the days of flashing sabers and bugle calls of glory were finished. From Gettysburg until the end it would be a bloody and brutal drive to crush Lee's legions into the filthy mud. Only when that was done would the butchery end. It was after Gettysburg that Hank Stephens became noted as a drinker in an army that generally used whiskey like water.

Most of the time, he considered that he had no problem in the whiskey bottle. Simply three or four drinks let him sleep, or relaxed his tension, or dulled the far thunder of the guns. They were really necessary when he made ready to crawl into his blankets at night, because he had a dream whenever he did not take them. The dream was always different, yet always the same. It wasn't complex, nor was it a panoramic nightmare with bizarre and horrible distortions of reality. It was, in fact, a simple dream. He always rode his horse in the dream, on a battlefield that was clouded with dust and smoke and mist. He was alone when the dream started; he could hear the guns and the shouts and screams faintly, as from a distance. Then, in the haze, he would see two men–one a Federal trooper, the other a rebel cavalryman. They hacked at each other with sabers, or blazed away with pistols. They were always different in dress, appearance, size. Their horses were brown, gray, black. Sometimes they were silent; sometimes they cursed, roared, screamed savagely. Always, however, the ending was similar. The face of one man or the other would suddenly explode into a shapeless mass of blood and bone, and he would scream lingeringly and terribly as he died. That was when Hank Stephens would wake up, shivering and wet with sweat, with his nerves screaming for a drink of whiskey.

To sleep without the dream–that was one reason why Stephens drank so heavily. The other reasons were ordinary: he liked the taste of whiskey; he now needed it to keep his hands from shaking and to give him the relaxation he had to have to do his work; drinking was a fixed habit bolstered by the other reasons. He supposed that the bottle had kept the eagles from perching on his shoulders. Kil had suggested that it had kept him from a brigade. That wasn't true; Hank would refuse a brigade even in the dim likelihood that Meade and Pleasonton would offer him one. The rigors and burdens of command, he believed, would betray him. He would try to use a brigade as a battering-ram, and would get every man killed with ruthless abandon.

How was it with Jud Kilpatrick, that the rebel scream brought a grin to his lips? Was the dream of glory always beckoning, to blind him to all else? Didn't Kil ever dream? Or worse, didn't he lie shuddering in the darkness, seeing the bodies sprawled in the dark red mud, hearing the agonized bleating of the wounded? Did he ever stare into the night, hearing young Farnsworth at Gettysburg protesting bitterly against the charge that Jud had ordered, and hearing his own–Kilpatrick's–harsh voice saying: "If you don't take them in, I will." Farnsworth had yelled, "Take that back!" and Jud had done so, and then Farnsworth had led the charge and been killed, while Kilpatrick watched calmly enough.

No, these things didn't bother Kilpatrick, who had never made a secret of his ambition. Hank easily recalled the early days of the war, when Hugh Judson Kilpatrick commanded the 2nd New York Cavalry and his adjutant was his erstwhile classmate, Lieutenant Henry Stephens; Hank brought clearly to mind, as he often did, the midnight conversations when Jud's long ugly face glowed with promise:

"Make a record for yourself–that's all there is to it. I've got a good start already–the first officer of the regular establishment wounded in the war. It was in all the papers. Now this regiment, and next a brigade! This is what I went to the Academy for. You watch me, Hank. I'll fight any time and any place, and the whole country will know my name. I'll bet you don't know who the next President will be, do you?"

Hank grinned. "I figure the one we've got now will get himself elected again."

"After the war," Kilpatrick said impatiently. "I mean after the war, after Lincoln."

"You tell me who, Jud."

"The general who gets his name in the papers the most number of times. It won't be me. I know that. I'm too young. But while he's getting himself into that job, I'm going to get to be Governor of New Jersey. By God, I am! When they're looking around for a governor, they'll remember Kilpatrick. I wish this damned regiment was New Jersey. And then the second President after the war, Hank–why not another general? Why not the general who happens to be Governor of New Jersey? Why not?"

Hank remembered how often, sometimes obliquely and sometimes directly, Jud had stated his goals. Even back in Academy days, he'd been active in New Jersey politics. He'd spent some of his leaves making stump speeches in rural Jersey areas.

And now, Hank thought, he's going to get his big chance. He has planned and schemed and connived for it, and Lincoln has given it to him. If he succeeds, not only will the whole country know his name; the people will scream it from the housetops.

The general who rode into Richmond could name his own price for the triumph. And Jud had named his long ago. How would it sound? President Hugh Judson Kilpatrick.

Hank laughed softly, and Kate moved restlessly in response. She moved her arm from his chest. He leaned forward and kissed her gently, but she did not awaken. It was just as well that she didn't; he was tired and at peace. It was a rare moment for him.

He lay supine again and closed his eyes, but he didn't go to sleep. In spite of his intention to live only in the present during this weekend, his memory slipped back to poke and probe among the years that lay scattered as they were instead of as they might have been.

In the early summer of 1860, the village of Peekskill was a middling prosperous Hudson River town. Its houses, shops, and factories perched on a dozen different levels on the east bank of the river. Its wealth was divided between new business and old fortunes. The town sometimes rested quietly on its notable history as a center of Revolutionary activity. At other times it showed a hustling energy to gain recognition as an important part of Westchester County, instead of remaining the rural cousin in the neglected northwest corner of the county. It was a pretty place in those days, and during the summer, the highlands in the area blossomed with vacationers from New York.

Hank Stephens' family, while not the wealthiest in the village, was one of the most prominent. Dr. Daniel Stephens, in addition to attending a good share of the local aches and pains, was a director of the bank, former school trustee, and four-term town supervisor. His two daughters, in their twenties, were married to fine young men, and his son was in his third year at the United States Military Academy–a career choice that Dr. Stephens might not have picked for his only son, since he was a peaceful and gentle man who abhorred the thought of war, but one in which he could take some quiet pride because his son was doing excellently both as cadet and student.

Dr. Stephens' world was securely established. His wife was, as he was fond of saying, still the prettiest girl he'd ever seen. There were enough young doctors in the town to keep him from working too hard, and he had time enough for his civic interests. He had joined the new Republican Party, leaving the rapidly expiring Whig organization, with no indication yet that such radicalism was going to cost him his post as supervisor. Matter of fact, his plurality in the village election of 1859 had been only ten votes below what it had been in 1857.

Best of all, in this summer of 1860, his son was coming home from the Academy for a long leave, and if there weren't more sick people than usual, he and Hank would do a bit of bass fishing at Lake Oscawana, where the doctor and his family had enjoyed a summer cottage for many years. Dr. Stephens looked forward to that pleasure, neglected since

Hank had left for West Point. A man wanted company when he went bass fishing.

Hank, a few miles up and across the Hudson, didn't think much about the fishing, although it came to mind a few times in the last warm days of the scholastic year. Mostly he thought of a summer devoted to getting fat on his mother's cooking, after three years of the plentiful but uninspired food of the Cadet Mess. He could see himself lying in the sun without a thought in his head, or taking a canoe out on the lake, or just lazing around in old clothes. He would shrug off the stiffness of three arduous years of constant academic and military regimentation. Perhaps he might even decide whether he would actually make the Army his career, or turn to engineering (he was alternately third or fourth in his class) or to the law. He had two years to make up his mind, in the Academy's current five-year course. At least once during the summer, he was going to have a couple of old school friends out to the lake overnight, and they would talk about old times while they polished off a bottle of whiskey. He'd had only three drinks in his life, all during Christmas leave the year before.

The morning that he was to leave for home, he saw Kate Palmer at her father's quarters near the Plain. She was packing to leave also; Major Palmer was going to spend the summer in Washington working on his principal life's interest: a book that would contain campaign and battle maps covering the entire history of the United States Army, from the gathering of the Continentals at Boston to the recent struggle in Mexico. A widower for many years, Alfred Palmer had retired to scholarship that was neatly divided between his classes in military topography and his book. Hank Stephens often wondered whether Major Palmer actually intended ever to finish the book. Certainly it could have been completed years ago; Palmer himself admitted that he had examined, and had copied or discarded, every military map that could possibly be of use to him. However, lately he had been talking of visiting England to work on the British sources for the Revolution and the War of 1812.

"You'll come to Washington for at least a week, Hank," Kate Palmer told him that morning. "Father says it's a big house and there will be plenty of room. I want you to come. You can even bring Kilpatrick, H. J., with you."

Hank grinned. "I get enough of him all year."

"You'll come, won't you?"

"I'll try, Kate. I'll see what my family has in mind."

"At least a week," she insisted. "I'll have a party, and we'll ride over in Virginia–Father has lots of friends with good horses, and we'll go boating and picnicking, and we'll have colonels in to dinner who will all want to grab you for their staffs two years from now—"

Hank laughed again, shaking his head. "You've got that wrong. Jud says that he and I are going to be sent to the plains to chase Indians. No Engineers for me, simply because I'm Jud's roommate. Jud and I, chasing Comanches. Custer will be our orderly."

"You'll be an Engineer, Hank."

"I dunno. Colonel Hardee took a dim view of the last scrap that Jud had. I aided and abetted by holding his coat and furnishing a handkerchief for his bloody nose."

"Oh, Kilpatrick!" she cried in exasperation. "He's nothing but a wild abolitionist. He probably votes Republican."

"I will, when I vote. So would you, if you could. Admit it."

"Maybe so. But at least you don't go around punching people in the eye because they talk States' Rights."

"He doesn't hit 'em in the eyes," Hank said mildly. "Usually he can't reach up that far. He aims for the chin, and has to jump to hit it. He's not so bad, Kate. He's only had one fight since Easter."

"He'll pick on the wrong man some time," she said vehemently. "Royce told me just the other day that he's taken his last sneer from Kilpatrick, H. J."

Hank shrugged, the laughter fading from his eyes. The less she said about Royce Farnham, the better he'd like it. It seemed to him that Farnham spent most of his free time at the Palmers' quarters. Hank was fairly sure of himself; he and Kate weren't engaged, but they were close enough to it that he tentatively planned a graduation-day wedding in the Cadet Chapel. Matter of fact, he intended in September of his last year to make time reservations for the use of the chapel in June. There were of course about a half-dozen other cadets who perhaps had hopes of a chapel wedding to Kate Palmer, and all of them were constant visitors at Major Palmer's quarters, but Farnham was the clearest present danger. He was handsome, wealthy, intelligent, and had the easy casual grace that so infuriated Jud Kilpatrick, and was at least part of the reason for Kil's frequent brushes with the Southerners. Hank was sometimes most grateful that Kate Palmer had been born a Yankee, because Farnham's easy scorn for the Northern commercial culture and his supercilious assumption that the tradesmen and pettifoggers would eventually knuckle down to the landed Southern gentry, quite often had Kate Palmer sputtering with indignation. What's more, Farnham would be graduating in a few days, and would be assigned to a post somewhere. Luck might post him a thousand miles away.

"Farnham does a little sneering himself," Hank said evenly. "I'll have to admit, though, that he does it like a Southern gentleman, with just a twist of the lip and an arch to his eyebrow. He doesn't snarl and spit the way Jud does."

"You all ought to stop it," she said. "The Corps is divided right down the center, half of you pounding at abolition and the other half insisting that the states must be sovereign."

"I'm prepared to stop for the whole summer," Hank said with a grin. "Over in Peekskill, it's just a matter of Democrats and Republicans, and the Democrats generally walk along with their heads down for fear somebody might speak to 'em and scare 'em out of a year's growth. I heard there were eleven Democrats by the last count. When should I plan for the Washington visit, Kate?"

"Anytime," she said. "Just tell me in one of your letters that you're coming, so I can plan things for us to do." She tossed her dark hair back from her brows and said casually: "I'll have to know beforehand, so you and Royce won't be stamping on each other's toes."

"What's he got to do with it?"

"He's going to be posted to Washington. One of his uncles is a Congressman from South Carolina. Royce is going to be assigned to duty at the War Department. Or so he says."

Hank glowered. "Whose idea was it that I might stamp on his toes, Kate? Yours or his?"

She flushed. "I shouldn't even answer that, but I will. Royce Farnham's comings and goings are not my concern, and you know it."

"I suppose he didn't know you'd be there all summer? Does he have invitations for riding and picnicking, too?"

"This conversation has gone just about far enough."

"No, it hasn't," he said quickly and harshly. "Not when you tell me you're going to spend the summer with Farnham."

"You'd better leave right now," she said. She turned and left the room. He stood there foolishly, cap in hand. He heard her light steps, running, on the stairs leading to the upper floor of the house. He went into the hall, standing at the stair well. He called once softly, tentatively: "Kate!" The answer was the banging of a door above.

He should have stayed. He knew it then, and he had full reason to know it later.

Anger gripped him. He crossed to the door, jerked it open, and thumped down the steps of the front porch. He stalked angrily back to barracks, scarcely noticing other cadets who hurried along the walks on errands connected with summer leave or summer camp. His mind was filled with images of Kate with Farnham. Kissing, embracing–gradually progressing toward the same sweet but maddening frustration that he and Kate had known for months now, each wanting to know the other physically, but both under the discipline of a society that prohibited a man from knowing a woman until the magic words of a preacher bound them together forever. If he had not been angered by the view of Farnham's opportunity to court her through the long pleasant weeks ahead, he might have braced himself to the knowledge that Kate would do nothing with Farnham that she would not do with him. Yet all he could visualize was Farnham's handsome features and charming ways, and he convinced himself that Kate would succumb to them.

In his room, he grabbed his bags, said good-bye shortly to several cadets he met in the hall and on the stairs, then walked rapidly down the winding hills to the water front, where the steam launch for Garrison across the river was filling with cadets and a few officers. He didn't look back to the left as he crossed the Plain, or he would have seen Kate standing on the side veranda of the Palmer quarters, waiting to beckon to him whenever he turned to see her.

There were men in the launch who would board the train with him at Garrison Station, then journey for days by train or boat or both to reach their homes in the West or South. Some would have only a few hours, at most a day, reaching destinations in the Eastern States. Hank Stephens was on the train for just seventeen minutes, from the time it chugged into Garrison Station until it came to a creaking halt at the water-front railroad depot in Peekskill.

His home-coming was not so much an occasion for celebration as would be those of cadets from distant parts of the Union; his family had seen him often in his three years at the Academy. Sunday visits to West Point were not at all unusual for them.

There was a party, however. His married sisters had arranged it for him, inviting eight of his old school friends from the Peekskill Military Academy, where most of the village's young men received any secondary education their parents thought necessary. (Hank had chosen PMA over a half-dozen preparatory schools in New England, mostly because some of his friends had picked the local school, and his decision had influenced his choice of career, for the commandant of cadets at the Peekskill school had influenced him to obtain the appointment to the Point.) The party was held on Hank's second night at home. One of the girls whom his sisters had invited was Caroline Blackburn.

He'd forgotten her entirely in the three years since he'd last seen her.

There hadn't been much to remember. Pig-tailed yellow hair and big blue eyes and a scrawny figure and too much height–that was about all there was to Caroline at age seventeen. She had lived with her widowed mother and her mother's brother in a big house on the way up the hill to the grounds of the Peekskill Military Academy. Her uncle, Adam Preston, was one of Peekskill's prominent attorneys. He was a long lean man with saturnine features who had a reputation for brevity and brusqueness in court and out.

Caroline was often seated on the porch of the Blackburn house when the PMA boys went home in the late afternoons. She never spoke to any of them, but just gazed incuriously as they went by. It became habit for them to try to get her to talk to them. They stopped at the gate and called questions to her about matters of no moment; she never said a word in answer. In the fashion of adolescents, they attributed her silence and her immobility to some unspoken romantic, even sexual, invitation. Each day they grew bolder, and then they discovered the reason why she never gave a sign of hearing them. One of the town boys, a shade bolder than the rest, suggested from the gate that he come up on the porch with her. "It's getting dark, Caroline. Don't you want company up there?"

Mrs. Blackburn immediately burst from the doorway behind Caroline's chair. She scolded the abashed young man with a shrill tongue, tossing reflections upon his breeding and character until the boys moved themselves hastily out of earshot. Next day, the headmaster called them all into his office and lectured them sternly for making indecent proposals to an innocent young lady. After that, they passed Caroline's house at a distance, on the other side of the street. She sat there quietly almost every day, watching them come and watching them go. Hank Stephens often had the uncomfortable feeling that he was the one she was watching particularly. After a time he went homeward alone, by another street.

It didn't seem to be the same girl at the party. Hank didn't recognize her before he heard her name. She was charming and talkative and graceful. Above all, she was beautiful. Her yellow hair was done in an intricate mass of curls and ringlets, piled high above shapely face and flashing eyes. She seemed to be wearing more rouge than was customary for Peekskill young ladies, and about her was a trace of tantalizing perfume, delicate rather than heavy, but deliciously permeating. She was wearing a green party dress that was unlike that of any other girl's–at least between waist and throat. Matter of fact, all the young men noticed immediately that there was less of it in the upper part of that area than there should have been. At one point early in the evening, she was discussing the downriver view that could be seen from the cupola atop her house. "Yes," said a young bank teller named Bill Beach, "if one leans over far enough, I imagine that one can see Tarrytown."

The rest of Caroline Blackburn's body, although well covered in the current fashion, seemed to be slim and graceful. She danced as well as Kate Palmer, Hank decided when he finally had a chance to be her partner. The other young men had crowded and circled and darted around her like trout in a big quiet pool when a May-fly hatch begins. Hank's sisters intervened quietly to parcel out males to female partners, leaving Hank with Caroline.

The party proved to be neither splendid success nor dismal failure. It was simply a pleasant social gathering of old friends who had not seen much of Hank Stephens in recent years. In the minds of almost all who were there, nothing happened to distinguish it from any of a dozen others held that summer. However, none of them was in a position to see what happened.

Late in the evening, in the shadows of the wide front porch of the Stephens' house, where honeysuckle twined and twisted over trellises to form a deep pocket of darkness, Hank Stephens kissed Caroline Blackburn. A kiss alone rarely changes lives to any appreciable extent, but this one did. It was a deep, crushing, passionate kiss, with lips parted. Their bodies pressed tightly. Hank could feel her large firm breasts and swelling thighs moving against him. His body responded instantly to intimacy; he wanted to release her, but she held him closely, kissing him again almost frenziedly before she let him go. His head was swimming with the fragrance of woman and perfume, and his mind was hazed by sensuality. He held her warm hands and whispered hoarsely in a voice he scarcely recognized as his own: "I'll call on you, Caroline. Tell your mother I'll come tomorrow."

"My mother's dead, Hank. Didn't you know? Please come. Tomorrow. Early, before my uncle returns from his office."

He nodded, not knowing or caring that she couldn't see his assent in the darkness. Then he said something that popped up from the memories of the past, a question that would lead him far along a path that until this moment he had not even known existed: "You watched me, didn't you? From the porch, years ago?"

"Only you, Hank," she whispered. "Always you. Kiss me now, and we'll go inside with the others."

The shutters and the shades of the Blackburn living room were barriers to the light of the afternoon sun, the shutters closed and the shades pulled in the belief that darkness of itself is a cooling agent. In that dim atmosphere, where whispers seemed muffled by the drowsy stillness and where the rustling of silk against flesh was a faint sibilance, Hank Stephens was introduced to sex completely for the first time. He had known a town girl or two, and a farmer's daughter of the kind they told jokes about, and an Irish corporal's Irish wife at the Point who grudgingly and angrily and gracelessly supplemented the corporal's meager pay by selling herself to a few cadets each Saturday night in a secluded thicket, near Benny Havens' tavern down by the river, where she accepted the silver dollar from each man with a muttered: "Jaysus, Mary 'n Joseph, forgive me," a supplication which usually managed to remove any aura of sensuality from the act and rarely encouraged her customers to dare certain expulsion for another visit. Hank Stephens had gone to her once, and had been violently sick before he had walked a hundred yards on the return to the Plain.

Never before, however, had Hank Stephens been offered sex disguised and offered as love, with the honored and traditional trappings of murmured endearments, long sweet kisses, and the prolonged tactics of intended surrender on feminine terms.

As a result of the strategy that dictated the tactics, Cadet Stephens, who believed himself to be the victor, was actually the defeated. His male egotism told him he had overcome feminine resistance; he had really succumbed to superior resources and accurately directed fire power. Triumphant advance was in truth only a savagely thrusting salient from which his mobile striking forces could not retreat without disaster, and to which his reserves must be committed. Had he but known it then, he might have echoed that ancient Grecian ruler who mourned: "One more such victory over the Romans, and we are utterly undone." He would have been almost correct if he had, although in truth the catastrophe and the capitulation were already accomplished.

That was the strategic concept that dominated the battlefield of shadow and summer's warmth and sounds muffled by the heavy stillness of the afternoon. The tactical developments were quite another matter.

She drew him forward and retreated in her turn, at once enticing and alarmed, attracting him ever deeper into encirclement, until they were engaged in a fierce and almost savage clash of flesh that left him spent and gasping, shamed and contrite by reason of the rules of the society he lived in, and yet already imagining the next engagement. On the other hand, Caroline lay before him in the semidarkness of the wide, soft sofa upon which she had taken him, and she was smiling gently, looking into his eyes tenderly, and stroking his smoothly shaven face with silken finger tips.

There were many questions that he might have asked himself, and if he had answered them properly, his capitulation might have been avoided. They never entered his mind, however. He did not speculate on why she had worn the enveloping brocaded dressing gown and no other single stitch of clothing; he failed to remember the admonitions of his contemporaries in amatory adventure to observe the signs of virginity; he did not wonder where and how and when she had assimilated the techniques she had demonstrated with such mastery. He was completely fascinated by the splendors of full firm breasts, rose-tipped, by columned thighs that gave no sign of the amazing strength contained within them, by the discovery in the half-light that the blond hair that crowned her lovely face was perhaps not so naturally blond as it seemed.

He had no questions; he posed himself no queries; he planned no orderly retreat, and so his ultimate defeat was assured before the conflict was fairly under way.

There were those who could have told him, had he been experienced enough, sophisticated enough, wise enough to have generated the inquiry. The word would have returned to him in one fashion or another. Bill Beach, the young teller at the bank, knew Caroline Blackburn. The tactical officer at the Peekskill Military Academy, whose wife preferred to live in Baltimore, might have supplied details, and his colleague, a lank-haired saturnine young poet who taught English composition at PMA, might have added to the story. A pair of elderly sisters, old maids both, whose actual knowledge of what was going on behind the blinds of the Blackburn living room could only be fragmentary, nonetheless kept constant vigil at curtains parted only enough to allow an outraged eye to peer forth as the participants in feverishly imagined orgies came and went. In point of fact, when Hank opened the gate and walked toward the porch that sultry afternoon, an aging female voice called from the sentry post: "Edna, come quick! Come see! She's got Dr. Stephens' son!"

There was a most important and available source of information that Hank Stephens might have tapped, if he had known enough to have resorted to it. This was represented by Adam Preston, Caroline's uncle, who lifted his eyebrow and curled his lip slightly when he was introduced to this latest young man. Being taciturn by nature, Preston said nothing of significance to young Stephens about any subject whatever during the several casual meetings they had in succeeding weeks. He might have, however, if he had been asked. And he might not. It would have depended entirely upon his feelings toward Caroline at the moment. She was a good housekeeper and a fine cook, and she was reasonably circumspect in her adventures. There was no conflict between them most of the time; indeed, there was little communication. He was really rather sorry for his niece. He remembered with strong distaste his late sister's hysterical ravings and rantings about modesty, the dangers of rape, the disgusting demands of men upon chaste human females, the constant grating orders that flowed at the adolescent girl: "Don't speak to boys; they're all disgusting . . . Pull your skirt down . . . Button the collar of your waist . . . Put your corsets on . . . Shutter your windows . . . Undress with the lights out . . . Call a policeman if a man speaks to you . . . Don't ever let one of those nasty boys touch you. . . ." On and on it went. His niece's behavior now seemed almost logical to him. Out of pity and hope of reformation, he might have allowed her to snare any man she could. On the other hand, Dr. Stephens was an old friend. His son was a young man of character and intelligence. If Adam Preston were to be questioned at the right moment, he might say: "Stay away from her, young fellow. She will ruin you."

The question never came up.

Hank Stephens never went bass fishing with his father that summer, although he spent many of his days at the summer cottage at Lake Oscawana. It was a favorite place for him and for Caroline. There were no near neighbors to observe them. They could do as they pleased, and they did. Their activities centered in sex; it dominated the daylight hours that they were able to spend at the lake. They were often at the cottage three times a week, although the trip with a fast team took an hour and a half each way.

Hank Stephens gave no thought to the future, beyond the gloomy prospect of returning to the Academy at the end of the summer. He was completely lost in sensuality. (In later years, his bitterness toward Caroline was ever tempered with the memory of what she had taught him about physical love.)

He did not write to Kate Palmer, after dispatching one short note stating that he would not be able to visit Washington that summer, adding a cursory apology for his rude conduct toward her on his last day at the Point. She answered the letter politely, accepting his excuse for not coming to visit, but not mentioning his apology.

Occasionally, he would vaguely consider that he and Caroline Blackburn had to arrive at some decision for the future, but she never seemed to think of tomorrow. All her whisperings of love were tuned to the present–today was important and tomorrow might never come. If it did, then it would be today once more.

The summer sped swiftly. Suddenly they were in the last days of

August. He was required to be at the Military Academy on September 1, a Monday. Suddenly, in a summer of todays, tomorrow came. He told her that he had to return to the Point. They were out on Lake Oscawana, sunning themselves on blankets atop Goose Rocks, in a stretch of shoal water where jagged boulders thrust upward from the lake bottom to make a picnic spot for vacationers.

"You can't," she said simply. "I'm going to have a baby, Hank."

It was November before he discovered that she was not pregnant at all. She told him late on the night of November 6, the day that Lincoln was elected. Adam Preston came home from the town's Republican headquarters to say that the clicking telegraph already had given word that there was no hope for Douglas. The Illinois lawyer was surely the victor. He and Hank opened a bottle and sat in the kitchen drinking whiskey and water until the bottle was half-empty. Then Adam Preston went quietly upstairs to bed. Hank stayed there, sipping at his drink, wondering if there would be a war as the Southrons threatened. If they proved to be that stupid, then his life would change once more. The country would need his three years of rigid discipline and rigorous training. He almost hoped that the South would choose the road to war. With only two months of his marriage gone by, he knew already that it was a failure. He and Caroline had nothing in common once their bodily hungers were satisfied. They had already engaged in several sharp arguments, each resulting in a day or so of sullen silence between them until reconciliation came with a sudden fierce love-making.

There was no pleasure or satisfaction for Hank in his work, either. Upon his resignation from the Academy, he had taken up the reading of law in Adam Preston's gloomy office, where he had discovered within a few days that the legal profession was to his mind a dry, musty, airless and dark cul-de-sac in which he was bound to shrivel and become desiccated.

There was no doubt about it. Sitting there with a few drinks in his belly, he knew what he wanted. He wanted a war, or an insurrection, or at least a time of long continued tension–any of these would put him back in the Army where he belonged. If it lasted long enough, he might even be given a place in the permanent establishment.

Oh God, he thought, let South Carolina mean what they say! Let all those Southern bastards like Royce Farnham do exactly what they are shouting about.

These were reasonable thoughts for a West Point cadet who had resigned because he had to, and who was quietly getting drunk at his kitchen table in anticipation that the election of a prairie lawyer to the Presidency was going to change his entire life. He didn't yet know, of course, what war was really like. He hadn't seen in all his twenty-four years a single person killed by violence; he'd never heard a horse scream in anguish; he'd never seen an eighteen-year-old boy sitting on the ground staring at the ragged red stump of his right arm and crying for his mother. He'd never had the dream of the two troopers hacking and blasting each other, nor had he yet seen the face explode in his dreams.

He wanted the South to carry out its threat. That would give some exciting purpose to his life.

Maybe he'd get killed. He didn't think much about that. It wouldn't matter. He already knew that he didn't love Caroline, and he suspected that she didn't love him. He found himself thinking of Kate Palmer—Kate Palmer Farnham now; she and Royce were married in Washington in the middle of October. Farnham was an aide to Jefferson Davis, Secretary of War in Buchanan's Cabinet.

He sat there and sipped his whiskey and pitied himself for all he had thrown away, and he consoled himself by dreaming that he could at least retrieve a part of it when Royce Farnham declared war on the United States of America. He smiled at that thought. Not what he meant, at all! When South Carolina declared war. That's what he meant. When South Farnham declared war on Abraham Lincoln.

Caroline came into the kitchen to stand with arms akimbo before him, staring at him angrily, telling him coldly to get to bed before he got too drunk to stand up. She wasn't about to put him to bed.

He grinned at her and told her that they had a new President, and that there was going to be a war with South Carolina, and that he and Hugh Judson Kilpatrick would lick the entire state all by themselves.

"You're drunk," she said coldly. "Go to bed and sleep it off."

"You're in a delicate condition," he told her amiably. "You're the one who ought to go to bed, my dear. I'm going to sit here and work out a few problems in military strategy. The siege of Charleston, South Carolina, my dear."

"You fool!" She tried to pull him to his feet. "You have to go to work tomorrow."

"No, I don't. Tomorrow I'm going to join Mr. Lincoln's army."

"Hank, I'm getting very angry. Go to bed before you get sick."

"Not me. You go to bed. You need rest in your condition, my dear."

"I'm not in any condition, you damned fool! I'm no more pregnant than you are." She ran from the room, leaving him staring after her, his mouth slack with the effects of the whiskey, but his eyes showing the sudden pain of understanding. After a while, he began to weep soundlessly, his head on his folded arms. He fell asleep there, remaining until a cold wind rising at dawn rattled the shutters to awaken him.

He never asked her for the truth—had she lied to him from the beginning? Had she honestly believed she was pregnant? Had she lost the child in an early miscarriage? Had she loved him, or at least desired him, so much that she could not have waited for graduation? Had she been so callous as to believe that the Academy was only another boys' school? He never asked, and she never told him.

In the spring of 1861, a month before his class was hastily graduated from the Academy and sent to the battle lines in Virginia, Henry W. Stephens went to Washington, D.C., where a short meeting with Senator Ira Harris of New York and a longer meeting with Colonel Alfred Palmer in the War Department resulted in his commission as Second Lieutenant of Cavalry in the Army of the United States. In June of '61, Captain Hugh Judson Kilpatrick was wounded at Big Bethel, the first officer of the regular establishment to become a casualty. In July of '61, Henry W. Stephens was commissioned captain himself, in the brand-new 2nd New York Cavalry, called the "Ira Harris" Cavalry. His commission was the result of that short meeting with the Senator in the spring. In September of '61, Lt. Colonel Hugh Judson Kilpatrick took command of the 2nd New York, and whooped with delight while he pumped the hand of his friend and erstwhile classmate, Captain Henry W. Stephens.

"You and me, Hank," Little Kil's voice rasped happily, "we'll whip those Southron sonsabitches together. You and me, we'll ride to glory, Hank."

Kate Farnham began to cry when she awakened. Hank was neither surprised nor perturbed. It happened almost every time they were together. He understood why she wept even though they never talked about it. It wasn't necessary to talk. She was crying because she believed there was no hope for them. She knew that he didn't love his wife, and had probably not been in love with her when he married her.

Hank had no way to comfort her. He lay quietly beside her, holding her hand gently, waiting until the quiet sobbing died away. He knew what would happen then. She always asked the same question, in one form or another.

"How is the war, dearest?"

He told her then of his doubts and fears about Kilpatrick's wild scheme, that it would be fruitless. He said again that he knew how the war must end–not with guidons streaming and cavalrymen riding triumphantly through the streets of Richmond, but mercilessly, terribly, in a bath of blood such as the world had never seen.

"We can help," he said calmly enough. "If we get into the city, we can kill them all–the whole nest of traitors, Davis and the rest of them. We can burn the city and its stores and war plants and docks and ships, and the houses too, because traitors live in them. We can kill and destroy, and it may help some. It just might make Lee surrender a month or two sooner. It just might."

"Kill them, Hank?" she whispered. "You mean that?"

"I mean it," he said without passion. "I don't know whether Jud does. I don't know whether the President does. I think Mr. Stanton might. He's a hard man."

"You're not, Hank," she said softly and gently. "You never were. I know how much you hate it all."

"Hating has nothing to do with it," he said. "If we're going, and if we get there, we might as well make a good job of it."

They lay quietly for a while in the darkness of the midnight hour, without speaking, each of them sadly dreaming a dream that neither of them believed could ever come true.

Again, without words, they turned to each other and made love once more while the fire died to glowing ashes in the fireplace and while the great city quieted after its customary noisy wartime evening, to rest and gather strength for the busy wartime day tomorrow.

After a time, they also slept, hands clenched and bodies touching, as if each wished to ensure the presence of the other upon awakening.

5

The squad of troopers lounged comfortably on the seats and on the wagon tongues of several ambulances that were parked in the vast open-front wagon shed. One of them whittled with painstaking care at a small slab of pine, fashioning breasts and belly and thighs of a woman out of the soft wood. Halfway through the process, he had stopped for a minute and stared at the small half-formed doll in his hand, turning it over and over. Then, with a swift slash of the sharp knife, he had cut off the already shaped head, and had continued his careful work on the body. Two other troopers were playing cards witlessly by simply matching euchre hands that each dealt to the other in turn. The other men were talking about women and drinking and war.

It was late afternoon. A cold drizzling rain was falling. Beyond the shed, toward the village of Brandy Station, a grunting locomotive was preparing to shunt livestock cars onto the short spur of track that led to the wagon shed. The troopers watched disinterestedly as the train's brakeman waved hand signals and yelled incomprehensible directions to the engineer. One of the troopers said casually to another: "I'll bet them sonsabitches get good money for that." The other one nodded. "Nobody shootin' at 'em, neither."

From one of the livestock cars came the questioning whinny of a horse. The troopers' horses, tethered in the shed, all lifted their heads.

"Remounts, in February!" said one of the troopers disgustedly. "You can't tell me, Sarge, that that don't mean something. You can't tell me that it don't mean trouble."

The sergeant in charge of the squad carefully considered the stub of cigar he was smoking. He turned it over and over, studying it dubiously. "I ain't told you nothing so far," he said mildly. "You been doing all the telling."

"Sure. Suppose you put it all together instead of me," the trooper answered vehemently. "First Little Kil and Major Stephens traipse off to

Washington. Johnston says they seen the President, by God, all very secret. Then Kill Cavalry comes back here looking like the weasel coming out of the hen house. And Johnston swears up and down and sideways that there's something cooking, only he don't know what it is. Stephens wouldn't tell him, he says. And then Kil races over here to headquarters every day, talking to Meade and Pleasonton and every goddam general in the goddam Army. And Stephens comes back from Washington, where Johnston says he got hisself laid as usual, and he works all night, every night, on papers and maps, and locks 'em up when he's done. And drinking all the time with that sad go-to-hell look on his face. And we draw new equipment, and the farriers are going all day long on new shoes for the goddam horses. And now we got remounts sent down from Washington, in the middle of the winter. You can't tell me all that don't mean nothing!"

"It might mean spring is coming," said First Sergeant Ben Turley, grunting the words as he heaved the stub of cigar out into the rain. "Anyway, Simmons, you been with this outfit long enough to know we get remounts whenever we can." He grinned. "Kil didn't earn his nickname for nothing. I bet we got the highest remount rate in the whole Cavalry Corps."

"Nope," Simmons said abruptly. "Something's cooking, all right."

The other troopers who were listening nodded agreement. The card-players and the whittler paid no attention.

"You take my advice, you'll just let it cook," Turley said. "And don't pay no attention to Johnston, neither. He's got a big mouth."

They're not stupid, Turley thought. If they got a look at some of those maps of Major Stephens', they'd know as much as I do. Good thing they don't. This camp would be buzzin' like a hive of bees, and within a day or two the word would be across the Rapidan. The rebs would sure relish the chance to sit there waitin' for us. Richmond! Jee-sus, Little Kil must of gone crazy altogether.

The string of cars creaked and groaned to a halt before the shed. Turley left the shelter of the building, stepping ankle-deep into the mud outside. "Let's go, boys," he said. "Now we'll see what the government's paying a hundred and fifty-nine greenbacks for this winter."

A heavily bearded lieutenant of cavalry and four troopers clambered down from the caboose at the end of the train. Turley saluted casually and identified himself as First Sergeant, Company B, 2nd New York Cavalry. The lieutenant nodded sourly, looking around him in disgust at the mud and the rain and the drab countryside. He took a sheaf of papers from his blouse pocket.

"Here you are, Sergeant. Sign for 'em."

Turley smiled. "Little previous, ain't you, Lieutenant? I ain't seen 'em yet."

"Well, goddammit, man, they're all there. In the cars. Forty remounts."

"Yep. Maybe so, Lieutenant. Have your boys trot 'em out, and if all of 'em are horses, and all of 'em have got four legs and two eyes, and none of 'em don't break a leg coming out of the cars, then I'll sign for forty horses."

The lieutenant glared, cursed, and then shrugged. "Get those nags out of there," he yelled to his men.

Within a few minutes, the horses stood in the thick mud beside the tracks, some of them docile and others very skittish from the effects of the rough, noisy ride on the cars. Turley looked them over as his men clipped long lead lines to halters. They were a good bunch this time, some better than others, but all of them big enough and young enough and healthy enough, at first glance, for the rigors of cavalry service. There didn't appear to be a single plow horse in the lot.

"They look pretty good for a change," he said to the lieutenant, who was impatiently proffering the papers.

"General Wilson's doing," the officer said. "A few weeks and he's changed the whole procurement system. Any horse contractor that doesn't furnish according to specifications, Wilson jumps all over him. Say, Sergeant, you people are really in a rush down here, aren't you?"

"What rush is that, Lieutenant?"

"These horses, and all the rest of them coming down from Washington. Every order says: 'Expedite delivery to the Third Cavalry Division, Army of the Potomac, at the siding, Brandy Station, Virginia.' Somebody must be in a hell of a hurry to get started on the rebs. It's only February, for God's sake."

Turley smiled, taking the papers from the lieutenant, and touching the point of a stubby pencil to his tongue. "We're hell on horses, sir. You know that we call the general Kill Cavalry."

The lieutenant shook his head, assuming an air of secret knowledge. "No, no, Sergeant. Maybe you fellows haven't heard about it. I guess I shouldn't be telling you. But who's got a better right to know? We've got horses listed for Custer, too. I don't envy you. A big raid in bad weather."

Turley's lips closed to a wide, tight line. He made a show of studying his signature on the receipts. Goddammit, he thought, does everybody know about it?

"What raid is that, Lieutenant?" he asked carefully.

"You fellows and Custer," the officer said, lowering his voice to a whisper. "They say you're going to hit Stuart at Charlottesville. It will be the biggest cavalry fight of the war."

"I'm glad you told me," the sergeant said, relaxing and smiling. "It helps to know where you're going."

"Don't let on I told you," the lieutenant said.

"Don't worry. I won't. I won't tell a soul."

That's just fine, Turley thought, as he took leave of the officer with a salute that was not much more than a wave of his hand. Too bad for Custer's boys to have the rebs know they're coming, but just fine for us. Because if I can hear it from a lieutenant who does his fighting in the bar at the National and at Willard's, then Lee and Stuart know it already. And that's fine. Custer will catch hell, but we may just ride all the way in without a fuss.

"All right, boys," he said to his men. "Climb up and let's get these beauties back to Stevensburg. Look 'em over as we go along. If you want to swap, do it before we turn 'em in at the stables. I'll take that ragged chestnut with the mule's ears. He looks about as ornery as I do."

They started for the cavalry camp, clopping liquidly through the soft mud of the road. They were coldly miserable in the rain. In every direction stretched the company streets of the Army of the Potomac in winter quarters, with huts of all descriptions curling wood smoke into the heavy atmosphere. There were plenty of infantry soldiers abroad in spite of the rain, and the squad of cavalry rode to the accompaniment of the foot soldier's invariable gibe at the cavalry trooper: "Mister, here's your mule!"

Passing the slab-sided depot at Brandy Station, where a locomotive with a string of passenger cars puffed lazily at rest, the squad saw a young cavalry colonel hand a pair of crutches to an orderly, then swing awkwardly into the saddle of a handsome, well-groomed black horse. The orderly adjusted the right stirrup to contain the boot of what was obviously a wooden leg.

"Who's he, Sarge?" Simmons asked. "He ain't but a baby, and a colonel already."

"Name of Dahlgren," Turley said. "Used to be on Hooker's staff. I didn't know he was a colonel."

"What regiment has he got, I wonder? With a wooden leg, looks like from the way he holds it. How can you serve in the field with a wooden leg?"

"Maybe he's staff again. Maybe Pleasonton. He don't mean anything to us. Let's get these nags to home before they melt in the rain."

A few hundred yards along the road to Stevensburg, the boyish colonel with the wooden leg rode rapidly by the long train of horses, spattering mud as he went. A string of soft curses followed his stiff-armed salute as he rode past Turley at the head of the column. Turley glared after him. The sergeant's right arm was still lifted, not so much in salute as to wipe the mud from his face. "You ignorant young bastard!" Turley muttered.

In the chill darkness of the February evening, Ben Turley had his men stable the new horses. He then dismissed the squad and reported to Company B's headquarters, where he found Captain John Mitchell and Major Henry Stephens talking over coffee and cigars. Jack Mitchell was a lean veteran of a half-dozen compaigns and scores of skirmishes. He was popular with the troopers of Company B because he wasn't a glory hunter. He never volunteered his troopers for hazardous missions, although Company B seemed to collect enough of them because Mitchell was a careful and conscientious cavalryman. He and Hank Stephens were close friends, partly because Mitchell was one of the few officers in the regiment who didn't treat Hank with stiff suspicion and reserve because he was a West Pointer. Mitchell seemed to feel that West Pointers weren't much different from anybody else, which was a rare attitude in an army that tended to automatic status assignments of its officers into two groups, "Pointers," and "the rest of 'em."

Sergeant Turley spoke to Mitchell first. "Forty remounts, sir," he said. "All prime and all in good shape."

Mitchell nodded, glancing at the shipping list that Turley put on the field desk. "Any that look real good, Ben?"

"A big black, sir. Kind of ugly, but he looks strong. Want me to hold him out for you?"

"Black? The hell with him," Jack Mitchell said. "I've been in this army too long for that. I can hear the reb sharpshooters now, calling their shots on the fellow that's riding the big black horse. I'll look 'em over tomorrow, Ben, and I'll pick me out a dirty old brown plug that looks as if he used to pull an ice wagon."

Stephens spoke up quietly. "What are the men saying, Sergeant?"

"Same as usual, sir. 'Where we going, Sarge? Come on, Sarge. Tell us the story.' They think there's a raid coming up, Major. They don't know where or when." Turley told the two officers about the rumor given him by the lieutenant from Washington.

"Good enough," Stephens said. "If that one crosses the Rapidan and gets to Stuart's ears, he may move in toward Charlottesville and wait for us. Too bad for Custer. Good for us."

"We could make sure they hear it," Turley said. "There's a half-dozen swapping parties back and forth every day, sir. You know that."

Stephens nodded that he knew, then shook his head to the suggestion. "No, for two reasons. The rebs aren't stupid; they would take a dim view of any story that was planted by pickets swapping coffee for tobacco. And if they really believed it, they would certainly be waiting to rip Custer to pieces. Everybody will be better off if they're just puzzled." Stephens eyed the sergeant speculatively. "Exactly how much do you know about all this, Ben?"

Turley was silent a moment. He knew what Stephens was driving at—by gauging the amount and accuracy of Turley's knowledge, the major would have a pretty good guideline to the speculations of the other non-commissioned officers, and in turn, how much the men would know before many more days went by.

"Before I answer that, sir, can I ask how many copies of those maps are around this camp?"

Stephens tapped the locked field desk. "I have this set, and General Kilpatrick has another."

"All right, then. I saw the maps, so I know where we're going. But unless you and the general have been showing them around, nobody else knows. Only what I said: new equipment, horses being shod, remounts coming in—they know there's going to be a raid."

"Hell, Hank," Mitchell said, laughing. "I don't even know as much as the sergeant seems to. All I am sure of is that we're going across the Rapidan. You're worrying too much about it."

"Somebody has got to worry. Kil sure won't."

"You need me any more tonight, Major? Captain?"

Mitchell shook his head. Stephens said, "No, Ben. Good night."

Turley remounted his horse and rode through the cavalry camp, bearing west along a muddy road in the general direction of Culpeper Courthouse. There were few riders abroad in the miserable weather. He met a party of pickets of the 6th Michigan of Custer's brigade, and a little later was challenged in a half-hearted manner by men of the O.D.'s party, completing its day-long circuit of the cavalry picket line of twenty-five miles along the Rapidan.

As he rode, Turley tried to shake off the sense of oppression that seemed to hold him in a loose grip. He was tired from a long day's duty, but not overly so, and he was a veteran of almost three years' service in the cavalry; the duties of a day in winter quarters shouldn't have taxed him.

I'm catching it from Stephens, he thought. This Kilpatrick scheme has got him on edge. I don't blame him. I wish I'd never got a look at those damn maps.

They had been easy to read, the night that Stephens had fallen asleep over them with a tumbler of whiskey in his hand. Turley had helped the major to sprawl on his cot, then had locked up the maps for the night, but not without looking at them first. The details had startled him—Force A and Force B, and the symbols had indicated that five hundred men in Force B would swing south and west of Richmond and come riding in through the back gate. You don't split a big cavalry force deep in enemy territory. That would be Rule One in a book of tactics compiled by First Sergeant Benjamin Turley. And just suppose the rebs closed that back gate, expecting company. Just suppose old Jeb or Wade Hampton closed it with a division of cavalry.

"Goddam," whispered Turley into the rain that tapped with chilling fingers at his stiff poncho. "I just hope I ain't included in that Force B. Matter of fact, I just as soon stay to home and mind the store."

He made a conscious effort to brighten his appearance and his spirits, as he turned the horse into a winding drive that led to a big house set on a knoll looking toward the distant Rapidan. The house was aglow with yellow light. An old dog barked two or three times in a gravelly voice as Turley's horse began to trot friskily in anticipation of feed and shelter. The sergeant whistled once softly to quiet the dog. He rode past the house and stabled the horse with practiced speed.

It was a double house, in effect. Beyond the main and older portion of the dwelling, a small wing had been added. It had a separate entrance. Turley headed that way. As he passed the wide veranda of the main section, a soft voice hailed him. "Good evening, Sergeant."

"Hello, Mr. Barr," he answered.

The man stepped into the dim light cast by a lamp inside the hall. He was small and slender, almost frail, with a thin, kindly face. "I thought I heard guns across the river," he said. "I stepped out on the porch to listen. Is there fighting yonder, Sergeant?"

"Not that I know of, sir. Nothing from our side, anyway."

"My imagination, I suppose. It's a little early in the year for fighting. Well, good night to you, Sergeant."

"Good night, Mr. Barr."

Turley walked the few remaining steps to the small porch of the lesser wing of the house.

Nice old codger, Ben thought. Got this damn big plantation and all the fences gone for campfires, and all the shrubbery trampled into the mud, and thousands of horses stripping his fields of anything they can grip with their teeth. And no word of complaint. He rents us the rooms for five dollars a month and never curls a lip at us for being dirty thieving Yankees. We're lucky, Emma and me.

The door opened while he was removing his boots on the porch. His wife held it wide, smiling at him. "Hello, Ben. You're right on time."

The smell of baking floated through the open doorway, along with another nose-wrinkling aroma. He sniffed audibly, trying to identify it.

"Chicken and dumplings," she said.

"Where'd you get the chicken?" he said, stepping over the sill and taking her in his arms. He kissed her gently.

She didn't answer his question, but held tightly to him, then kissed him with vigor.

"Hold on," he said gruffly, laughing. "Let me get inside."

She stepped back, sighing and brushing herself. "Now I'm all wet from your poncho."

"Your fault," he told her, grinning. "You could of let me take if off before you grabbed me."

She moved away from him, taking off her damp apron and eying it ruefully. Then she looked solemnly at him. "Ain't you even going to ask me, Ben?"

"Ask what, Emma? Good Lord, let me get in the house and get dried off. Besides, I asked you. Where'd you get the chicken?"

"Traded with Mr. Barr. He was saying he had too many roosters with the young chickens, so I gave him a pound of the quartermaster's coffee for two of them. Go ahead. Ask me, Ben."

"Yes, dear," he said softly. "You all right now?"

"No, I'm not," she beamed. "I marked off another day on the calendar. That's fifteen over my regular time." Suddenly she frowned. "And that's not the way to ask. 'You all right now?' As if there was something wrong with the chance that maybe we're going to have a baby."

He looked at her in concern. "Well, there is something wrong with it if you get in the family way down here in Virginia."

"I know. I know. As soon as I'm sure, I'll go back to Peekskill. Dr. Stephens can take care of me just fine when the time comes."

He crossed the warm kitchen to the door at the left, leading into their bedroom. He put away his poncho and boots, took off his blouse, and slipped his feet into a pair of worn carpet slippers. Emma came into the room behind him.

"You haven't got the duty tonight, Ben?"

"No, dear," he said without turning around. "Sixth Michigan. The poor bastards. It looks to rain a lot more before it lets up."

"Come and eat," she said. "And take a big drink of whiskey first. You don't want to come down with something in this weather." She paused, then said musingly, "Ben, I don't feel a bit different. You think I should?"

He grinned. "Now how the hell would I know, Emma? I ain't used to asking women in that condition how they feel."

"Seems I ought to feel different, somehow. If it's so, and not just another false alarm. We done just what the doctor said."

Ben groaned mockingly. "We sure did, Emma. Goddammit, there was days this last month when I thought I wouldn't last out the day. And then comes the night, and here we go again! I must be getting old."

"Don't swear, Ben," she said absently, as she led the way to the kitchen. Suddenly she turned, flushing. "You sound like it was a chore, like picket duty, or something."

He laughed. "It sure to God ain't like picket duty. More like skirmishing and then a battle." He pursed his lips and whistled the bugler's "Charge." He put his arm around her and led her to the table, feeling her softness and warmth against him. "I love you, Emma, and I hope just as much as you do that you're going to have a baby. Now you dish out the chicken while I scrub my hands. I'm hungry as one of Jeb Stuart's troopers."

Ben Turley was a big man who liked to eat, and especially he liked his wife's cooking. This had been a good winter for him, since his wife had pulled up stakes at home and had come down to the Army. It was almost like living at home, having her there. It was even better in some ways; the first sergeant of a troop of cavalry had pretty good pickings that didn't have to be accounted for—things like coffee and tea and other staples, as well as a man detailed now and then to cut firewood for Emma and for the Barrs. He could always send a trooper out with provisions, or to string clotheslines, or to repair the rickety furniture with which their quarters were furnished.

Ben sat down at the table, ready to tear into the chicken and dumplings, thinking of the men back at camp who were likely having the eternal beans and salt pork for supper. He was grateful to Emma for the food and lots of other things. He always had clean clothing and carefully pressed uniforms. He had his hair trimmed neatly. There were a dozen other things he was thankful for.

It had been her idea to come south from Peekskill to Virginia; he'd written to her and said there were lots of women around winter quarters —officers' wives living in Culpeper, and nurses, and workers for the Sanitary Commission and the Christian Commission. Next thing he'd known, he'd had a letter saying she was on her way, and then he'd had to scurry around until he'd found these quarters with the Barr family.

It was a good living she provided for him, all right, and he'd miss her when she had to pack up and head back north in the spring. He had all the comforts of home, and he had his own woman to keep him in warm pleasure through the cold nights that were so lonely for so many hundreds of thousands of other men in the camps along the Rapidan. He was grateful.

He hoped that she would get her wish. There was nothing else that would keep her happy and contented up home while he soldiered with Kilpatrick.

He wondered about their chances, though. They'd been married five years, and she hadn't ever got in the family way, and not through lack of trying, either.

His mind switched back over the years to the consultation he'd had with Dr. Stephens, the major's father. That had been a year after he and Emma had been married, when all she'd talked about was getting pregnant. He'd gone to the doctor to find out if there was any good reason why she didn't.

The doctor had asked a lot of questions, personal questions about the way they were in bed, and how often did they do it, and things like that which were embarrassing, in a way, to talk about to another man, even though he was a doctor. Then he'd examined Ben, shook his head, and asked some more questions. As soon as Ben understood what the doctor was searching for, he'd told him the truth. There'd been a Mexican girl, when he was in the war down there. He was just a youngster, and he'd picked up an awful dose from that girl.

Dr. Stephens had nodded. "Maybe, Ben. We don't know too much about these things. That may be it. The medical journals say so. They say sometimes a disease like that will leave you sterile. I dunno, to tell you the truth. I can find out, maybe, by writing a few letters."

Ben had shaken his head slowly. "Leave it lay, Doc. We'll keep trying, me and Emma. It don't seem possible to me, what you say. Anybody will tell you that it ain't no worse than a bad cold."

"Did you think you had a bad cold?"

"Hell, no. Wasn't any doubt in my mind."

He thought about it once in a while. He'd even questioned an Army surgeon about the probability that he could not engender children, posing the question as if asking for a friend. The surgeon had shrugged, said he didn't think it very likely that a simple dose would have that result. Hell, it wasn't much worse than a bad cold, was it? So Ben had always figured that Dr. Stephens was talking through his hat, in a manner of speaking.

Of course, there was nothing wrong with Emma. She'd been a widow when he'd married her. Her husband and her three children had all died of diphtheria. Actually, he'd met her through Dr. Stephens. He remembered how it had been. Stephens had been worried about her, after her family had all died. He said that if she didn't perk up and quit mooning about the dead children, she'd wind up in the asylum. Her husband had been a quiet man who'd worked briefly for Ben Turley, who was foreman in the iron foundry in Peekskill. Dr. Stephens said that Turley ought to go see her, and try to comfort her, and maybe perk her up a little. They were all members of the Methodist church together–even though Ben hadn't set foot inside for years. He'd called on her one Sunday five years before, and that had been the start of it. They were married within three months, and he'd never regretted a day of it.

Their only regret was shared–that she had not yet produced another child to help her dim the memory of the terrible week in which her entire family had died. Ben knew that she still grieved deeply. Sometimes he'd waken in the night to find her weeping. There was no way to soothe her.

Sometimes he was slightly annoyed to know that during their fierce love-making, she was often thinking only of the happy prospect of having a baby. At other times, he'd grin to himself and say, why the hell not? That's what we do it for, ain't it? That's what the Good Book says.

He hoped for her sake that this time she'd missed her monthlies for the right reason. But he was less optimistic than she was. It had happened before. She was in her thirties; Doc Stephens had said that lots of women didn't follow the calendar.

"What are you thinking, Ben?" she asked as he sat with a chicken leg held between thumb and forefinger, halfway between his plate and his lips.

He smiled at her. "Lots of things," he answered. "Got a new horse today. Big mean-lookin' bastard. Thinking about what we're going to name that baby you say you're going to have. How about Hugh Judson Kilpatrick Turley?"

"Never! I wouldn't name a mongrel dog after that ugly man. You don't mean it, do you, Ben?"

He laughed aloud, then took a big bite of chicken, tearing the flesh from the bone with strong tobacco-stained teeth. "I don't mean it,

Emma. Third thing I was thinking–cup of coffee and then it will be bedtime. I'm damned tired tonight."

"You are, Ben?"

He laughed again. "Not that tired, sweetheart. Never that tired."

She blushed happily, then seemed thoughtful. "How come you got a new horse, Ben? You always told me that remounts were the first sign of campaigning."

"Little Kil's going to take us on a ride, Emma."

She suddenly looked frightened. "Where, Ben?"

"You know I won't tell you," he said softly. "Shouldn't of even said that. Pour my coffee, Emma, and then we'll go to bed."

6

The brilliantly lighted ballroom had been constructed of raw timber by carpenters from the ranks of the II Corps for the single purpose of providing a place to hold that corps' Washington's Birthday Ball. The big building, more than a hundred feet long and about half as wide, was jammed with generals, field officers, and politicians from Washington, all beaming in the company of gaily dressed ladies. There was also a large number of junior officers in attendance, but not many of them had the chance to talk to, let alone dance with, a female all through the happy evening.

Hank Stephens and Kate Farnham managed to have two dances together. Most of the time Hank stood against the wall, watching her swing in the arms of colonels and generals. Kilpatrick danced with her, and so did George Custer, in spite of the fact that his bride of thirteen days, Elizabeth Bacon of Monroe, Michigan, was scarcely ever out of touch with his magnificently gold-laced sleeve. That was a bright spot of the evening for Hank, to see how Mrs. Custer was watching jealously every turn of the waltz that her darling "Autie" had with Kate Farnham, even though at times it was difficult for her to follow them, since she herself was being borne about the crowded floor in the eager arms of Hugh Judson Kilpatrick. Little Kil danced with many ladies during the evening, and some of them were critical of him for it; the wife whom he had married on graduation day in 1861 was dead and in her grave for only a few months.

In the main, it was a painful evening for Hank Stephens, as had been the evening before, when Kate had come down on the train from Washington, and as tomorrow would be. He almost wished she hadn't come. He hadn't known that she would be there; she'd had a belated invitation from Senator Harris and his wife to join their company of young ladies from Washington.

Hank knew quite well that his unhappiness was completely selfish.

He wanted her to himself alone, and there had been no chance of that, nor would there be. She was quartered in a rambling farmhouse a mile or so from Brandy Station, with a dozen other young women. So far the only physical contact they had managed was in dancing; he didn't see how he could last through another twenty-four hours without crushing her to him. They had whispered to each other some few words of love, but that only made his longing for her harder to bear.

Good God, he told himself angrily, use your head! Let her have a good time. Just watch her and be thankful that she loves you and that she came here at all. Don't be a damned fool about it.

She rejoined him at the wall after enduring a cumbersome waltz with General Pleasonton, who somberly bowed to Kate and to Hank before he walked away, his short beard bristling and his brow wrinkled, as if dancing were a punishment inflicted upon him by the War Department.

Hank and Kate were immediately joined by the Custers, and were introduced to the pretty, sharp-eyed bride by the Beau Sabreur of Union cavalry. Hank noticed with amusement that Custer's long golden locks had been shorn for the wedding, but that the general's self-designed velvet uniform was made more ornate than ever by the addition of large golden stars on the rolled collar, probably embroidered and sewn into place by the bride. Hank also decided in a matter of seconds that Kate and Libby Custer weren't going to be the best of friends. Each was examining the other without any show of warmth.

"You're looking well, General," Hank said quietly to Custer.

"I'm just fine, Hank. How are you?" Custer said absently, frowning slightly as he listened to his wife saying sweetly to Kate: "Autie tells me he knew you at the Academy, Mrs. Farnham."

"Autie?" questioned Kate, just as sweetly. "Oh, you mean Fanny. That's what they called him, you know."

"Now, Kate," Custer said quickly. "Don't start that again."

"Whatever did they call you that for, my dear?" Libby Custer asked her tall and very masculine husband.

"Just a nickname," he said gruffly.

"He was so pretty," Kate explained. "Golden curls and a rosebud complexion."

"How interesting," said Mrs. Custer. "And now he's the youngest general in the entire Army."

"And still the prettiest," Kate said.

Mrs. Custer was about to reply, but her husband took her arm and led her off to dance.

"The general's wife is a snip," Kate said immediately.

"You were pretty snippy yourself." Hank grinned.

"I hope we're never posted with her. She and I will tear each other's hair out."

"Who is we?" he asked unhappily. "You and I? You and Royce? You and your father?"

"I'm sorry, Hank." She touched his hand gently with her fingers. "It was just a manner of speaking. Shall we dance?"

He shook his head. "Let's go back to your quarters. Maybe there will be nobody there."

"No, Hank! You know better than that." She whispered to him: "Anybody might walk right in on us. Isn't there someplace we can go?"

"None that I know of. Let's get out of here, anyway."

They rode an Army ambulance along the muddy roads to the country house where she was staying. Any hope that they had of being alone was dashed when they saw many lights in the building, where a half-dozen young officers, who had not been invited to the ball, lounged in the parlor and the dining room, waiting patiently for the ladies to return from the dance.

"I'm sorry, Hank," she said again, as they stood in the darkness of the porch. She kissed him with passion. "I want you, too, you know," she whispered. "When will you come to Washington? After the raid?"

"Yes. As soon as I can."

"When will it be? Do you know?"

"Depends on the weather. End of the month, maybe."

"Do you feel any better about it?"

He shook his head. "Worse, if anything."

She took his hands and held them tightly. "Then I'll tell you something that you can take with you, and remember every time you think of me. I've made a decision, Hank. When the war is over, I'm going to get a divorce from Royce. There will be a terrible scandal about it. There always is. People will think all kinds of things about us, won't they?"

"Most of them true," he said gently.

"Yes. I won't mind. My father will be hurt. Your family, too. We'll both get divorces, Hank, and then we can go to California or England or someplace where nobody will know us. Maybe we can live right in New York City. It's such a big place. Anyway, I've decided. Does that make you happy?"

"Of course it does, my dear." They kissed each other passionately, paying no attention to one of the young infantry officers who came out on the porch to smoke a cigar and stood staring curiously and probably enviously at them.

She whispered to him before he left her: "See if you can think of a place for us to go tomorrow, darling. I'll stay another day if you can find a place."

He rode back to Stevensburg on the dark quiet road, letting the horse pick its way as it would. Unhappily, he tossed her words back and forth in his mind. Divorce. She'd made the decision, finally. They would go where nobody knew them. She would divorce Farnham; he would divorce Caroline.

The only trouble was, he was afraid that now it was too late.

He hadn't had the courage to tell her the truth, just as he had avoided telling her during the fall and winter whenever he saw her in Washington. The fact that they must face was that Caroline was going to have a baby.

It had happened a few days after Gettysburg. She had written to him that she wanted to see him. She needed his advice about some commercial properties that her mother had left her. She didn't want to take her uncle's counsel; he said keep the buildings, but she wanted to sell. Besides, she said, she and Hank ought to talk about the future. She knew he no longer loved her; they ought to talk about it, and see what should be done.

He had arranged it. Kilpatrick had a chore for him: go to Philadelphia to inspect a new saddle that a harnessmaker had written glowingly about. If the saddle was any better than the standard McClellan model, Kil said, they'd outfit the division with it. They'd call it the Kilpatrick saddle. "Go take a look, Hank. I'll trust your judgment."

Caroline came to Philadelphia. He met her at her hotel for dinner. She introduced him to the manager glowingly as her husband, and then to the desk clerk and the maître d'hôtel in the dining room. She clung to his arm possessively.

While they ate, she talked about the property. He discovered immediately that the estate was not the reason for this meeting. She'd made up her mind long ago that she was going to sell it. She didn't even ask if he thought it the proper thing to do.

Then she began to talk about their marriage. He'd had several drinks, and their effect was to make him listen in morose silence while she talked softly.

She hadn't changed, she told him, in spite of the arguments, the misunderstandings. He was her husband and she loved him. She hoped that he would come home after the war with the resolve to try to forget any mistakes they'd made in the past. Wouldn't he join with her in trying to make a go of it? He still loved her. She knew he did. She would be kind to him and gentle. She vowed she would. She had a wonderful idea. When the property was sold, she would have a lot of money. They could take a long trip to Europe. They had never had a honeymoon. A trip like that would be the best way to start all over again. He'd think about it, wouldn't he?

He tried to tell her bluntly, but he couldn't manage it. Instead, he asked a question. "Suppose there was somebody else for me, Caroline?"

She understood, she said. She smiled sadly. "I'd be foolish to think that some such person might not come along. You're an attractive man, Hank."

He started to speak, but she held up her hands charmingly to stop him. "I know she might exist. I know that Washington has many lovely women. But remember, Hank, that we were so much in love. It *was* good, wasn't it? It can be good, still. I need you, Hank."

He never remembered quite how she managed it–there was talk of a quiet drink and more conversation–but after dinner he found himself in her room. A bellboy brought a tray with whiskey, ice, and water. She kept talking while Hank fixed them each a drink. She said she wanted to change her cumbersome gown, weighted with bustle and acres of petticoats. She went into the dressing alcove as if to change modestly out of his view. He couldn't decide whether she was aware that he could see her in the mirror on the dressing table.

He didn't move to another chair. He sat there, watching her. She stripped all her clothing from her body and then stood before the mirror, brushing her hair with vigorous strokes that made her large breasts sway. Finally she put on the handsome brocaded dressing gown that she had worn that first day long ago. She came into the room and smiled at him.

"Are you all right, Hank?" she asked softly. "Anything you want?"

He put his drink down slowly before answering. Then he stood up and told her in short words what he wanted.

She laughed merrily. "Why not? We're married."

Within a month of their meeting in Philadelphia, she wrote to tell him that she was pregnant.

Thinking about it now, as he rode through the darkness to Stevensburg, he felt shame and guilt, as if he had been unfaithful to Kate with his own wife. He hadn't thought about the imminent birth of the child very often in the intervening months, as if he were deliberately keeping it from his mind in order to avoid a sense of guilt during the visits to Kate in Washington. Sometimes he cursed himself for not telling Kate the truth. Now he would have to, and their hope for happiness would end.

He damned himself for a pure fool–for having gone to Philadelphia to meet Caroline, for the drinks he had taken, for not understanding that she was seeking a new hold upon him, for watching the display of her body that had aroused him so swiftly.

He would have to tell Kate about it soon–perhaps after the raid. He dreaded the moment, and he kept refusing to face it.

In the cavalry camp at Stevensburg, he stabled his horse and walked through the mud to the headquarters tent of the 2nd New York Cavalry. He thought it unlikely that he would be able to sleep immediately, so he lit the pair of lamps that illuminated the tent, put some coal on the banked fire in the potbelly stove and opened the draft a bit, and took a quart of whiskey from the wooden cabinet that housed the records of the regiment, along with oddments of equipment such as broken spurs, rusty sabers, tarnished buttons, tattered guidons.

He then unlocked the field desk that was set close to the stove for working comfort on nights like this, and took from it the leather map case that held all the planning for Kilpatrick's scheme. He poured himself a half tumbler of whiskey and started to work. He would work and drink for an hour or so, and then he might be ready to sleep.

As he opened the map case, he could hear distantly the hourly call of a sentry: "Twelve o'clock, and all's well." The last word trailed into the night, and was immediately followed by the more distant voice on the next post, mournfully echoing: "Twelve o'clock, and all's well."

He took out the first of the papers that were enclosed in the case, viewing it unhappily. Kilpatrick was strong on theatrics; he wanted Hank to have a speech ready for his command at the start of the expedition. It should contain the plans for the raid, so that each man would know exactly where he was going and why, and, Jud had insisted, it should have the full flavor of passionate rhetoric, so that it would read well when the history of the expedition became a major glory in the archives of the war. "Pour it on, Hank," Jud had said. "Use plenty of words like gallantry, courage, desperation, sacrifice, fearlessness. You know what I mean. When we get back, every paper in the country will run our story on the front page. Make three copies. One for me, one for yourself, and one to leave here with the division records, just in case."

"Just in case what, Jud?"

Kilpatrick had grinned coldly. "They'll be shooting at us, Hank."

Hank Stephens started to read the draft of what he had written so far. It was headed: "Headquarters Third Division Cavalry Corps," and he had left a place for the insertion of the date the expedition started. The salutation was simple: "Officers and Men":

He smiled humorlessly as he read along. It was far from simple once it got rolling. He was following Kilpatrick's orders:

> You have been selected from brigades and regiments as a picked command to attempt a desperate undertaking–an undertaking which, if successful, will write your names on the hearts of your countrymen in letters that can never be erased, and which will cause the prayers of our fellow-soldiers now confined in loathsome prisons. . . .

He picked up a pen and dipped it into the inkwell, and then let it hover over the word "loathsome." What was it that the President had said? ". . . that dreadful island in the James . . ." Might it not be better to use that? No. Had to include Libby as well as Belle Isle. He put the pen down and continued reading.

> . . . to follow you and yours wherever you may go. We hope to release the prisoners from Belle Island. . . .

Isle? Island? Leave it. Island was the common word.

> . . . first, and having seen them fairly started, we will cross the James River into Richmond, destroying the bridges after us and exhorting the released prisoners to destroy and burn the hateful city; and do not allow the Rebel leader Davis and his traitorous crew to escape. . . .

That was pretty strong language. Maybe too strong; Kilpatrick would have to approve it.

Hank read the sentence again. It expressed his philosophy as another grim year of brutality opened. Smash them, crush their army, destroy their cities, devastate their land–leave them nothing to fight with. Hurt them in every possible way and bring the bloody business to an end as quickly as it could be done.

How would that exhortation stand, however, if women and children were to die when the city burned? How would it look if some raging trooper hacked Jeff Davis to pieces with his saber? The whole world would shudder and say that the butchery was ordered. He could see the newspaper editorials blazoning the outrage: "These men of Kilpatrick were not soldiers. They were assassins, barbarians, thugs."

Hank picked up the pen again, but he did not put it to the paper. Instead he put aside the speech, taking another drink while he sought a document in the map case. This one was completed. It was Hank's instructions to Captain Mitchell of the 2nd New York, who would lead a detachment along the north bank of the James, while Hank led the main body along the south bank. There were specific details about scouts, pickets, skirmishers, communications, crossing of the river, burning of the bridges. Finally he reached the section having to do with the taking of the city:

> The bridges once secured, and the prisoners loose and over the river, the bridges will be burned and the city destroyed. The men must keep together and well in hand, and once in the city it must be destroyed and Jeff. Davis and Cabinet killed.

It wasn't properly literary, but it was to the point. Hank sat back in his chair and thought about it. How likely was it that they could capture Davis? It wasn't a strong probability, even assuming the raiders got into the heart of the city without fierce fighting. Davis was a soldier, and many of the men around him were soldiers. They would probably put up a desperate resistance, and would have to be taken, if they were taken at all, in hand-to-hand combat. The chances were heavily against all of them surviving without harm.

He had written it, he remembered, in still another place, in pencil on the pages of a pocket memorandum book, which he now took from the map case. He found the place immediately, among a series of reminders to himself of the details of the expedition. The words stood out boldly enough: "Jeff. Davis and Cabinet must be killed on the spot."

What the hell! Let Kilpatrick decide. It was his responsibility, and the glory that came with success would be his. To whom would the shame of failure belong? That was another question entirely.

Hank finished his tumbler of whiskey, poured another, and then picked up the slim black pen. He began to write once more on the draft of the exhortation to the troops:

> The prisoners must render great assistance, as you cannot leave your ranks too far or become too much scattered, or you will be lost. Do not allow any personal gain to lead you off, which would only bring you to an ignominious death at the hands of citizens. Keep well together and obey orders strictly and all will be well; but on no account scatter too far, for in union there is strength. . . .

All right, Hank told himself. You studied rhetoric for two years at the Academy, now let it roll out in the phrases that the politicians and the newspapers will love. He dipped the pen into the inkwell again and jabbed it at the paper, scratching out the words, while a favorite expression of his mild-mannered father ran through his brain: "That, sir, is a worthless mixture of tosh and balderdash!"

> With strict obedience to orders and fearlessness in the execution you will be sure to succeed. We will join the main force on the other side of the city, or perhaps meet them inside. Many of you may fail; but if there is any man here not willing to sacrifice his life in such a great and glorious undertaking, or who does not feel capable of meeting the enemy in such a desperate fight as will follow, let him step out, and he may go hence to the arms of his sweetheart and read of the braves who swept through the city of Richmond. We want no man who cannot feel sure of success in such a holy cause. We will have a desperate fight, but stand up to it when it comes and all will be well. Ask the blessing of the Almighty and do not fear the enemy.
>
> H. W. Stephens,
Major, Commanding.

There you are, Kil! Goddammit, unfurl the guidons, let the bugles blow "Boots and Saddles," and let's ride off to glory.

He sanded the paper to dry the thick black ink, and he sat staring at it while he drank from his whiskey tumbler. The words faded and swam on the paper as he stared morosely at them, until the letters reformed again in his mind, making different words, the words he would like to say slowly to his men when they assembled to ride out:

> Officers and Men: We're going on a raid. We're going to ride like hell to stay ahead of the reb cavalry. If we're lucky, we'll get to Richmond before they cut us off. The general and the main body of troops will pound into the city from the north. We'll swing south, just five hundred of us, and sneak in the back door. First we free the prisoners on Belle Isle, and herd the poor sonsabitches into the city. Then we burn the damn place, kill Jeff Davis and anybody else that's wearing a frock coat or a reb officer's uniform, and then we get the hell out of there, if we can, before Stuart or Hampton makes mincemeat of us.
>
> That's all there is to it. It's a stupid scheme, and a lot of us are never coming back. I'm sorry to have to lead you into such a stinking job. Take care of yourselves. You do your best, and I'll do mine, and maybe we'll be lucky. Anybody who gets lost or cut off, head

for the Peninsula and General Butler's army. That's the shortest route to safety. God keep us all.

He smiled slightly. He'd be reduced to farrier if he tried anything like that. Maybe being a farrier wouldn't be so bad. Farriers had no problems beyond maintaining the agility to duck an occasional kick from a mean horse and keeping enough soap handy to free themselves of the smell of manure. He'd wager that farriers had no dreams of battlefields and ghostly cavalrymen.

He yawned and stretched and sensed drowsiness creeping upon him, partly from the whiskey and partly from the glow of the fire. He decided to stretch out here in the headquarters tent of his regiment, instead of walking the several hundred yards to Kilpatrick's headquarters, a big farmhouse where Hank had a room of his own.

As he turned toward the cot that stood against the back wall of the tent, he heard horses in the company street outside, and the sound of voices. He recognized Kilpatrick's sharp tone trying to be friendly and casual. Jud was always failing in the attempt to be comradely instead of commanding. Idly he wondered, as he waited for the visitors to enter, why he'd ever been so close to Jud at the Academy. Propinquity, he supposed. And Kilpatrick had always amused him, just as Custer had with his flamboyance. He'd never cared much for Custer, however. Matter of fact, he'd never considered Custer very bright. Kilpatrick was. No doubt about it. In spite of the fact that the Third Cavalry Division was the most slovenly in the Army of the Potomac, and in spite of the outrageous discipline, or lack of it, in the outfit, as well as the generally disgraceful condition of horses and equipment, Hank Stephens had to admit that Kilpatrick was probably the most capable division commander that the Federal cavalry could throw against Stuart and his superb string of generals.

Kilpatrick came stomping into the tent, scattering thick red mud on the rough boards of the flooring. A bleak smile cracked his long ugly face. "Saw the lights, Hank, as we were returning from the ball. I told Ulric that you'd be working on our plans. So here you are."

Behind Kilpatrick, Colonel Dahlgren came stiffly through the tent flaps, thumping the floorboards heavily with his wooden leg. He maneuvered and maintained his balance with a pair of dark canes. "Evening, Major Stephens."

"General. Colonel." Hank nodded to each of them. He gestured toward the whiskey bottle. "Would you have a drink, Colonel?"

Dahlgren shook his head, declining. Kilpatrick, as was his custom, took a long, speculative, disapproving look at the bottle, and then frowned at Hank. Finally, he shrugged slightly, turning his attention to the desk.

"You've got everything ready, Hank?"

"All the paper work. You'll have to read it and approve it, General. There are a couple of things we'll have to discuss. Language for the official records, mostly."

Kilpatrick nodded. "I'm sure it reads well, Hank. You were damn near 3.0 in composition and rhetoric all the time. I'll go over them the first chance I get. Hank, we've got a kind of problem, Ulric and I, and I'm glad we found you awake. Might as well get it settled right now."

Hank waited. He noted that Dahlgren looked slightly uncomfortable, as if he didn't relish the thought of airing the problem, whatever it was.

"It's just this, Hank. Your end of this expedition is vital. I don't have to tell you that. Your success in getting into Richmond will probably determine how soon the resistance against my force will crumble. If the rebs have your troopers at their backs and my men with artillery smashing into them along the broad front, they'll likely fold up and skedaddle. Without you inside the city, though, I'd be in for a rough time of it before we broke through their lines. You understand all this, of course."

Kilpatrick seemed to be hesitating, as if he were dodging the issue. Hank almost smiled. His mind went back several years. He could see Cadet Kilpatrick running his horse at a high jump and swerving aside at the last moment. He could see Jud at saber play, pressing an advantage until his opponent was desperate enough to move forward without caution; then Jud would suddenly back up and go on the defensive. He could remember Jud sitting down with confidence to a quiz, pencil flying and lips moving as he facilely manufactured answers for easy questions; then the face would cloud and the lips would tighten as he hit the first hard one. At such times, Hank had learned, Jud responded simply and swiftly to encouragement: a shout of "Put 'im up and over, Jud!" as he approached the jump; a cry of "You've got him, Kil!" as the sabers clanged; a smile and a wink across the classroom when the worried face lifted from the quiz paper.

Remembering, Hank volunteered the encouragement. "Yes, General, I understand how important Force B is to the operation. You have some changes in mind, I take it?"

"That's right, Hank. Ulric and I have been discussing it. We think that your role is so important that the expedition might fail if anything happened to you. Might, this is, if there were not somebody along equally capable of leading the men into the city. Another field officer of proven merit and ability."

Kilpatrick paused again. Dahlgren was looking at the field desk as if he were mightily interested in the leather-bound map case. Hank helped once more. "Yes, General. Somebody like Colonel Dahlgren."

"Exactly," Kilpatrick said. "If one of you should fall, the other could carry on. I had counted on taking Ulric with me, until we began to speculate on the possibilities. Then, reluctantly, I suggested to him that he ride with Force B. He agreed."

Hank nodded slightly. He didn't say anything for a few seconds. He was raging within. Even though Kilpatrick's words had skirted the main point of this discussion, it was as plain to be seen as the shining eagles on Dahlgren's shoulders. Major Stephens was about to be removed from command; Colonel Dahlgren was about to relieve him. He took a deep breath, thinking: Why not? You don't want the responsibility; you don't want to be blamed if it fails, and you don't want the glory if it succeeds. You've hated the job all along. Let him have it now, gracefully. Then you can just go along for the ride.

"I see, General," Hank said softly. "Colonel Dahlgren is the senior officer, so he will of course have the command."

"That's right, isn't it?" Kilpatrick said with little artfulness, but managing to display a crooked grin. "I guess Ulric had better take the reins. He'll have your guidance and counsel, of course, Hank."

"He will," Hank said. He turned to the map case. "I'll turn these papers and maps over to you, Colonel."

Dahlgren held up a protesting hand. "Not tonight, Major. Not tonight! Continue as you were, please. You've devoted an enormous amount of time and energy to this. I'd be obliged if you'd finish and then let me have all the documents."

"As you wish, Colonel."

"Well, Hank, we'll leave you now," Kilpatrick said. "Get some sleep, and we will, too. Big day tomorrow." He turned to Dahlgren. "The Third Division will stage a charge during the II Corps' review tomorrow. It will be most impressive. Sabers shining, guidons streaming, hoofs thundering; we'll frighten the ladies to death."

"If you don't mind, General," Hank said, "I'll let Mitchell take my battalion tomorrow. He handles them as well as I do."

"Whatever you say," Kilpatrick said agreeably. "Take a day off, Hank. You've been working hard."

"Good night, Major," Dahlgren said pleasantly.

"Good night, Colonel. Good night, General."

He stood there, staring at the field desk absently, until the sound of horses' hoofs, clopping in the mud and the squeaking of saddle leather faded into the night. Then he picked up the bottle and poured himself a drink. He held the glass high to the light. "Here's to you, Jud," he said softly. "You don't have to be an ungrateful, mean son of a bitch, but you are. And here's to you, Colonel Dahlgren. Little Kil has set you on the road to glory. I hope you ride it to the end. And here's to Major Stephens, who drinks too much and can't be trusted to tell the difference between glory and perdition."

He set down the glass after drinking, picked up the slim black pen, and pulled to him the address to the men of Force B. With slashing strokes, he crossed out the signature: "H. W. Stephens, Major, Commanding." In its place, he wrote: "U. Dalhgren, Colonel, Commanding." He looked at the result unhappily, then sighed. It wouldn't do anyone any good to be childish about it. He pulled fresh paper from the desk and picked up the pen again. Carefully but swiftly, he copied the address. At the end, he wrote the signature just as any adjutant in the Army might do: "U. Dalhgren, Colonel, Commanding." He didn't know that his writing was so similar to Dahlgren's that an expert might have had difficulty in telling the two apart. He also didn't know that he had spelled the colonel's name wrong.

On the twenty-third of February, when the Third Division of Cavalry was busy to a man with the chores of brushing uniforms, soaping saddles and gear, and shining weapons to brilliance so that the assorted generals, politicians, and pretty ladies could be impressed by their unaccustomed smartness, Hank Stephens was nowhere near the grand review.

He was with his love in an old-fashioned country inn near Culpeper, where the amiable proprietor was quite unconcerned about Yankee officers who brought their "wives" for the day, so long as they paid in greenbacks for the room, the food, and the whiskey. Hank Stephens and Kate Farnham had a splendid day of love that was intertwined with long happy whisperings upon her part of a future in some distant pleasant clime, together for all time. There was little response from Hank, other than to kiss her when she wanted to be kissed and to join with her whenever she wished. There were two important subjects on his mind, however, and they stayed there until the end of the long day.

He told her one of them: "We'll ride out on the twenty-eighth, Kate, if the weather holds."

The other one he kept within himself, and it was still unsaid when she was aboard the train that would take her and the bevy of lovely ladies back to Washington: "Caroline is going to have a baby, Kate." He would tell her that harsh fact when he returned from the raid; he had kept it from her for so many long months that a few more days would not matter.

7

Trooper John Watkins sat on a stump behind the hut in which he had lived all winter with five men of his company. The air was pleasant enough for late Saturday afternoon in February, in Virginia. The temperature was far enough above freezing that his hands were comfortable while he wrote letters to his folks. He didn't mind the chilly breeze that stirred occasionally; he was dressed in woolen cavalry breeches and two heavy shirts. Two or three times, however, the pale sun broke through the low overcast, and Johnny felt with pleasure its warmth soaking into his neck and shoulders. He was writing his letters with a soft pencil, using his mother's gift, a calfskin writing case, as backing for his paper.

The letter he was working on was to his father. For several minutes now, he hadn't added a word to it. He just sat there, thinking about the two letters. They were as different as day and night, black and white, up and down. His mother's had been written first; it was now folded and tucked into the writing case, ready for mailing. Not a single one of its many sentences reflected the mind of a nineteen-year-old cavalryman who had learned in the past year to smoke strong rebel cigars, to appreciate a couple of ounces of pop-skull whiskey on a Saturday night, to call his messmates affectionately either "Sam, you ole bastard," or "Sam, you ole sonofabitch," to refer to what his mother, if she ever were forced to, might call "horse manure," as plain old "horseshit," and to whistle suggestively, along with his comrades, at any female, white or black or yellow, between the ages of twelve and sixty, who might be seen in camp or on the march.

It was a chore to write the weekly letter to his mother. He never knew what to say. He had to belabor his brain for the phrases that would not shock her, upset her, make her worry. Matter of fact, if you looked at it fairly and squarely, he had to lie to her.

He wrote: "Our chaplain spoke well on the subject of moral laziness at Sunday services," instead of: "Most of us who are not on duty lie abed on Sunday mornings, some of us plain lazy and others sleeping off the bite of Saturday-night's whiskey."

He wrote: "Three of my tentmates and I were invited to tea at the home of a prominent merchant of Culpeper," instead of: "Four of us went to Culpeper, bought two quarts of whiskey from a fellow who runs a stable, and then the other three lined up and changed their luck for twenty-five cents apiece with the colored woman who keeps his kitchen, but I was scared and maybe disgusted, so I just got quietly drunk."

He wrote: "There is talk that the general is planning a brilliant maneuver that will bring us all glory without danger," instead of: "The boys say the Old Man is about to take us out and get us all killed or captured."

Why did he have to lie? Why must he fill page after page with sweet words about how he missed her, and missed his home, and how gentlemanly his messmates were, and how splendid his officers? He knew why. He knew that his mother had never faced reality in her life: whenever he thought of her, he brought up an image of the child-wife in Dickens' *David Copperfield* (which he had read aloud to her just two years ago), and he suspected that she had the same image of herself, since she had asked him to read about Dora again and again. His mother was adept at pouting, pirouetting, weeping soulfully, lisping, speaking baby talk, nibbling but never eating, tiptoeing, giggling but never laughing, sipping but never drinking, blinking rapidly to express admiration or amazement, and literally scores of other trivialities.

Sometimes he wondered why his father had ever married her, and then he sometimes speculated on the act that had conceived him—how had that been managed, in what inconsequential series of tiny birdlike flutterings and chirpings? Sometimes Johnny wondered what had finally decided his father to leave them and live elsewhere, first in New York and then in Washington. That had been ten years ago; Johnny remembered no scenes or quarrels or outrages—one day his father had been there as usual, and the next day he was gone. Mrs. Watkins never talked about it, expressed no sadness, regrets, nor recriminations; she would pleasantly explain to anyone that "Mr. Watkins is in the hotel business in Washington, you know," in a tone that implied that his affairs in that city were quite temporary, that he was expected home at any time, or that she and Johnny were about to board the train to stay with him.

Her entire life was, in Johnny's view, a trifling charade, an everlasting game, and he had long ago decided to play it with her to her heart's content. So he lied to her in his letters, because he was sure that if he didn't, she would have been prostrate with shock. He was convinced that she viewed the war as a distant panorama of bugles, flags, and bright uniforms, in which young cavaliers like her darling Johnny tilted at one another in the fashion of Walter Scott's *Ivanhoe,* but in which nobody ever truly got hurt or killed. In truth, nobody ever died in Mrs. Watkins' world; from time to time, someone she knew might "pass to his reward," but death was a word she could not acknowledge. If he wrote the truth to her, about the blood and the stink and the filth and the fleas and lice, she would surely faint away, and then take to her bed for days or weeks until she managed to obliterate the terrible words from her mind.

And again, why did he have to lie to his father? John Watkins, Senior, wrote to his son on an average of once a week, and Johnny always tried to reply. The father's letters were just as ridiculous as the mother's, in their own fashion. John Watkins seemed to think that his son was a hard-bitten veteran of countless cavalry clashes, some kind of modern paladin upon whose slashing saber and death-dealing carbine the preservation of the Union depended. His father's letters were filled with speculations upon strategy and tactics, reflections upon the personalities and characters of generals who were only names to his son, tales of valor and derring-do that had been related to him at Willard's bar. Mr. Watkins' war was one of deathless rallying cries shouted by conquering legions, of thundering artillery, charges like Pickett's at Gettysburg, of splendid historical pronouncements (*The Father of Waters again goes unvexed to the sea. . . . There is Jackson standing like a stone wall*). He had used those and many more in his letters. Johnny had often speculated, while reading his father's pontifical prose, how his messmates might have discussed the great events his father was so fond of.

"I see Grant has took Vicksburg. He must be a stubborn son of a bitch. Goddam good thing for us he's out west."

"That Jackson was a mean bastard. Jesus, I'm glad I didn't join the infantry where I'd have to face him. This way, I got a horse can run faster'n I can."

Johnny Watkins studied the latest letter from his father. Talking to Major Stephens and the general. Says the general spoke highly of me. Goddammit, I never was closer than twenty yards to Kilpatrick. That's a lie, one way or another. He doesn't know me, and I don't know him. I'll bet Stephens can't even call my name, and I'm in his regiment. Why does everybody have to lie all the time?

He stared at the paper. Maybe I'll tell him the truth, this time.

Dear Pa:

If the mud gets any deeper, we'll be swimming in it. That is, if it doesn't freeze. Then we could skate on it. The bugs are worse than ever. I got spots all over me from bites. The food is rotten. It gives you the trots more often than not. All officers are fools, and most of them are drunken fools. My tentmates think about three things: women, whiskey, and avoiding duty. War is a rotten business. Kilpatrick's taking us out and we're all scared of getting killed. The rebs are scared, same as we are. I hate it, Pa. What ever made you think I love it? Did you ever get shot at, Pa? And, goddammit, Kilpatrick doesn't know me! He never heard of me, Pa! Why does everybody lie about everything? Just answer me that, Pa, in your next letter.

He wouldn't write it. He'd never write it. The same old malarkey:

Dear Pa:

We are going raiding, so we hear. We look to capture General Lee and bring him back to Mr. Lincoln. You will be reading of our deeds in the papers soon. I am well and hope you are the same. . . .

Johnny Watkins sighed. Ah, the hell with it, he told himself. I'll write to him when we get back from the raid. He doesn't really care, anyway. If he cared, he would have stayed with us ten years ago. He just likes to tell the customers that he's got a son in the cavalry. "My boy is with Kilpatrick. Was talking to the general about him just the other day."

You ought to face the truth, Johnny thought. Face it! Ma is one kind of a fool, and Pa is another. And I'm a third kind, thinking all the time about people telling the truth to each other, as if anybody ever would. It's a rotten war. I wish I was shut of it.

But I'm not, he thought. And I'd better get my butt off this stump and look at my gear. Clean and reload my revolver. Put a new edge on the saber. Tighten that butt plate on the carbine. Three pairs of clean socks. Extra shirt. What else?

"Johnny, we're going to Culpeper. Come on." The voice belonged to Sam Foley, who was tall, lean, and sallow, showing little effect of almost three years of Virginia's wind and weather. He was accompanied by Willie Leech, a fat lazy boy about Johnny's age, and Fred McAfee, a burly farmer from Poughkeepsie, who was generally placid and amiable and a slovenly soldier. Foley and McAfee were both in their mid-twenties. These three were the men whom Johnny had accompanied on that previous trip to Culpeper.

"We been looking for you," Willie said. "We didn't want to go without you. Gonna get us some whiskey and have another whack at that nigger woman."

"Nobody leaves camp," Johnny told them. "You heard the order. They say we're pulling out tomorrow."

Foley, who wore corporal's stripes on his shirt sleeves, took a piece of paper from his pocket and let it flutter in the breeze. "Orders," he said, grinning. "Officers' laundry. It says: 'Pass work party of Cpl. Samuel Foley and three troopers to Culpeper Courthouse and return, February 28, 1864. Captain John F. B. Mitchell, 2nd N. Y. Cav.' So, come on, Johnny. You're the third trooper."

"Thanks. I'll stay here," Johnny said.

"She ain't so bad," McAfee said quickly. "You can even go first, can't he, Sam?"

"Sure," Foley said. "Last chance, Johnny. Little Kil takes us out tomorrow. Whiskey and a woman before we go. Come on, boy."

Johnny shook his head. "I've got too much to do. Go ahead. Bring me back a slug or two of whiskey, if you want."

"I think he's scared of the nigger woman," Willie Leech said. "He wouldn't touch her last time, neither."

"Yeh," said McAfee, the placid follower. "You scared, Johnny?"

Johnny started to flare for a moment, and then the memory of his thoughts about truth returned to him. Why not tell the truth once? Why not try it?

He looked at them for a few seconds without answering. Then he nodded. "Yes. I'm scared. I don't want to catch the claps, or whatever you call it. More than that. I got no wish for rolling on a dirty bed with a dirty woman, nigger or white. If I got to go with a whore, I want a clean one. I want a pretty one. I want it to mean something. I don't want it in a dirty room on a dirty bed."

The truth had no effect. Foley just laughed. "Whatever you say, boy. You want to be a Sunday-school teacher all your life, it don't matter to us. We'll bring you some whiskey. You get a chance, clean my weapons, will you, Johnny?"

"And don't bother with the whiskey, either," Johnny flared. "I don't even like it!"

They laughed again, and they walked off through the mud. Foley said again that it was a wonder that Johnny Watkins didn't teach Sunday school right in camp. Johnny could hear Leech's voice floating back in argument: "I think I'm right. He's scared 'cause she's a nigger."

Johnny Watkins slammed his writing case together in anger at himself, at his messmates, at the whole goddam war. There, Ma! There you are, Pa! There's your war. Rotten whiskey and a poor stupid colored woman who's got to do what the boss says. That's war for you.

"What's the matter, Soldier?" asked a calm voice.

Johnny looked up into the eyes of Major Henry Stephens, who was passing between the huts to the next company street.

"Nothing much, sir. Just the way you get, sir. Disgusted with everything."

Stephens nodded. "I know what you mean, Soldier."

Johnny hesitated. "Major, did you– When you were in Washington, did you talk to my father? At the bar in Willard's?"

"Yes. You're Watkins? I spoke to him. A pleasant conversation."

"Did he talk to the general?"

Stephens nodded. "He did." The major eyed the trooper shrewdly. "General Kilpatrick stretched a point in saying he knew you, Watkins. He said you were a good trooper. Did your father tell you that?"

"Yes, sir. The general doesn't know me, Major."

"Maybe not. But your father was pleased. His mind was probably relieved to know that the general has his eye on you."

"Yes, sir. I understand. Major, tell me one thing more. What the hell are we doing here? I know, the war and all. Got to lick the rebs. Got to save the Union. All that. But what are we doing here? Why doesn't everybody stop, before we're all dead?"

Stephens smiled. He held up his hands as if to bar the question. "You won't get the answer from a major of cavalry, Watkins. I don't know where you'll get it. If this raid troubles you, you might talk to the chaplain."

Johnny shrugged. "Words, sir. Chaplains have been talking for almost three years, and we're still killing each other."

"Yes. I guess you're right. I can give you three words that help some of us. They were drummed into us for years at West Point. Three words. Duty, Honor, Country. The West Point code. They may help you. I think they keep some of us going in the worst of this terrible business."

"Yes, sir. Thank you, sir. I didn't mean to bother you with all this talk."

"No bother, Watkins. I'm glad you brought those three words back to my mind. They may help in the few days ahead of us. Have you been assigned yet for the expedition, Watkins?"

"Yes, sir. Detached service, sir. A bunch of us. What does that mean?"

"It means you'll go with me, Watkins. I'll be glad to have you. Carry on."

Sergeant Caleb Alexander Johnston, formerly of Yonkers, New York, and now of the provost's guard, Third Division of Cavalry, Army of the Potomac, acting as chief clerk to Major General Hugh Judson Kilpatrick (the general's "dog robber," according to his comrades), was mad at the world. Or at least he was angry with all that part of the world within the limits of the cavalry camp in Stevensburg, Virginia.

Goddammit, Kilpatrick wouldn't say where they were going.

He wouldn't even tell the oldest campaigner of them all, who'd been with him since the 2nd N.Y. had been formed back in '61.

Richmond, for Christ's sake! The whole camp was saying Richmond, and had been for a week. Even the official communications that had been flying like leaves in the wind between Brandy Station, Washington, and Stevensburg–even they said Richmond. But Caleb Johnston was smart enough to disregard them.

If he could only get a look at Little Kil's map case. The general kept it locked away, however, in his trunk, for which he had the only key. Three times today, Saturday, Johnston had asked for the key on the pretext of preparing extra clothing for the raid, getting the general's binoculars, cleaning his Navy model Colt's .44. Each time, Little Kil had said he'd take care of those things himself.

What am I supposed to tell the men when they ask me, Johnston groused. Richmond! That's what everybody's saying. That's just the story that's supposed to get to the rebs. By God, he's got to tell me pretty soon. We're moving out tomorrow, and how will it look if I don't know where we're going? Look as if I don't amount to a goddam around here, that's what. Dahlgren knows, and Stephens knows and even Captain Mitchell knows. All the goddam officers know and his own chief clerk doesn't! Is that fair?

Johnston turned around on the cracker box he was sitting on, putting his back to the desk at which he was listing regiments and detachments under the headings Force A and Force B. He didn't even know what the hell they meant, except that Kilpatrick would lead the big one and Dahlgren the smaller one. Johnston eyed the general, who was standing near the Franklin stove in the center of the tent, sipping absently at a cup of thick black coffee.

"General, don't you think it's about time you told me where we're going?"

Kilpatrick looked at him in surprise. "Good Lord, Sergeant. Where have you been the past few days? Richmond, of course. You know that. I've said it a dozen times in the past twenty-four hours."

Johnston stared at him. He read no guile in Kilpatrick's face, heard none in his tone. "My God, General, you really meant it?"

"Of course I meant it, man."

Johnston's expression was at first puzzled, then chagrined. "If that's so, General, then the word is all over camp. I bet the rebs have heard it by now."

Kilpatrick shrugged. "We'll be fast enough to beat them there, and fast enough away to stay ahead of them until we get to Butler on the Peninsula. And if we have to fight, we'll fight."

Johnston's face then became sullen. "All I got to say, General, is we ought to have better security around this place. I heard that Richmond story a week ago. Matter of fact, I heard it the day we was in Washington to see the President. Now that ain't a way to keep a secret, General. You know it ain't."

The general laughed and went back to thinking while he sipped his coffee.

Johnston was thinking too. He'd gone to all the trouble of speculating at length on the target for the raid, and he'd settled on Charlottesville, a prime Confederate storehouse of food and war matériel. He'd been noising Charlottesville around camp for the past week, scoffing at the Richmond rumors. Now he'd look like a fool. Goddammit.

Suddenly Johnston grinned. No, he wouldn't look like a fool. He'd manage to look like a fellow who was in the know all the time. Anybody asked him about Charlottesville, he'd wink knowingly, and say the one magic word: "Security." They'd think he'd deliberately told the false story to cloak the true one, and they'd think he and the general were pretty damned smart. He wondered how many had believed the Charlottesville tale.

At least one man had. That was Jesse Morrow, correspondent with the Army of the Potomac for the New York *Herald*. Morrow had reasoned that, with a couple of drinks under his belt, Johnston had been talking straight from the horse's mouth (the horse being Kilpatrick, of course) when he said the big raid that everybody was talking about was aimed at Charlottesville. Morrow had written the story and sent it to his paper, where it had arrived on February 25. Morrow's editor, however, hadn't believed it. He wanted further word before he'd print a rumor. His wariness of rumors didn't stem from the possibility of men being killed because of them; he just didn't want to seem a fool for printing them. He'd had the story set into type, however, just in case.

The typesetter, a quiet little man who had worked for the *Herald* for fifteen years, had read the story with interest. At his noontime break for lunch, he'd left the *Herald* building and walked rapidly seven blocks along New York City's teeming streets to a telegraph office in the railroad station. He'd sent a telegram to his brother in Baltimore:

THE IRISH JOCKEY PLANS TO VISIT SISTER CHARLOTTE.

The quiet little typesetter had smiled at the telegraph clerk, saying gently: "Our family doesn't approve of the fellow, you know."

The clerk didn't bother to answer. He wasn't interested in the customers' family affairs.

The brother in Baltimore had then sent the message to a third brother, who occupied a desk in the Confederate War Department in Richmond.

While Johnston, in Third Division Headquarters in Stevensburg, was reflecting that his Charlottesville story hadn't been so bad after all, it was being discussed far to the south. Most of those concerned were inclined to believe it. The information from New York had always proved quite reliable, whenever it had arrived on time. Furthermore, there had been a flurry of information about troop movements in the past twenty-four hours on the northern side of the Rapidan. They seemed to involve bodies of both infantry and cavalry drifting westward as if to strike in the direction of Charlottesville.

General Wade Hampton, informed of the spy's message by courier, and discussing it at a staff meeting at his headquarters, was in the minority. "I don't believe it," he said in his cultured voice. "It's probably a diversion. Kilpatrick may be putting on a show to shield somebody else's major thrust, or his destination is quite different from Charlottesville. In the first place, they wouldn't talk about it freely, if it really was Charlottesville. Since they seem to have talked freely, it's a ruse. I think it's Richmond. They have a fetish about Richmond. They think that if the city falls, they've won the war. I think it's Richmond."

No agreement was reached in the capital, other than the general acknowledgment that the Yankees were up to something, and that the something was probably a big cavalry raid.

Colonel Royce Farnham, aide to President Davis's military adviser, General Braxton Bragg, was one of those who disagreed with General Hampton. "I know Jud," he said with conviction. "He always was a blabbermouth. At the Academy, we used to say: 'Never ask Jud Kilpatrick what time it is; he'll tell you how to make a clock.' If he's in charge of a raid, and one of our good agents tells us the target is Charlottesville, then I think we'd better have General Stuart defend Charlottesville. Jud Kilpatrick simply cannot keep quiet about his plans and ambitions."

Judson Kilpatrick eyed with satisfaction the orders that lay on the table before him. He'd been afraid all along that Meade and Pleasonton would try to steal his thunder, but this communication from Meade removed all question of that. It was clear and to the point: this expedition was Kilpatrick's brain child, and for it he would have the responsibility. He would also get the glory.

Kilpatrick signaled to the mud-spattered orderly who stood at attention just inside the doorway of his office. "Here's your receipt, Soldier," the general said, hastily scrawling his signature in the red ink he was fond of using.

"Thankyousir," the orderly snapped in one burst of sound. He wheeled and left the room.

Kilpatrick turned his fond eye once again to the orders. He scanned them hastily, the stiff phrasing leaping into focus here and there on the pages:

> *. . . 4,000 officers and men and a battery of light artillery . . . utmost expedition possible on the shortest route. . . .*

He paused at the paragraph dealing with Custer's diversionary slash. He wouldn't trust Custer to cross the street without explicit instructions. On the other hand, he had Major General Benjamin Butler to rely upon. Butler was safely settled with a small army on the Peninsula below Richmond. Butler would be under orders to move up to threaten Richmond as Kilpatrick slashed in from the north. Butler's infantry and Kilpatrick's cavalry would overwhelm the untrained men who would defend Richmond. Kilpatrick thought that he could depend upon Butler, who was a politician and who needed no second invitation to be a participant in the attack that would end the war.

Kilpatrick once again turned his mind to Custer's specific orders:

> *. . . To create a diversion in your favor a powerful expedition . . . will be in full movement to-morrow, the 28th instant . . . in the direction of Charlottesville . . .*

There followed details about bridges, railroads, infantry movements. Clear enough, even for Fanny Custer.

Kilpatrick grinned. He could imagine Custer ranting about favoritism, about his own abilities, about what he would do to Richmond if the damned politicians gave him Kilpatrick's chance.

The general's eyes slipped down the page. The final paragraph was the one that would secure Hugh Judson Kilpatrick's place in the history of the United States. He had already read it twice since the orderly had arrived ten minutes ago with the orders, written by General Humphreys, General Meade's Chief of Staff. Now he joyfully read the paragraph once more:

> I am directed by the major-general commanding to say that no detailed instructions are given you, since the plan of your operations has been proposed by yourself, with the sanction of the President and the Secretary of War, and has been so far adopted by him that he considers success possible with secrecy, good management, and the utmost expedition.

And that will do it, Kilpatrick exulted. The man who planned to capture Richmond, who organized and led the expedition, and who achieved that glorious result, is Hugh Judson Kilpatrick! He could actually hear the words booming in a great convention hall where the delegates of the magnificent Republican party had gathered to select their candidate. Behind the speaker who was holding forth so thunderously about "the man who . . ." were seated the stalwarts of the organization–ex-President Lincoln among them, nodding in satisfaction and approval–and in the audience the veterans were already on their feet, starting to roar for Little Kil, the man who took Richmond and ended the war.

For a brief moment, scarcely long enough to be counted as a fragment of time, Kilpatrick also realized that, while Meade had opened the way to glory, he had also absolved himself of blame for failure. The thought went flickering off; there could be no failure.

Dahlgren came thumping awkwardly into the room at that point. Kilpatrick greeted him happily, handing him the orders. Dahlgren read them swiftly, then smiled at the general. "We're ready to go, sir. Tomorrow night, then?"

"The road to Richmond, Ulric. We're ready."

"I brought my own orders for you to approve, sir. Address to the command, instructions for Mitchell, all the rest of it. Stephens did a good job, sir. With one exception, that is."

"Hank is a good man, Ulric. I've known him for many years. What did he do wrong?"

"Pretty strong language, General. I glanced at these. He threatens the rebs with hellfire and brimstone."

Kilpatrick laughed harshly. "That's what we're going to give 'em, boy. Here, let me see the damn papers."

The general scanned the documents that Dahlgren took from the inside pocket of his blouse. He nodded, after a time. "What it says about Jeff Davis ought to come out, if these things are ever published. They may be. The newspapers will want everything we've got. Copy 'em over, Ulric, and then I'll approve them. Leave out that stuff about Davis."

Working into the quiet hours, Ulric Dahlgren copied the documents for Kilpatrick's approval. When he'd finished, he put aside the new set for the general's signature. The originals were stuffed back into his blouse pocket.

The whole thing was only a matter of form, anyway, Dahlgren told himself. He wouldn't use these. Stephens' planning was all right, and they'd use his carefully selected routes and annotated maps, but the address to the command could go out the window. Ulric Dahlgren wasn't going to make a speech. He'd look ridiculous, and he'd sound pompous.

He had it planned. His five hundred would mount and wait in column. When they were ready, he would ride to the head of the column, with no fanfare or falderal. He'd raise his right hand, and sing out the marching command, deeply but casually, letting it roll back to them in a lingering cry of drawn-out syllables: "Fo-o-o-r-w-a-a-r-d Y-o-o-o-o!"

He had one more duty to perform in the quiet hours of this last night before the expedition. He took up his pen and wrote a short letter to his father: "I think we will be successful although a desperate undertaking . . . I will write you more fully when we return–if we do not return there is no better place to 'give up the Ghost.'"

Eventually he stopped writing, sitting with eyes half-closed. He was viewing tomorrow's long, dark column, setting out into the early winter's dusk, a spectral body of horsemen whose actual corporal presence was revealed only by the squeaking of saddle leather, the clank of equipment, and the soft thudding of thousands of hoofs in the yielding mud.

Sergeant Turley got permission from Major Stephens to ride out home. Emma would have understood if he didn't come home that night. She'd have known that the expedition had either left or that the men had to stand by their arms and horses. With everything ready in Company B, Turley requested permission to spend the night with his wife.

"Sure, Ben," Stephens said, "but don't tarry tomorrow. You'll be with us in the advance. We'll be way out in front, picking up that picket post the rebs have got at Ely's Ford."

"I'll be back at dawn, sir."

He approached the house uneasily in the crisp, clear air. He had to put on an air of unconcern, all the while he was wishing that someone higher up had put the kibosh on this damn-fool idea of Kilpatrick's. He didn't want to go. He was scared, this time.

Hell, you're scared every time, he told himself.

Now he had to make Emma think that this raid was only a harmless maneuver to keep the rebs stirred up.

Damn it, why had he ever told her about it in the first place!

All right, he thought, go on inside and get it over with. Get a good meal under your belt, too. If I know Little Kil, it will be hard lines for the next few days. No stops along the way for hot meals.

A thought about Emma struck him, and he grinned as he reached the steps. He wondered if she would want to tumble into bed after he'd eaten. This would be his last night home for a while. Good Lord, he would bet on it! All she had in mind these days, it seemed, was to make sure that they had a baby started. It was on her brain too much. He remembered how close she'd been to going balmy when he'd met her. She had never been what you'd call rock-solid practical, anyway. Always dreaming, sometimes moody, sometimes crying for no apparent reason. He'd always treated her gently because of those things.

Now she was probably all set with the baby. She was very late. She had the calendar marked day by day. It would be fine to have a youngster. He hoped it would be a boy. Benjamin Edmund Turley, Junior.

He opened the door and saw immediately that something was wrong. She sat at the kitchen table with her head on her folded arms. Nothing was cooking on the stove. The lamp was dim. He could hear her sobbing.

"What is it, Emma? What's the matter?"

She lifted her head; he saw her face wet with tears.

He crossed to her and took her in his arms. "What's the trouble, dear? Tell me, now."

It seemed that she couldn't get her voice through the sobbing. He waited patiently, stroking her back and touching her hair with his big hands.

"Tell me, Emma."

She did, finally. "Ben, we're not going to have a baby! Oh, sweetheart, I was so sure. All this time. I feel so bad about it."

He had the chilling thought that probably Doc Stephens was right about him. No baby now, nor ever. All right. She'd have one. They'd adopt one. People who couldn't have kids went out and got 'em from orphanages. Why not?

He held her close, tenderly. "You shouldn't get all het up, Emma. It's happened before. You know it has. You get your hopes so high, and then they come tumbling down. I'm sorry, Emma."

"I was sure this time, Ben."

He spoke as gently as possible. "Don't fret about it, Emma. Please don't. We'll have a whole crew of children. You wait and see."

"I don't want a whole crew," she sobbed. "I just want one."

"All right. Stop crying, now. You want to fix something to eat?"

She pulled away, concerned. "You're home, and no supper for you! I'm sorry, Ben. I just felt so blue."

"All right," he said, smiling. "Nothing that will take too long to fix. We were so busy, I guess I didn't eat since breakfast."

"Stew, left over from yesterday," she suggested, touching her face to get rid of the tears. "It's always better the second day."

"That will do fine."

"And tomorrow night I'll try to have another chicken."

He shook his head. "Not tomorrow night, Emma. Not for me."

She stared at him. "You're leaving tomorrow?" Her eyes were wide with concern.

"That's right. In the evening. We'll get a big jump, traveling all night." He almost added: "We'll need it."

She came close to him again. "Ben," she whispered, "you be careful, will you?"

He managed a grin. "I'm an old hand at being careful. Besides," he lied, "this trip won't amount to much. We'll go give the rebs a lick and a promise and come running back like rabbits."

"You come back to me, Ben. You hear?"

"Honey, this ain't any different from any other time I been out with the regiment. They ain't made the minnie ball that will puncture my tough hide."

"You stop that smart talk! It's not lucky to talk that way."

"No luck in it at all," he said, grinning again. "It's all in being a good soldier, and your husband, Emma, is the best soldier in the 2nd New York Cavalry, even if it's himself that says it."

She stared at him for a long time, then turned toward the stove. "I'll heat up the stew while you get washed."

"Emma," he said softly.

She turned to look at him again.

"I'm sorry about the baby and all, Emma."

"I know you are, Ben."

Libby Bacon Custer was angry, even though she didn't show it. Not angry with Autie; she could never lose patience or temper with her handsome boy general. Meade and Pleasonton and Mr. Lincoln and Mr. Stanton! What had they done? They'd given this splendid chance for fame and everlasting renown to that ugly little grinning monkey Kilpatrick, whom Autie disliked so much. And what was her sweetheart given? The silly job of riding to Charlottesville and back, just to fool the rebels.

If Autie could take the Michigan Brigade! He would be upon Richmond before the rebels could catch their breath. He ought to have the chance, instead of that foolish Kilpatrick. She could see her general now, handsome and debonair, riding through the streets of Richmond at the head of his Michigan legion. She could hear the bugles blowing and see the guidons streaming. With a grimace of distaste, she could see the Southern belles looking upon her darling with flirtatious eyes.

"Libby, have you got my hat and gloves?"

"I have them, Autie. Are you all ready?"

"Ready as I'm going to be," Custer said. "Off to play hare and hounds. Except maybe the hare will turn and get in a few bites himself."

"Now, you be careful, Autie. You're not supposed to take chances."

"Hell, no," he said disgustedly. "This is Kil's dancing party. I'm just a wallflower."

"Don't swear, Autie," she said automatically. "Don't you fret, dear. One day the whole nation will be talking about my darling."

"Come kiss me, Libby," he said, smiling at her with delight. He still couldn't believe his luck in gaining this lovely creature for his own. "At least Jud hasn't got anybody to kiss good-bye but one of the division mules."

"Take care of yourself, Autie," she whispered in his strong embrace.

"And you, my darling. I'll run the brigade ragged to get home to you."

She stood on the porch in the chill air after he had left her, standing there without regard for the temperature and the gray dullness of the day, until she saw the column of blue-clad troopers ride into the distance, with her hero tall and graceful in the saddle, leading them.

She whispered aloud into the dreary air: "Maybe that Jud Kilpatrick isn't so smart as he thinks he is. Maybe his great plan will turn out to be a failure."

Oh, my goodness! That isn't very patriotic. I don't care, she told herself vexedly. My Autie deserves the fame and the glory.

8

Along most of the eastern seaboard the weather was miserable on the twenty-eighth of February, 1864. In Virginia, the vast cavalry encampment at Stevensburg had been blanketed throughout the early part of the day with heavy fog that caused mixed feelings among the thousands of troopers who were awaiting "Boots and Saddles." Some men believed that the fog would delay the expedition, and like all veterans, they considered any delay in facing the enemy to be a blessing. Others were anxious to move out in the fog, considering that the troop movement would be masked from the sight of enemy eyes and therefore less likely to be interfered with. Major Henry Stephens was not as concerned with safety for the entire expedition (believing as he did that the rebs already knew that Kilpatrick was coming) as he was with the initial task of securing the crossing of Ely's Ford on the Rapidan. He was interested in silence and in secrecy, and the fog provided hope for both. He could picture the broad stream fully cloaked in the thick swirling whiteness, and since he had the responsibility for planning the attack on the secesh picket on the far side, he could see patrols moving soundlessly across the brown waters, edging like dark ghosts in a white world to the beacons of the rebels' campfires. In celebration of the shielding fog, he poured himself three fingers of whiskey and downed them with satisfaction. When the fog lifted later in the day, disclosing a bright sky that promised a moonlit night, he downed another three fingers of whiskey to ease his worry.

In the city of Washington, the fog lasted through most of the day, and as usual it tied up all the traffic—carriages locked wheels at intersections; horsemen knocked pedestrians sprawling; all the hacks disappeared as if by magic. Hotel porters and restaurant doormen vainly waved their arms to attract cabbies' attention. Kate Palmer Farnham waited quietly in the lobby at Gautier's while the handsome and youthful Brigadier

General James H. Wilson, Chief of the Cavalry Bureau, stood in the middle of the street like a porter, trying to hail a hack that would take her home. He had been the guest of honor at a Sanitary Commission tea, for which Kate Farnham had been the program chairman.

He found a cab for her, and came ebulliently back into the lobby, to find her gazing abstractedly at a huge rubber plant, as if she were many miles away and did not even recognize his presence. "What's the matter, Kate?" he asked.

"I am thinking of a man down in Virginia," she said.

"Yes, I know," he said. "This is the night they ride out."

In the village of Peekskill, New York, Dr. Daniel Stephens looked out of his office window at the heavy snow which was being whipped by northwest winds into drifts already above a man's knees. It was late afternoon, and the streets were almost deserted, as might be expected on a winter's Sunday, even without the wind and the swirling snow. He fervently hoped that no resident of the town had the bad manners and poor sense to fall sick in this storm.

He would spend the rest of the evening looking through a week's accumulation of newspapers, a medical journal or two, and if he was undisturbed, he would fall asleep on the big couch in the living room with a bottle of brandy (an ounce an hour was his prescription for a stormy night) and Hugo's *Hunchback of Notre Dame,* two French imports that were well calculated to put him to sleep eventually, although he was usually pleasantly stimulated by each of them, taken in moderation.

He wondered if it was snowing in Virginia. He wondered if his son had a bottle of brandy to comfort him on a cold night.

Dr. Stephens went into the kitchen, where his wife was fixing dinner. He was not surprised to find her standing at the window, looking out upon the growing darkness and the swirling storm. Three decades of marriage and doctoring had taught him that the mind of man was a strange and wondrous mechanism—he had been thinking of his only son a few minutes before; it was perfectly natural that his wife should have picked up his thought.

Dan Stephens put his hands on her shoulders. "He's all right, Sarah. And he will be, with the Lord's blessing. This year will be different. This will be the infantry's year. You know how I've studied the war. I'm sure that I'm right. This year the poor foot soldiers will have to break Lee's army into little pieces. It won't be the cavalry's year."

"I wasn't thinking of that so much, Daniel. Not the danger. I was standing here wondering if Henry is still drinking heavily."

Dan Stephens sighed. "On a night like this, Sarah, I hope he has a drink or two to comfort him."

"That's no answer, Daniel." He felt her shoulders stiffen beneath his hands. "When is that woman going to have her child?"

"Oh, Lord, Sarah. I dunno. Soon. I wish someone else could deliver it. But Higgins is sick, MacLeod is in Europe, Welch and Foster are in the Army. Goddammit, I have to take care of the whole town."

"Don't swear, Daniel," she said mildly. "Dinner will be ready in less than an hour. Are you going to take a nap?"

"Too dangerous," he laughed. "Soon as I popped off, the doorbell would ring."

"Not tonight," she said abruptly. "No house calls for you unless it's an emergency. Let the patients come here for a change."

"They're all emergencies, Sarah."

The doorbell rang.

The man who stood on the doorstep in the drifted snow was Bill Beach, the young bank teller who had been Hank's schoolmate and friend. "Doc, she needs you. Hurry."

"Come in, Bill. Can't let the heat out. Who needs me?"

Beach rushed through the door, dumping small lumps and clods of packed snow on the hall carpet. "Caroline," he said. "I guess it's the baby. She's in awful pain."

Stephens looked at him in momentary puzzlement. "Why did you come, Bill? What– Never mind. I'll get my bag."

He went into the kitchen. "Keep the dinner in the oven, Sarah. I'm sorry. It would have been a nice night to spend together."

"Who is it, Dan?"

"Caroline."

She nodded. "I'll get my coat and hat."

"Uh-uh," he said abruptly. "Nothing doing. I don't need you. I won't have any trouble handling it alone."

"You do so need me, Dan Stephens. I'm better at birthing babies than you are, by a long shot. And this is my own grandchild."

"Stay here, sweetheart. If I need you, I'll send young Beach after you."

"Bill Beach? Why Bill Beach? What's he got to do with it?"

That's a good question, Stephens thought. What, indeed? He's out there in the hall wringing his hands and biting his lips as if he were the husband. Why didn't her uncle come? Or one of the neighbors?

"I dunno, Sarah. He brought the word. I'll send him for you if I need you."

The trip should have taken about eight minutes, from the Stephens house on Washington Street, on the bluff above the river, to the big dark rambling house on the hill near the military school. The horse had trouble holding its footing on the slick streets, however, and Dr. Stephens had to make two detours to take advantage of lesser grades on side streets. Even though the sleigh runners slipped easily over the snow, the horse had to labor mightily on the hills.

"We should have walked," Bill Beach yelled, making his voice heard above the wind. "We'd be there by now. You get out and walk, Doc, and I'll bring the rig."

"I'm too old to risk heart failure or a broken leg on these hills. She'll wait for us, Bill."

"It hurts her something awful, Doc. She's scared."

"They're all scared, Bill, the first time. And it always hurts like hell. She'll be all right."

"She's all alone, Doc," Beach yelled into the doctor's ear. "Can't this old plug go any faster?"

"Alone? Where's Adam?"

"New York City. He'll be back on the midnight train. He's been there three days."

And you were keeping her company, the doctor thought. What the hell goes on here, anyway?

She wasn't all right. The doctor saw that right away. She was not far from unconsciousness when he examined her; he doubted that she recognized him. She writhed and moaned. His long experience swiftly arranged the facts for him. The baby was dead and could not be removed from her without surgery. He would have to be swift, precise, skillful. He needed help.

He left the bedroom. Beach was sitting on the stairs in the light of a glowing gas lamp. He jumped to his feet. Anxiety twisted his handsome face; his voice was high-pitched: "She all right, Doc? You need anything?"

Stephens nodded. He spoke rapidly. "How long has she been like that?"

"Sick? All day long, I guess. And yesterday. She said it was real bad. I wanted to get you earlier, but she said wait. She said the baby wasn't coming yet. She said she could tell. Then she fainted, like, and I ran for you."

"I see," Stephens said. "You take the sleigh and get my wife. Don't delay. I'll take care of everything else while you're gone."

Beach reached forward, grabbing the doctor's arm. "She's in trouble, Doc? Is it real bad? What's the matter?"

No harm in telling him, Stephens thought. Friend of the family–it's better if he knows what to expect, in case he has to tell her uncle when he gets here. He can tell Sarah, too, so they'll hustle back.

"She's pretty bad, Bill," he said soberly. "I'll do my best, of course. Now you get going and bring my wife. Speed's the thing we need."

Beach suddenly began to cry. Great sobs shook him. Tears rolled down his cheeks. "She's going to die! Oh, my God! Don't let her die!"

The doctor stared at the young man unbelievingly. The urgency of speed slipped from his mind for the moment. He reached for the young man's shoulders and shook him cruelly. "What in the hell have you got to do with this, Beach? Why are you carrying on like a maniac?"

"I love her," Beach sobbed. "Don't let her die, Doc. Don't let her. It's my fault. That's my baby. I love her. I always loved her."

"It's my son's baby," the doctor cried, gripping the other's shoulders fiercely. "You don't know what the hell you're saying. They were in Philadelphia. Last summer. You're lying, goddam you!"

"It's mine, Doc. Don't let her die. It's all my fault."

Stephens struck Beach heavily in the face. He struck him again. "You son of a bitch! While my boy is off fighting, you slimy cur, you crawl into bed with his wife. Rotten, filthy–"

He stopped, sharply cutting off his words. He released his grip on Beach. He breathed deeply and then exhaled. "All right, young man," he said as quietly as he could. "You go get my wife. As fast as you can. I'll do my best for her. Now pull yourself together, Bill. Let's both forget everything you said. I'm sorry I hit you. Let's get to the job that has to be done."

She was unconscious when he returned to the bedroom. There was nothing he could do. She was dead before he could prepare for surgery. The foetus–he couldn't think of it now as a child–had probably been dead for some time. Strangled by the cord, maybe. Something like that. For a moment or two, his intellectual curiosity told him to operate to find out. It might help him or his colleagues in another case. No. He knew what he'd find. It was pointless.

He covered her body with the white counterpane. He went downstairs to the dimly lit living room to wait for his wife and Beach. He'd send them back when they arrived. He thought grimly that he wouldn't let Beach in the house. She was Hank's dead wife, and the proprieties would be observed. He would stay with the body until her uncle returned.

Beach, he thought. Draft dodger. I'm the one who certified him as unfit for service. Right leg malformed as a result of childhood injury. Cannot be expected to perform the arduous duties of a soldier. Goddam him!

If not Beach, then someone else. I always knew it. You could tell it by looking into her eyes, watching her walk, listening to her voice. Whore! Adulterer!

All right. All right. She's dead. God willing, Henry need never know about it. Now I must carry out my final task. She died under my hands, and I must pray for her.

The doctor bowed his head and whispered: "Grant peace to her soul, my Lord, and grant happiness to her next to Thee. Forgive me for my anger and my bitterness. In Thy name I ask it. Amen."

Henry, my son, your wife is dead. Wherever you are tonight, maybe you will think to say a prayer for her. I am sure that it will be heard.

The doctor lifted his handsome head from meditation, running his fingers through his gray hair, then stroking his lined face as if to ease his weariness. He smiled sadly, shaking his head.

Whenever one of them dies, I pray. Maybe I ought to pray beforehand each time I'm called. But no, I have too much faith in my healing power; I never ask for the higher power until it's too late.

Hank, my boy, I'm sorry. Your wife is dead.

Part Two

9

Colonel Ulric Dahlgren rode the length of the column, from the rear to the point, his youthful face stern and sober in the fading light. He exchanged stiff salutes with officers he had never seen before, and who had never seen him. The object of the ride was to let the officers and men look him over, to let them see the crutches strapped to his saddle and the false right let set rigidly in the stirrup.

This was a ragtag bunch that he commanded, in his estimation. He would have preferred a full regiment—the 2nd New York, say, which had been Kilpatrick's own. He had followed Stephens' planning, however. He had five hundred men: picked detachments of the 1st Maine, 1st Vermont, 5th Michigan, and 1st and 2nd New York Volunteer Cavalry.

He checked his horse at the head of the column, where his staff, if he could call it that, was waiting for him to give the word. Stephens lounged in his saddle, his campaign hat low over his eyes, his weathered face looking drawn and haggard. Dahlgren eyed the major sharply, wondering if the man had been drinking. Kilpatrick had warned him about Stephens, but had added a bit of advice: "Don't worry about him, Ulric. Drunk or sober, he's the best you've got." Captain Mitchell, beside Stephens, was sleepy-eyed, carelessly dressed, completely relaxed. He was supposed to be a good one, too. Several other officers waited apart from the two New Yorkers, talking among themselves while they watched the young colonel.

"All right," Dahlgren said in a voice pitched a shade higher than normal. "You men rejoin your detachments. Major Stephens—are all units present or accounted for?"

"All here and ready to go," Stephens answered casually.

Dahlgren nodded to Sergeant Caleb Johnston, who was waiting to report to Kilpatrick. "My compliments to the general, Sergeant, and will you inform him that this command has advanced toward the Rapidan."

"Sir!" Johnston piped, saluting and wheeling his horse to dash off to

Kilpatrick, who was readying the Third Division to ride out an hour later.

Dahlgren adjusted his campaign hat in the approved Kilpatrick fashion, brim high on the left side and low on the right. While his hands were busy, he called to mind the scene he had witnessed that afternoon at two o'clock, when Custer took his Michigan Brigade on the road to Madison Courthouse and Charlottesville. The flamboyant boy general had led them away in a graceful canter, his big black horse prancing, and his gold-braided arm glinting in the sunlight as he pointed his saber forward and rolled out the command.

Like one of Napoleon's marshals, Dahlgren told himself. We can do the same thing, without any speeches to the troopers. And when we get back, by God, if I want a velvet uniform and both arms full of gold braid and hand-embroidered stars– All right, here we go.

Dahlgren not only made no speech; he made no remarks of any kind as he prepared to leave. He lifted his arm, pointed southeast toward the Rapidan, touched his horse with the spur on his left boot, and called out the marching order: "For-wa-ar-rr-d Yo-o-o-o!"

His horse moved out spiritedly enough, but after a few seconds he had to check the animal, because he was thirty yards ahead of the column, all by himself. He reined in and waited, watching with irritation as the long column of troopers humped and bunched and stretched and slowly lurched into movement, like an elongated caterpillar moving leisurely and ponderously across the ground. The way the troopers slumped and slouched and sagged in their saddles, one would think that they were returning from a five-day expedition, instead of starting one. Stephens and Mitchell were as bad as the most laggard troopers in the column, shoulders hunched and bodies swaying with the jolting motion of their identically ugly, dirty brown mounts, both of which looked as if they should have gone to the glue factory years ago. Dahlgren thought to himself that this was a hell of a way to start the ride that would change the course of the war. Both officers looked as if they were taking out a forage detail.

Dahlgren set his horse beside Stephens' mount, and he swallowed his chagrin at the unimpressive leave-taking. He couldn't resist, however, giving some voice to his disappointment: "You fellows seemed to have shared badly in the horse allocations of the regiment."

Stephens didn't answer, but Mitchell looked up in surprise, and then studied the ugly head and ragged mane of his mount, as if seeing the animal for the first time. "Hell, no, Colonel. I picked this beast out of two dozen. I wanted that bag of bones that Hank is riding, but he pulled rank on me."

"If those were the best, I'd hate to see the worst of the lot."

"You mean looks, Colonel?" Mitchell asked wonderingly. "Sure, these were the worst-looking ones we could find. They're good sound horses, though. Get us there and get us back on a bag of oats."

"I should think," Dahlgren said carefully, "that officers of field rank would exercise the right to choose mounts of the best quality."

"My God, no! When I take Company B at a reb position, I want to look like the company cook."

"What Jack means, Colonel," Stephens said in a lazy voice, "is that the reb infantry learned a long time ago that the way to break a cavalry charge is to shoot the officers before they get up close. Man who wears a clean uniform and waves a saber and rides a splendid animal is asking to have every sharpshooter fix his sights on him. Some day Fanny Custer is going to get his head blown off." Hank glanced sideways from beneath his hat brim at Dahlgren's immaculate uniform with its shining buttons and brilliant eagles. "Besides, Colonel, the general always keeps a pretty sloppy outfit. We've got a bad reputation for spit and polish. Anybody want a drink? It's going to be a cold night."

"No, thanks," Dahlgren said in a cold voice, staring vexedly at the bottle that Stephens pulled from his saddlebag. "Not too much of that, Major, if you please."

"No, Colonel," Hank said deliberately. "Just enough."

Dahlgren had had about enough of these two caricatures of officers. Sharply he issued an order, turning in his saddle to look along the ragged blue column of horsemen that straggled far back into the fast-spreading darkness. "Captain Mitchell, ride back along the column! Tell the men to stop the laughing and talking and yelling to one another. Tell 'em to fasten their cookingware securely–the rattling is enough to wake the dead. Tell that man to stop singing. Good Lord, this is a military expedition!"

"You want 'em to shut up now, Colonel?" Jack Mitchell asked in wonder. "Hell, we won't get to Ely's Ford until eleven o'clock. It's only about quarter past six. There ain't a secesh soldier this side of the Rapidan, Colonel."

"That's an order, Captain."

"Sir," Mitchell said smartly, wheeling his horse. He rode back along the column, chanting the commands in a loud voice: "No talking above a whisper. Tighten your gear. No noise from here on. Button your lips. Tighten up those pots and pans. You, man, stop that singing!"

The mournful strains of "Somebody's Darling" were snapped off instantly, although the sad lament seemed to float on the frosty air for a moment or two.

A joker deep in the ranks called out: "Hey, Cap, what'll I do if my horse breaks wind?"

Dahlgren didn't hear that, but he did hear a carrying voice–Vermont or Maine, he wasn't sure–sing out: "What's the matter, Captain, you got a hair up your backside?"

"Stephens," he said sharply, "get that scout Hogan up here. I want to be sure about Ely's Ford."

"Sure enough," Stephens said. "Hey, Martin Hogan! Pull up here, will you?"

Dahlgren was annoyed once more to find that the young Irishman, who had in three years made himself a splendid reputation as a spy and scout, had been riding two horses' lengths behind him. All Dahlgren had needed to do to summon him was turn in the saddle.

Nothing's going right, the colonel thought. My God, I'll have to get them straightened out. A collection of idiots, clowns, drunks, and slovens– I'm nervous, he thought. I'd better straighten myself out.

"Hogan, are you certain we can cross the river above the ford?"

"Crossed it meself on the Friday." The pleasant, musical Irish voice was another irritant to Dahlgren. Goddammit, would none of them take this thing seriously?

"And you're sure about the reb picket?"

"Hell, yes, General. One captain, one lieutenant, a dozen men. Cobb's Legion, North Carolina Cavalry. Captain's name is Young. Dunno the lieutenant's name. I was close enough to 'em to see the graybacks crawlin' on their collars. They got a farmhouse there, but they camp out by the river."

"I'm not a general, Hogan. I'm a colonel."

"That's all right," the Irishman said easily, winking at Stephens. "I call everybody General. Makes 'em all happy. Don't you worry about that picket. They had two gallons of whiskey hid in the bushes on Friday. Happens that they been tappin' the kegs today, we'll scoop 'em up like fish in a net."

"We'll have to get them all," Dahlgren said. "If one man gets away, they'll know we're coming."

"Jay-sus, General," Hogan exclaimed, "don't you think they know already? With Sedgwick moving the II Corps, and Custer riding out, and us running around like chickens when a weasel's in the henyard– Hell, they been watchin' us for the last week. They know we're coming. They just ain't sure where we'll hit, that's all."

"Very well, Hogan," Dahlgren said. "We'll stop well short of the ford. You'll take a patrol up to look it over."

"Or be looked over," Hogan said. He turned his gaze upward to the bright stars and the great slice of moon that glowed in the eastern sky. "I sure hope the rebs have been tappin' those whiskey kegs. This ain't much of a night to sneak up on a sober man, is it, General?"

The moonlight beamed its brilliance upon the Rapidan, turning the dark brown surface of the water into a broad silver carpet that crinkled and rippled with the passage of the horses. One of the flanking parties, led by Captain Mitchell, with Hogan as scout and guide, splashed across far upstream from Ely's Ford.

The troopers were nervous as they crossed the open water in the moon's glow. Every man let his horse have its head, holding the reins lightly with his left hand, while his right rested on or near his carbine or his holstered pistol. Each pair of eyes was fastened on the dark mass of trees that lined the far shore, watching with dread for the orange flashes of flame that would mean the rebs had set up a turkey shoot.

Johnny Watkins felt sweat drip from his armpits and run coldly down his rib cage. He was frightened. A man didn't even have the advantage of speed out here in the treacherous stream where his horse could not run, but had to pick its way over the uneven bottom. He made up his mind to hit the water if the shooting started. Damned if he would sit high in his saddle to give 'em a target. Maybe not, though–it might be better to drop down alongside the horse and hang on until the horse made it back to shore.

"If there was any of the sonsabitches over there," McAfee muttered, "they'd of opened on us by now."

Up front, Hogan turned in his saddle, laughing. "I told you it would be easy. Come on now, boys. There ain't a living thing on that yonder bank but frogs and the coons that are a-huntin' 'em. Put your nags to the bank with spurs when we get there. It's steep and slippery."

"Don't be so goddam cheerful," Mitchell told him. "These are veteran troopers, Hogan. They got a right to be scared. Good reliable cowards, every man of 'em. And that includes me. All the heroes are dead or promoted to general by this time."

"Ah, hell, Captain," Hogan grinned. "I told you fellows that the rebs would be settin' round a campfire, swiggin' whiskey and tellin' stories. I bet they're all drunk when we get there."

"Drunk or sober, they can squeeze a trigger. Let's hump it a little and get into the trees. I feel naked out here. I'm still not sure that the whole goddam Army of Northern Virginia isn't sitting on that shore, laying a bead on us."

Hogan chuckled. "You listen to me, Captain. I'll take you to Richmond and back again and you'll never even get shot at. I know every reb in this country by his first name." He changed the subject abruptly. "That boy colonel of yours. What's his name?"

"Dahlgren."

"Yeh, that's it. He don't know a hell of a lot, does he? And he's awful nervous. Who gave him this job?"

"How the hell do I know? You talk too much, Hogan."

"All you boys are nervous. You just listen to Martin Hogan, and you'll have no trouble. Up the bank now. Here we go."

Every man in the detachment breathed easier when he was within the comforting darkness of the trees. Hogan led them downriver on a narrow trail that followed the bank. After ten minutes, he halted the column. He was all business now, serious and sober. "We go in on foot from here. The ford is about three hundred yards. Leave five men with the horses, Captain. We take 'em any closer, they're apt to whicker. When we get close enough to see the campfires, then we'll spread out and circle 'em. With this moonlight, you'll be able to see all right. Watch my signals for spreading out. All right, Captain?"

"All right so far," Mitchell said quietly. "You men shoot any rebels that try to run for it. Don't let any of the bastards pull foot. Hear me?"

The troopers murmured understanding.

"Ready your pieces now," Mitchell said. "I don't want to hear levers or hammers clicking and snapping when we're ready to jump 'em. And for Christ's sake, don't fall and discharge your piece. I'll shoot the son of a bitch who does."

"He means it, too, I do believe," McAfee whispered to Watkins.

Johnny Watkins grinned and nodded. He tried to act unconcerned, casually checking his Spencer. Levered and cocked–he set his thumb between hammer and firing pin, so that no accident could discharge the weapon. He felt sick at his stomach, as usual. He hoped he wouldn't vomit.

The capture of the Confederate picket was actually as simple as Hogan had predicted. Mitchell's men came walking in from the right, encountering a party of troopers from the 5th New York, who had crossed the river at another fording place. More than forty men suddenly appeared from the trees and brush around the rebel campfires. Not a shot was fired. The rebels didn't even rise from their blankets or from their seats on saddles around the three glowing fires. They stayed where they were while the Yankees surrounded them. There were sixteen of them, fourteen troopers and two officers, just as Hogan had said. He was even right about the drinking. Several of the secesh captives were dull-eyed and foolish-looking.

Hogan whistled shrilly in the direction of the river, cupping his hands around his mouth to make the sound carry. Within a minute, the point of Dahlgren's column rode into the campsite, led by Hank Stephens, who dismounted and approached the rebel captain. Hank nodded curtly in response to the officer's slight bow. The Confederate put both hands to his waist and unbuckled the frayed belt of braided cord that tightened his tunic and held his sword. He held out the sword to Hank Stephens.

"Keep it," Hank said abruptly. "You had no pickets out?"

The officer held the sword awkwardly, as if he didn't know just what he should do with it. Captain Mitchell reached forward and took it from him. The man stared in amazement as Mitchell pitched sword, belt, and scabbard into the surrounding shrubbery.

"I asked you a question, Captain," Hank said. "No pickets? Why not? Didn't you know we were coming?"

"I didn't think there was a Yankee within ten miles of the river," the captain said, shrugging. "My mistake. In payment for it, I will be forced to accept your hospitality for the rest of the war. I trust that General Lee will force that conclusion swiftly. My name is Young, Cobb's Legion. May I know whom I have the honor of addressing as my captor?"

"Jesus Christ!" Mitchell said. "No wonder we caught you sleeping. This is a war, not a goddam tea party. May I know whom I have the honor–"

"My name is Stephens," Hank said shortly. "Captain, you'd better get your men on their horses." He glanced at Mitchell. "Jack, detail a detachment to take them back to Kilpatrick. Send enough men to make sure that none of them try to run for it. Let Turley take 'em back. If Dahlgren wants to talk to Captain Young here, tell Turley to take care of it."

"Major, I have a question for you," said the Confederate captain affably. "I'd like to know why you have crossed the river. It's a shade early for the spring campaign."

Stephens shook his head, denying an answer. He turned away from the rebel to remount his horse.

"Major!" the rebel called angrily now. "Common courtesy, at least–"

Stephens swung on him. "Captain, you got caught with your pants down. I'm damn glad of it. I won't tell you who we are or why we're here. I won't tell you anything. Now, good-bye to you, sir. I hope you fare well in whatever prison they put you in."

"After talking to you, sir, I know what treatment I may expect. You don't even have the common decency–"

Hank erupted. "War isn't decent, you fool. War is a dirty, filthy mess, and the sooner it's done with the better. You people started it, and now you're going to pay for it. You will pay in prison, Captain, and your army will pay in blood. You're going to be pounded to pieces, and the sooner all of you traitors realize it, the better off you'll be. Maybe the rest of your crew will have the sense to surrender and end the slaughter. I don't like rebels, Captain, and especially I don't like rebel fools that think this war is something out of the pages of Sir Walter Scott. Didn't anybody ever shoot at you, for God's sake? Let me tell you something, Captain. You're going to prison. You're lucky. Because this is the year that we're going to drive you and smash you and whip you, and there won't be any common decency in it. It will be pure brutal power. You're well out of it, Captain. And now good-bye."

The column rode through the night, headed straight south. Kilpatrick with the main body was more than an hour behind, not yet having moved his entire three thousand troopers across Ely's Ford. Dahlgren's column made good mileage, with the restless young colonel falling back occasionally along the line of trotting horses, chanting encouragement as if he had five hundred recruits instead of selected veterans: "Close up! Keep in column. Don't straggle, men. The general's on our heels. Close up. Secure your gear. This country is full of rebs. No noise. Close up."

He kept his voice at a shrill whisper, although the troopers had long since returned to normal conversational voices. Any reb patrols close enough to hear voices would have been attracted by the myriad thumps, bangs, clanks, and creaks that a large body of horsemen threw upon the still night.

The weather was changing as the night began to wane. Riding with Stephens and Mitchell, the scout Hogan glanced upward now and then, critically studying banks of scudding clouds that were thickening the moonlit sky in the northwest. "Going to rain like hell," he said finally. "Twelve hours, maybe. Give or take an hour or so."

"Been thinking the same thing," Mitchell agreed. "I wasn't sure, though. It's hard to tell weather in this godforsaken country. Back home, when the clouds come rolling in over the Catskills like those yonder, we're in for a good soaker."

"How far will we be when it starts?" Hank Stephens asked.

"Pretty damned far," Hogan answered. "Maybe Beaver Dam."

Hank remembered the maps. Beaver Dam was a station on the Virginia Central Railroad, and the goal of the first twenty-four hours' ride. "All right with me if it rains," he said. "If we get jumped, their paper cartridges are apt to be wet. Nothing like a nice heavy rain to put secesh soldiers out of action."

"I'd just as soon it held off, though," Mitchell said. "I hate to ride in the rain. Jesus, how I hate it!"

Hogan was a talker, and when he left them to drop back along the column where Dahlgren rode, the two officers welcomed the silence. They rode without words for several miles. Jack Mitchell seemed to be exercising the veteran cavalryman's ability to doze in the saddle. Hank Stephens' mind was free to wander.

He thought longingly of Kate Farnham, wishing that he had used a friend's prerogative to ask Jim Wilson for a post in the Cavalry Bureau. If he had, he wouldn't be riding through the chill night along a lonely road in Virginia, without even the solace of a whiskey bottle, although he had two in his saddlebags. He had already decided that he'd better hold off on the drinking until this expedition was finished. In the first place, he'd have to stay alert all the time. This was rebel country, and any bend in the road might hide a brigade of secesh cavalry and a battery of guns. In the second place, Dahlgren evidently was nervous in the command, and Hank wasn't inclined to put very much faith in a nervous man's judgment. It would be best to stay sober and keep his senses sharp.

He thought unhappily about his wife. She was well along in her pregnancy. What was his duty? She claimed to love him and need him. She was willing to forget the past. Could he therefore leave her and the child to seek his own happiness? He would do it, of course, if he made the decision. That was the problem. He didn't know to which path his understanding of duty and honor committed him. Kate loved him and he loved her. Caroline said she loved him and there was no doubt that she would need him. The child would need him.

He decided that he must try not to think about the dilemma any more until he returned from the expedition. He was committed now to the third of the three words of the code: country. He knew that he had better keep his mind on present happenings, because he wasn't sure of Dahlgren's steadiness. If the boy colonel got them into serious trouble, he would surely have to lean on Hank Stephens to get them out of it.

Hank looked up at the sky, where the bright stars had vanished behind the growing cloud cover, where the brilliant moon flashed on and off like a gigantic signal light as the dark clouds scudded across the sky.

Hank called softly to Captain Mitchell. "Say, Jack, I wonder what Wade Hampton's doing right now?"

Mitchell's answer was muttered sleepily: "I don't give a good goddam, long as he ain't saddling his horse to take after us."

"Not yet, Mitch," Hank said softly, "but maybe tomorrow. I sure to God hope we didn't miss a picket or two at Ely's Ford."

They hadn't missed any pickets at the crossing of the Rappahannock, but they missed three gray ghosts hidden in the brush. These were three of Wade Hampton's "Iron Scouts," whose habit was to roam for days behind the Federal lines, picking up all kinds of useful information. They were a picked band of irregulars, able woodsmen and tough fighters. Two of them, young men named Hugh Scott and Dan Tanner, watched from cover as the main body of Dahlgren's command crossed the river. They rolled a pair of logs into the cold water, paddled across to the other side, ambushed a couple of troopers and stole their horses, and then mingled with the column until they had a good estimate of numbers and had heard the magic word "Richmond." As soon as they could, they fell away from the raiders and rode hard through the night eastward toward Hampton.

The leader of the Iron Scouts, a Texas sergeant named George Shadburne, came upon Kilpatrick's column between Stevensburg and Ely's Ford. He calmly counted the regiments in the brilliant moonlight, estimated the total number of men, looked over the guns that trundled along with the column, and finally headed downriver toward Fredericksburg to tell Hampton that the Yankees were out raiding, and from the direction they were taking, they would strike deeply toward Richmond.

Near the head of Dahlgren's column, Johnny Watkins and his tentmates were riding with a stranger. This was a civilian Negro entrusted to their care by Sergeant Turley. The fellow didn't seem to know much about riding a horse. He couldn't seem to adjust very well to the jogging, and before very many miles had gone by, he was complaining that his legs and backside were being blistered and bruised.

Several times Johnny edged his horse alongside the Negro's, to give the man some pointers on how to adjust his posture to the horse's gait, but the man's only response was to moan softly that he was used to a mule for short distances, and that he didn't know if he could stick to this horse all the way to Jude's Ferry.

"Where's Jude's Ferry?" asked Fred McAfee.

"I dunno where it is from here, Cap'n, but I know where it is when I'm there."

"Goddammit, so will I know where it is when I get there," McAfee said. "What town is it near?"

"Just a ways from Goochland, Cap'n."

"And where the hell's Goochland?"

"Where I was born, Cap'n. I hope I can stick to this here horse until we get there."

"What are you doing with us, anyway?" Willie Leech asked the Negro. "You the colonel's dog robber? Who are you?"

"I'm a freeman," the Negro said. "I know the river you gonna cross, Cap'n. I take you across hit."

"You ain't even going to get there," Sam Foley said. "Your ass will be bleeding before morning unless you learn to stop bouncing up and down in that saddle."

"I get the hang of it pretty soon, Cap'n," the man answered. "Jes' leave me be. Can I hang on—"

"Yeh. You'll be all right," Foley said. "The hell you will."

"He's just plain stupid," McAfee said with conviction to Johnny Watkins, not caring whether the Negro heard him. "I don't think he's got all his buttons."

Johnny was inclined to agree, but he didn't say so. He worried about the fellow, who turned to him every once in a while to ask: "Where we now, Cap'n?" Johnny always had the same answer: "Damned if I know." Johnny wondered if the man's brains were rattling around in his skull, to make him keep asking the same question.

Sometime in the early morning, the Negro looked at Johnny once more, as if about to ask the question. But he didn't. Instead he said: "Now I know where we is at."

"Where?" Johnny asked casually. He really didn't give a damn.

"Can't you smell hit?"

Johnny sniffed the air. So did the other three troopers. They looked at one another inquiringly. They all smelled something evil in the air.

"Whatever it is, it sure stinks," Foley said.

"Dead hosses," the Negro said. "Dead men, too. You dunno where we is at, Cap'n?"

"Where?" Johnny asked.

"This here is Chancellorsville," the Negro said. "Was hit daytime, you see the bones and all. The frost th'ow um from the ground. Dey don't put um down deep."

"Jesus," Foley said.

Dahlgren's column rode through the village of Spotsylvania Courthouse early the next morning, stared at by a few early risers among the residents, who generally went on about their business without any show of emotion.

"Now the word will be out," Dahlgren said to Stephens as they rode at the head of the column. "They'll know we're on our way."

"If they don't know already," Hank said.

"How could they, Major? We captured all the pickets and got a twelve-hour start."

"We got a start, anyway. I won't say it's twelve hours until we're in the streets of Richmond."

They rode through the village in the growing light, pressed on for two miles where they swung right, toward Frederick's Hall Station, a stop on the Virginia Central Railroad. At eight o'clock in the morning, Dahlgren called a halt, so the men and horses could be fed.

The Negro guide, whose name was Martin Robinson, was stiff and sore from more than twelve hours in the saddle, but he made no complaints when he more or less fell from his horse and lay dolefully on the cold ground.

"You got to keep them feet in the stirrups and ride easy," McAfee told him gruffly. "You got anything to eat, friend?"

"Wisht I had some," Martin said. "That horse riding makes a man hungry."

"Salt pork and hardtack," McAfee said. "Share if you like."

"Thankee, Cap'n. I take some po'k. I dunno what them little pieces of wood taste like."

"Goddammit, that ain't wood. That stuff is crackers, hardtack, hard bread. Look here," McAfee said, showing a biscuit with the maker's initials that had been stamped into the dough. "See what it says? 'B.C.' That means these things was baked before Christ."

"Maybe they was," the Negro said soberly. "I jes' don't want none right now."

"Jesus, you are stupid, ain't you?" McAfee told him.

The main column under Kilpatrick rode into Spotsylvania at about the same time that Dahlgren's men were resting miles ahead. The troopers of the 17th Pennsylvania Cavalry, still feeling frolicsome after twelve hours in the saddle, spotted an elderly woman herding a flock of fat geese across the road ahead of them. She was only an old secesh woman who didn't matter a damn to hard-bitten Yankee cavalrymen. One trooper drew his saber and put spurs to his horse, and his comrades followed suit, whooping. They rode at the gallop among cackling, frantic birds. Feathers flew from flapping wings, heads jumped from twisting necks, and bright-red blood spurted in fountains. Every goose that lost its head was grabbed by a grinning trooper.

The old woman, who had been herding the geese with a long-handled broom, swung it frantically among the slashing sabers. The troopers laughed at her screams. Captain Kurtz of the 17th Pennsylvania leaned from his saddle, laughing: "Madam, I'm afraid that Yankees are hell on poultry."

She took a swipe or two at him with the broom, yelling at the top of her lungs, before she retreated into her barnyard and slammed the gate. In lonely outrage, she stood and watched the last of her geese gathered by blue-clad arms. "You're nothing but a pack of nasty, thievin' Yankees," she shouted through her tears.

10

The train was a short one—a locomotive pulled a tender and three cars. The engine chugged wearily along the tracks of the Virginia Central Railroad, passing through long stretches of pine woods as it approached Frederick's Hall Station, more than halfway to its destination at Orange Courthouse, headquarters of the Army of Northern Virginia.

The engine seemed to threaten to quit at any moment. The drive shafts screeched and rattled, for want of grease; the wheels clanked and thumped over the worn rails and the rough roadbed; the cars were badly in need of repairs and paint. Some of the windows were cracked. The entire train clattered a protest against the mechanical deficiencies of the Confederate States of America in February, 1864.

It was, however, the best locomotive and the best trio of cars that the trainmaster of the Virginia Central had been able to muster in Richmond on the morning of February 29. As a matter of pride, it had to be the best in the yard. If any comfort could be provided, the commanding general of the Army of Northern Virginia deserved it.

General Robert E. Lee sat in a seat alone in one of the cars, map case beside him, a portfolio of correspondence open, and his eyes far away, as if he could see along the many miles of track ahead to the ranks of ragged and gaunt men to whom he was returning. He had been in Richmond to confer with the President about the progress of the war, the plans for the campaign to come. The word had been forwarded from Washington by the efficient Confederate espionage system that Lincoln was going to get himself yet another general to lead the Army of the Potomac. This one had an awesome reputation for stubbornness, earned in the Western war. He would hammer and pound with his vast army. The question was: how much hammering could the Army of Northern Virginia endure?

The general shook his head as if to free himself of sober thoughts, but instead he attracted the attention of one of his aides in a seat across the aisle.

"Sir?" the young officer said, jumping to his feet.

"Sit still, Major. Make a note, please. I would like private reports from all officers who were contemporaries of Grant at the Academy, or who served with him in Mexico and elsewhere. Particularly from General Longstreet, who knows him so well. His character, personality, habits —you know what I want."

"Yes, sir. Of course, sir."

The general looked out the window. "Coming to a station. Where are we, Major?"

"Frederick's Hall, sir. More than halfway, General."

The general nodded. He continued to look out the window. His eyes had the faraway look once more.

Hank Stephens was the first to see the smoke of the train. It was distant; with the rising wind that rustled the pines, he wasn't sure that he could distinguish the puffing and snorting of the engine. He pointed out the smoke to Mitchell. "Virginia Central. Going to the reb army. Troops or supplies. Be good to grab it."

"What the hell would we do with it?" Mitchell grinned. "Ride it back into Richmond? My God, that would surprise 'em, wouldn't it? Have a train roll into the yards and have five hundred Yankees pile out of it?" Mitchell laughed at the idea.

"Burn it," Hank said. "Take any food first, of course."

"S'pose it's loaded with troops?"

"Loaded?" Hank shook his head. His voice was somewhat sardonic. "Our information is that there are only clerks and bookkeepers in Richmond. They're not sending them out to headquarters."

He spurred his horse ahead to join Dahlgren, who was riding with Martin Hogan. The two were talking seriously.

"Colonel," Hank said, interrupting. "Train ahead on the railroad." He pointed toward the distant puffs of smoke that rolled above the pine woods on the horizon. "Shall I take a company and see what they're hauling?"

"Hell, no," Dahlgren said sharply. "That's Frederick's Hall, Major. Artillery depot for the rebs' II Corps. Probably five thousand infantry to protect the guns. Good God, we can't risk discovery just to capture a railroad train."

Hank shook his head. "No risk, Colonel. I'd ride like hell west until we cut in toward the smoke and stop the train. We'd intercept it five miles the other side of the town."

"Nothing doing," Dahlgren said. "Our objective is Richmond, not a rebel railroad train. Forget it, Major."

Hank nodded. "Whatever you say, Colonel." He dropped back to rejoin Mitchell.

"Do we go after it?" Mitchell asked.

Hank grunted.

"S'pose that means no," Mitchell grinned. "Too bad, Hank, but maybe just as well. What would you do with a trainful of clerks and bookkeepers?"

"Don't laugh. There might be something worth keeping on that train."

A few minutes later the riders on the point surprised a quartet of reb artillerymen, out foraging in the countryside. A little farther on, they picked up a dozen more. Immediately thereafter, the head of the column closed in upon an ordinary-looking farmhouse which was being put to surprising use. The house attracted attention because there were eight or ten saddled horses at its hitching post. The Yankees had interrupted a rebel court-martial in session in the building, and from it poured a mixture of judges and judged, accusers and accused. There was a chagrined lieutenant colonel named Jones, three captains, four lieutenants, and a ragged bunch of enlisted men. All the prisoners were questioned, some of them separately from the rest. Dahlgren left no doubt about what he wanted to know: how many troops at Frederick's Hall? The answers were varied, but all the variations were on the side of strength. Plenty of cavalry, plenty of infantry, artillerymen in great numbers–they were all stationed in the rebel camp to protect the guns.

Negroes from nearby farms were brought in at about the same time; their answers to questions indicated lots of guns–"Dey got bof big guns and little guns" and many soldiers. "Infantry?" The Negro wasn't sure, but they "got stickers on the ends of the guns."

The officers of the court said that there were plenty of troops in the rebel camp–infantry, artillerymen, cavalry, special battalions of sharpshooters.

"What did I tell you?" Dahlgren said angrily to Stephens. "And you wanted to chase a train, Major. Goddammit, we'll have to ride around them."

"I think that every man jack of them is lying like hell," Hank said quietly. "Ask Hogan what he thinks, Colonel."

Hogan shrugged. "I been through here a time or two. I never saw more than a handful of rebs. Artillerymen, mostly."

"We'll go around," Dahlgren said abruptly. "Let's ride."

The column headed along secondary roads toward a way station on the Virginia Central, a place called Bumpass Turnout, swinging wide around the artillery encampment as they went, while rebel scouts ranged along the column at respectable distances of an average half mile. There were almost one hundred artillery pieces in this winter park of the II Corps, and there were only one hundred and twenty sharpshooters to guard them. As Dahlgren's column began to recede in the distance, Brigadier General A. L. Long, commanding the artillery of the II Corps, grinned delightedly and immediately resolved to ask for a couple of regiments of infantry to be rushed to him in case the Yankees should come back.

Just above Bumpass Turnout, the column hit the track of the Virginia Central, and for an hour or so the troopers were dismounted, tearing up rails, stacking the ties, and lighting great bonfires that billowed smoke across the countryside. As the fires leaped, the troopers laid the steel rails over the fierce flames to heat and warp them so that they might not be used to repair the tracks. While the troopers were busy with their destruction, a train approached from the west, stopped when the engineer saw the blazing ties, then backed hastily in the direction whence it came.

The troopers remounted and rode on as soon as the damage to the railroad was complete. As night fell on the road to the next objective, the South Anna River, the threatening storm broke in driving rain that was mixed with sleet and wet snow. The column pushed on through the darkness, halting only once during the night for rest and cold food. Fifty troopers lost their way in the storm and wandered all night before they found the tracks of the column and rejoined it in the morning.

On parallel roads eastward, Kilpatrick was pressing with the main force. He crossed the Virginia Central at Beaver Dam Station, where his point riders captured the man at the telegraph key before he could tap out a warning to Richmond. As the storm began to rage, Kilpatrick's troopers burned the railroad depot, water tanks, fuel supplies of cordwood for the trains, and various storehouses around the station. They destroyed the switches, ripped up spur tracks, tore the main tracks of the line from their bed, and gleefully cut down telephone poles for a half mile in each direction.

Clothed in ponchos and bowing their heads to the wind and the stinging sleet, they rode south again. Kilpatrick was at the head of the column, fretting because his signal officer, Captain Joseph Gloskoski, could not launch rockets into the dark sky–rockets that were supposed to be the means of communication between the two commands.

"Goddammit, I don't even know whether he's run into trouble, or is riding free and clear on schedule," Kilpatrick groused to Brigadier General Davies of the First Brigade. "They might have been jumped, or turned back–who knows? I'll tell you one thing. He's got to be in the streets of Richmond at ten o'clock tomorrow morning."

"He'll be there, Jud. He's got picked men, and only five hundred of them. He's probably at the James already, resting for the ride into the city in the morning."

"He'd better be there. Can't we push a little faster, Henry?"

"Not in this storm, Jud. We're all right. We'll make it."

As the column rode on through the driving storm, the dozen or so troopers at the point were the targets of occasional bushwhackers. Every half hour or so, the long column bunched and milled at the dull reports of muskets up ahead, where flashes of fire in the darkness indicated a makeshift barricade manned by a few ghostly figures that fired once and ran off into the pines and brush.

Kilpatrick was furious at the frequent delays, but he had to submit to them rather than risk casualties by bunching a company of cavalry in an assault upon each barricade. Instead, the entire column waited while the men on the point rode wide around the obstruction, scattering the mixed militia and civilians who briefly posed opposition. At one barricade, the rebels were regular soldiers, who held their ground for several minutes before Yankee troopers surrounded them and demanded surrender. Ten rebel soldiers and two lieutenants were captured.

In spite of the bushwhackers, however, the men rode miserably through the night, trying like seasoned troopers to sleep slouchingly in the saddle whenever they could, shoulders bowed to the driving, slashing sleet, and exposed skin surfaces becoming raw and tender.

Shortly after dawn, Dahlgren's weary and rain-soaked command reached the Kanawha Canal along the James River, about twenty-one miles from Richmond. Here Dahlgren sent Mitchell with about one hundred troopers, mostly from the 2nd New York, along the canal on the north side of the James. Mitchell's mission was to destroy locks in the canal, and all the canal boats he could find, and to burn all the mills and factories that lined the busy waterway and to destroy all the grain. Mitchell took with him the prisoners, the single ambulance, and the spare horses, in order to send them to Kilpatrick at Hungary Station on the Richmond & Fredericksburg Railroad. With everything that would burn flaming behind him, Mitchell was to dash into the city to rejoin Dahlgren.

The rest of Dahlgren's four hundred troopers, in the meantime, would cross the James at a ford to be pointed out by the saddle-sore Martin Robinson.

Mitchell's men rode onward slowly, burning and pillaging as they went. Along the river below Goochland Courthouse, they came upon some of the finest estates in Virginia. They fired granaries, barns, and corncribs; they broke into the big houses and roistered in the wine cellars. There were troopers who rode toward the rebel capital drinking fine wines from silver goblets and refilling them from ancient cut-glass decanters.

Although the schedule called for Dahlgren to be upon the streets of Richmond by ten o'clock in the morning, he made an unscheduled stop. He rode with his staff and a half-dozen troopers along the tree-lined drive of a splendid plantation house which an inconspicuous sign named Sabot Hill. He explained to Hank Stephens: "This is the home of the reb Secretary of War, James Seddon. His wife is an old family friend. I'm stopping to pay a courtesy call."

He dismounted clumsily at the veranda, and, using his crutches, climbed the steps. A handsome woman, elegantly dressed, stepped out of the doorway. She seemed not at all disturbed to find four hundred Yankee troopers in her drive. Calmly she surveyed Dahlgren's clumsy maneuvering on the steps.

"Do you need help, Colonel?" she asked in a low musical voice. She motioned to a Negro behind her in the doorway. "Help the gentleman."

Dahlgren shook his head. "Thank you, ma'am. I'm all right. You are Mrs. Seddon?"

"I am."

"I'm Colonel Dahlgren. Ulric Dahlgren."

She smiled then, warmly, stepping forward. "Of course," she said. "I should have recognized you. This is a pleasure, Colonel. Will you come in, please?"

"A moment, ma'am," Dahlgren said. "Major Stephens, will you come, please, and meet Mrs. Seddon?"

Hank dismounted and climbed the steps. He bowed stiffly to the elegant Mrs. Seddon, who touched her skirts in the faintest of curtsies as if that was all an unshaven and mud-spattered Yankee major deserved. Hank was irritated by the slight disdain he thought he detected, by the arrogance with which Dahlgren had ordered him to dismount, even though the word "please" had been used, and most of all by Dahlgren's delay in pressing on for Richmond. By this time of morning, Kilpatrick might already be hitting Richmond's defenses.

The reason for the stop at the Seddon plantation was apparent in Mrs. Seddon's next words. "You know, of course, Colonel, that I am most anxious for news of your father. Do come in, and you, Major. I will have a servant fetch some wine, and you can tell me all about that distinguished gentleman, the admiral, whom I find it difficult to picture except as I knew him so many years ago, before you were born." It was all said charmingly, graciously, as if this were an ordinary social call being made in the days when this plantation must have been a center of Virginia society.

Dahlgren smiled. "I have often heard, ma'am, of Miss Sally Bruce, from the admiral." He looked at Hank. "Mrs. Seddon, Major, was a schoolmate of my mother's, and she also knew my father."

"Come now, Colonel Dahlgren! You know that he was my beau, and your mother stole him completely away from me. It is most amazing to me that the son of my two old friends is a colonel of Yankee Cavalry. Come inside, please." She turned to the Negro servant. "Wine for the gentlemen, Charles."

"Thank you, ma'am," Hank said evenly. "Not for me. Colonel, I'll get the column moving. I'll leave a squad to wait on you."

"Where is it that you're going in such a hurry, Major?" Mrs. Seddon asked, again using a slightly different tone with Stephens from the one she had used with Dahlgren, as if the distinction between the son of old friends and any other Yankee officer should be made clear.

"To capture your husband, ma'am," Hank said in as quiet a voice as he could manage. "He is one of our objectives."

She laughed musically but artificially, as if the Yankee major had told a joke that she neither appreciated nor understood.

Hank bowed again, turned and left the porch. Dahlgren and Mrs. Seddon went into the house. Dahlgren had given Hank an angry look but had made no comment about Hank's remark on Secretary Seddon.

Once again the column lurched into movement, with the troopers on the point leading the way down the broad hill that sloped to the valley of the James River. Hank pulled out the gold watch that his father had given him upon his appointment to the Academy. It was already past nine o'clock. They didn't have a chance of keeping the rendezvous with Kilpatrick. The only thing to do was keep pressing for the city and trust Kilpatrick to keep the reb troops busy on the Brook Turnpike north of Richmond.

The first task ahead, however, was to cross the James, in order to reach the bridge in the town of Manchester–the bridge that crossed the channel between the southern bank of the river and the prison pen on Belle Isle.

Hank swiveled in his saddle. "Sergeant Turley!"

"Sir?" the call came back from far down the column.

"Bring up that guide."

Immediately Turley came cantering along the line of troopers, his left hand gripped upon the bridle of Martin Robinson's mount, while the Negro clung to the saddle and moaned with every jolting step his horse took.

"What's your name?" Hank said.

"Robinson, Cap'n. Martin Robinson. I'm a freeman, and a bricklayer by trade. Used to belong to Mr. David Mimms at Goochland, Cap'n."

Hank unfolded a map of Goochland County, refolding it with one hand to show the James River section west of Richmond. He held it across for Robinson's eyes, steadying it as well as he could. "All right. Show us where we cross the river."

Robinson shook his head. "I can't read, Cap'n. I know where we's at. I was born and raised here. 'Bout three miles to Jude's Ferry. That's near a place they calls Contention. You crosses there to git over to Powhatan County."

Hank put the map away. He looked searchingly into the guide's face. "You're sure? One hundred per cent sure?"

"Born 'n raised, Cap'n. Back yonder. Now I lives there, not far from Jude's Ferry."

"A ferry?" Hank said abruptly. "What do they need a ferry for, if it's a ford?"

The Negro looked puzzled. "The name is Jude's Ferry, Cap'n. What you mean?"

Hank tried again. "Does everybody cross there? Mounted? Wagons? Buggies?"

"All the time, Cap'n. I be glad when I gits you folks there. This here horse nigh to killed me."

"Have you crossed the ford this winter?"

"Don't cross 'er much in winter, Cap'n. There ain't much work in Powhatan County in winter. Don't lay much brick in winter, Cap'n."

"Goddammit," Hank said, venting his irritation on this seemingly dull fellow. "You'd better be right about the ford. If we have any trouble, you'll pay for it, Robinson."

"I'm a Linkum man, Cap'n. I lead you right there. You go right over the river. I seen 'er times when you ain't hardly gonna get your feet wet going over."

"In the summer," Hank said.

The Negro nodded. "Summer is the best. I seen 'er running high in the spring, lots of years. Runs pretty high iffen it rains."

Stephens looked at Turley. "Sergeant, how much rain would you estimate in the last sixteen hours?"

Ben Turley frowned. "Storm came out of the west and northwest, Major. The streams were high when it started. The Rapidan was damned high when we came over. This storm has run off a lot of snow in the western mountains. Depends how long it would take that water to get down here. Sixteen hours? maybe. Wouldn't surprise me none if the goddam river has lifted as high as a whore's skirt on a Saturday night."

"Take a squad and take a look."

Fifteen minutes later, Turley came back from his ride to the riverbank. His face was somber. He reined in beside Stephens.

"High and brown, Major. Snow water. You've seen it back home in the spring when the Hollow Brook floods all that flat land down through Putnam Valley and Van Cortlandtville. You can't cross this bastard where I looked at it. I dunno about down below."

Stephens turned to Robinson again. "How far are we now from the ford?"

"Ain't but two miles, Cap'n. You won't have no trouble. Git a little wet, maybe."

"You'd better be right."

Dahlgren came cantering along the column a couple of minutes later. He nodded coldly at Hank. "I was not taken with your attitude toward Mrs. Seddon, Major."

Hank nodded in return. "I don't give a goddam if you were or not, Colonel. She's just another rebel to me. I think we've got some trouble ahead."

"Don't change the subject, Stephens. You were damned rude, you know."

"Jesus, Colonel, forget it, will you? This is important. Turley went to look at the river. It's running high and fast."

"We'll cross at the ford. Right ahead, I believe. It's called Jude's Ferry."

"If we can. I wouldn't trust that colored boy to come in out of the rain. He's not very bright, Colonel."

"We'll soon see. My report of the expedition, Major, will contain a full detailing of your conduct toward Mrs. Seddon."

"I expect that it will, sir. Now listen to me, Colonel. We've got a mean job ahead. We're going to be fighting in maybe two, three hours. Let's get along together until we get back to Stevensburg."

Dahlgren nodded slightly. "You're a good officer, Major. I will also put that in my report. All right. Why don't you ride ahead and take a look at that ford? Take the Negro and at least a dozen troopers. The rebs may have patrols out."

Hank swore softly to himself as soon as he saw the river. The water was reddish brown. Debris of all kinds floated swiftly downstream. The current looked deep and strong. Hank noticed the high-water marks of other seasons, set precisely for the experienced eye by bits of flotsam, mainly grass and leaves, that were caught in the branches of the brush along the bank of the river. There were also bands of color on the trunks of trees at the water's edge, where high water had swirled in past years and deposited layers of reddish-brown silt in the crevices of the bark. The water of the river now was creeping toward those high levels.

Robinson stared placidly at the swirling water. "She has riz up some, Cap'n. Them solgers yonder going to get wet some."

Hank didn't even bother to reply. He looked at Ben Turley, then nodded his head at the river. "Let's give it a try, Ben."

Turley frowned. "Never make it, sir."

"We won't know until we try. Let's go."

They were ten yards into the current when Hank knew that the attempt to cross here would be futile. His big ugly horse was moving slowly in heavy water that already reached its belly, and the water was getting deeper and the current swifter. Five yards more, and suddenly Turley's horse lost its footing, downstream of Hank, and Turley was free of the animal and being carried rapidly with the torrent toward Richmond. Troopers on the shore immediately galloped downstream to get ahead of the flailing sergeant in order to throw a picket rope to him when he came within reach.

Hank's mount continued to pick its way over the ford, and since he was now in the center of the river, Hank let the horse have its way. He couldn't turn now and come back. His legs and thighs were soaked and he began to shiver. The water was, he supposed, about thirty-five to forty degrees in temperature.

Now the horse had to swim, and Hank was completely wet and miserable. He held to the pommel of the saddle with both hands. He knew that he would drown if he were thrown free of the horse in the center of the current. He couldn't swim with boots, blouse, poncho, and the rest of his heavy clothing.

The horse found bottom with its pistoning hoofs, and a few moments later it scrambled into the shallow water of the far shore. Hank immediately looked downstream. Turley was ashore. His horse was being led to him by a mounted trooper.

First things first, Hank thought. I'll freeze to death if I don't get rid of some of this water.

He stripped, then stood shivering while he wrung the water from his clothing. He dressed again, miserable in the heavy sodden uniform. Then he gave his attention to the north shore of the James.

Dahlgren had come up with the column. Hank could see the colonel at the edge of the water, crutches held in his armpits. Dahlgren was shouting something, but Hank couldn't hear a word above the sound of the river. He cupped one hand to his ear to indicate that he was unable to hear. Dahlgren turned his back to the river, evidently issuing orders.

There was an immediate reaction. An officer spurred forward from the column. Hank recognized him by his horse, a big gray mare. It was Lieutenant Reuben Bartley, of the Signal Corps, who carried in his saddlebags the rockets that were to have answered Captain Gloskoski's signals from Kilpatrick's column. Bartley also carried a pair of semaphoric flags. He stepped to the water's edge. His arms began to move rapidly. The flags jumped up and down, high and low.

M-O-R-S-E-?

Hank contrived a pair of flags with his hat in one hand and his wet map case in the other. He sent the answer back.

Y-E-S

C-A-N W-E C-R-O-S-S-?

N-O

W-H-Y N-O-T-?

N-O F-O-R-D—2-0-0 W-I-L-L D-R-O-W-N

C-A-N Y-O-U G-E-T B-A-C-K-?

Y-E-S

As he prepared to push his reluctant horse back into the river, Hank saw Dahlgren remount on the far bank. Then the distant figure of the colonel moved toward a man who stood alone near the water's edge. Hank could see that it was the Negro guide, Martin Robinson. Dahlgren was leaning from the saddle, apparently shouting at the man, because his right arm was chopping the air before the man's face. Hank reined his horse, to watch the scene. He was puzzled. He saw Dahlgren's arm lift high in the air.

Robinson suddenly turned and started to run stumblingly along the riverbank. Three or four troopers cantered after him and caught him quickly enough. They brought him back to Dahlgren.

The colonel leaned far from his saddle and took something from the horse equipment of a nearby trooper. He tossed it to the men who held Martin Robinson.

Hank Stephens suddenly understood what it was that Dahlgren had reached for, what it was he intended to do.

"Good God," Hank whispered, spurring his horse immediately toward the surging river. "Don't do it, you young fool!"

11

The troopers who had chased Martin Robinson along the riverbank were Johnny Watkins and his messmates. Johnny thought the fellow was a fool for running. The colonel was trying to scare him to get the truth out of him. Obviously this was the wrong ford; there must be another one that was passable, and the Negro was trying to keep them from finding it by insisting to the colonel that this was the ford at Jude's Ferry.

Sam Foley caught Robinson by leaning from his saddle and grabbing the man's coat collar. Willie Leech reined his horse in front of Robinson and leveled his carbine at the Negro. "Move another step," Willie growled in his best hard-bitten cavalry manner, "and I'll blow your head off."

Watkins and McAfee followed the other two troopers as they hauled Robinson at a stumbling run back to Dahlgren. The colonel's face was drained of color and his lips were tight as he glared at the terrified Negro.

"The Old Man looks madder'n hell," McAfee whispered to Johnny. "I bet that nigger thinks he's really gonna get himself strung up."

"The rebels probably paid him a pretty good price to steer us wrong," Johnny said. "Seems funny to have a colored fellow as a spy, doesn't it?"

"He'll talk now," McAfee said. "Like the colonel says, there's got to be a ford here somewheres."

Dahlgren leaned to a nearby trooper's saddle and pulled free a long picket rope. He tossed it to Sam Foley. "Hang him," he said abruptly.

"No, Cap'n, no!" Robinson screeched. "That there is the ford. I swear it. That's the one we uses. I can't he'p it if the water has riz up, Cap'n. You ain't gonna hang me, Cap'n?"

Foley let Willie Leech hold the Negro while he proceeded to fashion a noose in the picket rope.

"What for, Cap'n?" the man cried. "I done what you said. Bring you to Jude's Ferry, you said. I brang you, Cap'n. Don't kill me, suh! Please.

I got me a family. I'm free, Cap'n. I ain't no rebel. You foolin', ain't you, Cap'n?"

Dahlgren continued to stare at the man coldly. The colonel's face was still white and strained. His jaws were clamped tightly. Several officers moved up from the column. Their faces were anxious, but none of them spoke. They grouped behind Dahlgren.

"Proceed, Corporal," Dahlgren said abruptly. "Hang the man."

"Jesus, please!" Robinson screamed.

No one else in the group around Dahlgren said anything at all. There were perhaps fifty men in the column who were close enough to hear and see what was happening. They passed the word back in whispers. All down the line the column seemed to shiver with a wave of motion that passed along it, as men stood high in their stirrups to try to see what was happening up front.

Foley and Leech dismounted. Foley threw the noose around Robinson's neck while Leech held his squirming body fast. The Negro was moaning now, pleading for his life. Matter-of-factly Foley motioned Leech to drag the man back until he stood under a big lower limb of an oak tree about twenty yards from the river's edge.

A captain from the 1st Vermont spoke flatly with the twang of his homeland: "Don't hang that man, Colonel."

His words, breaking the silence around Dahlgren, loosed a flood of comments from the other officers. Most of them opposed the hanging. Only one, a major from the 5th Michigan, snarled approval: "Hang the rebel son of a bitch!"

"Shut up!" Dahlgren cried harshly. "Goddammit, I'm in command. I said the man hangs, and hang he will." Then he regained control of his composure. "Do you gentlemen realize what he's done by leading us astray? I'll tell you in a few simple words. He has condemned those poor fellows on Belle Isle to stay there. We can't reach the island unless we cross the river. I said hang him, and I mean hang him! Proceed, Corporal."

"Hold on, Colonel," said the Vermont captain. "Talk a minute. I think he's just a stupid colored boy who did his best for us. He couldn't help the flood waters. Hold on a minute, sir."

"Hang him," Dahlgren ordered.

For a moment, it looked as if the Vermonter was about to speak again, but then he shrugged and reined his mount away to return to the column. The Michigan officer also rode back, talking to the man from Vermont. His comment carried clearly above Robinson's wailing to the group around Dahlgren. "What the hell! He's only a nigger, ain't he?"

Near the oak tree, Johnny Watkins watched in horror as Foley and Leech proceeded with their orders. "My God, Fred," he said to McAfee, "he means to do it!"

"Sure looks like it," McAfee said laconically. "Too bad that fellow is so dumb he don't know another way across this here river. Save his life if he did."

"That's it," Johnny said urgently. "He's just stupid. We know that. We rode with him. I'm going to tell Colonel Dahlgren."

McAfee grabbed the bridle of Johnny's horse. "You shut your mouth, boy, if you know what's good for you. That man's gonna hang, and there ain't anything you can do about it."

McAfee held the bridle while Johnny's horse pranced at the restraint. Then McAfee echoed the Michigan officer: "Don't be a fool, Johnny. He ain't nothin' but a nigger."

Four troopers jumped to the ground at another short order from Dahlgren. Foley held Robinson while the four newcomers took hold of the rope that Foley had tossed over the branch of the tree. Robinson's moaning was suddenly stilled as the four troopers and Willie Leech pulled up the slack on the rope. Then they all hauled together and Martin Robinson was strangling in mid-air.

When he reached the north side of the James once more, Hank Stephens paused long enough to make sure that the Negro was dead. The long line of cavalrymen was passing by in a column of fours, most of them looking up curiously at the body spinning at the end of the rope. Hank spurred past company after company until he reached the point, where Dahlgren was riding alone, his face grim and drawn.

Stephens reined in beside the colonel. "Why did you hang him, Colonel?"

"Treason," Dahlgren said.

"He was only a harmless fool," Hank said quietly. "You had no reason to do that."

"Harmless! The purpose of this expedition is lost because of that harmless fool of yours, Major. The best we can do now is to try to get into the city from this side of the river. They'll be waiting for us. He probably planned it with them all along. Tell me he was harmless fool, Major, when the rebel guns begin to cut us down."

"Hear me, Colonel," Hank said soberly, keeping his voice low so that no other officers or troopers could hear him. "I'll have to report this to General Kilpatrick. Killing him was absolutely unjustified."

"Report and be damned to you, Major!"

There was nothing more for Hank to say, since he was powerless to act. Dahlgren was in command. Hank fell back and rode with the troops, worried deeply that Dahlgren was frightened and therefore inclined to panic.

Captain Mitchell, with the bulk of the detachment of the 2nd New York, left the towpath along the canal in early afternoon. His men were boisterous. They had burned and pillaged through several hours, and now they moved out on the river road and spurred after Dahlgren. They caught up with the column at a crossroads about eight miles from Richmond, where Dahlgren's command had halted because of the capture of three wagonloads of corn. The troopers made coffee and fed the corn to their mounts, while Dahlgren conferred with Mitchell.

Mitchell came to share Hank's coffee. He jerked his thumb in Dahlgren's direction and said, "He's jumpy, Hank. Can't say I blame him. No way we can cross the river now. Say, what'd you hang the nigger for?"

"Dahlgren said he was a traitor."

"Jesus, he must be worried even more than he looks. No call to hang a man because the river flooded. That poor fellow couldn't help it."

Mitchell suddenly stopped talking. He lifted his hand and pointed to the northeast. He grinned. "Kilpatrick!"

Hank heard it, too. Every man in the command turned and looked in the same direction, as if they could see the smoke of the fieldpieces that had suddenly started to pound in the distance.

"Give it to 'em, Kil!" Mitchell laughed. "Hey, boy, now we'll go in. Right into Richmond while Old Kill Cavalry keeps 'em busy yonder."

Hank shook his head. "Listen," he said quickly. "Try to count."

Mitchell cocked his head as if that would help him to hear better. Then he nodded. "We brought six guns. That's about twenty a-booming. Well, what the hell! Nobody ever thought they'd throw flowers in our path."

Dahlgren's voice carried to them, shouting orders to get the column in the saddle. In the midst of the hustle to get riding again, three horsemen in gray uniforms came galloping to the crossroads from the direction of Richmond and were captured before they could wheel their horses to attempt escape. They seemed cheerful enough about their fate, grinning when they said that they reckoned they'd been captured by the very

Yankees they'd been sent out to serve picket watch against. They were militiamen of General Custis Lee's Richmond City Battalion. These men, with all the others who had been captured since Dahlgren had started south from Ely's Ford, were sent northeast under guard of twenty men, heading toward the sound of Kilpatrick's guns. With them went the ambulances and the led horses.

At the head of the column, Ulric Dahlgren lifted his saber high and called out the command to ride for Richmond: "At the gallop, yo-o-o-o!"

The gallop lasted only a few minutes, however, before it slowed to a steady trot. The horses were as weary and road-worn as the troopers. They plodded along the Three-Chopt Road, strung out in a long and irregular column of fours.

It was now late afternoon, and speed was imperative. Unless both Dahlgren and Kilpatrick were inside the city by nightfall, and unless resistance could be quelled before darkness hid the defenders, the raid would fail almost entirely. Hank Stephens considered the prospects as he rode. They could set the city afire, certainly, but fire brigades could control the flames in time if there were no street fighting to hinder them. The chances of capturing or killing Davis and his subordinates would be small in the darkness, when any resourceful men could escape through or hide in a city that they knew well. The prisoners on Belle Isle would probably have to stay there. By the time Dahlgren's cavalry fought its way through the city to the Manchester bridges, enough guns and troops could be mustered by the rebels to make any attempt to reach Belle Isle a bloody and fruitless affair. No more could Libby Prison, where Federal officers were held captive, be reached by the raiders, since it was well downriver from Belle Isle and protected by lines of fortifications that would be heavily manned.

Even clerks and bookkeepers, Hank thought, could hold us through the night. In the morning, we'd be an additional twelve hours late. Add that to the seven or eight hours' delay today, and we'd be cooked. Hampton coming down from the northeast; Stuart riding in from the west.

He told Mitchell how he felt about it. "We haven't got much time," he said soberly. "Get in there, do as much damage as possible, join Kilpatrick tonight, and run like hell for the Peninsula and Butler's lines. The whole reb cavalry will be on us tomorrow."

Mitchell nodded agreement. "I'll be damned if I like night fighting. One man behind a fence in the darkness is worth ten men riding horses in an open street. You can't see the son of a bitch that kills you."

Mitchell looked up at the gray dreariness of the sky. "We've got maybe an hour's light left. How far into the city, Hank?"

Stephens shook his head. "I dunno, and I can't hold a map steady at this pace long enough to pick out landmarks. Shouldn't be more than five miles. And it shouldn't be long before we hit some rebs. Maybe right up there." He pointed to several stands of trees that bordered the plank road along which the blue column was now pounding.

As he spoke, a puff of smoke made a momentary dot among the dark trees and the report of a musket shot reached them a second later. The troopers of the 5th Michigan, riding the advance, immediately began to open up their column into a line of battle, pushing their horses across ditches and rail fences into the fields and scattered wood lots that bordered the plank road. Drawing sabers and revolvers, they rode for the trees, which now spurted smoke in a dozen places. The rattle of the muskets suddenly increased as the wave of Michigan cavalry rolled toward the line of woods. Troopers now were firing revolvers and yelling savagely. The Michigan men reached the trees, vanished among them, and just as suddenly as the muskets had started to bang, they became silent. Now the other detachments formed into line of battle and pushed into the woods–New York, Vermont, and Maine all following Michigan.

The rebels in the wood lot, nondescript fellows of all ages, began to file into the road with the urging of the Yankee troopers. Two or three dozen of them, mostly wearing makeshift uniforms, and all of them dismounted, were put under guard. The rest had fled through the fields and woods toward the next line of defense, nearer the city.

Five minutes later, the rebel skirmishers opened fire again, and the procedure was repeated–a charge of yelling cavalry, a sudden end to the musketry, a score or so of milling prisoners.

The only way to get through the hidden defenders was to charge right over them and round up as many as could be found. One detachment after another galloped ahead to attack. Always the running rebs faded into the growing darkness, although almost two hundred of them straggled under guard along the plank road behind the cavalry.

The winter dusk changed swiftly into darkness, and now only the orange flashes of secesh muskets could be seen. The Federal troopers were using their sabers now, slashing at any running figure they could ride down. The rebel casualties were heavy, but there were blue-clad bodies scattered all along the borders of the plank road. In the darkness, many of the prisoners walked away and disappeared.

About two and a half miles from the point where the 5th Michigan had first been fired upon, and about the same distance from the city proper, the rebel fire suddenly became intense and concentrated. It was Hank Stephens' opinion that the rebel forces had been rallied with the view to fighting it out in the darkness. As he led the 2nd New York in a charge on the line of musket flashes, he thought that this was the rebels' last gasp. If the column burst through this final stand, it would be in the streets of the city within a few minutes. If Kilpatrick were pounding down from the north, tremendous damage might be done to the priceless treasures of the Confederacy: the Tredegar Iron Works near the James, the mills and warehouses along the river front, the state armory, the gas works, and dozens of government buildings of all kinds.

On the other hand, Hank thought swiftly, if Kilpatrick is lallygagging, we're gone up.

It turned out that Dahlgren did not consider this the rebels' last stand outside the city; he thought that strong reinforcements, too strong for night attack, accounted for the sudden increased volume of musketry. His bugler sounded the Recall, almost too late for the 2nd New York to turn back from the rebel position.

Dahlgren's voice rolled out shrill commands over the crackle of secesh muskets: "Fall back on the plank road! All units keep together! Don't bunch up on the road! 2nd New York, under Captain Mitchell, take the rear guard! 2nd New York, acknowledge!"

Mitchell shouted a long answering call: "2nd New York to the rear, sir!" He leveled his revolver for a final shot at the hidden rebels more than a hundred yards away, and rallied his troopers to take the rear guard.

Hank Stephens spurred furiously to the road, where Dahlgren was sending the detachments into disorderly retreat along the route they had covered just a few minutes before. Hank fought his temper while he struggled to control his prancing horse. "Listen to me, Colonel," he said urgently. "That's their last line. Why don't we re-form in line of battle and go right in over 'em? Kilpatrick will be waiting for us. We can roll right through those rebs and do the job we came for. The whole goddam city can be burning in an hour. Let's go in, Dahlgren."

"Too many of them," Dahlgren answered. "Major, take the point. We're heading for Hungary Station on the railroad."

"I'm telling you, Colonel, we can cut right through 'em! Let's not quit and run for it, Colonel!"

Dahlgren shook his head vehemently. "No, no. You have your orders."

Hank gave up the fight. "Yes, Colonel," he said wearily. "Whatever you say. You're in command."

He rode rapidly ahead past the various disordered detachments until he was almost a quarter mile beyond the first sizable body of troopers. There he found the dozen or so horsemen who had, willy-nilly, been sent ahead when the Recall had been sounded. Among them was a small group of 2nd New York troopers headed by Sergeant Ben Turley. There were also Michigan and Maine men in the small advance party.

"I'm in command up here, Sergeant," Hank told Turley. "Let's keep together, but don't bunch up. There may be bushwhackers along the fences."

"Where we going, Major?" Turley asked.

"Back the way we came, Ben. Who are the men with you?"

"Watkins, Foley, and them other two cronies. I dunno who these others are. Michigan and Maine, they say. Where's our outfit, Major? We lost 'em in the charge and the colonel sent us out here."

Hank laughed sourly. "Rear guard. We're up here and the rest of the detachment is back there."

"I'll tell you one thing, Major," Turley said harshly. "That goddam boy colonel has messed us up for fair. Jesus, I hate to think of what the rebs will do to us tomorrow, when they find us."

"All right, Ben. We'll take care of tomorrow when it comes. Let's just keep moving and keep our eyes open. Don't let any of the men get too far out in front. We could finish this expedition riding through Virginia all by ourselves."

"Do you know where to go, Major? I don't even know where the hell we are now."

"We'll head for Hungary Station, on the Richmond & Fredericksburg Railroad. That was the rallying point in case anything went wrong."

Turley grunted humorlessly. "In case anything went wrong. Holy Jesus, I don't know what else could go wrong."

The weather could. As they rode through the black night, the cold rain of the past few days started once more, and then it changed to snow and sleet that lashed horses and men.

North of the city during the early hours of the day, Kilpatrick had kept to the schedule fairly well. By ten o'clock, the hour when Dahlgren should have been releasing the prisoners on Belle Isle, the main force of cavalry was columned on the Brook Turnpike, about five miles north of Richmond.

West of him and to the rear, Kilpatrick could hear guns booming heavily at Ashland, where he had sent Major Hall and five hundred men to attack a rebel troop concentration. He grinned when he heard the secesh artillery, because the sound of guns would assure the concentration of Richmond's defense forces in that direction. The way into the city would be clear of Confederate troops in numbers sufficient to halt his hard-riding cavalry. He hauled out his great turnip watch and checked the time. If all had gone well with Dahlgren, Federal horsemen would have the city in their hands within the hour.

By God, Kilpatrick thought triumphantly, I'm on my way!

All right, he told himself, play it according to the rules now, even if they are clerks and bookkeepers. Advance guard and skirmishers first, and then bring in the column in battle line to roll over 'em.

He began to issue commands rapidly, tersely, in good spirits. He gave the advance to Brigadier General Henry E. Davies, Jr., who normally commanded the First Brigade of Kilpatrick's Third Division.

"Go in and flush 'em, Hank," Kilpatrick said happily. "Dismount your troopers and drive 'em out into the open. You get 'em running, and then we'll be right in behind you to ride 'em down."

Davies grinned. He was a slim young man with pouched eyes and tight little goatee and brush mustache, who wore the Kilpatrick hat with a vengeance—even higher on the left side of the brim than Kilpatrick wore his, and so low on the right that it covered his ear.

"Keep close on my heels, General," Davies said. "If my boys get the rebs to running, I won't be able to stop. We'll go right into the streets of the city to call on Mr. Davis before he takes it in his mind to pull foot."

Kilpatrick shook his head abruptly, frowning. He'd imagined the scene too many times to accept any tomfool notions about it, even though they came good-naturedly from a trusted subordinate. "Hold up and wait for us at the city limits," he said harshly. "They'll fight like tigers once we get into the streets. You hear, now? Wait for me, Davies."

Jud Kilpatrick would be damned if he would change the playscript. He would take Jefferson Davis into custody himself—personally. And if Davis chose to fight, Jud Kilpatrick would be in at the kill. He could see the headlines screaming the news; he could feel the laurel wreath upon his brow; he could hear the words booming in a jam-packed hall: "I give you the man who captured the Confederate capital; I give you the man who personally made a prisoner of the hated traitor, Jefferson Davis; I give you the man who struck the Confederacy to its knees in the daring raid that won the war; I give you the next President of these United States of America; I give you General Hugh Judson Kilpatrick!"

Davies rode forward with his brigade, somewhat subdued by Kilpatrick's sudden words of caution. Fight like tigers, would they? How could they? There probably wouldn't be more than five or six hundred altogether, and with Dahlgren slamming in from the south—where in hell was Dahlgren, anyway? They should have heard the sound of fighting within the city long ago. What had hit Kilpatrick, anyway, to make him change from smiling exuberance to frowning suggestion of resistance?

All that Davies could do was to try the rebs and see. He'd be damned careful until he found out how strong they were. The expedition had come too far to stumble into any disasters now.

Davies moved slowly, while Kilpatrick, now impatient once more, waited with the main column. The guns were still pounding at Ashland, and that was a reassuring sign. It was raining intermittently, a cold and driving rain that occasionally turned to biting sleet.

Far along the Brook Turnpike, Davies and his brigade began to run into rebs. Bushwhackers banged away at them from distant thickets and fences. Some of them were captured before they could run and were rounded up in pairs, trios, and quartets.

Finally, the advance guard hit the rebs in force. Far distant, across open and level country that stretched for perhaps a thousand yards, the raw earth of breastworks was raised in rain-darkened and red-hued symmetry. Davies immediately halted his command.

Binoculars picked out the muskets leveled and waiting along the silent line of breastworks, which rose to both right and left of the road. There was no place for Federal guns to be swung into action on the level land without fear of quick destruction from the rebel battery of fieldpieces that commanded all the broad approach to the breastworks as well as the long straight turnpike. On the left of the rebel works, two guns enfiladed the open ground. A sweep of the field glasses to the rebel right showed four more guns waiting for the Federal advance.

Davies hesitated. He sent couriers back to Kilpatrick with the word, while other couriers swept forward to him to demand on behalf of the general what the hell was holding up the advance.

Davies again used the field glasses, then let them swing on their lanyard while he used his good eyesight to survey the terrain. It was impossible, to his mind, for the effective use of cavalry. If he sent the troopers pounding straight down the pike into the rebel works, they would be slaughtered by the cannon. The fields on either side of the road were soft and muddy from the combination of the rains of the past days and the downpours of this day. The land was also slashed by wide, deep ditches. A brigade of cavalry would flounder to destruction under musketry and cannon fire while the horses mired themselves in the mud.

Davies took a long time in surveying, going forth bravely enough into the open land in order to sweep the entire rebel position with his glasses. He finally made a decision, in the length of time that it took two more couriers from Kilpatrick to pound forward to ask what the hell was holding up the parade.

Davies dismounted five hundred of his troopers and sent them forward on the far left in skirmish order. He depended on ground contours and farm buildings in that direction to allow the troopers, under command of Major Patton of the 3rd Indiana Cavalry, to bring fire to bear on the rebel artillery. An attack upon the enemy's right by Patton's command would enable a second unit of dismounted men, the 5th New York Cavalry, to advance as skirmishers on both sides of the road. Meanwhile, the rest of the brigade would remain mounted, ready to sweep along the road and hit the enemy's center with irresistible force as soon as the Confederate cannon were engaged with the dismounted skirmishers.

It was a sensible plan, based upon sound military thinking, and promised good results if Davies ever got around to put it into action. If there were truly only five hundred clerks and bookkeepers in those breastworks, as all information had indicated, then Davies' attack would certainly crumple them and send them lickety-split back into Richmond.

The trouble was a combination of couriers and cannon. Davies, struck with caution by Kilpatrick's reference to "tigers," sent back reports that indicated concern about the evident strength of the Confederate defenses. Kilpatrick, in turn, asked for action. So Davies, urged by the frequency of couriers, moved his skirmishers cautiously into the field of fire of the secesh cannon. The guns immediately opened fire, one after another.

These were the guns that Dahlgren and his men, far to the southwest, heard as they neared the city of Richmond.

The closer that Davies' men approached to the breastworks across the uneven ground, the more Confederate guns began to fire. The musketry now added its brittle crackle to the rapid thudding of the cannon.

Kilpatrick brought up the Federal artillery, all six fieldpieces, to pound the rebel works while the dismounted troopers advanced across the level ground.

Jud Kilpatrick was alone for a few minutes while his field officers and staff raced hither and yon to bring the horse artillery into position smartly and efficiently. He stood in his stirrups to give himself the added height that he needed to sweep with his field glasses the open ground across which lurching lines of blue were advancing unevenly. He could see the gaps in the skirmish lines where a trooper here and another there stumbled and lay still in the mire.

He studied the secesh position, taking a veteran's estimate of the number of rifles firing—a hell of a lot more than he'd been led to expect. He scanned the rebel fieldpieces that were banging away in disciplined order; those guns were well manned and effectively placed. No clerks and bookkeepers were slamming shells into the breeches. Those were trained artillerymen.

He studied his own skirmish lines, where the weary troopers were slogging through the mud and muck, making dreadfully slow progress across the open land. The rebel fire from the breastworks was taking a steady toll; the fieldpieces weren't causing many casualties, but the bursting shells caused sections of each skirmish line to linger in the temporary shelter of ditches and slight ground depressions. Every time a shell screamed and flashed, scores of men threw themselves to the ground, even though three years of war had taught them that the only shellburst they need fear was the one they couldn't see because it was right on them.

Why the hell didn't they get a move on? Kilpatrick knew that the rebel line could be turned and then be disintegrated if a few hundred of his troopers would hit it hard. They were too damned slow. Too slow!

Where was Dahlgren? Those rebs were getting reinforcements. He could see files of fresh men moving into the breastworks. Where in the hell was Dahlgren? The rebs would act like ants when the nest was broken into if Dahlgren were behind them. They'd run this way and that, backing and filling, if they got word from the city that the Yankees were inside and raising hell.

He should have known better. Goddammit! A boy. Nothing but a boy, and a one-legged boy at that. Should have left Hank in command. I know Hank. Drinker or no drinker, he knows how.

Kilpatrick could remember Academy days. In an instant, scenes flashed across his mind—scenes in which Hank Stephens urged him to bear down on assignments that baffled him, to push a horse to a high jump, to use a small man's abilities to their maximum in the physical world of the Academy, to breathe deeply and grin and summon new courage when the regimentation became almost unbearable. Jumping Jesus, Kilpatrick thought. I wish I had Hank here now.

A courier came hell-bent from the rear, saying that Hall was meeting ever stiffer resistance. "He says, General," the man panted, "that the Johnnies are bringing men up by train. He says listen and you'll hear the train whistles blowing all the way back in Richmond. He says these we're bumping into ain't Home Guards. Army of Northern Virginia, Major Hall says."

Kilpatrick nodded, then sent the man back with orders to Hall to fall in on the main column.

Train whistles! How the hell am I supposed to hear train whistles with the rifles popping and the guns banging?

Now the skirmish lines were moving slower. They'd never reach the damned breastworks!

Army of Northern Virginia? How the hell could there be any of Lee's veterans down here? How? But, by God, if they were–

Three or four thousand would do it. That many could hold up a cavalry column for hours, days. Hold up, hell–they could whip as many cavalrymen as he had, with Dahlgren thrown in. Where in hell was Dahlgren?

For that matter, where was Ben Butler, who was supposed to sashay up from the Peninsula to threaten Richmond from the east?

Again Kilpatrick swept the field of battle with his glasses. His own guns were thumping now and he could see the shells bursting harmlessly against the breastworks. The skirmish lines were moving even slower. The rebel musketry and cannon fire now seemed sharper and more authoritative than ever. Clerks and bookkeepers. Hell, no! That was certainly a big detachment of reb veterans. He wondered again where the hell they had come from. Hampton had been behind him and to his left when the column was making its dash down through Virginia. Could Hampton's cavalry have sneaked into the city, dismounted, and manned those earthworks? Were those Hampton's fieldpieces ripping up his lines? He didn't think so. He knew Hampton, or thought he did, and he believed it unlikely that Hampton would unhorse his men. Who the hell was it, then? If not Hampton, who? Custis Lee and his Home Guards? If it was, then not a single spy was worth the powder to blow him to hell.

His glasses showed him more men, and more men behind them, all filing in double time toward the rebel breastworks.

His attack was stalled now. The firing continued, but his men were pinned into the depressions and the ditches. They moved forward only in spurts, a few men at a time, simply following their officers' shouted orders to straighten out the lines.

Kilpatrick lowered his glasses. His staff and several field officers from the main column that waited on the pike were now gathered near him, some sitting watchfully on steady mounts, others busy controlling horses that were frightened by the harsh gunnery. For a few seconds, while his officers waited for some decision, Kilpatrick's chin fell within the folds of his greatcoat's collar. To the casual observer, he might have lowered his head to take a moment for deep thought, for careful decision. He might almost have been praying briefly. His shoulders were slumped as if to protect his face from the rain.

Kilpatrick was quitting. He wouldn't have called it that. In the few seconds during which his head was bowed, he found several good reasons for the action that he was about to announce to his staff. Dahlgren had disappeared. Ben Butler had failed to show himself. The rebs were veterans of the Army of Northern Virginia. The secesh guns and musketry were deadly. The rebs who fired them showed no signs of panic under the pressure of his veteran troopers in the skirmish lines. He told himself that an attempt to enter the city at this point would end in bloody failure. His men were bone-weary. His horses were jaded. Somewhere to the rear, Hall was being forced to retreat under pressure. Tomorrow was another day. It was getting dark. His troopers would be severely hampered in the streets of Richmond at night, even if they could smash the rebel defenses. Pull back, he told himself. Pull back and see what happens tomorrow.

Where in hell is Dahlgren?

Kilpatrick lifted his head. His face was grim, as usual. His mouth was a tight line, as usual. His shoulders were square. He sat high in the saddle. He was the image of the finest cavalry leader the Army of the Potomac could wish for.

His words were sharp, biting, commanding, as usual. "Send a rider to Davies. Tell him to fall back on the main column. Turn the troops and start 'em for the Chickahominy. We'll cross over and rest tonight."

His orders were repeated in singsong clarity. The knot of officers exploded as riders dashed off in several directions. For a few moments once again, Kilpatrick was alone.

He could hear the voice once more, the phantom voice that thundered in some vast hall somewhere in the nation, sometime in the future. The words were almost the same; he couldn't quite fix them in his mind, but they repeated several times the phrasing, ". . . the man who . . ." and then some deed of great valor. There were several of these, heard dimly in the instant's turning of his mind toward the scene, and then he heard the end clearly: ". . . I give you the next President of the United States of America; I give you. . . ."

He didn't catch the name, but he knew it wasn't Hugh Judson Kilpatrick.

12

Tall pines grew thickly in stands that bordered the road. Their heavy wet branches sagged with the downpour and drooped darkly across the road. The horses brushed against the branches and the troopers' bodies touched them also, with the result that every man in Dahlgren's retreating column was drenched with water again and again. The branches bent even lower when the rain changed to sleet and heavy snow, and it was almost impossible for the men on the point to determine where the road was in the darkness.

Turnings or forks of the roadway had to be called back from the point to the men in the column, many of whom were sound asleep in their saddles. The sleepers had their horses guided by their alert companions around the turns and into the proper forks. Even with one man helping another, many troopers were jolted into wakefulness when their mounts stumbled into the ditches along the road.

The horses were thoroughly jaded now. Most of them had grotesquely swollen withers; many had split and cut hoofs; a majority of them had suppurating saddle sores. Occasionally a horse would stumble and fall in a ditch, to lie there unhurt but worn out and refusing to rise. Then his rider would draw his revolver and shoot the animal. These dismounted men then stood by the roadside, waiting for the end of the column, where a couple of dozen led horses were available.

The darkness of the stormy night, combined with the heavy driving snow, brought a danger that all the officers were well aware of–the chance that the column would break into segments and that small groups of men would wander off by themselves on the many woods roads that forked to right or left. Throughout the early hours of darkness, when the wind was blowing fiercely and the sleet was lashing unprotected flesh, the officers of every detachment moved back and forth along the column, calling commands of caution: "Close up! Don't lose the men ahead of you. Close up! Stay awake and stay alert. If you lose your company, sing out. Close up!" The trouble was that the troopers ceased to listen. Sometime before midnight, a break in the column developed about a quarter of the way from the point to the end of the long line. Nobody noticed it particularly. The troopers riding at the head of the longer segment of the column were mostly asleep. Their horses carried them along at a pace set by the animals, not the riders. Before many minutes had gone by, the gap in the column had stretched to a couple of hundred yards. Nobody was aware of it. Captain Mitchell, senior officer among all the captains and lieutenants who were riding this far back, was far to the rear with the detachment of the 2nd New York.

Far ahead, at the point, Hank Stephens and Ben Turley debated a fork in the road at the precise moment when the gap in the column reached its greatest length.

"The right bears too sharply toward the Chickahominy, Ben," Stephens said, looking at his pocket compass by the light of a flaring sulphur match. "The left seems to head straight for Hungary Station, or at least where I think Hungary Station is. What do you think?"

"The right is the better road, sir. What I can see of it, it's wider and has got a better surface."

"You think we ought to take the right, then?"

"If you leave it to me, then yes, Major. We'll hit Kilpatrick either road. You got the compass. We get too far east, we can swing north again."

"All right. Take 'em to the right, Ben."

Dahlgren rode up to them while they were talking. "What's the problem, Major?"

"Right or left, Colonel. I say left, direct to Hungary Station; the sergeant says right, toward Kilpatrick and the Chickahominy." Hank grinned to himself in the darkness. If he knew Dahlgren by this time, the boy colonel would take up for the sergeant.

"Right, Major. That's the sensible course. We'll cut Kilpatrick's trail somewhere before we hit the Chickahominy."

Sure we will, Hank thought. And how will we see it in the darkness, assuming it isn't covered by snow or washed out by rain?

"Yes, sir," he said aloud. He called back the order casually: "Column, right by fours, right." Officers and sergeants picked it up and sent it back through the moaning wind until it was lost in the storm.

The command reached a half-dozen officers, perhaps a hundred and ten men, and a few Negroes who were trudging wearily in the mud to keep up with "Linkum's solgers" who were leading them to the kingdom coming and the year of Jubilo.

The command did not reach the main part of the column, far back in the darkness. The leading riders of that larger body never saw a fork in the road, had no idea that they were supposed to go anywhere but straight ahead, didn't realize that their section of a long column had suddenly become the point of a shorter column.

Captain Mitchell discovered the splitting of the column some time later, when he sent the adjutant of the 2nd New York, Lieutenant Mattison, forward with a message for Dahlgren, who might as well have vanished from the face of the earth.

Mitchell pushed his weary troopers, after he lost contact with Dahlgren, to catch up with the head of the column, but when dawn came, he discovered that nobody was ahead of him–nobody but rebels. All through the morning of that day, from the vicinity of Hungary Station through his crossing of the Chickahominy to his eventual meeting with Kilpatrick's main body at Tunstall's Station, Mitchell was plagued with rebels. They stood and fought him; they bushwhacked his point riders; they hit his rear guard and ran when the rear guard charged; they lay in wait for him wherever the road passed through thick pine groves. He lost several dozen men during that long hard ride to reach Kilpatrick; in one charge he lost twenty.

He reached Kilpatrick at dusk of the day following his separation from Dahlgren, bringing with him about two hundred and sixty of Dahlgren's original five hundred. The bantam general listened in silence to Mitchell's report, and had only one question: "Where is Dahlgren?"

Mitchell had only one answer: "General, I'll be goddamned if I know."

The long night ride for Dahlgren and his men was dreary and uncomfortable. Time and again Hank Stephens hauled out his compass and dry matches to take a bearing on the Chickahominy at Dunkirk. His maps of the area north and east of Richmond showed a ferry at that village. He knew that Mitchell's maps would likely lead him to the same crossing, and the severed sections of the column might join again.

Hank considered it almost imperative to find Mitchell. That was a more important immediate goal than seeking the safety of Kilpatrick's numbers. In spite of the complete isolation of this band of cavalry because of the enveloping cloak of heavy wet snow, Hank Stephens was certain that dawn might mean disaster. Every man in three counties between the ages of sixteen and sixty would be out with the Home Guard, hunting for Yankee cavalry detachments. By this time, Wade Hampton was certainly down from Fredericksburg with his veteran cavalrymen, although Hank thought it likely that Hampton's scouts would lead the reb troopers directly to the big force under Kilpatrick. Nonetheless, these few score weary troopers who rode the dark forest with Dahlgren might find themselves in the gray dawn facing Hampton's disciplined ranks drawn up in line of battle.

There were no incidents during the long and miserable night ride. The horses plodded on; the men slept in their saddles. Hank Stephens rode with the first set of fours at the point, where Ben Turley helped him keep the vigil of the compass that had to bring them eventually to the Chickahominy. Ulric Dahlgren rode with the second set of fours, silently through most of the long night because his leg stump was raw and throbbing mercilessly after his fifty-odd hours in the saddle.

Several times during his sporadic periods of wakefulness, Hank Stephens thought of what might have been. With two divisions instead of one, Kilpatrick might have slashed into Richmond in swift triumph, instead of retreating somewhere eastward in desperate flight from Hampton. With direct speed and dispatch, instead of delay and indecision, the smaller column could have smashed the flimsy defenses of Richmond along the plank road and could have liberated the Belle Isle prisoners and destroyed the rebel war plants along the James.

Without conceit, Hank knew that if he instead of Dahlgren had commanded, the column would have gained the city.

Even if Kilpatrick had failed against the northern defenses, as he apparently had, the smaller second column would have been inside the rebel stronghold, destroying and burning. Even though escape would have been unlikely, the damage would have been done. War plants in flames, shipping burning all along the water front, the city demoralized, and most important of all, Jefferson Davis killed or captured.

Hank considered that most of the command would have been lost, but they would have done the job they came for. Davis and his Cabinet and his main officers of government—could the rebs have survived a blow like that?

Most of the attackers would be dead, and survivors would probably have been hanged out of hand, but the war would be nearer to an end.

It was too goddam bad that it hadn't worked as it had been planned, because some of the command—or most of it—would be killed tomorrow.

Hank hoped that it wasn't snowing or raining when the end came. He had never pictured himself getting killed in a storm. It wouldn't seem right, somehow. It was a miserable prospect.

"Fork in the road, Major," Turley said wearily. "Get out the goddam compass."

Dahlgren rode up and sat silently while Hank made a tent of his poncho to shield maps and the flame of the sulphur match from wind and snow.

"Right fork, Sergeant," Stephens said quietly. "We'll hit the river before dawn if we're lucky."

Dahlgren laughed. "Lucky," he repeated. "What do you think we'll find in the morning, Major?"

"Rebs," Hank said. "Lots of rebs, Colonel. Buzzing like flies in the stables in July."

"Yes," Dahlgren said. "We'll need the luck."

The column resumed its weary journey. Dahlgren rode beside Hank for a hundred yards or so without speaking. Then abruptly he reached across the short space that separated them, touching Hank's arm. "Stephens, I suppose you believe that a man should admit a mistake?"

"I guess I do, Colonel."

"All right. You and I haven't seen eye-to-eye on this raid. But my report to the general will give you the highest praise. Captain Mitchell, too. If we've failed, it was through no fault of my officers."

"Thank you, Colonel."

"It's the first time I've ever failed at anything I put my hand to," Dahlgren said bitterly. "By God, if we'd managed to get inside the city–"

"I was just thinking the same thing, Colonel. We could have raised some hell."

"They'd have sure known we were there," Dahlgren said. "Jesus, this weather is the worst I've ever campaigned in. This damn horse is almost dead, and I'm tired and freezing, and my butt is rubbed raw, and the stump of my leg feels as if it's on fire."

Hank reached back to his saddlebags, lifting the flap of the one on the right. He pulled out a bottle of whiskey. "I've had this since we started, Colonel. I guess this is the time for it."

"Hell, yes. Open it up, Hank."

Stephens dropped his reins to the pommel of his saddle, freeing both hands. He pounded his palm against the base of the bottle to start the cork, which he then pulled with his teeth. He handed the bottle to Dahlgren. The young colonel took a long drink, coughing with the bite of the whiskey when he swallowed it. He shook his head in dismay, but then took another drink. He handed the bottle across.

"That fires up my blood. Thanks, Stephens."

Hank tilted the bottle to his lips and took two swallows. Then he tapped the cork back into the bottle. "Any objection to giving the rest to the men, Colonel? It won't go far, but it might help some of 'em."

"Go ahead."

"I've got another bottle," Hank said. "I'll give 'em that one, too."

He coaxed his horse to move to the side of Turley's mount, and gave the sergeant the bottles. "One swallow to a man, Ben, as long as it lasts."

"Yessir. 'Preciate it, Major."

Hank fell back to Dahlgren's side. The colonel was slumped in his saddle. "I'm about to doze off," Dahlgren said. "Keep me on the road, will you, Stephens?"

"All right, Colonel. I'll wake you when we hit the Chickahominy or at dawn, whichever comes sooner."

They rode slowly through the storm. The colonel dozed, but Hank stayed awake, staring into the shifting curtain of snow as if he might see what lay ahead.

Tomorrow will be a son of a bitch, he thought. I wish I had another drink to go with that first one.

Far to the north, beyond the Rapidan, George Custer's lovely and vivacious bride preened before a mirror in a farmhouse near Brandy Station. Her husband's orderly had just left after bringing her the message that Autie was back, safe and sound, from Charlottesville. He'd be along as soon as he could, the orderly had said.

She admired herself in the mirror. She was glad she was pretty. She was an asset to her tall handsome husband. When he became a national hero, she would grace the dinners and the parties and the balls. How exciting the future would be!

She could scarcely wait for him to come to her, but she knew she'd be a fool to run off to meet him at General Meade's headquarters, where he was reporting on his expedition. This had been their first separation since the marriage; how wonderful to anticipate the next few hours! She blushed prettily into the mirror as she thought of the big bed upstairs, but then she smiled.

Autie, hurry up!

Finally, he arrived with the drumming of horses' hoofs and the pounding of boots across the wooden veranda. The door burst open as if a wind of hurricane strength had struck it, and his splendid baritone made her shiver: "Libby, my darling!"

She was in his arms then, holding him close in spite of the mud-spattered uniform, the bristly blond beard, the strong smell of horses. The lamps flickered in the wind that blew through the open door that they paid no mind to while they kissed and kissed again.

"Autie, I missed you so!"

He laughed joyously, but his reply was not of love. In point of fact, it had nothing to do with their love; it was entirely about his grand adventure with his other love–the cavalry of the Army of the Potomac.

"I hit him, Libby! Jeb Stuart, goddam us all! I hit him hard, and I beat him again! I'm the only damn cavalryman in the whole goddam army can beat him! I didn't lose a man, Lib. Not a single trooper. And I cut right through Jeb Stuart and left him there with his mouth open! Not a man. Libby. I didn't lose a man."

"Don't curse, Autie. You know how much I dislike it. What else did you do, my darling?"

"Why, goddammit, what didn't I do! I burned a bridge, and captured some artillery, and burned some flour mills, and I caught me a wagonful of bacon and we'll have some in the morning, and I picked up fifty prisoners, and I marched one hundred miles in one and one-half days, and, by God, I brought back five hundred secesh horses! That's what I did, so now you can kiss me again!"

"How wonderful, Autie. How splendid!" She kissed him. "And what of Kilpatrick? Have they told you?"

He shook his head with a frown. "Nothing. There's not a word but rumor. And rumor says that he didn't get into Richmond. Nothing official yet, but the telegraph from Washington says that he didn't make it."

"I knew he wouldn't," she said with some satisfaction. "They should have sent you, Autie, instead of that mountebank."

"By God, next time they'll know who to send, Libby. And, by God, before I'm through, the whole country will know the name of George Armstrong Custer."

"Of course, darling. Now I have a nice dinner fixed for you, Autie. Come and be a gentleman and not a hard-riding cavalryman."

"To hell with dinner," he grinned.

"What, then?" She didn't look directly at him.

He scooped her up in his powerful arms and headed for the carpeted staircase that led to the second floor. "You know what." He kissed her hungrily, reaching with one booted foot for the first step of the staircase. "Tell you what the troopers say, Libby. One trooper looks at his riding partner and says, 'What's the first thing you're gonna do when you get home?' The other trooper says, 'Tell you what the second thing is. Second thing is, I'm gonna take my boots off.' "

"Autie, you're terrible!"

He laughed boyishly and carried her along, taking the stairs two at a time.

A dozen scouts who had ranged the countryside between Kilpatrick's column and the city of Richmond brought back to the general some discomfiting reports. They swore up and down and sideways that the rebel forces who had manned the breastworks on the Brook Pike were all that the city could muster, that there had been no regulars of the Army of Northern Virginia among them, that there had been no trainloads of reinforcements, nor indeed, any trains at all.

"And now, goddammit, General, you can ride right back in there!" one of the scouts insisted. "I just come most of the way on the Mechanicsville Turnpike, and the only rebs I seen were stragglers and forage parties. It's as wide open as a whorehouse door on a Satiddy night."

Jud Kilpatrick believed him. Ever since the order for withdrawal, he had been damning himself for refusing to accept the final responsibility for sending his column into heavy fire where many men would die. He had weighed certain casualties against the city as a prize, and he had turned back from glory.

Kilpatrick wasn't afraid. His courage was as strong as his wiry little body; his bravery had been tested in a score of engagements with the rebels. All that Kilpatrick lacked was the final ounce of resolution that might have ensured his ambitions.

Now, knowing that it had been a mistake to withdraw in the face of what had seemed to be withering fire, and knowing that there might just be one final chance to ride to everlasting glory, Kilpatrick issued several brisk and decisive commands. Couriers and staff officers swung to saddles and raced to deliver the general's orders. It was now night, in fact, already ten o'clock.

Lt. Colonel Preston, 1st Vermont Cavalry, was to select five hundred troopers. Major Taylor, 1st Maine Cavalry, was to take five hundred more. In two detachments, these officers would gallop through the storm into the heart of the city. The rest of the column, with the artillery, would cover the bridge over the Chickahominy and the Mechanicsville Turnpike.

One thousand weary and miserable troopers got up from the warmth of campfires and saddled their mounts, cursing the storm and the general and the sergeants who had kicked them to their feet. They were mounted and riding out in column within a matter of minutes after Kilpatrick made his decision. The rest of the command moved more slowly, but soon all the troopers were on their feet and tending to their horses.

The two detachments moved out and started down the pike toward Richmond. The rest of the command started to file in disorderly columns toward Meadow Bridge on the Chickahominy, where the six fieldpieces were already in position to sweep the pike with shells if Preston and Taylor ran into trouble.

Then, faintly through the noise of the storm, the general heard the popping and crackling of carbines from the north, where the Second Brigade had posted vedettes along the roads that approached the Chickahominy from the direction of Hanover Courthouse. A minute or two later, a courier pulled his horse to a halt before Kilpatrick.

"Colonel Sawyer's complements, sir, and he reports that our pickets are under fire. Mounted rebs, sir. The colonel says they ain't Home Guards."

Kilpatrick started to fire questions, but obviously the man knew no more than he had reported in three sentences. He was still proclaiming his ignorance when another courier came from Sawyer.

"Colonel Sawyer says to tell you he's pulled in our pickets, sir. Lots of rebs. He says it's Hampton."

"How does he know that? Is he sure?"

"Damned if I know, General. I seen 'em, lots of 'em. They're cavalry, and they act like they know what they're doing."

"Well, what are they doing, man? Speak up!"

"Pushing up hard. I told you, General, that they already drove in the pickets."

Kilpatrick's mind was almost instantly made up for him when he heard, while the courier was still talking, the dull thump of a field gun northward, followed within the timing of a quick breath by another. Home Guards would have neither the talent nor the training to wheel fieldpieces behind a cavalry skirmish and to fire them in unison against an enemy in motion. Disciplined artillery at night meant the Army of Northern Virginia. That was Hampton, sure enough.

The general sent orders that would bring back Preston and Taylor and their thousand men. He gave the commands that would bring his main force of weary troopers straggling into a change of front on Hanover Courthouse. A couple of regiments complied promptly, but the darkness and the driving snow and the clinging mud and the worn-out horses all combined to produce chaos for most of the outfits. On the periphery of the big camp there were still groups of troopers who had not yet struggled out of sleep to mount their horses. Here and there clumps of them sat on the ground, ponchos over their heads, the reins of their mounts clutched in their hands, all of them sleeping in misery. An officer who was stretched flat on the wet snow finally struggled to his feet when his orderly shook him a half-dozen times. He put his foot into the stirrup to mount his horse, but went tumbling when the saddle slid with his weight because the girth had not been tightened. When it was properly fixed, the officer mounted and began spurring the horse, which pranced and bucked, but didn't move toward the skirmishing. The horse was tied to the tree under which the officer had been sleeping.

The rebel guns thumped regularly, first one shot and then another. In the scattered pine woods and fields on the northern edge of the Federal camp, Sawyer's troopers were being routed by hard-riding rebels who came screaming out of the night from all directions at once. The guns kept firing their evenly spaced pairs of shots, until each of them had fired seven times.

The Yankees didn't know it, but the fourteenth shot was the signal for Hampton's cavalry to deploy in skirmish order on foot. They slipped like dark ghosts among the pine trees, firing and reloading and running between shots, driving the disorganized masses of Kilpatrick's troopers back into the light of the roaring campfires that they had built to keep themselves warm in the bitter night. Silhouetted by the glare of the fires, the Yankees were splendid targets for Hampton's veterans.

The rebels' fun didn't last long. Kilpatrick took charge, and his swift commands brought some order to the milling mass of Federals. The rebels kept pressing, firing from good cover, and Kilpatrick ordered a slow withdrawal, regiment by regiment, leaving the campfires and much food, scores of horses, piles of equipment, and all his seriously wounded to the grinning men of Hampton's cavalry. The Yankees took up the march eastward toward Old Church and Tunstall's Station, and eventually the Peninsula, where Ben Butler had an army to protect them.

About thirty-three hundred men under Jud Kilpatrick took the dark road through the storm, the road that would be lined with bushwhackers all day tomorrow, the road that Hampton might dispute in the morning, but the road that must finally get them out of the mess that their general had got them into.

By the light of the campfires in the camp that the Yankees had abandoned so eagerly, Confederate Major General Wade Hampton sat cheerfully on his horse and looked benevolently at his ragged and gaunt but grinning heroes as they raced around to grab Federal luxuries, or tried to catch splendid Federal horses.

One of them whooped at Hampton as he went by: "'Y Gawd, we done it, Gen'ral. We whupped 'em, didn't we?"

Hampton nodded and laughed. Whupped 'em, indeed! By one count taken late that afternoon, there had been two hundred and ninety-four men and officers in his entire command. He wondered how many Kilpatrick had commanded. By the light of the fires, he had judged the Yankees at between three and four thousand.

'Y Gawd, we done it, the aristocratic Hampton told himself.

13

The dawn gave no comfort to Dahlgren and his men. The dirty weather continued. The roads were fluid with sticky mud and slush. The men were worn out, sodden, sick, and scared.

Dahlgren and Stephens didn't know it, but Hampton's troopers were between them and Kilpatrick. Mitchell had seemingly vanished from the red earth of Virginia. Dahlgren's small command, who now wandered through the pine woods and scrub oak and low-lying marshes, were entirely on their own.

The gray cold dawn brought trouble to the Dahlgren column, or at least the daylight revealed trouble that had probably been dogging them through the night. The first sign was a volley of shots that rattled ineffectually from a stand of pines far ahead. None of the troopers on the point heard the bullets whine, so they grinned at the foolishness of firing at targets out of range, and they even laughed when, while the smoke of the shots was still curling among the pines, a dozen or so men on foot were seen racing for the safety of a larger pine woods far to the left of the road.

The bushwhackers were no laughing matter, however. All through the long day, they peppered the column from woods and brush and fence lines and from the far banks of streams. Most of them were dismounted, and they were the least dangerous, because they usually fired at ranges far too great for their weapons. Some of them were mounted, however, and they chanced ambushes at effective ranges, even though they pounded away on their horses immediately after they fired their volleys. Dahlgren's command was saved from suffering any serious casualties because the mounted bushwhackers shot from their saddles, and the shots were almost invariably wild, although a few horses and one trooper were wounded during the morning.

At McClellan's Bridge, they crossed the high and muddy Chickahominy early in the morning. The bushwhacking continued on the far side of the river. Now the rebels were bolder. There were more of them, most of them were mounted, and they could be seen from time to time, on the right and left flanks, paralleling the march of Dahlgren's column. The colonel kept a squad out on either side of his march as flankers, and now eight men rode at the point.

"All Home Guards," Hank said to Dahlgren. "I wonder where Hampton is?"

"Busy with Kilpatrick, I hope," the colonel answered wearily.

The column reached the flooding Pamunkey River at Hanover Town Ferry at eight o'clock that morning. The flatboat was on the other side. Two troopers volunteered to swim the strong current to get the boat. When the boat was brought across, more time was consumed in stretching the tow rope across the river. It took the better part of two hours to ferry men and horses across the swollen river.

There was one more river to cross, the Mattaponi, which would surely be as high and difficult to manage as the Pamunkey had been. Hank Stephens' maps again were studied. He and Dahlgren agreed that they had better head for Aylett's Ferry on the Mattaponi, where the maps showed a flatboat crossing. On the other side, however, the party would be in King William County, sparsely settled and wooded and swampy, as was its neighbor to the east, King and Queen County. The column wouldn't be able to head directly on Kilpatrick's probable trail with the expectation of catching up with him that day. Nor was there much chance of meeting General Butler's forces on the far side of the Mattaponi. On the other hand, Dahlgren said, to head south after Kilpatrick would mean that they would run headfirst into Wade Hampton.

"Better to go it alone across the Mattaponi than try to fight reb cavalry," Dahlgren said.

"Whatever we do, we're in trouble," Hank said. "These Home Guards will swarm after us. I'd bet there's two hundred around us now."

"Hampton scares me," Dahlgren said. "Home Guards don't."

"All right, then," Hank said. "Aylett's Ferry it is."

There was no boat at Aylett's. There were plenty of rebels, popping muskets from cover. Ben Turley searched the riverbank for a hundred yards in each direction, finally discovering a big old rowboat that could hold a half-dozen men in one crossing. The horses waded and swam, attached to picket lines that were gripped by the troopers in the boat. The crossing took an hour. It was two o'clock in the afternoon before the final boatload was over the river. Stephens crossed with the first group; Dahlgren waited for the last trip. Each of them, while the rowboat labored over the floodwaters so many times, was busy directing troopers in flank operations to keep the swarming rebels from attacking the crossing points. Here at Aylett's many of the scores of Negroes who had followed them so far under such miserable conditions, were left behind.

The worn-out horses and the weary riders moved away from the river on a rutted road that several of the Negroes declared would lead to King and Queen Courthouse. The flat land stretched for miles ahead, unbroken except for the endless stands of green pines and the barren thickets of scrub oak.

The column traveled for almost four hours on the lonely road, constantly harassed by hidden snipers, by motley groups of mounted Home Guards who threatened to skirmish, by roadblocks of trees and brush that always indicated an ambush. Several of the flankers were captured by the rebels during the afternoon. Many of the accompanying Negroes vanished into the forest, finally frightened away by the constant cracking of muskets and carbines and by the evil whining of bullets through the pines. It rained intermittently, and the wind whined in the treetops.

Near a crossroads hamlet called Mantapike, the column stopped just after dark, because some of the men on the point had discovered corn and hay in a barn beside the road. The troopers dismounted, built campfires, tended their horses and fed them, and then had their first hot meal in thirty-six hours, of corn and odds and ends dredged from saddlebags. The men and horses were almost finished. Some troopers fell asleep with their food in their laps; a few were so exhausted they couldn't eat.

There were about one hundred men in the command now. There were still a large number of Negroes. A third of the troopers were completely out of ammunition, another third had only a few rounds left. None of them had any food remaining after they'd eaten.

Dahlgren allowed them to rest for three hours. Most of the men fell into instant deep sleep in the barn. They were all lucky that the swarming Home Guards did not attack; all of Dahlgren's pickets, seemingly alert, were asleep on their feet.

About nine o'clock, Turley made the rounds to get the men moving. It was snowing again, and the wind was blowing, and the men who stumbled out of the barn cursed bitterly when the snow and sleet lashed their faces.

Hank Stephens charted the route that would take the column through the rest of the night, a route that hopefully by morning would bring them near Ben Butler's vedettes. With luck and without too much delay by rebel bushwhackers, Dahlgren's party would be approaching safety along the north shore of the Mattaponi River.

The column rode out slowly into the familiar misery of the storm. The men on the point anticipated being challenged by three scouts who had been sent to check on the road ahead. No challenge came; the three troopers had disappeared.

Although Dahlgren and Stephens had no way of knowing it, their selection of an escape route dumped them out of the frying pan and into the fire. They had made the great circle to the northeast largely because it would take them away from Hampton's veterans and into the pine barrens and swampy lowlands that lay between the Rappahannock and the Mattaponi, country that soldiers frequently passed through but did not linger in. On that stormy night in early March, however, there were soldiers, plenty of them, in King William County and in King and Queen County. They weren't all Home Guards, either, which accounted for the sharp skirmishing and determined bushwhacking that had lasted through the day. There were detachments of several units of the Army of Northern Virginia on armed furlough in their home counties. Notable among them was Company H, 9th Virginia Cavalry, commanded by Lieutenant James Pollard. They had been gathering from all compass points during the day.

Pollard was intelligent, brave, and accustomed to partisan warfare. He didn't need Stephens' maps, or any maps at all. He knew his county well. When the Federals stopped to cook meals and feed their horses and grab a couple of hours of sleep, Pollard abandoned his haphazard pursuit of them that had resulted in intermittent skirmishing all day long. He took his lean and ragged troopers across country on a short cut that brought them out at a crossroads called Mantapike Hill, near the Mattaponi.

Lieutenant Pollard was most pleased with his strategy. He was very confident, also. He sent out pickets to watch for the approach of the Federals; he placed his men in ambush among the pines that lined the narrow road; he thereupon went to a nearby farmhouse to take a nap. He therefore missed most of the excitement.

The Federal column rode, as usual, in sets of fours, even though the road was narrow. The men no longer made any attempt at silence; few of them cared to do any talking, but the sergeants called out constantly: "Close up. Don't straggle. There's rebs all around. Close up." Mess kits clattered and sabers rattled; the hoofs of a hundred-odd horses in liquid mud made perhaps even more noise than they would have made on a dry and dusty road. Fully a third of the command coughed loudly and monotonously and painfully; a few of them were actually running the high fevers of ambulatory pneumonia.

The four riders in the first set of fours were Privates Watkins, McAfee, and Leech, and Major Henry Stephens. Crowding close behind them were Dahlgren, Ben Turley, Sam Foley, and a lieutenant from the 5th New York. His name was Merritt.

Sometime after eleven o'clock and before midnight, Hank Stephens called back softly to Dahlgren, who was riding directly behind him: "Coming to the Mattaponi pretty soon."

"Then what?"

"Left on the river road and stick to it all the way to West Point. We ought to hit Butler's vedettes anytime after dawn."

"I hope so," Dahlgren answered wearily. "I think this horse is just as sick of me as I am of him."

Merritt suddenly spoke up for the first time in an hour: "Colonel, what was that?"

"What do you mean?" Dahlgren asked casually.

"Noise," the lieutenant said. "Something. Sounded like rifle hammers being drawn."

"Halt," Dahlgren commanded in a whisper. He turned and sent the word back. The long line of horsemen began to bunch and bulge because the command didn't travel swiftly enough. Far to the rear, the Negroes began to moan, as they had at every halt; they had many more fears to contend with than their cavalry escorts–they were afraid of the dark, ghosts, rebels, the weather, these strange bearded saviors who took pleasure in cursing them. The Negroes were afraid of everything in this wild country on this dark night.

Somebody yelled, "Shut those goddam niggers up, will you?"

Ahead of the column and to the right, among the pine trees, a man moved and a dry pine branch broke beneath his foot. Another man cursed him softly. Several rifle and carbine hammers clicked immediately. The noise was clearly heard by the men on the point.

"More Home Guards," Dahlgren said, pushing his horse forward to Hank's side. "They're bound to do some shooting, but maybe we can scare 'em out of there and put 'em on the run."

"Pull back first," Hank whispered urgently. "We're jammed up on this narrow road. Ditches on each side."

"No," Dahlgren said. "I'll challenge 'em." He again pushed his horse forward, drawing his revolver from its holster. He shouted with authority: "You rebs, surrender or I'll shoot!" He didn't wait for a reply, but leveled the heavy Colt's .44 Navy model revolver and pulled the trigger.

The hammer fell and the cap flashed, but the damp charge didn't explode.

Then the reply came, certain and terrible, as the pine trees spurted flame and smoke. Half a hundred rebels fired squarely into the point riders.

Dahlgren was smashed from his saddle as if by a giant ram; five balls ripped into his body. He was dead before his body settled in the mud.

Sam Foley died in his saddle. Willie Leech screamed and fell under his horse's slashing hoofs. Fred McAfee didn't die immediately; he took a ball in the mouth and another in the belly, and he just clung to his saddle, knowing they'd fire again and hoping they'd hit him in the heart and kill him. A ball ripped through Johnny Watkins' side. Another killed his horse. The animal, falling to the left, threw Johnny Watkins into the ditch. He lay there, stunned, not knowing what was happening.

Stephens, behind Dahlgren in the line of fire, wasn't wounded. His horse was hit twice in the head, however, and the animal fell into the mud, pinning Stephens in the saddle. He struggled to get free, while the rebs fired another heavy volley.

Ben Turley escaped the first fusillade. He drew his revolver and fired methodically at the flashes in the pine trees until the weapon was empty. Then he turned his frantic mount and surveyed the disaster. He saw immediately that the colonel was dead. He saw Stephens struggling. Turley swiftly dismounted, took a second to grab Sam Foley's revolver from the dead man's holster, threw his own away, snapped a shot at the rebels, and then bent to haul the horse from Stephens.

In a moment, Hank was on his feet, testing the leg that had been pinned by the horse and finding it unhurt. He also drew his revolver and fired at the orange flashes of the rebel weapons.

Ben Turley went down in the third rebel volley. As many as half a dozen balls hit him one after another, one making him stagger, another spinning him around, a third knocking him to his knees, and the rest smashing him to the ground.

Hank Stephens didn't see the sergeant die. He was looking for Dahlgren, but he couldn't find him. He didn't think of looking at the ground. He probably wouldn't have seen the colonel, anyway. The handsome face and thin blond beard were buried in the mud.

The column was in chaos. Horses reared and screamed, bucked and kicked. Dead men and wounded men were pounded by steel-shod hoofs. The band of Negroes had started to run at the first volley. Some of the troopers were following, others were trying to control their horses. A few of the men up front were firing at the rebels. The main body of the column, however, was trying to get off the narrow road that served as a funnel for the rebel marksmen's volleys. There were deep ditches on either side of the road, and there were rail fences beyond them. The troopers milled, trying to force their mounts into the ditches; other men made the situation worse by trying to flee to the rear through the plunging, bucking horses.

Hank Stephens raced back on foot to try to restore order. He shouted commands to fire on the rebels, to get off the road, to fall back out of the range of fire in good order. Jumping into the ditch at the left side of the road, he tore down the rail fence, three sections of it, and then jumped aside as the mounted troopers forced their horses over the ditch and into the neighboring field.

The rebel fire slackened somewhat now, since it was being returned, and since the road was clearing. In the field, Hank issued orders to the troopers to form line of battle on a small knoll on the rising ground above the Mattaponi River, and about seventy of the disciplined troopers who survived turned their horses there and waited. Hank managed to catch a riderless horse, and once mounted, he took charge of the line of battle, abandoning the men still in the road, the fleeing Negroes, and the wounded, whose screams and moans could be heard. The rebel fire ceased completely now, as if the enemy didn't know where the Federal troopers were.

Hank surveyed his command as well as he could in the darkness. He'd guessed correctly; there were about seventy troopers in the waiting lines. All day long men had been complaining that they were running out of ammunition. Hank's first order was to check his fire power.

He was dismayed by the return. There were thirty rounds in the entire party. There was one cartridge left in his own revolver and none in his saddlebags.

He abandoned his first plan, which had been to charge the rebs with heavy fire and slashing sabers, to break through the ambush by sheer force and ride with the survivors for the safety of Butler's lines. A body of cavalry couldn't ride over a heavy concentration of dismounted men without fire power. Thirty rounds would be worthless. Furthermore, if they did manage to break through, his command would have to ride about twenty-five miles to safety, without ammunition, in a country that obviously swarmed with Confederates.

What to do next? He was already forming the only plan that would get any of them to safety. First, he had to check officers. "Did any of you see the colonel go down?" he asked quietly.

"Yessir," the lieutenant named Merritt, from the 5th New York, answered. "I did, sir. Dead. Hit right away by a lot of shots. I could see blood all over him."

"All right," Hank said, "officers form here in front of me."

Five men rode forward, all lieutenants, including young Bartley, the Signal Corps officer who had hoped to fire rockets when the Dahlgren command stormed into Richmond.

"Sergeants come forward," Hank said.

Eight men joined the officers.

"There's only one thing to do," Hank said. "Dismount and split up and run for it. Each of you take a small party. Take three or four men apiece. Divide any food you have. Head southeast. Travel at night and hide out in the daytime. It's maybe twenty, twenty-five miles."

"Sir?" one of the sergeants said.

"Yes, what is it?"

"I'd rather do it a-horseback, sir. Can I take three men and try?"

"Any of you can, but I advise against it. They're all around us, and they're mounted. They'd have you before morning. We've got to sneak away, and we've got to make 'em think we're still here."

"Maybe you're right, Major," the sergeant said.

"We haven't got much time," Hank said sharply. "Now listen to me. Every man with a horse is to drive his saber into the ground and tether his horse to it right on this knoll. They're watching us. If they see the horses, they won't be in any hurry to attack. They don't know we haven't got any ammunition, and they do know we have Spencer repeaters. They won't rush us tonight. Any questions?"

There were none.

"All right, then. Two things more. Every man is to take his Spencer, withdraw the magazine tube, bend it and twist it and throw it as far as he can. Then remove the chamber mechanism and smash it. Then leave the carbines. That's the first thing. Second, every man is to leave everything right here but his sidearm and haversack. If you don't see to it that your men travel light, the rebs will track you by the discards along your trail. Understood?"

There was a murmur of agreement.

"All right. Finally, they'll probably put dogs on you tomorrow. If you hear hounds baying, take to the water as often as you can. Wade streams and swim ponds and travel in swamps if they have water in 'em. Dogs can't follow you through water. Is everything understood? We haven't got much time. They'll try to move in, even if they don't attack. We've got to get out of here fast, before they circle us."

A weary voice spoke from the line of mounted troopers. "Major, kin

I stay right here and give up to the Johnnies when they come get me? I just can't go it a-foot. I got me a wrenched ankle and it's swole as big around as a wagon tongue."

"Reb prisons are pretty miserable places," Stephens said.

"Can't help it, Major. I couldn't go a mile."

There were many other men who immediately voiced the same request. They were too worn out to go any farther. When all the men had made their decisions, there were only about a dozen who elected to try to escape the rebels. Stephens reluctantly gave permission to stay and await capture to all who asked for it, knowing that most of this small command would be in reb hands by morning, anyway.

Within the next five minutes, the horses were tethered in lines, the Spencers broken and tossed aside, and useless equipment abandoned. The few men who were leaving went around shaking hands. Hank Stephens spoke to the two dozen Negroes who had gathered with the survivors on the knoll. He told them to make their own way south to the homes they had abandoned. The kingdom was not coming; this was not the year of Jubilo.

The several escape parties began to slip away on the eastern side of the open ground, crawling on hands and knees through the pines and brush. In groups of three and four men every two minutes, they vanished into the darkness. Finally, all who wished to escape were gone, excepting Hank and Bartley and young Merritt.

There was no sound from the rebs on the road, other than the occasional drumming of a horse's hoofs as the rebel commander sent off a courier. Hank supposed the rebels were waiting for dawn and reinforcements before proceeding to wipe out the rest of Dahlgren's command.

"Good luck," Hank said to the men who had elected to stay.

Most of them gave the identical reply, "Good luck, Major."

On hands and knees, and sometimes slithering on their bellies when they heard voices in the distance, the three officers crawled for the better part of an hour, making perhaps a half mile, before they got to their feet and began to walk through the pine barrens.

14

The wound wasn't bad, not so bad. Lying in the ditch by the side of the road, Johnny Watkins reached inside his greatcoat, then under his blouse and shirt. The blood wet his fingers. The ball had entered the flesh below the ribs on the right side. It had gone right through, tearing a rough hole in his back as it ripped its way free. He shuddered when he felt the exit hole. At least the ball wasn't in him. Everybody said it was hard lines when the ball stayed inside a man. The wound was bleeding quite a bit, but it didn't hurt too much. Not yet, anyway. The edges of it felt numb as his fingers touched them.

Nossir, the wound wasn't so bad at all, at all.

Mother, he thought, I've got the best kind of wound to have, if a fellow has to have one. But I didn't get it with guidons streaming and bugles blaring. Father, I wasn't charging the enemy with a cry of glory on my lips. No, dear parents. I got it this way: some dirty rebel sonofabitch shot me from ambush. Some dirty stinking Virginia bastard shot a hole in me, and I never saw him.

Johnny Watkins began to cry. Now it hurt. Oh, Jesus Christ! Now it hurt him.

Everybody has left me. I'll die here in this goddam Virginia ditch. Oh, my God!

Then blackness swept over him.

He woke up after a time. He didn't think he'd been out very long. The pain had changed now. It hurt like hell, but suddenly he realized that he'd had pains like that before. Like a broken arm, maybe. Or like the slash from the ax when it had slipped from the piece of kindling and bit into his foot.

He'd been right the first time. The wound was not so bad. He thought he could ride with it, if he could manage to get on a horse. There were riderless horses plunging and bucking and screaming on the road, but he wouldn't be able to catch one of them, even if he weren't wounded.

He lay where he was, trying to think about what he was going to do. He was surprised to find that he was very calm now, even though his wound throbbed badly. The pain was frightening because he knew that it might mean he was about to die. Well, all right. Nothing he could do about dying.

There was a lot of talking up ahead, and suddenly a pine torch flared. A half-dozen voices cried out in alarmed anger at the light, and a swiftly snapped order from an officer caused the man holding the light to dip it into the mud and slush on the road.

Johnny heard wounded men moaning, and in the brush and timber nearby he heard shouts and sharp commands, and every few seconds a gunshot or two, some close and some distant. Once there was a fusillade, perhaps six or eight muskets banging raggedly. This was followed instantly by a shrill scream that quickly died away.

They got him, Johnny thought.

They'll get me, too, he figured, if I get up and run. They'll either grab me or shoot me. So that's out. I couldn't run, anyway. I don't want to get shot again, and if they're going to grab me, I might as well let 'em do it right here in this ditch.

Comes to that, I don't want to get grabbed, either. Best thing is just to be dead.

A group of soft-speaking rebels walked slowly past his resting place, looking at the sprawled blue-clad figures on the road. They were looking for wounded men. One of them told another to go take a look at the Yankee in the ditch. Johnny lay absolutely still.

The rebel didn't step down into the ditch. He crouched at the edge of the road, peering at the huddled body. Johnny held his breath so no telltale vapor would rise. The rebel studied him for perhaps five seconds, then rose from his crouch. "He's dead," the man said to the others.

The rebs went off down the road. There were few shots now from the surrounding woodland and fields. Most of the excited shouting that had followed the initial clash had died away. There were groups of men in no particular order scattered everywhere on the road. Rebs and prisoners, Watkins decided. Everybody's quit fighting.

Now the wound was aching severely. He thought about the bleeding. It didn't seem to be pouring out of the wound, but his entire right side was wet and sticky. He thought of dying, and panic gripped him again. He had to force himself to lie still. He had to think.

He would have to choose from the alternatives. He drummed them up to his attention:

First, he could call out to the rebs and give himself up. That would get him to a doctor, but it would also land him on Belle Isle eventually. He'd heard all about Belle Isle and had seen some of the few living scarecrows who had somehow escaped and made their way through the lines. It seemed reasonable to believe that a wounded man would die if they put him on Belle Isle.

Second, he could get up and run, if he could manage to run. It would probably be more of a stumble. He might find one of the loose horses. He might also get a minnie ball square in the middle of his back.

Third, he could lie here and pretend to be dead. It had worked once. When things quieted down, he might be able to sneak away. Trouble with that was, the next reb who looked at him might step into the ditch to take a closer look. Then it would be off to Belle Isle for Johnny Watkins.

Fourth, he could sneak away right now, if no rebs were so close they could see or hear him.

He liked that fourth choice, everything considered. If he had a little luck, he'd be into the timber and on his way. If he didn't, they weren't likely to shoot a crawling man. They'd come up on him and cover him without shooting. So he'd be captured, but at least he would have made a try. The danger in the fourth choice, as he saw it, lay in the nature of his wound. How bad was it? Would he bleed to death somewhere in the pine woods? He didn't think so. First chance he got, he'd patch it up to stop the bleeding. After that, he'd just keep going until he got to General Butler's lines on the Peninsula. It wasn't so far, from the maps he remembered, and he was healthy and strong, even with the wound. The way he looked at it, anything was better than Belle Isle.

So, he thought. Just so. All right. Let's haul your butt out of here, Trooper.

He lifted his head very slowly and tried to make out any near figures on the road. The sleet was now changed to snow, further lessening the visibility.

Six of one, half dozen of the other. He couldn't see them, but they couldn't see him, either.

Using his elbows and forearms as pistons, he pushed himself up the bank a few inches at a time. The nearest cover was a tangled clump of brush a few yards away at the top of the ditch. He sure to God hoped that there weren't any berry bushes in there.

There weren't. It was scrub oak or something like it. He couldn't tell in the darkness. The leaves beneath him seemed to be rustling unbearably loud, but he knew that was his imagination. The floor of the thicket was wet enough to deaden the noise of his passage. Besides, the men on the road were talking and rattling equipment.

Within the brush, he halted and listened. There was nobody near him. He waited a full minute, during which a few shots were fired in the distance, toward the river. There were shouts in that direction.

He began to crawl the other way, heading vaguely north as he remembered direction. He went slowly for a half hour, as best as he could figure it. All sound had died away. There wasn't any more shooting. His elbows and arms were stiff and sore, and his hands were ripped and scratched in a dozen places. Finally, he stopped crawling and managed to get himself painfully to his feet. He tried a few steps. He could walk–not well but capably enough to move along slowly.

He took off his greatcoat, then his blouse, then his shirt. The cold wind flayed him; the snow picked at him icily. He was about to rip his shirt into winding lengths when he heard the sound of a man running through the woods. Johnny stepped into the shelter of a big pine tree, standing close to the bole. He could see nothing, but he knew the man passed him about ten yards away. The fellow was going hard, his breathing harsh and uneven, as if he'd run all the way from the road.

Johnny knew it must be a Federal, but he didn't call out. One thing was sure–the man was frightened, by the sound of him as he went by. He might have a gun, and might let a shot fly. The bullet could find a mark, or the report might draw rebs. The other thing was, if the man wanted to run, let him run. Noise would only draw pursuit, and Johnny couldn't run with him, anyway. Let him go.

The sound of the fugitive died away. Johnny ripped the shirt and tied the lengths together, shivering uncontrollably in the cold. He wiped away as much blood as he could, then bound his waist so tightly that pain from the wound seemed to turn his mid-section to fire. He put on the blouse, then the greatcoat. He began to walk.

He had a vague idea of direction and destination. He knew that he should go straight north for a few hours–maybe the rest of the night, to get himself out of reach of the rebels who had staged the ambush and of those who would be rushing in as reinforcements and searchers during the night. There would be hundreds of them combing the countryside along the Mattaponi and its tributaries, picking up the scattered survivors of the ambush. When he got far enough north, then he could strike east and south, and just keep going. Sooner or later he'd come to Butler's picket lines, or perhaps run into a Federal scouting party somewhere in the barren lowlands. He had no hope of meeting up with any of Kilpatrick's raiders. They would be mounted, and far ahead of him. At any rate, north and then east by south were the directions to safety.

He could walk without too much discomfort, although he didn't try for speed. Every few minutes he reached inside his clothing to test the bandages for bleeding. There didn't seem to be much, although the wound was now hurting badly, as if he had a bayonet through his side that was twisting and turning with every step.

Johnny tried to remember the details of stories he'd heard veterans tell about the Peninsular campaign under McClellan. There would be mud and swampy lowlands and great stretches of piney woods and brush country. He would have to figure that he was going to run into that kind of country, although he would be north of McClellan's route of almost two years ago, when the general had foundered on the road to Richmond. At least he would have woods to hide in by daylight, and woods roads heading southeast that he could travel at night. Three nights afoot ought to put him within reach of Butler's lines.

During the rest of that night, he kept going in the storm. He was cold and wet and miserable. He saw nothing but trees and brush, heard nothing above the wailing of the storm. He was confident that he was heading north, with perhaps a slight bearing to the east. Without stars or moon to guide him, he was nonetheless confident enough of his skill as a hunter to keep him going in the right direction. He had roamed the hills of Westchester and Putnam Counties back home throughout his youth, and he had always been interested in natural things. He knew how to figure his course. The storm had come out of the northwest; whenever he was in a clearing or on the crest of a low ridge, he made sure that the sleet and snow was biting into the left side of his face. He stood still to watch the snow catch along the left side of his greatcoat. He was all right, if the wind hadn't changed. He studied the sluggish courses of brooks and rivulets that he came upon occasionally; they all flowed generally in the direction whence he came. That was proper; so close to the Mattaponi, they must feed it.

When dawn threw dim gray light into the woods, he looked for shelter. He found a rock outcropping hidden in a clump of gnarled pines. He drank a few mouthfuls of rain water that had collected in a pothole among the rocks, and he ate two of the four hardtack biscuits that he'd had in his shirt pocket. Then he curled under an overhang of rock where the pine needles had drifted with the wind. He went to sleep, shivering.

Billy Littlepage, thirteen years old, was introduced to war and its horrors during that stormy night near Mantapike Hill. The trouble was, he didn't see much of war beyond a lot of noise and a lot of gun flashes, nor did he experience any horrors during that fighting. The entire action was most disappointing to Billy.

He was a soldier, too, and they should have let him participate. He was a regular member of the Home Guard of King and Queen County, enlisted by his schoolmaster, Mr. Ed Halbach, who was the captain. All the members of Mr. Halbach's company were schoolmates, ranging in age from Billy's thirteen to men of seventeen, who, in Billy's opinion, ought to be off in the Army of Northern Virginia. That was where Mr. Halbach would be, but he was a sickly fellow and the Army wouldn't take him. That was why Mr. Halbach had organized the company; he said he'd fight for his country, by God, even if it was at the head of a bunch of beardless boys.

The chance to fight had come early that night, when Lieutenant Pollard, a real soldier with a ragged uniform and a rusty saber, had led his gaunt men through the hamlet of Stevensville, on the way to set an ambush for the Yankee raiders whose coming had the whole country up in arms.

Mr. Halbach, properly called Captain Halbach when he was in the service of his country, had presented himself to Lieutenant Pollard, girded with a saber equally as rusty as the lieutenant's, and had offered the services of his company in laying the damned Yankees by the heels.

"Sure enough," Pollard said casually. "Where's your company?"

"Round 'em up in five minutes, sir."

"How many you got?"

"Fourteen, maybe fifteen," Halbach said.

"Jesus," Pollard said. "I thought we had some slim companies in the Army, but goddammit, yours takes the prize. Where are they?"

"Well, sir," Halbach said lamely, "I guess most of 'em have gone to bed, if they've finished the chores."

"Christ, man, I can't wait," Pollard told him. "Get as many as you can and come after us. We'll lay for 'em down where the creek cuts into the Mattaponi."

Halbach scurried around for his soldiers, but of the few he could reach in the next several minutes, none could get permission from his parents to march off to war. Playing soldier on the green was all right for schoolboys, but getting shot at–nothing doing!

The crowning blow to Halbach was when the school trustee, whose son was a sergeant, glared at the teacher in amazement: "Halbach, you're a stupid son of a bitch, and I'm going to remember this when it comes time to pick a teacher next year. Goddammit, man, you can't take children to fight Yankees!"

Halbach mostly objected to the language the man used. Everybody in the village knew that Edward Halbach was training to be a minister of God.

Billy Littlepage's parents weren't home. They'd gone to King and Queen Courthouse earlier in the day to buy a new plow. Billy, of course, enthusiastically volunteered for hazardous duty.

So the Stevensville contingent of the army of retribution ran down the road after Company H of the 9th Virginia Cavalry, and, puffing and blowing from the hard run, they took their places in the ambush. Captain Halbach looked sick from the exertion of running, but Billy was a tiger. He had his father's ancient muzzle-loader and he was ready. Or at least he thought he was ready until he started to load the rifle. Then he discovered that he had powder but no balls.

What the devil! He loaded the weapon with a big charge of powder and looked around in the darkness for a vantage point. If he couldn't shoot any Yankees, he could scare some of them to death!

The veteran troopers of the 9th Virginia, however, weren't going to fight Yankees in company with a little boy. Billy hadn't any more than settled in a prone position behind a big pine when a sergeant sent him back to join the horse guard. All his shrill arguments came to naught, when Lieutenant Pollard growled, "Shut up that goddam noise!"

Captain Halbach wasn't any help, either. He wouldn't even talk back to the sergeant–and him a captain! Halbach told Billy to go to the rear as he was told.

Therefore Billy Littlepage didn't participate in the great battle, but only heard a lot of noise and saw a lot of gunfire, and held desperately to the picket ropes of plunging, rearing horses.

After the fighting was all over, nobody seemed to care much what Billy did. He wandered out on the road, and there he saw his first horrors of war. There were dead men all over the place. There were a few who were wounded, too, and their screams and moans and groans made him feel sick. He didn't go near any of the wounded; he wandered among the dead.

Billy knew enough about Yankees to understand that every man among them was either a millionaire or darned close to it. He saw his present comrades busily stripping boots and coats and weapons and wallets and stuff like that from the bodies of the millionaires, and he wished that he had one to work upon. A fellow could get rich, sure enough.

He walked around in the darkness near the spot where the head of the Yankee column had stopped, and there he found his own millionaire, lying face down in the mud at the edge of the road, with a coating of snow already beginning to cover the body. Billy rolled the body over. By gosh, an officer! Little birds embroidered on his shoulders–must be a captain at least.

Billy didn't know it, but he had found the only body that might in life have eventually claimed the status of millionaire. Billy had under his eager hands the body of Ulric Dahlgren, whose father, Admiral John Dahlgren, had invented the noted artillery piece bearing his name.

The first quick search gave Billy a splendid gold watch, a billfold jammed with greenbacks, a silver pocketknife, and a fine leather holster and belt, although he had to probe in the mud for a minute or two before he found the revolver that fitted the holster. Billy had a shock when he went for the man's boots. The damn Yankee had a wooden leg. The bloody wounds hadn't bothered Billy, but that horrible wooden contraption did. He was about to make off with his loot because he felt as if he was going to vomit, but he controlled himself long enough to make another search of the man's fine woolen tunic. He found nothing else of value excepting a cigar case. He missed a gold ring on the left hand of the dead man. Finally, Billy took a bundle of papers and a notebook from the inside breast pocket of the tunic. He stuffed them into his shirt.

When Captain Halbach braced his only soldier about being a ghoul for searching dead bodies, Billy said nothing about watch and greenbacks. He turned over the cigar case, knowing that the schoolmaster liked a good cigar, and then he pulled the papers and notebook from his shirt. "Must be important," Billy said, "because he was a big officer, with gold birds sewed to his shoulders."

"Good work, soldier," said Captain Halbach.

"Thank you, sir," said Billy Littlepage.

Back in the road where Dahlgren's body lay, a more careful searcher found the gold ring on the finger. He couldn't get the ring off, so he took out a razorlike pocketknife and hacked off the finger.

All night long Stephens, Bartley, and Merritt walked through the pine barrens, fording creeks and runs, skirting several bogs and a long pond somewhere north of King and Queen Courthouse, always taking their direction from Hank's compass. They couldn't get lost, Hank knew, if they followed the Mattaponi, which flowed southeasterly. Somewhere within the next twenty miles, they had to run into Butler's pickets.

At dawn, the three men selected a pine grove that stretched for hundreds of yards in every direction. They moved to its approximate center and threw themselves down to sleep out the day. Toward dusk, they awakened chilled and sore and ravenously hungry, but ready to travel at least ten more miles before the next dawn. Hank figured that ten miles would put them into disputed territory, where any pursuing rebels would think twice before following, since Butler's vedettes ranged widely on the Peninsula and the contiguous arms of land that reached to the sea.

They had traveled a mile or so beyond the thick pines when they came upon a habitation. It wasn't much of a place—a small weather-beaten house with a rail fence, a few outbuildings that sagged for want of repairs, a few chickens scratching at gravel, a pair of huge pigs in a pen behind the house. As the three men approached, a dog started to bark fiercely. They could see him tied to a chain near the woodshed.

Hank wanted to go around. Merritt wanted to ignore the dog and see if they couldn't snatch a couple of chickens from the yard and maybe some corn from the outbuildings. Bartley insisted that it was a Negro shack, and he wanted to walk right up and ask for food.

Hank's view, the sensible one that their presence would be reported within a few hours, was finally agreed to by the others, and they were about to walk into the falling night, when two people came out of the shabby house. They were a man and a woman, and both of them were elderly, and seemingly incapable of traveling any great distance in a hurry. They stood in the yard, apparently wondering why their dog was barking.

Hank still wanted to move on, hungry or not, but the others now insisted that even if the old folks were rebs, they wouldn't rush off at night to give warning, and it was entirely possible that they wouldn't even bother with an alarm tomorrow. Hank finally agreed to approach the house.

The old people, man and wife, were named MacFarland, and they didn't seem at all upset by the Yankee uniforms. They offered food in plenty, and sleeping room in the barn. They were very cordial to the strangers, asking many questions about the war. They didn't seem to know anything much about it, although the old woman asked curiously why "you Yankees have come down here to take our niggers?"

Hank was uneasy. They were too friendly, and the woman didn't seem in any great hurry to get the food together for the hungry Yankees, even though there were pots steaming on cranes in the big fireplace.

He had reason to worry. While Mr. MacFarland was greeting the three strangers, Mrs. MacFarland, more spry than she looked, had scooted into the other room of the house to tell her servant, a young Negro girl, to run to the big house and get Captain Bagby. "Tell him we got three of them Yankee raiders," Mrs. MacFarland had said. Then she had sauntered back to the main room and had been as nice as pie to the visitors.

Ten minutes later, the fugitives were seated at the table, about to pile into a big meal of salt pork, potatoes, and cabbage, when the door burst open and what looked like half the Home Guard of King and Queen County loomed in the doorway.

Captain Bagby was a remarkable man. He owned a vast plantation, was landlord to the MacFarlands, was a conscientious Home Guard officer, and was, moreover, pastor of a Baptist church in the vicinity. He and his men had been with Lieutenant Pollard at the ambush, and he'd spent the succeeding hours in beating the bushes around the countryside for the Yankee villains who had escaped.

He took them to his big house where a better dinner awaited. The three Yankees sat at a splendid table, loaded with provisions, but they were somewhat uncomfortable because Captain or Reverend or Landlord Bagby kept his cocked revolver at hand.

He said a lengthy grace, sprinkling it with Biblical quotations about peace and love and thanksgiving, all the while he had his revolver leveled across the table at his guests. They didn't appreciate his benediction; they had their eyes fixed on the finger that was curled around the trigger.

He talked a lot during dinner, monopolizing the conversation. His manner was most pleasant, although he castigated Dahlgren, damned all Yankees to hell-fire for eternity, called Mr. Lincoln an ape and a clown, accused his prisoners of being barbarians, and called upon the Lord to witness that the Confederacy was upon the point of crushing Yankeedom forever.

"Most of you have been caught," he told them at one point in this one-sided conversation. "Greatest excitement ever to hit this countryside. All the folks were out today. Men, women, children, dogs—all looking for Yankees. You gentlemen are lucky. You get a good meal and a comfortable bed before you start for Richmond. I have some fine cigars, by the way. Would you each care for one with your port? Then let us retire to the library, if you will precede me, gentlemen." He waved them toward the door with his cocked revolver. "And by the way, I'll have to inconvenience you for your weapons, your boots, your ponchos, your watches, and all else of military value. War is war, you know. My poor fellows are almost barefoot. I believe your boots will fit me, Major. I'll give 'em a try when we get to the library."

Merritt protested. "You can't take our boots and clothing."

The cocked revolver swung toward Merritt. "Why not?" Captain Bagby asked.

Merritt shrugged. "I guess you can, at that."

Hank had one question. "You mentioned our starting for Richmond. Will you furnish the horses?"

"Horses, Major? Horses? You ought to know that the Confederacy hasn't enough for our cavalry. No horses, Major. You'll walk. It's only forty miles, more or less."

15

Johnny Watkins woke in the late afternoon. The storm was ended, and the sky was gray and cold, layered with thick clouds. His body was stiff and chilled, and his wound hurt badly. He had trouble getting to his feet, and when he managed it, he felt light-headed. He remembered how years ago he had got up from bed after a severe case of measles. He'd felt this way, dizzy and awkward. He'd fainted, that time, and his mother had kept him in bed another three days. He waited now to see if he would fall. He stayed on his feet, but the light-headedness remained.

Johnny had thought he was damned close to freezing until he touched his face with his hands. It was burning. Fever, he thought. You expected it with a wound.

He ate the two remaining pieces of hardtack, and then he drank a lot of water from the pothole. That would keep him going until morning. He ought to be somewhere near food by morning. Maybe he could steal something. He'd learned how to forage in the cavalry.

He struck out again as the light began to fall, heading into the pine-covered lowlands. He thought he was making good time; actually he was traveling very slowly, with short lurching steps. Whenever he fell or stumbled across an obstruction, he blamed it on the darkness.

Tomorrow night, he thought, I'll go on the roads. The night after that I'll run into Butler's pickets. Then I'll be all right. Food, and a bunk to lie in, and a doctor to plug up this hole in me.

He managed a grin, although the effect was that of an animal snarling. Well, he thought, it's not an arm or a leg, anyway. They can't cut it off if it festers.

Veterans were always talking about the best parts of the body in which one might be wounded. He knew he had one of the favorites. "Right where the meat rolls around your belly," the old-timers said. "That's a damn good spot, long as it ain't too far in. Or get a ball in the shoulder, long as it don't smash up the bones, or get one in the fat part of your ass. Those are the best. Anything else them goddam butchers will cut off and throw away."

Somehow, Johnny Watkins kept going most of the night. Stumbling and falling, in great pain at times, he kept his feet plodding forward as he talked to himself or whistled without sound through chapped lips. He thought he was keeping track of the distance. Every few hundred yards he would think of the ground he had just covered, and would say to himself softly: "That's another mile since the last place I counted. Just about a mile." He was proud of himself when he stopped for a rest during the night. He didn't know it, but he was having hallucinations now. He thought there were two of him. The first one, the one he had actually withdrawn from, was the fellow who was lying on the cold earth, trying to rest his weary body. The second one, the one who was standing above him, looking down at the prone body, was really Fred McAfee, who hadn't been killed in the ambush at all, but had somehow become invisible to rebs or anybody else. He even talked like Fred McAfee.

"You come twelve miles since dusk," he whispered, shaking his head in admiration. "Keep it up like that, Johnny boy, just till morning, and dang if we won't be having breakfast with old General Ben Butler." (He had really managed two miles since the night fell.)

Several times he had thought he'd seen lights in the distance, and often he'd heard the barking of dogs far away. His McAfee-self warned him now:

"Jes' keep away from them dawgs," he muttered. "And don't go near nobody or no noise, lessen you hear a Yankee voice holler out at you: 'Who goes there?' When you hear that, you just holler back, calm as you please: 'This here is Private John Watkins, 2nd New York Cavalry.' Then they'll give you coffee and good hot soup with meat in it and a bed and a doctor. And then you'll be all right. And they'll say to you: 'Why, it's just fine to see you, John Watkins. We all thought you was gone up. Wasn't you with Dahlgren and Stephens and Fred McAfee and them?' And you'll say: 'I sure to God was. I come back. Dahlgren is gone up, and Stephens is gone up, and old friend Fred McAfee is gone up–even though he come part of the way with me; you tell 'em that, Johnny–but Watkins ain't. Watkins is all right.' And then you'll have some more of that soup. You're all right now, Johnny. It's about time for me to go now and see what's off yonder. Good-bye, Johnny."

The figure on the ground stirred and croaked: "Good-bye, Fred, old friend, old messmate, old trooper." Then he got to his feet again and stumbled along.

He came to a rail fence when the night had almost ended. He blundered into it, catching at it to keep himself on his feet. He stood there swaying, thinking about the fence.

"Just have to go over it," he mumbled. "No trouble. Climb up this side and get down on the other side. That's all."

He grabbed the top rail firmly and put one foot, then the other, on the bottom rail. He swung his right leg over the top rail. He felt himself falling, but there wasn't anything he could do about it. He went down hard, scraping his face across the rough rails. His wound flashed pain through his body. Then his head smashed into a half-buried boulder, and he was knocked senseless.

The day was bright when he came back to consciousness. He couldn't see much more than the light, for his eyes were crusted with fever matter. He heard a voice, though, talking to him, urging him to wake up.

"All right," he whispered through cracked lips. "Watkins, Private Watkins, 2nd New York Cavalry."

The voice asked him if he could get up. It was a young voice, a boy's voice. What was a boy doing with Butler? Maybe a drummer boy. There was something about the voice that worried him, though.

"Who are you?" he breathed harshly, trying to get his eyes open, tuning his ears to hear every syllable of the reply.

"It don't matter who I am," said the voice, and now Watkins was sure.

It was a goddam secesh voice, that's what it was. This was a rebel. One of Stuart's young troopers, or maybe a Home Guard boy.

Johnny Watkins wanted to cry. All this way for the two nights, and here he was almost having breakfast with General Ben Butler, and the sons-of-bitching secesh had caught him.

"Christ Jesus!" Watkins whispered. "Belle Isle."

Libby Prison was a large brick building with a street frontage of one hundred and forty-five feet on Cary Street at Twentieth in the city of Richmond, and a depth of one hundred and five feet. It was isolated from other buildings, and was three stories high as it fronted Cary Street and four stories high at the rear above the James River.

The prison offices and supply rooms were on the street floor, and on the upper floors were nine rooms, each one hundred and two feet long and forty-five feet wide. These rooms housed more than a thousand Union officers.

The three prisoners who were brought in by Captain Bagby were assigned space in the long corner room on the second floor, where barred windows at front and rear and seven windows at the side gave views of the city of Richmond. Bartley found friends from the Signal Corps; Merritt was hailed by fellow officers of the 5th New York Cavalry; Hank Stephens saw no one whom he knew.

He was pleased to be left alone. He was dog-tired after walking almost thirty miles in two days; the prisoners had been allowed to ride the last ten miles in a wagon that was taking straw into the city. He'd had some sleep on the baled straw, but he needed much more. He was worn out.

He slept so long that he missed being assigned to a mess roll, and he faced the prospect of no food for his first twenty-four hours in the prison. An elderly captain of Indiana infantry who shared floor space with him in a corner of the huge room remedied that fault by giving Hank his rations. The captain was sick, and had to vomit every few hours, so he willingly gave up his food. Hank offered to pay him for it–he managed to hide twenty dollars in greenbacks in the split leather of his belt, and the money had escaped the careful search of a turnkey named Ross in the reception room downstairs. Ross had skillfully examined every man who denied having money or valuables; not many hiding places had escaped him. The Indiana captain had refused the money, however.

"No good to me, son," he whispered. "I'm dying. They'll be coming to take me to the hospital pretty soon. I hope to die here first, with my comrades."

Hank sensed that there was no comfort to be given, so he thanked the old man for the food, ate it, and then walked around to survey his surroundings. There had been glass in the windows, but there were now only a few panes left. Even with the cold winter air pouring through the openings, the prison stank of dirty men and sick men and rotten food.

Managing not to step on any sleeping men, and avoiding the card games and the letter writers, Hank viewed the city from each of the windows. The view at the front was not inviting–empty lots and dingy commercial buildings, and beyond them many roofs and chimneys. The rebel guard tents were in a vacant lot across Twentieth Street. From the side windows, the scene wasn't much more exciting–more rebel tents and another big warehouse-type building like the prison, which had formerly belonged to Libby & Son, ship chandlers and grocers.

From the rear windows, however, Hank could see the dock below, the canal and the high and muddy James River. Over the river there were open fields and some houses, and far downstream he could see rolling hills. There were factories on the far shore, and upstream was the village of Manchester. Our first target, Hank thought.

He saw the second targets for Dahlgren's raiders, the two bridges that crossed the James from the south shore to Richmond. They were long and white above the brown water. In the distance upstream, he could see a big island, and he knew that was the third target. Belle Isle.

He turned away from the window. He wouldn't stand there looking at it, knowing that an unforeseen storm and floodwaters on the James had kept five hundred cavalrymen from freeing the poor devils who rotted there.

He turned his attention to the prison routine. He was invited to join a mess with officers from Massachusetts and Maine. He discovered a classmate named Stanton in the next room, a fellow from Rhode Island whom he'd never liked at the Academy, and whom he didn't like now. Stanton had been fat and greasy and slovenly as a cadet; now he was skinny and greasy and slovenly.

Stanton laughed bitterly when he saw Stephens. "Well, Hank Stephens, by God! These sons of bitches nabbed you, too. You musta been with Jud on this raid of his."

"That's right, Alex," Hank said.

"I'll be goddamned. Old Cadet Sergeant Stephens, the pride of the Corps, in a reb prison with File Closer Stanton. Jesus, how the mighty have fallen."

Hank had little to say to Stanton after refusing to buy necessities at astounding prices. Stanton seemed to be a kind of sutler; he had for sale such items as paper, ink, books, sugar, salt, Richmond newspapers, and even a small cake of soap, which he offered for five Yankee greenbacks or fifty dollars Confederate.

Later Stephens discovered that he could do well with his greenbacks if he invested them wisely. Pen and ink and paper would be his prime investment. Letters could go out and be launched on the cartel route through General Butler on the Peninsula, but nobody knew whether they were delivered in the North. He would write to Kate Farnham as soon as he could.

Kate Farnham. He'd scarcely thought of her at all since the expedition had ridden out. There hadn't been any time for thinking about the past.

Now I'll have all the time I want, he told himself, taking his place against the wall of the Twentieth Street side of the prison. All the time in the world, until it's ended.

Many of the prisoners were going to sleep although the sun was still hanging in the western sky toward Belle Isle. Hank settled himself on the thin blanket he'd been issued. He wondered for a moment as he lay there if the prison was infested with vermin. Of course it was.

He looked across at the Indiana captain, who was sleeping heavily.

How are the bedbugs, Captain? Hank asked silently. How are the lice and fleas?

Kate. Are you thinking of me tonight? Have you heard how we failed? Do you yet have any idea of where I am?

He was about to doze off when he suddenly came awake again with another thought: By God, I bet I'm a father, or will be any minute. Boy or girl?

He smiled at the thought. His mother would be delighted. So would his sisters. He hoped that Caroline would be happy and content with the baby. If he ever got out of this place, if the war ever ended, he would go home to Peekskill. The baby could be the reason for the survival of the marriage, if it did survive. He wasn't sure that a child was sufficient reason for two people to stay married when they lacked love and compassion. Yet he was fairly certain that the birth of a child was reason enough to try to keep the family together. Without experience, he had no way of knowing what was best. At any rate, he had a subject for speculation during day after endless day in this place. Boy or girl? He wondered how long it would be before letters could reach him from Peekskill. He made a mental note to ask about the speed of the mail service. He wondered when the baby would be born. Caroline's few letters had been vague about it. He could count it off on his fingers, but he didn't know whether it was exactly nine months. It seemed to him that his father had often spoken of seven-month babies, and also of births that were evidently quite overdue. The Academy and the Army were not the best schools for learning the facts of obstetrics. He just didn't know.

At any rate, there would be a child. Boy or girl?

The room suddenly came alive as a bright light appeared in the doorway. Every prisoner began to hoot and catcall. When the lamp advanced into the room, the jeers became louder. Hank could see a tall Confederate officer behind the beam of the bull's-eye lamp. The man waited patiently motionless, until the hooting died away.

"Major Henry Stephens," he called.

Hank pushed himself up on his elbows. "Here," he answered.

The lamp and the officer crossed the room. The glare hurt Hank's eyes and he turned them away. The officer then covered the lamp, and Hank could see that he was tall and slim, and was dressed in a fine gray uniform.

"I'm Major Thomas Turner, commandant of the prison," he said. "I wasn't here when you were brought in."

Hank made no reply, but he got to his feet.

"There's no problem right now," Turner said affably. "I just wanted to locate you. You'll be an object of interest up at the Capitol, I'm sure. You were Dahlgren's second-in-command, weren't you?"

"I was."

Turner laughed. "You tried to get all these people out of here, and landed in here with them. Too bad, Major. Now that I know where you are, I'll send for you when we need you. Do you have any idea of what they're talking about at the Capitol, Major?"

"No, I don't."

"They say they're going to hang you Dahlgren people, Major. Good night. Sleep well."

Lieutenant James Pollard didn't have time to read the papers that the schoolmaster-captain gave him. Pollard was too busy chasing Yankees. However, Halbach wouldn't be denied. He followed Pollard for several hours, insisting that the papers were important.

Finally, to get rid of the schoolteacher, Pollard glanced through the documents. He saw what they were right away–careful plans for the expedition that had ended a few hours before on a muddy road in a storm. They were interesting, all right. He read parts of them. Then, leaping at him from the page, the fateful words made him whistle ". . . destroy and burn the hateful city, and do not allow the Rebel leader Davis and his traitorous crew to escape . . ."

Then Pollard had an argument with Halbach, who claimed that the documents were his responsibility, and that he would see that they got to the right hands in Richmond.

"You go to hell, friend," Pollard said. "I'll take 'em in myself."

Halbach bowed to the inevitable. "I'll go with you."

"You go back to Stevensville and teach school. Leave the soldiering to soldiers."

Later that day, Pollard stood before his commanding officer, Colonel Richard L. T. Beale, 9th Virginia Cavalry, who was hunting Yankee raiders near Old Church on the southern side of the Pamunkey. Beale peered through spectacles at the damning words.

"By God, Jim, you take these to Hampton. Get on your horse and get going."

"Where is he?" Pollard asked sensibly.

"Damned if I know. If you don't get word of him, go right into the city and give 'em to Fitz Lee."

Pollard didn't find Hampton, who was also chasing Yankee raiders, but he found Fitzhugh Lee, who was the next man to read the incriminating words that would prove to all the world that the Yankees weren't gentlemen and cavaliers, that chivalry was dead in the North. Fitz Lee also examined Dahlgren's wooden leg, which Pollard had brought with him as a curiosity.

Fitz Lee left the leg with Pollard, but went to the President's office to show him the Dahlgren papers. The President was in conference with his Secretary of State, Judah P. Benjamin.

Mr. Davis read the papers quickly aloud, pausing to smile over the words: "Jeff Davis and Cabinet must be killed."

He looked up with a quick grin: "That means you, Mr. Benjamin."

After reading them, the President handed them back to Fitz Lee. "Have them filed, General, if you please."

Fitz Lee took them to Adjutant General Samuel Cooper with the filing directive, and said to Cooper, "They need no comment." General Cooper disagreed. He thought they did need comment. He showed them to prominent Confederates. The President's military adviser, General Braxton Bragg, was one of those who studied the papers. He wrote to Secretary of War Seddon: ". . . the papers are of such an extraordinary and diabolical character that some more formal method should be adapted of giving them to the public than simply lending them to the press. My own conviction is for an execution of the prisoners . . ."

General Josiah Gorgas was another. He wrote in his diary: "What beasts and murderers. Hereafter those that are taken will not be heard of."

Secretary Seddon was a third. He wrote to Robert E. Lee: "My own inclinations are toward the execution of at least a portion of those captured at the time Colonel Dahlgren was killed . . ."

The Richmond newspapers went wild. The *Whig* editorialized: "Are these men warriors? Are they soldiers . . . ? Or are they assassins, barbarians, thugs who have forfeited (and expect to lose) their lives? Are they not barbarians redolent with more hellish purposes than were the Goth, the Hun or the Saracen?"

Braxton Bragg was for hanging them out of hand and publishing the facts later. His chief aide, a handsome and quiet-spoken cavalry colonel from South Carolina, didn't give a damn much one way or another. His only comment was, "I wish we had Kil in Libby. That would be one hanging I would enjoy. Let's see whom we do have, General. Do you have a list?"

General Bragg handed over several sheets of paper. "All the officers are on that first page."

The colonel glanced at the first page. His eyebrows went up, and he whistled softly. "And lo!" he said, "Ben Adhem's name led all the rest."

"Who?" asked General Bragg. "Ben who? What the hell are you talking about, Farnham?"

"An old friend of mine, General," Farnham smiled. "An officer I knew at the Academy. A close friend of Kil's. I think I'll pay a visit to Libby, sir. In the morning, right after breakfast. Kil got off scot free, and

Dahlgren is dead, but you may have a prime candidate for the gallows sitting right in Libby Prison."

"What's his name? Ben what?"

Farnham shook his head. "Henry Stephens, General. As close to Kil as you can get. Or," the soft voice added, "perhaps as close as anyone would ever care to be."

Farnham picked up a pair of black brier canes from the floor beside his chair. They were identical, with shining gold handles and brass ferrules. He got to his feet and started for the door, dragging one leg and then the other, supporting himself heavily on the canes. "I'll see you in the morning, General."

News traveled swiftly through the North. By Thursday evening, March 3, General Butler had telegraphed about Kilpatrick's arrival within his lines on the Peninsula. Brigadier General James H. Wilson happened to be with Secretary of War Stanton when the wire came. It mentioned that Colonel Dahlgren and Major Stephens were lost and presumed prisoners. A later despatch from a Union spy came in by courier; it said that a one-legged colonel and his principal officers had been killed in King and Queen County.

The New York *Times* had had a correspondent with Dahlgren. Both the *Times* and the *Tribune* published accounts of the raid, speculating on what had happened to Dahlgren.

In the city of Peekskill, New York, Dr. Daniel Stephens read the sketchy accounts of the raids, and, for the first time, knew that his son had probably no knowledge that his wife was dead and buried. Three telegrams had gone from Peekskill to the Third Division of Cavalry of the Army of the Potomac. Now Dr. Stephens knew that the wires were probably sitting at headquarters awaiting his son's return from the Richmond expedition.

He shunted aside the dread thought that came into his mind as he read the newspaper accounts. What had happened to Dahlgren? What had happened to Hank Stephens?

There was one thing he could do. He could find out. Hank had good friends. Jim Wilson, Chief of the Cavalry Bureau, for one.

Hank was all right. Dan Stephens was sure of it. Sure of it! Damn the newspapers! Why didn't they get the whole story and get it right?

"Dan, where are you going?" his wife demanded, catching him at the hall closet reaching for his hat and coat. "It's bitter outside."

"Downtown to get some cigars, my dear."

"You've got cigars. Plenty of them. Where are you going?"

"Haven't got the right kind," Dr. Stephens said gently. "I'm just going to walk down by the river and back, my love. Take a walk and get some cigars."

He did both, because he wasn't a liar. He also went to the telegraph station, which was down by the river at the train depot. He wrote the telegram carefully, addressing it to Brigadier General James H. Wilson.

PLEASE ADVISE WHEREABOUTS OF MY SON STOP MAJOR HENRY STEPHENS SECOND NEW YORK CAVALRY STOP IF PRACTICABLE SUGGEST LEAVE STOP HIS WIFE AND CHILD DIED RECENTLY

DANIEL STEPHENS

"You want M.D. on the end of your name, Doc?" the telegrapher asked. "Won't cost you no more."

"Just as it is, Sam."

"Sure enough, Doc. First time I ever seen that word there—practicable. You sure she's spelled right?"

"Just as it is, Sam."

"All right, Doc. You're having trouble finding Hank, ain't you? Sad about his wife. I'm sorry for your trouble, Doc."

"Thank you, Sam. When may I expect a reply, assuming that General Wilson answers immediately?"

"Oh, God, Doc, it's hard to say, what with this Army traffic on the wire these days. Might take yours four or five hours to get there; might take his a couple to come back. Say six-seven hours, figuring his is an official answer. I'll send it up to the house, Doc."

"Don't do that, Sam. I'll come down, say seven hours from now. That will be at eight o'clock tonight. Hold the answer for me."

"Anything you say, Doc. By the way, I've had this goddam pain in my back for weeks, Doc. Right here. Like to cripple me if it keeps up. What do you think, Doc?"

Stephens looked around the bare telegraph shack that shivered and shook in the wind. "Don't sit in drafts, Sam."

At eight o'clock, when he was supposed to be visiting a patient, Daniel Stephens arrived again at the station. Sam looked up at him and nodded soberly. He handed over a yellow sheet.

REGRET TO INFORM YOU MAJOR STEPHENS MISSING IN ACTION AGAINST THE ENEMY STOP DETAILS NOT AVAILABLE AT THIS TIME STOP SUGGEST STRONG POSSIBILITY OF CONFEDERATE CAPTURE STOP WILL INFORM YOU AS WORD ARRIVES STOP BE OF GOOD HEART STOP HANK IS A TOUGH ONE

JAMES H WILSON
BRIGADIER GENERAL

"Thank you, Sam," Dr. Stephens said quietly. He went to the door.

"I'm awful sorry, Doc," Sam said. "Keep your chin up like it says there."

Stephens nodded and went outside into the snap of the bitter wind. I'll have to tell her, he thought. We will have to comfort each other. He walked up the hill from the station with his shoulders bowed. His step was slow. Tears flowed down his cheeks.

It was almost twenty-four hours before Wilson had further word in Washington. Richmond sent the news by flag of truce down the Peninsula to Butler's vedettes, and Butler then sent it on to the War Department. Dahlgren was dead and Stephens was in Libby Prison. The first action that General Wilson took was to write another telegram to Peekskill:

MAJOR HENRY STEPHENS REPORTED CAPTURED BY CONFEDERATE ARMY STOP I TOLD YOU HE WAS A TOUGH ONE

JAMES H WILSON
BRIGADIER GENERAL

Wilson's second action was to put on his greatcoat and campaign hat and step outside to the street, where an orderly had a horse ready before Wilson finished putting on his gauntlets. He grinned to himself. The Cavalry Bureau had some snap and dash to it these days. The only damn trouble, he told himself as he mounted, is that I wish to God I were in the field. If I'd had Kil's chance—

He rode the few blocks to Colonel Palmer's house on Seventeenth Street, where the old butler, Howard, welcomed him gravely. "Good day, General. Will you step into the library, sir, and I'll tell Mrs. Farnham you are calling."

Kate came running into the room a few seconds later. "What is it, Jim? Hank? It's Hank?"

He nodded soberly, then hastened to say, "Not bad, Kate. Captured on the raid."

"Oh, God, I thought he was dead. Oh, my God, Jim. Don't ever scare me like that again."

"I'm sorry," he said. "I knew he was missing yesterday, but I didn't have the courage to come and tell you. We just had word a half hour ago that they've got him in Richmond, probably in Libby Prison."

"Not many die in Libby, do they, Jim?"

He shrugged. "Some men die in all prisons. Hank will be all right. He's in good health."

"He wasn't wounded, was he?"

"Not that we know of. The rebs didn't mention it. Dahlgren is dead, and Kil has failed completely. There's one thing more, Kate."

She looked at him steadily, nodding. "I can tell from your tone that this is bad. What, Jim?"

"We got word of what the Richmond newspapers are saying. All of 'em are screaming for the execution of anybody who was with Dahlgren. They captured his plans for the raid and they're furious. Evidently he wrote that he was going to kill Jeff Davis and his Cabinet."

"Execution? Soldiers? That's nonsense, Jim. They weren't spies."

He shook his head. "The papers call 'em assassins, barbarians, thugs. It's apparently an official view. I don't know whether it goes as high as Davis and Lee. We'll do all we can, Kate. I expect the War Department is already busy working on it. We'll have the President in on it, too. You know that. I wouldn't worry too much, Kate. It's only a wild threat."

"They're going to hang him? They can't do it. They can't. He was doing his duty."

"As I say, they probably are just talking the way they do all the time."

"I'm going to Richmond, Jim. Get me a safe conduct."

"Kate! What are you talking about? How are you going to get to Richmond? You're out of your head."

"No, I'm not, Jim Wilson. You get the safe conduct. Go to the President if you have to. Arrange my passage on the first river steamer to go to the Peninsula. You have spies going back and forth all the time. You can send the wife of a Confederate colonel."

"It's a dangerous trip, Kate. Too dangerous. Forget it, please."

"Do what I say, Jim Wilson! I'm going. I just hope in God's name that I get there in time."

He argued for fifteen minutes more, but he couldn't talk her out of it. Unhappily, he agreed to arrange for her passage and safe conduct through the lines.

Kilpatrick wished that Major General Benjamin F. Butler would go to bed, or at least go someplace else. Goddammit, this preliminary report of the expedition had to go to old Sobersides Pleasonton, who would say to everybody who would listen: "I told you so, didn't I?"

Kilpatrick had been trying for an hour to write the thing, but Butler kept interrupting. Kil couldn't be rude; these were Butler's luxurious quarters in Fortress Monroe, down at the end of the Peninsula.

"How much have you got so far, Kil?" Ben Butler asked. He leaned back to listen, taking a sip of dark-brown whiskey and a puff on a long green cigar.

For the fourth time, Kil read the beginning of the report:

"I left my camp at Stevensburg with 3,585 men, 6 guns, 8 caissons, 3 wagons, and 6 ambulances. I have now 3,317 men, 3,595 horses. . . ."

That was as far as he was able to read, because Ben Butler started to laugh again. When Butler laughed, the room shook and the furniture rocked. Finally Butler choked and coughed, then wiped his eyes with a big red bandana.

"By God, Kil, you take the cake! You're the goddamndest liar in the whole goddam army. You claim to come back with more horses than you started with, and yet you got the tar kicked out of you, and you had men walking when you got here. By God, you have the gall to tell Pleasonton you now have more horses than you had men to start with. You're a prize, Kil."

"It's true, General. You see—"

Butler roared again. "Don't try to explain it. By God, just leave it as it is. I can just see that bastard Pleasonton taking a pencil and a piece of paper and begin subtracting and adding men and horses. You'll have the simple-minded son of a bitch in the asylum before you're done."

Irritated though he was with Butler's interference, Kilpatrick began to grin. Butler nodded, slapping his knee with a beefy hand, and the two of them laughed together.

"I'll admit," Kilpatrick said, "that we brought back some three-legged horses, and some one-eyed horses, and some with holes in 'em. . . ."

Butler rocked with glee. "But, by God, it amounts to more than you started with, no matter how you look at it! Tell me this, Kil—are you going to say in that report how many men Wade Hampton had that night when he scared the bejesus out of your three thousand? Are you going to tell Pleasonton that? Three hundred skinny rebs tied the tail to your goddam kite!"

Kilpatrick's eyes turned cold and his thin mouth tightened. This wasn't joking any more. This was his reputation that Butler was talking about.

"Oh, Good Lord, Kil, I won't spread the word," Butler said affably. "But it will get around. You can be sure of that. You'd better fish for another command, boy. Folks will start comparing. Your division runs from three hundred of Hampton's troopers, and Custer takes a brigade right through Jeb Stuart's whole goddam cavalry corps and doesn't lose a man."

Kilpatrick lashed back. "I noticed, General, that you didn't show up when we could have used you."

"Hell, I never intended to, son. That was your raid, and you were welcome to it. If you'd got into the city and done some good, I'd have been there with five thousand men before you could say Jack Robinson. I would've taken a little of the glory; I didn't have any mind to share your troubles. Goddammit, Kil, you don't understand politics. Nobody bothers me down here on the Peninsula, and that's the way I want it. Once a month or so, I take three or four newspaper reporters and some soldiers and I sashay up toward Richmond, shoot some guns and raise a little hell, then back I come. Lee's got all he can do with the big army up on the Rapidan. He knows I'm no serious trouble to him. I'm satisfied just to get my name in the papers every few weeks. That'll get me elected to Congress, and it will make me governor of Massachusetts after the war. That's all I want out of life, unless folks think enough of me to run me for the big job later on. Let me tell you something else, Kil. It never hurts a fellow to stay out of trouble. Look at that do-nothing bastard George McClellan. Sure, we all liked him, and knew he was a damned good man, but by God, he was even more cautious than I am. If he saw five rebs boiling coffee, he'd turn the Army of the Potomac and run. And what's he doing now? Getting ready to run against Lincoln this year, that's what. He never made any trouble for anybody, and it may get him the big job. That's politics, Kil."

Butler paused, then spoke seriously. "I get a lot of rumors down here. Every mail from Washington brings me rumors, all kinds of 'em. You know about Grant coming in as the boss, of course."

Kilpatrick nodded. He'd heard that as a rumor before he'd left Stevensburg. Now it was fact.

"All right. They tell me he's bringing Sheridan with him to command the cavalry. That's a rumor. Pleasonton is out. That's a rumor. Wilson takes a division. That's a rumor. I've got lots of 'em."

"What division for Wilson?"

"Yours, Kil."

"And what happens to me, in your rumor factory?"

"Sherman gets you in the Army of the Tennessee."

"All rumors?" Kilpatrick said calmly.

"All rumors, Kil. I got lots of spies up in Washington. Lots of 'em."

Kilpatrick nodded. "So, according to your rumors, it doesn't matter what I tell Pleasonton. I'm going to Sherman and Pleasonton's going out on his backside. All right, then–I returned with three thousand five hundred and ninety-five horses, ten more than I started with."

Ben Butler doubled over with laughter once more, before calming himself in order to have another drink.

An orderly poked his head into the office. "Beg pardon, General. A lady to see General Kilpatrick."

"Well, I'll be goddamned, Kil!" Butler said. "I knew you were a ladies' man, but hell, you've been here such a short time–how'd you do it?"

"The lady is from Washington, General. She's got a safe conduct to Richmond. Mrs. Farnham, General."

"Show her in," Kilpatrick said. "Your pardon, General. I know the lady."

"I bet by God you do!" Butler shouted. "Show her in, son," he said to the orderly.

Kilpatrick went swiftly to meet Kate when she entered the office. "He's all right, my dear. We had word. He's in Libby Prison. What in the world are you doing here?"

Kate took his hand briefly, then nodded to General Butler. "I'm going to Richmond. Jim Wilson told me they were going to execute the prisoners. Royce is in Richmond. He'll save Hank."

"They aren't going to hang anybody, ma'am," Butler said genially. "That's just the usual rebel balderdash. If they hang anybody, I'll hang a few myself and they know it."

"They'll be all right, Kate," Kilpatrick said quickly. "You don't have to go to Richmond. You won't get out again, you know. They aren't as generous with passes as we are."

"Hank is there. I'll stay there until he's free."

"Well, little lady," said General Butler, "you can't leave for Rebeldom tonight, so sit you down and we'll give you a big dinner of oysters and clams and whatever you want. I'll see to it personally." The general stared at her delightedly; he didn't know who the hell she was, but, by God, she was a wonder. Now if he could get rid of that popinjay Kilpatrick, and if she wanted to get to Richmond badly enough, and he could convince her that only by his good graces could she make it, and if she were properly grateful– Well, by Jesus, this could amount to something!

The general grinned delightedly. She had the look of smoldering fire that he had noticed and taken advantage of so often among the ladies of New Orleans when he'd been earning his Confederate sobriquet of "Beast" Butler.

"Introduce us, if you please, General," Butler said to Kilpatrick, "and then we'll have a splendid dinner together."

Unhappily for Ben Butler, the little lady was thoroughly familiar with his reputation. She stayed as far from him as she could; Kilpatrick wouldn't take any hints; neither of them drank. General Butler had a very dull evening.

16

A prison orderly came upstairs to get Hank Stephens at nine o'clock in the morning. All the prisoners hooted and jeered, as they always did when a Confederate entered the room. The man paid the noise no mind, but led Hank downstairs to the street-level offices.

"You have a visitor," Major Turner said, grinning coldly. "A very important visitor in my private office."

Royce Farnham was standing in the small room. He supported himself with the black canes. He nodded matter-of-factly when Hank came in, as if they had last seen each other at breakfast in the Cadet Mess at the Academy. "Good morning, Henry. Sit down, please."

Hank took the straight-backed chair that Farnham nodded toward. He didn't know what to say to Farnham by way of greeting, so he said only his name, with a nod, "Royce."

Farnham made his way in obvious pain to Turner's walnut desk. He seated himself in the swivel chair with difficulty, laying his canes across the top of the desk when he was settled. "I got this at Kelly's Ford last November 7," he said. "Were you there, Henry?"

"No."

Farnham nodded. "You're 2nd New York, is that right? No, you weren't there. Well, this was a minnie ball right through the groin. It's killing me, Henry. Literally killing me. Too bad. I wanted to last through the end of the war. I wanted to see what kind of peace you will give us. You're probably pretty damned sick of the war, too. You always were a peacemaker, as I remember."

"I'm sick of it," Hank said. "I'm sorry about the wound, Royce."

"The hell you are," Farnham said calmly. "When I die, you'll have my wife. I could call you a few names, Hank. I could whip out a revolver and shoot you. Who would blame me? Goddamn you, Hank, and her, too. Did you think I didn't know? Did either of you think you were fooling me? I used to lie awake at night in camp or on the march, wishing I could be in Washington to find you two together. I'd have shot you then, Hank. And Kate, too. But not now. I'm not a man any more. And I'm dying."

"I'm sorry you knew, Royce," Hank said quietly.

Farnham nodded. "I guess I am, too. My spies in Washington were too efficient. Well, it doesn't matter now. I believe you when you say you're sorry. You lived by the honor code, didn't you, Hank? You wouldn't tell a lie, would you? Not even to save my pride. How did you reconcile your sleeping with Kate to the honor code, Hank? How did you fit it in?"

"I didn't," Hank said.

Farnham nodded again. "All right. Enough of that. No—one thing more. She doesn't get an acre of land when I die. That's all that's left, land. I'm assuming of course that you'll let us keep our land. Anyway, she gets nothing."

"She wants nothing."

"All right. Now to the business at hand." Farnham opened a portfolio on the desk. He took out the documents taken from Ulric Dahlgren's body. "You have a choice, Hank. You can attest that these papers are authentic. Or you can walk out upon a scaffold some bright morning in the near future. If you identify them as Dahlgren's, and attest that the objectives stated in them were his objectives and that he and Kilpatrick and all your officers and men knew them to be your objectives, then we will give you a safe conduct to Butler's lines. If you deny them, you'll be the first to hang for violating the rules and principles of organized warfare."

"They are not Dahlgren's," Hank said.

"I thought you didn't lie, Hank. However, I suppose the code allows a lie to an enemy. Don't you want to look at them? How do you know they are not Dahlgren's unless you look and see what they are?"

"I know what they are. I wrote them."

Farnham showed no surprise. He shifted his body in the chair with a grimace of real agony.

"You wrote them, Hank. I see. Well, that makes you a prime candidate for hanging, but it's not what we want. You're only a major, Hank, and it wouldn't mean a damned thing to have you identified as the author of these historic documents. It would do us no good at all to nail you to the cross. We want Dahlgren and Kilpatrick. We understand that Lincoln authorized your expedition personally. If we have Dahlgren and Kilpatrick, we have Lincoln, too. You have an election this year. If we can last until then, we'd be delighted to see George Brinton McClellan elected President of the United States. We could negotiate with him. After all,

Hank, he's a member of our closed society of West Point graduates. Our President is also, you remember. You see why we can't use you, why we need Dahlgren and Kilpatrick and Lincoln."

"I wrote them, Royce. I wrote them after Kil and I saw Mr. Lincoln. I wrote them before Dahlgren succeeded me in command of the second force. Actually, I don't believe he even read them."

Farnham smiled grimly. "You know, Hank, I believe you're telling the truth. But it isn't satisfactory. It won't do. We will not accept it."

"I can't help that, Royce. Those papers express my philosophy on this war. If I had the power, I would use every resource in the North to crush you this year. I would use every man, every cannon, every greenback–I would smash the Army of Northern Virginia. As those papers say, I would burn this hateful city. I would kill Jeff Davis and his Cabinet. That's what I intended to do when I had the command. I am only sorry now that Kil relieved me. I would have been in Richmond earlier this week and those things in those papers would have been done under my orders."

"I can see that we'll have to hang you, Henry. You're a menace to civilization." Farnham paused, smiling slightly. "Let's try again, Hank. All you have to do is sign a statement that you knew these documents represented Dahlgren's plans and Kilpatrick's tactics. You just have to say you discussed them with both of those officers. Then back you go to my wife, and you can live happily ever after."

Hank shook his head. "Kil gave me a free hand. Dahlgren, so far as I know, took those papers from me and never read them."

Farnham suddenly slammed the desk with his open palm. "It won't do you a damned bit of good, Hank! We'll hang you, anyway. And you know that we can make photographic copies. Any good photographer can do it. We will send them through the world. We'll blame Dahlgren; we'll blame Kilpatrick; we'll blame Meade. And, by God, we'll hang the blame right around the neck of Abraham Lincoln. That's what you're going to hang for, anyway. Why not walk out of here a free man, just for signing a statement? Think of Kate. She's waiting for you."

"I wrote them, Royce. Nothing you say can change that. Who will believe you, when they aren't even in Dahlgren's handwriting?"

Farnham grinned once more. "Oh, yes, they are, Hank. Evidently he'd started to copy them from your originals, but never finished. Part of them are in his handwriting. That's enough for our purposes."

It was Hank Stephens' turn to grin when he reached for the papers and studied them. He remembered his first copies of the papers. He hadn't corrected his spelling of Dahlgren's name, and now he saw it immediately. The address to the command, which Hank had written, was signed: "U. DALHGREN." Nobody in the North would believe that a man would misspell his own name. The rebel photographic copies would be considered forgeries.

"You won't change your mind, Hank? You can go free if you do."

"Nothing doing, Royce. I wrote 'em, and Dahlgren never read 'em, as far as I know. Maybe he started to copy them, but they were never read to the troopers, nor even to the officers. They represent only what I believe should be done to your city and your government."

"My wife will be heartbroken when she reads of your execution."

"You won't hang me, Royce. As you said, your own President is a member of the society. He knows the honor code as well as we do."

"I promise you, Hank. You'll hang."

Stephens shook his head. "Can I go now, Royce?"

"You can go."

"I'm truly sorry about the wound, Royce."

"Again, I suppose I believe you. Good-bye, Hank."

"Good-bye, Royce."

Kate arrived at Richmond with a Confederate cartel to whom she had been passed through Butler's lines. They had a spring buggy for her to ride in, and the journey was fair enough, with the pleasant company of three young Confederate officers and a dozen cavalrymen. Rarely was the war mentioned, and the young officers evidently saw nothing unusual in escorting the wife of a Confederate colonel from Yankeeland to her proper place at her husband's side in the rebel capital.

In Richmond, one of the young men quickly discovered that Colonel Farnham had rooms at the Spotswood Hotel at Eighth and Main Streets, close to the War Office. Kate told the room clerk who she was, and he gave her a key to her husband's suite. "He usually comes in about six, Mrs. Farnham. In the meantime, if there's anything we can do for you—"

"Nothing, thank you."

She went upstairs to wait. The suite was composed of a sitting room, a bath, and two bedrooms. That settled one problem.

She didn't even consider what his attitude toward her might be. She hadn't seen him in almost three years. She hadn't heard a word from him or about him in more than two years excepting that he had been promoted to colonel of cavalry. She didn't really care how he reacted to her presence. She was concerned only with the dreadful prospect that confronted her in the Richmond newspapers that she found on the table in the sitting room. They were going to hang all the officers and most of the men who had been with Dahlgren. The papers screamed their verdict. Certain officials evidently were urging them on to hysteria.

She heard someone coming about six o'clock, but she didn't know it was Royce. In the quiet hotel room, the sounds from the corridor were audible, and she was puzzled by the shuffling of feet and the thumping of the canes. She jumped up in alarm when the noise stopped at the door and the sound of a key took its place.

The door swung open. He stood there, and for a terrible moment, she didn't recognize him. She cried out in alarm.

"It's me, Kate," his cold voice said. "The room clerk told me you were here."

He shuffled inside and pushed the door closed with one of his canes.

"Not a very pretty sight, am I?" he said. "But you are as lovely as ever. By God, if I were still a man, I'd want you, you bitch. You goddamned whore! You–"

"Don't, Royce, don't!" she whispered.

"You shouldn't fear me," he said with composure returned. "I can't harm you. I can't even lift one of these canes to beat you. You deserve a beating, Kate." He made his way painfully past her to a chair. He lowered himself into it slowly, awkwardly. "I saw your man in Libby. Big and handsome and strong. We're going to hang him, Kate. Did you come to Richmond to watch?"

"In the name of God, Royce, what happened to you?"

"I got killed," he said harshly. "At Kelly's Ford, riding with Stuart, on the Seventh of November, 1863. I just haven't died yet. Not yet, but soon."

She shook her head. "The doctors–"

"They pray," he said. "That's all they can do. They pray, and they tell me to have faith. I'm rotten inside, Kate. It won't heal, and it keeps rotting. Oh, it's a bad wound, Kate. It bleeds and it rots and it smells." He glared at her. "Remember when I was a man? Remember how it was? No more, Kate. Look, goddamn you! Look!" With one hand he ripped his tunic free. Then he ripped his trousers open. With a tortured face, he tore at the bandages that were revealed. She cried out, going to him, but he fended her away savagely with a cane and continued to rip at the bandages with his other hand. Blood stained them suddenly, and then his hand fell limply at his side. He had fainted.

She fled from the room, running downstairs into the crowded lobby, where people looked curiously at her. The room clerk nodded when she asked about Colonel Farnham's doctor.

"Yes, ma'am," the fellow said. "He lives right here in the hotel. I'll send a boy for him."

The doctor was an elderly man in the uniform of a Confederate major. He clicked his tongue repeatedly, shaking his head each time. Then he said, "Oh, my goodness, the poor boy," repeating himself softly three times. Then, with Kate's help, he put Royce Farnham to bed.

He seemed to take Kate's presence for granted. "I'm glad you got here, my dear lady. The young man is very sick, you know. You are willing to be his nurse, aren't you?"

"Yes, Doctor."

"Not a very pleasant chore, I'm afraid. The wound continues to suppurate, you know. Foreign matter, I fear, of some kind. Most mysterious."

"He says he's dying, Doctor. Is he?"

He seemed to hesitate before answering, and then suddenly, his puttering manner was gone. He had seemed to be a genial man who radiated optimism and good cheer. Now, when he looked squarely at her, he was old and weary and bitter. "You're going to nurse him," he said harshly. "You'll see for yourself. The answer to your question is yes. He's dying. He might have lasted longer if he'd stayed in bed; he might even have recovered, although I doubt it. I'm sorry, Mrs. Farnham, but I've never seen a recovery in a case as far along as this. Whatever's in there will kill him, sooner or later. You have a dirty job ahead of you, ma'am, but I'm glad you're here. I couldn't spare an orderly to look after him."

"Thank you for your confidence, Doctor."

"I'm sorry. Sorry for you and for our country. We need all the young men now."

17

Johnny Watkins remembered that the boy had led him somewhere, not very far from the fence where he'd fallen, and then had helped him get to bed. Someone had fed him some soup. He'd slept for a while. From the tightness of bandages that were wrapped around his belly, he supposed that the wound had been dressed. That was good of them.

He opened his eyes to see what kind of place they'd put him into. It seemed to be a log cabin, a big one. People lived in it, for certain. There was clothing hanging on pegs along the walls; there was a big fireplace with pots hanging on cranes. From them came a good smell of cooking. He wrinkled his nose–it was some kind of game stew. Squirrel or rabbit or deer meat? A big table, hewn from rough timbers, stood in the middle of the room. The table was flanked by long benches, also hand-finished.

Johnny was lying in a bunk against the wall in one corner of the room, opposite the fireplace. He turned his head to see the rest of the place. A big flop-eared hound dog lay on the floor near the bunk. He lifted his head when Johnny moved. His long tail thumped on the floor. The only other sign of life in the place was a half-grown chicken that pecked industriously at the floor under the big table.

It's not a rebel jail, he thought. Not with a dog and a chicken. Not even a barracks or a hut in winter quarters. People live here. A woman's clothes on those pegs.

He lifted his head to look around further. Three guns were resting on wooden pegs tapped into the wall above the bunk. One was an old flintlock musket, another was a fowling piece with over-and-under barrels. The sight of the third weapon caused Johnny's blood to race. It was a Sharps breech-loading carbine, and hanging from the peg under the stock was a cartridge box marked "U.S."

Johnny pushed himself up with his elbows, then reached upward. He took the Sharps down, and removed the cartridge box from the peg. With a twist of the lever, he opened the breech and shoved in a cartridge. He threw the lever closed, readying the gun to fire.

The dog thumped its tail enthusiastically at the sight of the gun, but the animal didn't move.

Johnny found his clothes hanging at the side of the bunk. All he was wearing in bed was his set of woolen drawers. He dressed awkwardly and shoved his feet into his boots. He picked up the carbine and got shakily to his feet.

He started for the door, but his head began to swim and he had to fall back to the bunk. He rested there for a minute or so, breathing heavily with his eyes closed, fighting the urge to be sick.

Then he stood up again. He started for the door once more, but stopped when suddenly it swung open. He brought up the carbine and held it as unwaveringly as he could. A bearded man, middle-aged but slim and wiry, stood watching him. The man wore a broad-brimmed hat and butternut-stained clothing like the garments that most of the secesh infantry wore in these later years of the war.

"Get out of the way," Johnny said. "This is loaded."

The man said nothing. The hound got to its feet, stretched and yawned, then walked over to the stranger, nuzzling its head into the man's hand.

"I mean it," Johnny said weakly. "I don't want to shoot you, but you're not going to take me to Belle Isle."

The man still didn't speak. A head appeared at his shoulder; in the shadows, it seemed a young face, topped by dark curls. That's the boy who found me, Johnny thought. Wonder how many of 'em I have to get through. More than three, it won't do me any good to try. I can't load this thing fast enough.

The man turned to the youngster, speaking casually: "Go take it away from him. Put him back in that there bunk."

Johnny lifted the carbine purposefully to his shoulder. The trouble was, the muzzle kept going around in circles that grew larger and larger. A wave of darkness came across his eyes and his mind. He fought it, but he started to fall. The two persons in the doorway moved then, although he didn't know it. They came forward to catch him and ease him back to the bunk.

A few minutes later, he came back to his senses. He was clear-headed again. He turned his head to look around the room. The man was sitting at the table, contemplatively forking stew into his mouth. There was a plate of corn bread on the table. As Johnny watched, the man took a two-inch square of corn bread and tossed it over his shoulder in a high arc. The hound moved its head a few inches and caught the morsel deftly. The chicken scurried to pick up the crumbs that fell from the hound's jaws. The man went on eating.

There was a woman in the room now, her back to Johnny as she leaned over the fireplace, putting a kettle to boil. When she turned, he caught his breath. It was the boy who had found him, only it wasn't a boy at all. She was maybe seventeen or eighteen. She had an oval face flushed by the heat of the fire, with dark eyes and a wide brow. Her curls were tied tightly back, so that he could understand how he'd mistaken her for a boy when her face had appeared in the doorway. She saw him looking at her; she smiled, and instantly she became the prettiest girl he'd ever seen. She motioned at him with her hand, as if to tell him that he should stay right where he was.

"Pa," she said softly. "He's living again."

The man looked around casually. "Stay put," he said evenly. "You ain't fit to move far as the door. You was bad hit, boy."

"Where am I?" Johnny asked weakly. "Who are you?"

"Name of Foote," the man said. "Our name, that is. Place ain't got a name. Just the piney woods near the Mattaponi."

"You ready to eat?" the girl said in her quiet pleasant voice. "I'll bring you a plate of stew."

He nodded, suddenly realizing that he was very hungry. He sat on the edge of the bunk while she dipped his meal from one of the kettles. He puzzled silently. What did all this mean? Was the man a secesh soldier?

All right, Johnny thought. Eat first, and worry about getting away from 'em later.

She brought the plate to him, offering to hold it for him while he ate, but he shook his head, cradling it in his lap. "That's corn bread I gave you," she said. "You ever et it before?"

"Lots of times," he said.

"Pa told me you Yankees don't eat no bread but hard crackers. Didn't you, Pa?"

"My mother used to make it at home," Johnny said. Then he added: "Not as good as this, though."

"I thank you," she said solemnly.

He was hungry and the stew was good. Nothing more was said while they all busied themselves with the meal.

Finally Johnny put his plate aside. "You're not taking me in," he said in a level voice. "Not to Belle Isle, you're not. I'd sooner die right here than there."

The man looked at him. There was no way to read his face through the heavy dark beard.

"Get it straight now," the man said. "Go the way you come, when you're able. Do what you want. I wouldn't take you to Belle Isle, nor no place else."

"Where's Belle Isle, Pa?" the girl asked.

"It's a prison place. In the James River, down to Richmond."

She laughed quickly. "Oh, my, mister! Pa wouldn't take you to no prison. Not Pa."

Johnny thought a moment, then smiled. "You're Union people? I was lucky to find you."

"Union?" Foote said slowly. "No, we ain't Union. Nor we ain't Confederates, neither. We ain't nothing but ourselves."

"Your clothes," Johnny said tentatively. "They look like what the reb infantry wears. You're not in the Army?"

Foote seemed to consider the question. "I was, for a spell. I ain't no more." He closed the subject. "How was the stew?"

"Good. Very good. Tasted something like squirrel, but a lot richer. What was it?"

"It's rich meat," Foote answered. "Lots of fat in it. I hope it don't make you sick. It was coon."

"I've had coon before. It didn't taste that good."

Foote nodded at the girl. "Her cooking. Beats me how she does it. Her name's Elvira. Mine's Bill. What's yours?"

"John Watkins. They call me Johnny."

"You lay there, Johnny. Sleep the sun around if you want. That hole in your side is all right. Elvira fixed it for you."

Johnny felt his face heat up when he thought of the way he'd found himself in the bunk, wearing only his drawers. Damn, even his mother hadn't tended him like that when he was sick, not for many years.

"I gave you a scrub bath, too," she said. "You were mighty dirty, Mr. Watkins."

"It's very fine of you, Mr. Foote, to look after me," Johnny said hastily. "I thought you were reb soldiers. That's why I grabbed the carbine. I'll go as soon as I can travel. I don't want to get you into trouble with your own army."

The girl laughed as if that was very funny.

Foote didn't say anything for a time. Then he said: "Call me Bill. And one other thing. It ain't my army. I got nothing to do with it."

"All right." Johnny was about to say more, then halted. "All right. Whatever you say."

Bill Foote nodded, then started to fill a cob pipe. He looked at Johnny. "You smoke? Got another pipe if you want it."

"No, sir," Johnny said. "Cigars, sometimes, when I could get 'em in camp."

The girl got up from the table and walked to the bunk. Johnny sat uncomfortably, aware of the clean fresh scent that reminded him of hayrides and picnics back home in Tarrytown, when a fellow could put his arm around a girl and kiss her and be dizzied by the strangeness of it all. This one, for looks, beat all the girls back home and then some. Of course, he told himself sensibly enough, maybe he was figuring that way because he hadn't seen a young girl in many months. Just officers' wives and nurses and women from the Sanitary Commission, most of whom seemed to be middle-aged–thirty or thirty-five or so–and whores like that colored woman in Culpeper.

"You'll be more comfortable if you take off that uniform," she said. "You get under the blankets and sleep as long as you want."

"I'm all right like this," he said.

She nodded sober agreement. "Maybe you're right. You ain't very quick at moving around. If anybody comes, you got to hide without losing time. I'll show you."

"Who?" he asked. "Who might come?"

She shrugged. "Soldiers. The police soldiers. What do you call 'em when they take the part of police in the Army?"

"The provost's guard."

"Yes. They've come three–four times, thinking to catch Pa."

"I run off," Bill Foote said casually. "Coming back after that fight in Pennsylvania last year. Last summer."

"Gettysburg," Johnny said. "I was there, too."

"Yeh. That's where. They been looking for me ever since."

"Look, now," Elvira said. She knelt on the floor before the bunk. Johnny was instantly aware of the way the brown cloth of her dress stretched tightly across her back. He didn't want to see her thighs outlined against the cloth, but she'd told him to look, hadn't she?

She picked up a rusted horseshoe nail that was lying on the floor almost at Johnny's feet. "The nail is always here," she said. "Be careful you don't move it or kick it. You might need it in a hurry."

She inserted the point of the nail into an ordinary-looking knothole in the irregularly cut floor boards. With a quick twist of the nail, she lifted a section of the floor about two feet square. It swung upward on hidden hinges that squeaked shrilly.

"They ought to be oiled again, Pa," she said. "Some night there may not be much warning."

"I'll tend to it," Bill Foote said.

Elvira pointed into the dark hole that was revealed by the trap door. "It's big enough for you, if you lay yourself down." She looked speculatively at his breadth of shoulder. "You're lots bigger than Pa, but you can fit through the trap."

He nodded wonderingly. "Do they ever search? How come they don't find it?"

She laughed. "I stand over it, making as if I just got up out of this bunk. They just look around. There ain't no danger to me; they have officers and sergeants and such. They treat me fine. They don't ever do a good job of searching. It's been some weeks now since they came by. I expect they've given up on Pa."

"How do you know they're coming?" Johnny asked. "Don't they just break right in?"

"They try," Bill Foote said. He pointed at the hound. "Jake always lets us know." The dog's tail thumped the floor at mention of his name.

"He raises a ruckus when strangers come anywhere near the house," Elvira said. "He heard you at the fence this morning. Pa went into the hole, and when they didn't come, but the dog kept barking, I went out to look. And there you were."

"Chances are," Bill Foote said, "you won't need it. But if you do, jump in and keep quiet."

"I've got to ask one thing," Johnny said. "If any Federals come, or even one of our boys on the run like me, you get me out of the hole, will you?"

"You want to go back to the killing," Bill Foote said flatly.

"No," Johnny said, thinking of Major Stephens's words: DUTY, HONOR, COUNTRY. "I just want to go back to my duty, until the war's done."

Foote laughed harshly. "How many have you killed so far?"

"None. None that I know of. I admit maybe I hit a couple."

"I killed just one," Foote said. His voice dropped to a whisper. "There was a railroad that ran through a cut at that town in Pennsylvania, but it wasn't finished. I mean, they never laid the rails. We cut off a regiment of Yanks in a wheat field. There wasn't any way out for 'em but to leg it across that railroad cut. We had it covered, had it stone cold in our sights. The artillery got them a word for the way we had that cut covered, along it—all along it."

"Enfiladed," Johnny said.

"Yeh. That's the word. All of 'em in a row, like. So one of 'em slid down the bank on his backside, and I laid bead on him, waiting for him to get up."

"Pa," Elvira said. "There ain't no need to tell it again."

"Hush," he said gently. "I got to. Reckon I'll be telling it the rest of my life, can I get anybody to listen. So he got up, and I squeezed on him, and the minnie hit him a little higher'n where I aimed. It hit him in the throat."

"Pa, don't."

". . . and he sort of sagged all over, like all his bones come apart from each other. And then his mouth opened and he was screaming. Only he wasn't, you see, because how can you scream with a minnie through your throat? Now, that made me kinda sick, you see?

"So I turned my head, because I didn't want to look no more. Turned my head, you see, to where my boy, her brother Billy, was a-laying right alongside me. You understand, all them Yanks was running, but some of 'em was shooting back at us. Turned my head just in time to see my boy Billy get a minnie in the same place. Just about the same place. Had his head up to shoot. Billy screamed too, before he died, but I didn't hear him either."

Elvira was crying softly. Johnny listened to Foote's soft voice and stared in fascination at the drawn face.

"It was a judgment on me. I knew it, and I took it on myself, and I'll carry it all the way with me. So I left 'em, boy, after I seen Billy put into the ground. And I ain't going back. Never. I just up and quit 'em and came home."

"Yessir," Johnny whispered.

"You think you got to go back. Duty, you call it. All right. But don't kill nobody, boy. Don't kill nobody. Never."

Foote got up, crossed to the fireplace, tapped his pipe against the palm of his hand, dumping the ashes into the fire. "I'll sleep in the mow, Elvira. You sleep with one ear open for Jake. They might come looking for this boy or some of his friends."

Foote paused at the door, shoving the hound away as it tried to follow him outside. "You're welcome as long as you want to stay, boy."

18

Hank Stephens found reading to be the most rewarding way of passing time. The Richmond papers came in every day, each copy costing one dollar Confederate, plus five dollars daily to the turnkeys for distribution. Hank found his name mentioned almost daily; he was cast in the role of assistant barbarian and associate assassin. The papers howled for execution of Dahlgren's officers. He grimaced when he saw that Dahlgren's body, minus ring finger and minus wooden leg, had been put on exhibition. He learned that he owed his captivity to the military genius of James Pollard, lieutenant of Virginia cavalry. He found out that Kilpatrick had made it safely to Butler's lines.

Hank managed an objective view of his danger. Public indignation was high and rising. His chances weren't very good unless somebody at Cabinet level doused the frenzy. He was the prime candidate for Richmond's vengeance. One hanging would satisfy everyone. The other officers of Dahlgren's command weren't in much danger. Hank's common sense told him that Davis or Seddon would put a damper on the flames, but it didn't ease his mind to learn that his fellow prisoners were quietly gambling on his chances. The odds stood at two to one against him.

There were plenty of books to read in the Libby Prison circulating library, which operated efficiently enough on the simple principle of trading a book you had read for one you hadn't. Hank Stephens took no pleasure in checkers or chess, or in any of the never-ending poker games, so most of his day, after he had read the newspapers, was spent reading books.

During his fourth day in the prison, he was sitting below one of the windows that looked out on Twentieth Street, to catch the best light on the fine print of his book, when men on the Cary Street side of the room called his name. He didn't hear them at first; the book was both fascinating and nostalgic—*Diedrich Knickerbocker's History of New York,* by Washington Irving. One of the poker players beside him finally had to nudge him to get his attention. "Hey, Stephens, they want you up front."

He put the book down and got to his feet. Turner again? Royce Farnham? Did they have the noose made and the scaffold built?

"At the window, Stephens," somebody said.

The turnkey named Ross was standing there at the first window fronting on Cary Street. He grinned evilly at Hank and said, "A visitor, Major. Closest she can get is across the street. From the stink of this place, that's as close as she wants to get, I reckon." The man placed himself squarely in front of the window, blocking Hank's view. "Cost you one dollar Yankee to take a look, Major. That's two dollars altogether. She gave me one to bring you the message."

Hank was completely puzzled. What kind of a trick was this? This man Ross was known for his lack of character and conscience. Greenbacks were too precious to hand out to Ross just for permission to look out the window. Hank shook his head and turned away. Whatever it was, whoever paid a dollar to get his attention–he was damned certain he wasn't going to be swindled by Ross.

Ross laughed. "All right, Major. Give me the greenback. She says her name is Farnham. Mrs. Farnham."

Hank wheeled. He stared at the grinning little turnkey in amazement. Quickly he dug into the inside pocket of his tunic and pulled out his billfold. He thrust a paper dollar into the man's hand and then pushed him roughly away from the window.

They simply looked at each other for a long time. Neither of them moved. She was smiling up at him. She was perhaps fifty feet away, standing alone beside a lamppost on the sidewalk at the intersection of Cary and Twentieth Streets. Confederate soldiers of the guard lounged nearby, watching her with leering interest; pedestrians passed around her, looking curiously at this pretty girl whose head was lifted to stare smilingly at the second floor of the prison across the street.

After a time, Hank slowly lifted his hand to his lips, touching the tips of his fingers. She did the same, smiling.

Curious prisoners crowded behind Hank to see the lovely woman. There were only a few coarse remarks, because his fellow inmates looked at his face and understood the longing they saw there. One sallow young fellow from Connecticut stared out at Kate Farnham, then looked at Hank. He turned away, weeping for his own loneliness.

She stayed on the corner for fifteen minutes. Then she opened her handbag and removed something that glittered in the afternoon sunlight. She showed it to Hank, but he couldn't make out what it was. She seemed upset by his inability to understand. Then she smiled. She held the object to her ear, as if listening, and then showed it to him again.

A watch! She wanted him to note the time. He nodded vigorously, pantomiming the removal of his own watch from his breeches pocket and pretending to look at it. She smiled. She pointed at the ground she stood on, and looked at the watch again. Then she held up seven fingers and ticked them off, one by one.

He shook his head, puzzled. She went through the routine again.

"Goddamm it, Major," said a voice behind him, "she means she'll be there at this time every day."

He laughed then, and nodded vigorously. She clapped her hands to show joy at his understanding.

She touched her fingers to her lips, held them there for a moment, and then turned away and walked out of his sight.

The question of execution continued to rage. The Confederate Cabinet discussed it at great length, but made no announcements. Presumably every man in high position wondered, at least momentarily, what might happen to him at the end of the war if he had had any part in the hanging of Dahlgren's raiders. Bragg fumed; James Seddon tended now toward caution.

Seddon was the man who set in motion the chain of communications that would resolve the question. He wrote to Robert E. Lee:

> . . . General Bragg's views coincide with my own on this subject. The question of what is best to be done is a grave and important one, and I desire to have the benefit of your views and any suggestions you may make . . . as well as your judgment of what would be the sentiment of the Army on a course of severe but just retribution . . .

Then the word came back from Headquarters of the Army of Northern Virginia, quiet but positive, from the field desk of the man upon whose shoulders the fate of the Confederacy rested:

> I concur with you in thinking that a formal publication of these papers should be made under official authority, that our people and the world may know the character of the war our enemies wage against us, and the unchristian and atrocious acts they plot and perpetrate. But I cannot recommend the execution of the prisoners that have fallen into our hands. Assuming that the address and special orders of Colonel Dahlgren correctly state his designs and intentions, they were not executed, and I believe, even in a legal

> point of view, acts in addition to intentions are necessary to constitute crime . . .

That was the beginning of the end of the danger to Major Henry Stephens. No one in the Confederate Government had the temerity to oppose the views and wishes of Robert E. Lee in March of 1864. He was all they had left, he and his ragged, gaunt legions.

As Hank had supposed, the papers were immediately and publicly declared forgeries in the North. General Meade, upon receipt of the photographic copies from General Lee, by flag of truce, demanded of Kilpatrick the truth of the matter. He had his reply promptly:

> . . . Colonel Dahlgren . . . handed me an address that he intended to read to his command. That paper was indorsed in red ink, "Approved," over my official signature. The alleged address of Colonel Dahlgren published in the papers is the same as the one approved by me, save so far as it speaks of *"exhorting the prisoners to burn and destroy the hateful city and kill the traitor Davis and his cabinet."* All this is false and published only as an excuse for the barbarous treatment of the remains of a brave soldier . . .

Captain Mitchell went to headquarters at Brandy Station and told Meade personally that he had never heard the address nor seen the orders. Other officers and soldiers testified similarly. The misspelling of Dahlgren's name seemed to indicate the probability of forgery. The matter was settled, as far as the Union was concerned. General Meade so informed General Lee, and that was that.

But General Meade had something else again to say to his wife:

> This was a pretty ugly piece of business, for in denying having authorized or approved "the burning of Richmond, or killing Mr. Davis and Cabinet," I necessarily threw odium on Dahlgren. I, however, enclosed a letter from Kilpatrick, in which the authenticity of the papers was impugned; but I regret to say Kilpatrick's reputation, and collateral evidence in my possession, rather go against this theory . . .

At any rate, no one was hanged for barbarism in the city of Richmond, and the one Union officer most concerned paid the controversy no mind in the days that followed. Hank Stephens' life in Libby Prison was taken up with waiting for the noon sun to slide past the zenith, when he daily took his place in the window looking out upon the intersection of Twentieth and Cary Streets, where his love would soon appear.

19

Emma Turley had the news from Captain Mitchell when he returned on the first of the steamers that brought Kilpatrick's men and worn-out horses up from the Peninsula. Mitchell came out to the Barr place to tell her about Ben. She accepted the word quietly enough at first, without comment but with sudden tears rimming her eyes. Then Mitchell offered gently to arrange for her transportation back home to Peekskill.

"I'll wait," she said. "It will be up to me to see that he's buried proper." The tears rolled down her cheeks; she brushed them away hastily with the corner of her apron.

"I'm afraid that's not going to be possible," the captain said diffidently. "You see, Mrs. Turley, he wasn't with the main force. He was with Colonel Dahlgren, and none of those men who were—who were left behind could be brought out."

She looked at him as if she didn't understand.

"You know that they were cut off," the captain said. He wished unhappily that she would wail or weep or faint—anything but stare blankly at him. "The rebs took those men, Mrs. Turley. They've probably buried Sergeant Turley in Richmond." He tried again, wearily. "The government has some kind of program, ma'am. After the war, they'll bury him where you want him to be."

"You mean the rebs have got him? They won't send him back?"

Captain Mitchell shook his head. "Now don't you worry about the sergeant, Mrs. Turley. They gave him a decent Christian burial. When the war is over, the government will bring him home. They will find him in a Richmond cemetery."

"I'll wait here," she said. "They may send him through any day."

"Not much use in it, ma'am," he said, almost angry now. "They don't have any provision for that kind of thing."

"I'll wait," she said. "Major Stephens will see to it for me. He's an old friend of our family."

"Major Stephens can't do it," Mitchell said. "They took him prisoner, ma'am. He's locked up in Libby Prison in the city of Richmond."

She lifted her head suddenly, as if she had been alerted by the word prisoner. "How can you be sure about Ben? How do you know?"

"Some troopers from that detachment got through to Kilpatrick. One of them says he saw Ben go down, ma'am. He tried to help him, but it was too late. He said Ben was dead, Mrs. Turley. We questioned the troopers closely, about every detail. It's so, ma'am. I'm sorry, but it's so."

"I'll wait," she said. "For a while, I'll wait right here. He may come back any day."

He shook his head, not knowing what else to say.

Just as if she didn't even hear me, he thought. Say something to her, you idiot. What? Nothing. Nothing at all.

"Thank you, Captain Mitchell. I'll wait right here. You wouldn't want to stay for a nice dinner? I know what you had on that trip–salt pork and hardtack."

He refused. He left shortly, stopping to ask the Barrs if they wouldn't look in on Emma Turley. "He's dead," Mitchell said to Mr. Barr. "I told her and told her, and it looked as if she didn't even hear me!"

The Barrs were most kindly and comforting, and, because of their gentle voices, Emma began to cry. She didn't wail or fling herself about, but she cried steadily for a long time. Then she wiped her eyes and blew her nose and tried to smile. "If you'll let me keep the place," she whispered, "I'll wait here for Ben. There may be word any day. The rebs won't keep him there."

"You stay as long as you want, my dear," said Mrs. Barr, drying her own eyes. "I'm sure you will have good news about the sergeant."

The Barrs furnished her a horse and buggy, and each day she drove to Stevensburg or to Brandy Station. Captain Mitchell became short-tempered at seeing her every morning, and took to inspecting stables or picket lines in order to avoid her. At headquarters the officers and men soon began to dread her quiet appearance with the inevitable question: "Have you had any word yet about Sergeant Ben Turley who was with Colonel Dahlgren?"

They were kindly men, in the main, and they detested the task of smothering the bright unfailing hope that shone daily on her handsome face. To make it easier for themselves, and–they thought guiltily–for her as well, they gradually joined the futile game she played. One after another of them added a few words to his daily denial: "Maybe we will know soon, Mrs. Turley," or, "I suppose it won't be long now until we hear, ma'am."

Each of them eventually found himself hoping, like a raw recruit, for the bright spring day that must come soon, when the Army would flex its gigantic body and then stream out to the new year's campaign. They would leave her behind them, and they could stop lying to her, although they might have to lie to somebody else, life and the Army being what it was. They were uncomfortable with her now, because she believed what they said to her.

She knew better, of course. She knew he was dead. She'd been a widow before. Sometimes she would pause in her housework and say to herself: "You're a widow. You're a childless widow. You're a widow without a child." She tried other variations of the words. Often she would think about her other marriage. She would think of the dead children, of their lifeless faces and cold bodies, of their small coffins. She would remember how she had been left alone, all alone in a world that could not share her grief. She would then sit down and cry for a while.

Then she would get back to her housework and think about Ben Turley. Sometimes she would tell herself very sternly that she knew that Captain Mitchell had spoken the truth when he said that Ben was dead. Captain Mitchell knew what he was talking about. So did all those soldiers who told her kindly that there was no news of Ben, that there would be none. One day she even turned away from the headquarters of the Cavalry Corps without asking a single question. She knew what the answers would be.

She stayed on, however. She and Ben had been provident for the few years of their marriage, and he had always been a man of good habits. There was money enough to keep her. She had their savings sent down from Peekskill. It cost her little to live, and she found something to do to occupy her days. She became a volunteer nurse in the II Corps hospital at Brandy Station. They were glad to get her. Each day, after her visit to headquarters, she drove to the hospital and pitched in to do the hundred jobs that were daily routine on the wards. In the darkness she drove home; she cooked her supper and ate it in loneliness; she went to bed to dream of her husband and his love and his strength and of the baby they had never had. Sometimes she saw him lying sick and friendless in a rebel prison, and she woke up crying. Her heart went out to the men whom she served each day. She treated them tenderly because they were sick and friendless, too.

In spite of her frequent acceptance of the knowledge that he was gone forever, she sought out eagerly the new patients who came into the hospital, even though it was an infantry installation, and even though most of them were just sick soldiers, not wounded cavalrymen. There was always a chance, she told herself, that he'd made his way through the lines and that he was so ill he couldn't tell anybody who he was. When an occasional patient came in from General Butler's force on the Peninsula, she always questioned him about a cavalry sergeant who might have come through from the Dahlgren ambush. There was seldom any word of encouragement, but she kept asking. Once in a while, a sick soldier might say something like this: "Seems to me I seen a feller like that, ma'am. I'll try to remember." She would then pester him so that he would tell the doctors to keep her away from him.

As the days went by, her quiet grief for Ben Turley was slowly transformed into something else–a sense of loss that was centered not in him, but in the child that they had never conceived. Slowly, hazily, over a period of weeks, an obsession began to form. She and Ben had never had the child that would have meant so much to her now that he was gone; it wasn't too late, however, because she was alive and healthy and willing. When she had a child, it would be just as much his as hers. Why, she asked herself, should the child that would have borne his name be denied life and the love of a mother just because the rebels hadn't let Ben come back from Richmond?

It wasn't even a decision; it was simply circumstance, the way things happened. One night in mid-March, when the roads were hub-deep in mud, a big handsome fellow like Ben suggested that he drive the buggy home for her. She asked him to come in to share her supper. He stayed the night.

He didn't return; he was only a youngster, in spite of his size and seeming maturity; he was a boy from a New Jersey farm who was trying to act like a veteran. He didn't return because he was frightened of her and of the intensity with which she held him in the motion of love and called him "Ben" when his name was Allen and talked all the time about making a baby.

There were others, of course, who made themselves available. She didn't even think about it very much. She knew that a soldier would be waiting when she finished her work at the hospital. Night after night, an infantryman or cavalryman would drive the buggy home and come in for supper. The word got around with the speed of a crown fire among the troops at Brandy Station. Within two weeks, it was usual for a dozen soldiers to be loitering near the hospital, waiting for her. They were quiet about it, and their conduct was most decorous through the dark ride on the muddy road and during the course of the meal that was always prepared with the touch of home. All but a few of them seemed to understand that this was an arrangement strange indeed, and somehow they came to share the feeling that it should not be demeaned by coarse behavior. For many of the soldiers, one trip to the Barr place was enough; they were afraid of what they couldn't understand.

There were only a few obscene stories about her passed through the camp. The men who accompanied her generally didn't talk about what happened. A fortunate circumstance for Emma was that the brutes and the bullies and the riffraff simply refused to believe that there was such a woman. Furthermore, Emma probably wouldn't have chosen any of them. She picked big, good-looking men of gentle voice–most of them noncommissioned officers. They generally looked something like Ben Turley.

Any man who was asked about her was usually reticent. He would nod and say: "Go find out for yourself."

Her conduct caused a scandal, of course, even though there was no ugly clamor about it. The doctors in the hospital heard of it and considered discouraging her attendance on the patients. Headquarters knew about it soon enough, but the responsibility was passed back and forth from infantry to cavalry; Pleasonton regarded the woman as Kilpatrick's responsibility, while Kilpatrick pointed out that she was engaged in hospital work for the II Corps. General Humphreys privately told Kilpatrick to send her home, but the bantam general was too busy fretting and fuming about being relieved and sent to Sherman's army in the West to bother with a soldier's woman who was in infantry territory at Brandy Station, anyway.

It took some time for the Barrs to discover what was going on in the attached wing of their big house. They were quiet, reserved, and elderly, and once the sun went down, they didn't pay much attention to whatever might be happening outside their house. In truth, they couldn't believe that Emma was having visitors at night, but they finally convinced themselves when they watched soldiers leave Emma's house on several occasions in the dawn light to walk back to Brandy Station or to Stevensburg. They had known that Emma had taken up the custom of having soldiers who escorted her home stay as guests for the evening meal, but they'd assumed that these were friends of her husband who had called in sympathy. The Barrs were early-to-bed people, and they had no way of knowing that the callers were staying most of the night.

Even when they were certain, they did nothing for a time. They were gentle people, and they knew that the shock of Ben Turley's death had affected Emma deeply. Why else did she so frequently tell Mrs. Barr that she was hoping that she and Ben were going to have a baby? According to Mrs. Barr's reckoning, the time for that had certainly gone by.

Eventually they summoned courage enough to speak to her. They went together to tell her that she had to go. They met her as she was leaving her house to hitch up the buggy for her daily trip to Brandy Station.

Mrs. Barr made a faint and distressed suggestion that they would need the wing that Emma occupied for the accommodation of some relatives who had been dispossessed by the Yankees at Culpeper.

"That's all right," Emma said, smiling happily. "I was going to tell you anyway that I will have to go home soon. I'll hate to leave the hospital and my work and all, when there's always a chance that some news of Ben will come in, but I just have to."

"That is wise," said Mr. Barr.

"Well, I just have to," Emma said. "The sooner, the better. You see, Ben and I are going to have a baby. Isn't that wonderful?"

The Barrs didn't look at each other, nor at Emma. Mr. Barr scuffed the soft soil with the toe of his boot.

"I'll say good-bye at the hospital," Emma continued, "and I'll ship my things off by railway, and then I'll take the first train from Brandy that carries passengers to Washington."

"Are you sure, Emma?" Mrs. Barr asked gently. "About the baby?"

"Oh, yes. Absolutely sure. If it's a boy, I'll name him after his father. Benjamin Edmund Turley, Junior. I haven't decided on a girl's name. Anything but Emma. I hate the name of Emma. I'll have to give it some thought. Maybe Ben will come home in time to help, if those rebs let him go."

"Maybe he will," said Mr. Barr.

So Emma Turley took her leave of the Army of the Potomac. She rode the cars to Washington, and through to the Hudson Valley, where the boy, if it was to be a boy, would grow up happily in a community that remembered and respected his father, who had been one of the heroes of Kilpatrick's raid on Richmond.

20

Johnny's wound was painful. He had difficulty in moving around, but he thought that at worst he'd be laid up only a few days. He dressed the wound himself when Elvira was out of the cabin. He saw no signs of unusual festering around the raw holes in his flesh, and he no longer had a fever.

Only once did he have to duck into the hole under the trap door. He was reclining on the bunk, watching Elvira work around the place, when the dog Jake began to bay. For a second or two, Johnny paid no attention. The dog was outside with Bill Foote. He came alert, however, when Elvira dashed outside to secure the dog after whispering vehemently to him: "Get under that trap! Move!"

The intruders were a half dozen of the Home Guard of King and Queen County, looking for fugitives from Dahlgren's command. They came into the house, and faintly Johnny could hear Elvira talking to them. He couldn't distinguish any words.

He was in the hole under the floor for about twenty minutes while the rebs searched the outbuildings and environs. Finally he heard the thudding of their horses' hoofs as they moved away from the house. Elvira opened the trap for him a few minutes later.

"All right. Come on up. They've gone."

"Your father all right?" Johnny asked.

She nodded worriedly. "Probably. They didn't go into the woods. But they asked about him."

"What else did they say?"

"They've caught men from your bunch. I don't know how many. They said that your cavalry has all run away. They laughed about that."

"Pretty soon they'll laugh on the other sides of their faces."

The first time that Johnny ventured outside, he walked slowly with short careful steps. He paused frequently, giving himself his first opportunity to see what kind of place he'd landed in. It wasn't much, that was sure. The house was an ungainly log cabin with wide bands of light clay chinking between the logs. The roof was slapdash, of weathered gray shakes that looked as if the first twenty-mile wind would send them sailing.

There were three cleared fields that he could see, separated from each other by flimsy rail fences. The outbuildings–low squat barn and small granary–were also of log construction similar to the house.

He smiled slightly as he thought of what his mother would say about the people who owned this place. She would turn up her nose, surely, if she could see Elvira Foote walking around barefoot in the house, dressed in brown homespun. She would even laugh at the name "Elvira" as far as that went.

His mother wouldn't approve of any of this–his mud-grained uniform, the light-blond three-day stubble on his face, his boots scratched and torn. She would shudder at the ugly wound in his side; if she had known he was wounded, she would picture him nursing a bandaged arm or leg in a spic-and-span hospital, attended by kindly efficient doctors and gentle nurses whose devotion would shine from their plain faces. She wouldn't be able to picture her son at this run-down farm in the pine lowlands, dirty and bearded and wounded, with only a barefooted girl to care for him. She would shudder if he told her that he relished raccoon stew. So he wouldn't tell her; when he got back he would tell her that some kind Virginia Unionists had given him aid and comfort.

His mother wouldn't even understand the simplicity of these people. They said what they thought; they seemed always to speak directly and truthfully about everything.

Yessir, he thought, if she ever saw this place and me and Elvira and Bill Foote and old Jake, she'd keel right over in a dead faint.

Bill Foote came toward him from the barn, noting how Johnny was studying the place. "Ain't much, is it?" the man grinned.

Johnny flushed. He didn't want his thoughts known.

"I had hopes, when my boy was alive. It's good rich land. Dunno when I'll get to do anything with it, the way I have to keep close to a hiding place."

"What would they do if they caught you?" Johnny asked.

"Ain't going to catch me," Bill said. He motioned toward a rough bench near the cabin door. "Let's set and take the air. No, they ain't going to nab me, but if they ever did, I reckon I'd be put back into the Army. They ain't got enough men now, to afford to shoot any."

"Maybe, if they took you, they'd give you a job where there's no fighting, like with the quartermaster."

Foote clucked his tongue in annoyance. "Boy, you don't understand. I have quit the Army. No more Armies, be they gray or blue. I just quit, that's what I did."

"How old is Elvira?" Johnny asked, not aware that so sudden a change of subject was startling.

"She's old enough," Foote said. "I'd have to count it up. Seventeen or eighteen. But don't you start any thinking about her, boy, not when you're fixing to go back to the war. If you was to stay here, I wouldn't mind, I reckon."

Johnny flushed. "I didn't mean–"

"I know what you mean," Foote said. "Young lad like you, there'd be something wrong with him if he didn't think about that. Mind what I say. No tricks with Elvira, lessen you mean to stay."

"I've got my duty," Johnny said, for want of something better to say.

"There you go with that word again. It don't mean a thing. No man alive has got a duty to kill another man, or to help kill him, either."

Foote got up and went into the cabin. Johnny sat on the bench, thinking of his mother's reaction if she had heard *that* conversation.

Then he saw Elvira coming in from the barn, where she'd been feeding the chickens and the pigs. He watched her step lightly and swiftly, in spite of the cut-down men's boots she wore outside the house. The sunset glowed on her attractive face, and he heard her voice lifted merrily in a light dancing tune, one of those rollicking songs that were termed "mountain music" in the Army, mostly because back-country soldiers often whined them by the hour to the accompaniment of a banjo.

She saw him on the bench and stopped singing. "You come out by yourself?"

He nodded. "I feel pretty good. It hurts a little right now."

She stood before him, setting on the ground the buckets she carried. "I believe I'll sit here by you for a spell, before I get us some supper. After all that hard weather, this was a nice day. You ain't chilly, are you, Johnny? Sick folks shouldn't get chilled."

"I'm fine."

"Two days, three days," she said quietly, "and then you'll be gone and I'll never see you again. I'll be sad when you go."

That's nice of her to think that way, he told himself. After all, I'm a Yankee. "Oh, I dunno," he said cheerfully. "Kill Cavalry may bring us right back here one of these days. And I'll sure stop in to see you and your father."

"No, you won't. You get back to the Army and that will be the end of it. Tell me something about that Sleepy Hollow place you said you come from."

"What do you want to know about it? Where will I start?"

"Start with you. Have you got a girl friend there? Is she pretty? What's her name? What kind of nice clothes does she have?"

He thought for a few seconds. There wasn't any girl in the entire village, as far as he knew, who'd ever turned a second glance at him. He'd been young and very shy before he joined the Army.

"I never had a girl," he said. "Never gave it much thought until now."

"Now?" she asked. "You mean you do now? You mean me?"

He gave a lame answer. "Like in the Army. The boys are always talking. You know–"

"I don't know," she said. "Tell me."

"Well, we're riding through a town, maybe, and there's a girl. She doesn't even have to be very good-looking, but the boys begin to whistle and talk wise and such. You know. They do a lot of talking about it."

"What do they say?"

Jee-sus, Johnny thought. If ever I told her! "Ah, just smart talk."

"Did you ever kiss a girl, Johnny?"

He shrugged, thinking warmly of Elsie Shannon, back home, who lived on a barge on the Hudson water front with her parents. Elsie had provided his only sexual experience. She'd obliged everybody for ten cents apiece. "Sure, I've kissed girls," he said. "Times, I have."

"Why don't you kiss me then? Maybe it ain't right for a girl to ask and all, but I never have, and I always wondered what it was like."

"Sure," he said. He leaned across and pecked at her pursed lips.

"That's all?" she said. "You ought to borrow Pa's razor, Johnny. He don't use it since he grew the beard. I better go in now and fix the supper. Don't stay out here too long. It will get real cold when the sun goes down."

The Home Guard got Bill Foote the next morning at dawn. They came sneaking through the woods on foot this time, encircling the little farm. When Jake bayed his warning, Bill was on his way to the woods for a day's hunting. He started to run for cover, but he ran right into the soldiers.

Johnny was under the trap, and he didn't know what was going on, but he could hear Elvira's voice outside the cabin. She told him later that the officer in charge had come from the woods to tell her that they were taking her father back.

She begged the officer to let her father go, but her tears had no effect. These were hard times, the man said, and General Lee needed every soldier he could get. He'd go himself, if the rheumatism didn't hit him so bad when he had to sleep out.

She was crying when she opened the trap to let Johnny out. Briefly he considered chasing after the Home Guard detachment to give himself up, even if it meant Belle Isle. What good would that do, however? They wouldn't bargain with him–himself in exchange for Bill Foote's freedom. They'd just take both prisoners to jail.

Johnny consoled Elvira as best he could, but she quickly brought herself back to normal. Her father would be all right; he was smart and he had been a good soldier. Now he would keep his head down and stay safe until the war was over, and then he'd come back home. The war couldn't last much longer.

She was struck by sudden panic. "They won't shoot him, will they, Johnny? He always said they wouldn't. You think they'll shoot him?"

"Of course not. They need every man. They'll put him right in the Army."

"I'm glad you're here," she said. "I'd hate to be alone, right off. Maybe when you leave, I'll go live with Pa's sister in King and Queen Courthouse. I guess Pa wouldn't want me out in the woods alone."

They finished the day matter-of-factly, she working inside the house and out, while he rested most of the time. He took a bath in a big wooden washtub while she was out at the barn, and he shaved with Bill Foote's razor. He put fresh bandages on his wound, thinking that it looked all right for a body wound, if you had to have one.

She exclaimed with delight when she saw him. "You look real proper," she said. "You know you're handsome, Johnny?"

"Thank you, ma'am. And you're very pretty."

"No," she said, "but I'm going to do my best. I'm going to take a bath too, and comb my hair up on top of my head and put on my church-meeting dress and real shoes. Maybe then you'll want to kiss me again. I don't think we did it right that first time. Not the way I've heard said, anyway."

He could feel his body warm immediately, and he was at once excited and alarmed. She was innocent, and he'd have to treat her that way. She wasn't any Elsie Shannon from a river barge.

The days went by, and with them the experiments in kissing increased in frequency. They both knew what was happening, but they avoided bringing it out into the open. Sometimes they sat before the fireplace in the evening, holding hands and talking quietly, until his arm went around her shoulders, and then they would spend as much as half an hour clinging to each other while the dog Jake slept peacefully at their feet. Then, with lips puffed from the kissing, and with Johnny embarrassed by his swollen manhood, they would separate for the night. He would go to his wall bunk and she would vanish behind the curtain that screened her cot.

A week went by, and there was no longer any innocent experiment in their nightly kissing session. Matter of fact, it was no longer restricted to the hour or so before the fire. Anytime during the day that she came near him, he would seize her and hold her, and he was aware that he was no longer shamed by his instant reaction, but delighted when she pressed against him.

He gave thought to leaving; he could travel now, and his wound was healing nicely, although it sometimes itched severely. He put off his departure day after day, until, inevitably, the night that they went beyond kissing. It happened when his hand went to her firm high breast with its raised nipple beneath the homespun dress.

"Yes, yes," she whispered. "I love you, Johnny. Let's be like man and wife. Do you want to?"

He restrained himself for only a moment, thinking again that he must not take advantage of her innocent direct nature, but then he was carrying her to the cot.

After that, they made love whenever they wanted to, and they were very happy.

During the next three weeks, the thought of leaving her never forced its way to the front of his mind. He wouldn't even consider it. They were in love; they were happy as neither had ever been before; they were just like man and wife, as she put it. He agreed with that concept. He even gave it voice: "I'll marry you, sweetheart. Maybe not before a preacher yet, but I'll marry you now. I, John Watkins, take thee, Elvira Foote, for my lawful wedded wife, to have and to hold . . ." He couldn't remember the rest of it.

"And I, Elvira Foote, take thee, John Watkins, to be my lawful wedded husband, to have and to hold . . ." She began to cry in his arms.

"It's just as good as if the preacher said it, sweetheart," he told her gently. "It binds us forever. We're married now. Soon as we can, we'll make it according to the law. But we don't need any more than to swear it."

"Johnny, my husband. I love you."

"And I love you."

He believed it to be true—they were married. In the eyes of the God that he had been reared to respect and love, he knew that he was married.

The physical intimacy continued unabated in its fervor, but now it was a familiar excitement, no longer dominating his entire mind in all his waking hours. Naturally, his mind began to wander back to his predicament of being a Yankee soldier in Confederate country. As soon as he could contemplate his future with calm view, he knew that he could not stay long as a free man in the heart of Virginia. He'd be caught sooner or later. Who could say how long the war would last? Eventually someone would see him outside the cabin—some casual visitor, perhaps, or a Home Guard patrol passing through the woods.

He didn't want to leave, and he delayed the inevitable decision. The weeks went by; March gave way to the buds and green grass of April. Then one day they had a real scare. A Home Guard patrol rode up to the farm. Jake bayed, and Johnny dived into his hiding place. The Home Guards searched both house and outbuildings very carefully this time. They made no bones about it to Elvira; the officer in command pointed to Johnny's tracks everywhere about the house and barns. "He may not be here now," the man said, "but he's been here a lot, whoever he is. We'll get him. You better tell him, Miss Foote, to turn himself in. We'll be watching for him. You going to tell us who he is?"

She refused to answer.

Finally the patrol rode away, and Johnny came out of the hiding place. "I've got to go," he told her in sorrow. "They're sure to get me, and I'd be better off in the Army than in a reb prison. I'd better leave tonight."

"A few more days, Johnny? Will you stay a few more days? You can stay hidden, and Jake will warn us."

He wanted to say yes, but reason overcame desire. "They're watching. They may have men posted to try to catch me. I'll have to go tonight."

They made love once more after the sun went down, holding each other tenderly, then fiercely. She cried in his arms, and he felt warm tears well in his eyes and roll down his cheeks.

He dressed and made ready. She packed him enough food to get him to the foot of the Peninsula and Butler's army.

They kissed each other for the last time.

"It won't be long," he said sadly. "The war will end soon, and I'll come back to you."

"Husband and wife, forever," she whispered.

"Forever," he said. He became practical. "Tomorrow morning, you close up this place and go to your aunt's house in King and Queen Courthouse. You wait there for me. It's dangerous for you to be out in this lonely country by yourself."

"I'll wait there until you come," she agreed. "Now, you remember her name, Johnny. Mrs. Alexander Downes. Remember that. Although it ain't a very big place. You could find me easy if you forget the name."

"You wait. I'll be there. Soon as you hear that the war is over, you be watching for me. One day I'll come a-running down the road."

"I'll watch for you, Johnny."

"Good-bye for a while, Elvira darling."

"Good-bye, my husband, good-bye."

Johnny Watkins was something of a seven-days' wonder when he reached the Army of the Potomac. He'd long since been crossed off as missing in action and presumed dead. He was treated wonderfully well, and Captain Mitchell gave him a month's furlough because of his wound, even though he was fully recovered.

He found himself a hero when he returned to Tarrytown. His father came up from Washington to join in the festive occasion. His mother clung to him for days on end, always kissing him and touching him and caressing him. He felt like a fool when the mayor of the village arranged a parade and speechmaking in his honor in the square. The schoolchildren piped unendingly the verses of "When Johnny Comes Marching Home Again."

The main orator was a surprise. Senator Ira Harris, in whose honor the 2nd New York Cavalry had been called the "Harris Light Cavalry," happened to be in the nearby village of Ossining that day, and he came down to deliver a speech for one of his heroes. At the end of his speech, he fired his main gun:

". . . I take the greatest pride and pleasure in announcing to you that I have this day asked the President to nominate Private John Watkins to be a cadet at the United States Military Academy. May he have a long and distinguished career in the service of his country, and may we be ever thankful that we have such grand young men to fight for us against slavery and treason. I thank you."

The pressures upon Johnny Watkins were enormous. He could no more think of turning down the nomination and returning to the Army of the Potomac than he could think of slapping his mother's face.

He'd never known much about West Point, although he'd lived within a relatively few miles of it all his life. He knew none of its rules, but he supposed they wouldn't cause him any trouble or discomfort after having served as a veteran in the harsh discipline of the Army of the Potomac.

His first day at the Academy was frantic, hectic, discouraging, unhappy, wearisome. At the end of it, just before the bugle for lights out, he sat with his roommates, all dog-tired, but all reading the Blue Book, the cadet bible, to get some better idea of this fantastic new world. He read hastily the words that he had never seen before, skimming over them, to absorb as many rules as he could before the lights went out and another day of frantic adjustment dawned. He read on rapidly, and suddenly he stopped and cast his eyes back to read again:

". . . no horse, no dog, no wife, no mustache . . ."

No wife! He had a wife. He'd sworn it in the sight of God. Elvira was his wife. All they'd lacked was the words of a preacher. He was married. He didn't belong here.

But he couldn't leave now. Goddamm it, in spite of the harsh discipline, the strict rules, the regimentation far worse than the cavalry had ever managed to maintain, he had loved this first day. He knew he would love every day of the years to come.

Duty, Honor, Country.

If he stayed, he would be faithless to the second word of the code. He would be a liar.

He knew what he had to do. He must report himself to the tactical officer in the morning, right after breakfast. He would be out of the Academy by noon, on the train in the early afternoon, and back in the Army of the Potomac the next day, or at least the day after. All right. That was what he had to do.

He never got a chance to speak to the tac officer. He didn't get much of a chance to speak to anybody the next day. He was running all day long, with the lashing voices of upperclassmen to keep him moving.

That night he thought about it again while the Academy lay in darkness. He was married, wasn't he? He was a liar, wasn't he? He'd broken the honor code, hadn't he?

Not really married, of course, but just as good as married. They'd said the words together. Not really a liar, either, not yet. He just hadn't said anything about it yet. He'd speak his piece tomorrow.

The next night, having failed to make his confession, he pondered the marriage question once more. He wasn't really a liar. Marriages had to be formal; they had to be recorded in official books. It wasn't a marriage, really, without a preacher. He knew what he would do–say to the tac officer that he'd once stayed with a girl in Virginia, because he had to, because he was hiding from the rebs, because he was wounded. Would that be considered a marriage? Of course not, even if they had talked about it like children would: "Let's play we're married; you're the father and I'm the mother."

That was what he would do. He'd put it in those terms to the tac officer the first chance he got. Maybe tomorrow, maybe the next day.

He went to sleep much more quickly. His mind was at ease. He didn't have to lie about it; first chance that came along he would ask advice.

As soon as the war was over, and communications were resumed with the state of Virginia, he'd write to Elvira and tell her to wait patiently because he would be coming back to marry her.

As soon as the war was over. . . .

21

Kate Farnham was resourceful. After her first experience of bribing the turnkey to get a message to Hank, she quickly discovered that she could use the regular mail service. She wrote to him every day, so that he had a letter to read in the morning before he started to wait at the window for her appearance under the lamppost across the street.

Hank believed that Major Turner read all of her letters before sending them upstairs, so he was glad that she was circumspect in what she said. Most of her love and longing was hidden in sentences that always started, "Do you remember . . . ?" She would ask him to recall a date or a meal or a phrase. The memory would be one of passion shared. In all other respects, the letters were those of a lady to a friend of her family who happened to be in unfortunate circumstances.

Hank treasured every one, and read them many times over. His replies were few; he was hoarding his money for the extras in food that would preserve his health. Paper, ink, and postage service were all too expensive.

Each day she continued to come to the corner opposite the prison. She would stand there smiling up at him for perhaps a quarter of an hour before she left. The other prisoners sometimes would stand behind Hank to look at her, as if they could absorb the love that was passing between the man and woman. They referred to her as his "lady" and sometimes spoke about her as if Hank had been talking to her. "How was your lady today, Stephens?" or "Your lady was a bit late today, Major," or "Too bad your lady had to stand there in the rain."

Her letters told him the news that he couldn't get from the Richmond papers. Grant was bringing Sheridan east. Wilson had taken the Third Division of Cavalry; Kilpatrick was on his way west to Sherman.

She told him about Royce in careful language, saying that he was confined to his bed at the hotel; that the wound was no better, but perhaps no worse; that she and Royce got on "as well as we could expect, after so long a separation."

Most important, she told him gently the news that had been given to her by Jim Wilson before she left Washington. General Wilson had shown her the telegram from Dr. Stephens that said that Hank's wife and child had died. She made no comments about her own surprise and wonder; she said only that she was sorry to pass on such sad news to him.

He mourned for Caroline and the dead infant. He was sure that he had loved his wife in the beginning, and he had known her passion and had given himself freely to her. He was truly sorry that he had been the reason for any unhappiness that she had suffered. She must have been lonely during these war years. Certainly the prospect of a baby had brightened her future, as it had sustained him through some of the first long nights in this ugly building.

His grief was sincere and lasting, and he did not immediately think of the future for which Caroline's death released him. When the realization of his freedom to marry Kate penetrated his mind, he put it aside without rejoicing. Kate had Farnham, who would probably be an invalid for a long time. Hank knew he had no right to speculate on any future for himself and Kate.

He thought about the mistakes he had made. Caroline might have been much happier with another man who loved her for herself alone, not because of a silly quarrel with another woman. He had not been fair to her, even though he remembered that she had swiftly drawn him to her desires. He hadn't been fair to Kate, either.

He also speculated on how different his career would have been had he never married Caroline. He would now have stars and a division in the Army of the Potomac–he was a better soldier than Custer or Kilpatrick, as good as Wilson or Merritt or a dozen others of the wartime graduating classes. If he had not been so foolish during that summer's leave in Peekskill, he would have graduated, married Kate on graduation day, and gone out to the same swift rise in the early wartime years that had brought prominence to Kilpatrick. Of course, he might have been killed long since. The first ranking cadet of his class, Paddy O'Rorke, had been killed at Gettysburg.

At any rate, if he had not married Caroline and thus removed himself from the ranks of the regulars, he probably would not be here now in Libby Prison. He probably would be a division commander like Kil, instead of a major of volunteers. But she had been his wife, and he had once believed that he loved her. He grieved for her.

In one of her early letters, Kate told him also that she hoped to arrange a visit to the prison. He asked his fellows about that prospect, and they took a dim view of her chances.

Royce gave her the idea for the visit, in one of his coherent hours when he was wide awake instead of comatose and was for the time free of the effects of the opiate the doctor fed him regularly. "What does your lover have to say for himself these days?" Royce asked her as she was busy with her nursing duties.

She shrugged and didn't answer. If he continued to talk about Hank, she knew he would become bitter, cursing her until she would be forced to leave the room.

"I know you go every day to see him," Royce said. "Who signs the visitor's pass? Does Major Turner leave you two alone so you can fondle each other and talk about what you'll do when he gets out of there? When I'm dead, and out of your way? Is that what you talk about, Kate?"

"I have no visitor's passes," she said abruptly.

He laughed. "Well, by God, how do you get in? Are you whoring for Turner, is that it?"

She was silent, knowing enough by now not to answer any of his accusations.

"Do you just stand outside? Is that it, Kate?"

She nodded numbly, tears in her eyes.

He laughed again in genuine amusement. "I never thought you were stupid, Kate. Good Lord, right across the street is my commanding officer, Braxton Bragg, an old friend of your father's. All you have to do is step into his office, and you can have all the passes to Libby Prison you want."

Oh, God, she thought. Why didn't I think of that? But he'll stop me. He'll send word to General Bragg not to give me a pass.

He must have guessed her thoughts. He spoke again, and his voice was weary: "Do that, Kate, and you can see him. It doesn't matter to me. Go ahead. Christ, I always was fond of Hank in the early days. Do what you want, Kate."

Royce didn't say anything for a while, and Kate chanced a look at him to see if he had fallen asleep. She met his eyes, and it hurt her deeply to see the pain and the bitterness in them.

He spoke then, softly. "How long, Kate? Has the doctor told you?"

She shook her head. "I'm sorry, Royce. I'm sorry for everything."

"I know. I know. All right, Kate. I'll try not to talk about all this any more. You go see the general. He'll give you a pass."

Seeing Braxton Bragg was not simply a matter of crossing the street, since the general was on a tour of inspection of the Army of Northern Virginia. A pleasant clerk in the War Department, a man named John B. Jones, told her that Bragg would be back in four days.

On the fourth day she went over to the War Office once again, and spent ten minutes with the courteous general, who gave her the pass without even questioning why the wife of his military assistant wanted to visit Libby Prison.

She couldn't use the pass that afternoon, however, because when she returned to the hotel, Royce was in a coma again. She gave his bandage a quick inspection, crying out when she saw that it was sodden with blood. She ran for the doctor, who was always at lunch at this time of day in the hotel's dining room on the floor.

Royce was dead when they returned to his bedside.

Hank was almost frantic because she had not appeared in her usual place at the usual time. No letter came for him in the morning mail. Had Farnham stopped her visits? What had happened?

He took his post at the window long before noon on the next day. His fellow prisoners were aware that she had missed her daily appearance. "Your lady didn't show up yesterday, Major? What's wrong?"

He had no answer for them, nor did they expect any. Some of them stood behind him, or found places at other windows, to watch for her.

When the turnkey Ross came to announce a visitor for him, Hank was beside himself. He didn't want to leave the window just to answer some more damned questions about Dahlgren's intent. Probably some officious Confederate was downstairs, eager to find out the true story of the great raid on Richmond.

"Tell him to go to hell," Hank said, not taking his eyes from the street corner opposite.

"Ain't a him," Ross said. "It's a her. Same one, Major. She got a pass from General Bragg hisself. By God, you got powerful friends. We'll have to treat you fine, Major."

Hank brushed past the man and raced down the stairs. She waited for him in Turner's office. She was dressed in black, borrowed from the doctor's slim wife. She took his hands in hers and held them tightly. Neither of them spoke, while Major Turner stood nearby, as if regulations demanded that he be a witness to their meeting.

Finally Hank found his voice. "Kate, my dear."

She nodded, tears in her eyes. "I'm here, Hank. I'll stay. They'll let me see you once a week, for fifteen minutes."

Turner bethought himself of courtesy, bowed to Kate, and left the room, leaving the door open.

They went into each other's arms then, and kissed longingly. She was crying. He held her gently, stroking her hair and whispering that he loved her. Finally she pushed him tenderly away, so they could talk.

She told him that Royce was dead, and that the body had been sent that morning to South Carolina. She said that she would stay on in Richmond. The doctor had told her that she could nurse sick Union prisoners, that her services were sorely needed. "I'll come to see you once a week, my darling. I'll write to you every day."

He held her to him again, whispering: "How long, Kate? How long, my love?"

How long? The question was asked a hundred times daily in Libby Prison. There were arguments, discussions, even informal seminars on the progress of the war. There was no doubt that the Confederacy was crumbling, but its slow dissolution was no solace to these men for whom the war was already over.

The elderly Indiana captain who had given Hank his rations on the first day had recovered from whatever illness had stricken him, but he was gaunt and weak and wasted. He was still convinced that he was dying, but his hope now was to linger until he could get home. Each day he would wander from group to group, listening to the speculations about Lincoln's new general, to the rumors of rebel defeats and disasters, to the heated debates on Federal strategy. He sought out new prisoners who were trickling into the prison now that the armies were beginning to test each other in the springtime days. He sought the magic word, the answer to the everlasting question: How long?

No one could give it to him, but any man could tell him that the long months ahead would be bitter and brutal, that the rebels seemed bent on fighting to the end of their resources, that they must not only be defeated but crushed to the earth.

The old captain told Hank sadly that there was no hope that he could last, and as if to prove himself right, he fell sick again, lingered for two days, and died quietly during the night. He left his possessions to Hank Stephens–pen and paper, a worn Bible, and order book in which he had once started a diary of prison life, a ragged blanket, an ancient razor made of Sheffield steel. He also left Hank the question to which no one knew the answer: How long?

Hank knew that when the answer finally came, shaped by the red dust clouds of marching armies, by the rolling clouds of cannon smoke, by the blood darkening the earth, that he would return to some measure of happiness during a lifetime of love with Kate. He also knew, however, that all the future would be marred and tainted by these years. He knew that in dark hours through all of his lifetime he would see the men dying and hear their screaming and their moaning. He knew that there was the possibility that his old dream of the cavalrymen in combat might return to torture him in sleep. Wounds that had been ripped open during these years would be generations in healing. Hank Stephens might remain in the Army for which he had been trained so well, but he hoped that never again would he take his place in line of battle.

How long? Far to the north, a stoop-shouldered man in the uniform of a private soldier, with three stars sewn on the shoulders of the blouse, bent over maps to trace the routes his army would take when he was ready to move. His thick forefinger kept edging southward, ever southward. Grant had a half-million men and the vast resources of a great nation. He would use them to crush the Army of Northern Virginia.

How long? From the moment that the elderly Indiana captain died with that question in his mind, there were exactly three hundred and eighty-nine days until that Palm Sunday in 1865 when, at the McLean house in Appomattox village, the end came as Grant said courteously to Lee: "I met you once before, General Lee, when we were serving in Mexico. . . ."

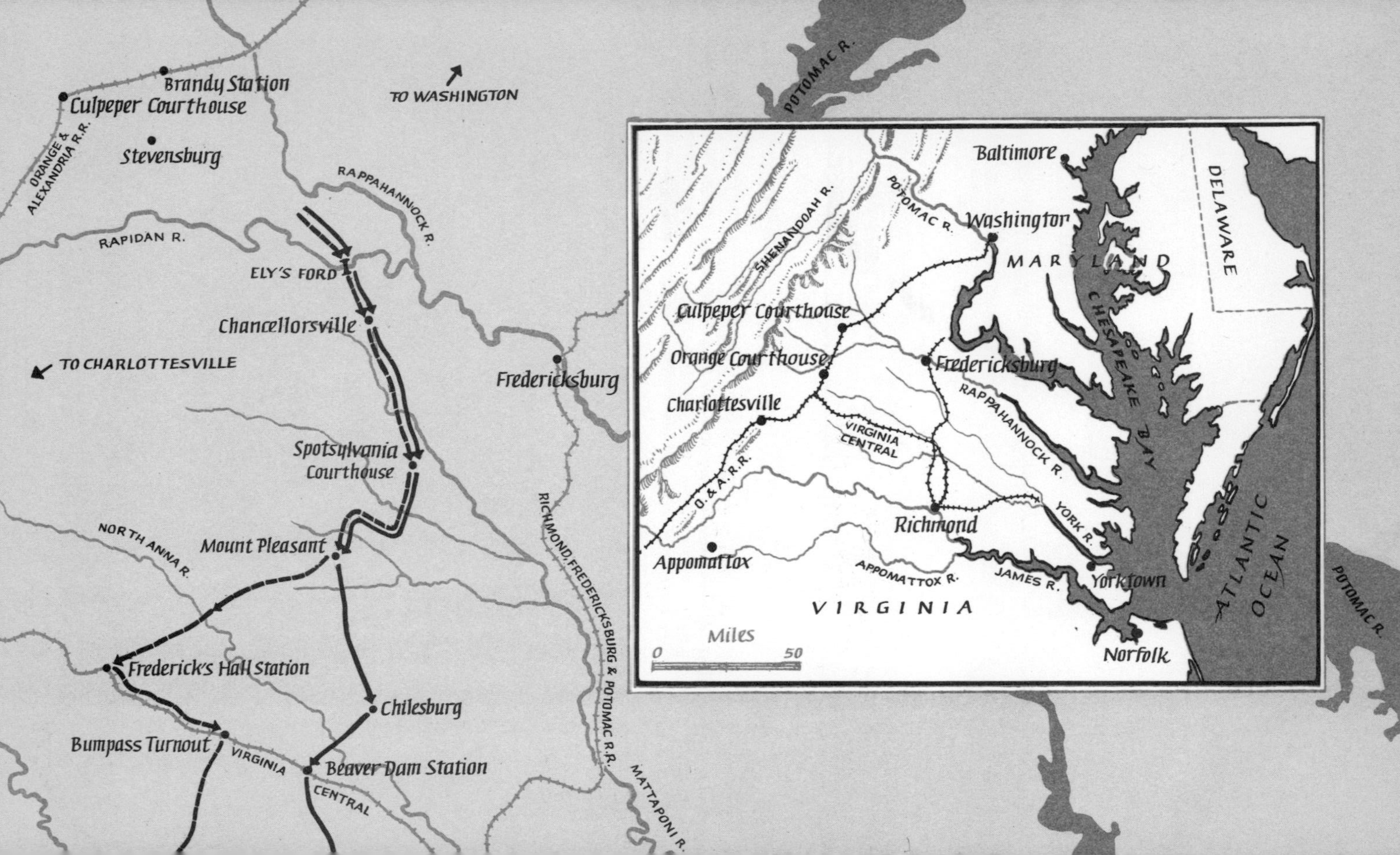

Brandy Station
Culpeper Courthouse
TO WASHINGTON
ORANGE & ALEXANDRIA R.R.
Stevensburg
RAPPAHANNOCK R.
RAPIDAN R.
ELY'S FORD
Chancellorsville
TO CHARLOTTESVILLE
Fredericksburg
Spotsylvania Courthouse
NORTH ANNA R.
Mount Pleasant
RICHMOND, FREDERICKSBURG & POTOMAC R.R.
Frederick's Hall Station
Chilesburg
Bumpass Turnout
VIRGINIA
Beaver Dam Station
CENTRAL
MATTAPONI R.
POTOMAC R.
Baltimore
DELAWARE
SHENANDOAH R.
POTOMAC R.
Washington
MARYLAND
CHESAPEAKE BAY
Culpeper Courthouse
Orange Courthouse
Fredericksburg
Charlottesville
VIRGINIA CENTRAL
RAPPAHANNOCK R.
O. & A. R.R.
YORK R.
Richmond
Appomattox
APPOMATTOX R.
JAMES R.
Yorktown
ATLANTIC OCEAN
VIRGINIA
Miles
0
50
Norfolk